ELEXIS BELL

A Blessed Darkness

A Blessed Darkness
Elexis Bell

Eager to stay up to date on the latest dark fiction from Elexis Bell?

Sign up for her newsletter at: www.elexisbell.com

Contents

Pronunciation Guide

Of course, you're welcome to pronounce the names as you see fit, but a few ARC readers expressed a desire for a pronunciation guide. So, this is how I pronounce them.

<u>Main Characters:</u>

Elairie Jooncourgahmas: Uh-lie-ree June-coor-guh-mah-s

Beluroan: Bell-oo-roe-n

<u>Cast:</u>

Aurujin: Ar-oo-jin (soft j)

Courg: Coorg

Deima: Dee-muh

Droucair: Drow-care

Evaerga: Ev-air-guh

Geeran: Gee-ran

Gourmaht: Goor-mah-t

Haedra: Hay-druh

Jaym: Jay-m

Kaimaer: K-eye-mare

Kaistrum: K-eye-strum

Kraimin: Cry-men

Oran: Or-un

Pakaibra: Puh-k-eye-bruh

Saerine: Say-reen

Traimon: Try-mon

Ultna: Ult-nuh

Vaerlin: V-air-lynn

Vourneima: Voor-nee-muh

Waergou: Wear-goo

<u>Gods:</u>

Baereen: Bay-reen

Doorma: Door-muh

Jemarie: Je-marie

Luxitore: Lux-it-or-ay

Nepiter: Neh-pit-er

<u>Locations/Geographical Features:</u>

Adalheid: A (like in apple)-dull-hide

Aivrard: Eye-v-rahr-d

Avaencery: Uh-vain-sir-ee

Banrould: Bahn-roold

Booran: Boo-ran

Cargam (mountains): Car-gum

Daernor: Dare-noor

Douhaen: Doo-hane

Draecon (river): Dray-con

Eadaion: Ed-dye-on

Hybar: High-bar

Kaern: Care-n

Nouvai (forest): New-v-eye

Romai (caldera): Rome-eye

Stravic (river): Stra-vic

Utmaer: Ut-mare

Vairsun: V-air-son

Vendaela (river): Vin-day-la

Viatlow's pass: Vee-at-low

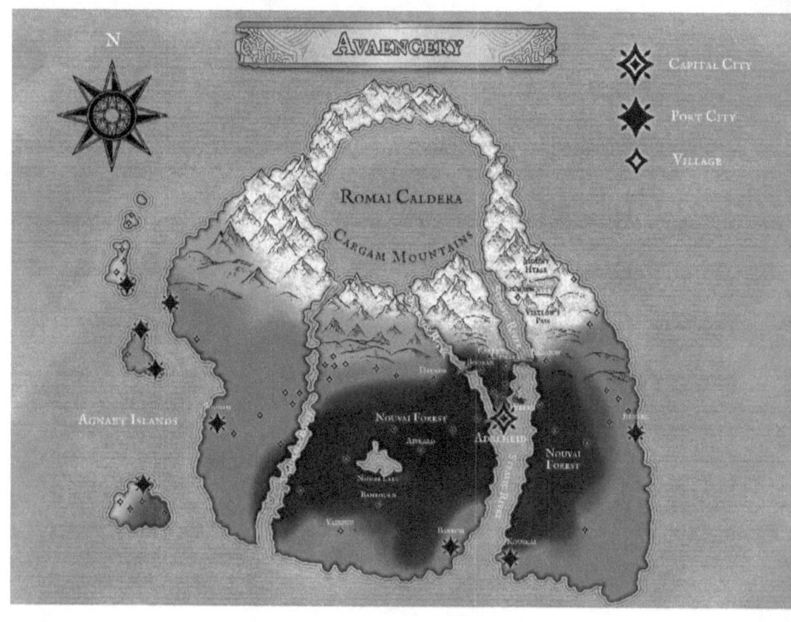

AVAENGERY
N
Capital City
Port City
Village
Romai Caldera
Cargam Mountains
Mount Hyaar
Viatlow's Pass
Agnaet Islands
Nouvai Forest
Adelheid
Nouvai Forest
Statue River
Aelard
Nothar Lake
Barrough
Vanrun

Prologue

Evaerga

Darkness creeps in around the edges of Evaerga's sight, closing it to a narrow tunnel, and her spirit soars over a shadowed forest and craggy mountains. The vision draws her into a cave, echoing with voices.

Her spirit hovers on the outskirts of a crowd, watching a man named Gourmaht. He saunters through the tunnels and caverns with his head held high, making his way to the biggest cave, his Command Room. She follows, heart in her throat and thankful for the safety of her vision to keep her from his sight.

He towers over the other Elves, lips curling up at the reminder of his superiority. Coal black eyes narrow, daring them to challenge him.

But they know better.

Their fear quickens her pace. Their thoughts echo through her mind, bloodlust with an undercurrent of terror.

Torches flicker in sconces along stone walls. Shadows play in the cavernous scar sprawling over Gourmaht's face, a remnant of a brush with earth magic. The damaged skin stretches diagonally from his temple, over his nose, reaching to engulf most of his left cheek, as if his face tried to split open, then decided against it at the last second.

Evaerga leans in, digging through the past for whatever atrocity left that mark behind, but a man calls out, drawing Gourmaht's attention. A chill runs over her spine as the dynamic between them washes over her.

Gourmaht looks down at his right-hand man, and Evaerga lets her gaze rake over him as well. Deep lines mar the man's ashen face, accentuated by the low light.

"What news have you this time, Waergou?" Gourmaht asks, surveying the man's savaged ear. A past riot stole its tip, robbing him of his taste for bladed weapons.

The vision supplies Evaerga with the knowledge that only his lethal talent for potions and magic keep him useful… and alive. She sucks in a deep breath, reading the tension in his face.

"Nothing good, I'm afraid," Waergou says, dropping his gaze. The torchlight flares brighter for a moment, sparkling on the jewel green spikes of his hair.

Fury rakes through Gourmaht. Heat ripples off him, and dread drags over Evaerga's nerves like sharp nails.

"Another failure? How many will it take?" Gourmaht hisses beneath his breath. He clenches his fist. "What happened this time?"

Waergou watches his feet and says, "They died again. They must have been weak, just as the last group was."

"No!" Gourmaht's shout echoes off the cavern walls, and silence descends in its wake. "Stop blaming them for your failure. You're doing something *wrong*!"

Anger radiates from him in hot waves of magical energy, and Waergou takes a step back.

Though only a hiss, Gourmaht's voice rumbles through the cave to reach the ears of every Elf present. "When Kaistrum used this magic, it mattered not how strong or weak the Fox Elf may have been. Their blood enslaved them. There was no resistance. There was no *hesitation*. None died before they could carry out the will of their Master."

Heat pours off Gourmaht as he picks up a scrap of parchment and shakes it in Waergou's face. It once held Kaistrum's recipe for the Blood Magic, but some of the ingredients and steps have been ripped away.

Evaerga's jaw falls open.

They can't...

No one could be that stupid, that horrible.

"Fix this. Or I will," he spits.

No one questions him. Heads bow and nod.

Gourmaht slams the paper down on a table and turns on his heel. A single strand of dark blue hair slips from the whip of his braid.

Waergou turns to face the Command Room as Gourmaht storms out, shouting, "Back to the scrolls. We must have missed something. Quickly. If we fail again, it'll be your heads, not mine."

Gourmaht smiles a twisted smile, savoring the fear in Waergou's voice. For all his bravado and shouting, the man knows he isn't safe.

It very well may be his head that rolls.

Gourmaht's mastery of all five types of elemental magic almost makes her pity the wretched poison maker.

Evaerga moves to follow the vile tyrant through the caves, but darkness encroaches on her vision. Her soul rushes across space and time, slamming back into her body. She gasps for air, hands trembling in her lap. Her heart pounds in her chest, battering her ribs. She closes her eyes in a desperate attempt to calm herself.

"They seek to renew the Blood Magic?" she croaks.

The words nearly choke her.

All the hard work, all the sacrificed lives, all the pain endured by so many to be rid of that wretched magic... Was it all for naught?

Desperate to occupy her mind, she analyzes her vision, picking at the details. Gourmaht's dark hair and eyes indicate Fox Elf heritage, known now as Blood Elves because of this exact magic. Yet, his skin was stark white like that of Light Elves.

And his ears didn't stick straight up like those of Fox Elves. They were out a little way from his head.

Realization dawns, bright and painful.

He's mixed blood. No Elf will be safe. All will fall as easily as dropped pebbles.

Including Evaerga's daughter.

Her stomach plummets.

Elairie... A slave?

The thought makes her sick.

Footsteps sound above her, and her eyes dart up to the kitchen ceiling. Evaerga traces her daughter's path through her room, preparing for another night of guard duty.

Knowing Elairie would guess something troubles her, Evaerga rushes off to bed. Strands of hair the color of fresh mulberries fall in front of her eyes, and she brushes them aside with a sweep of her hand.

Fear follows her, clawing at her heels with every step she takes. A chill creeps into her heart and flows through her veins. Ice water pours over her soul.

Very dark times lie ahead, of that she has no doubt. And something tells her that Elairie will be right in the middle of it.

Chapter 1
Elairie

The night reaches for me, but it slips off my shoulders as I step into the jail building. Ultna sits rigid at the front desk, frowning at the candle before him. The tiny flame joins forces with the fire in the hearth, sending flickering shadows over his scowl.

Is there someone in one of the cells?

It's been peaceful lately, but maybe something happened.

Vaguely, I wish Mother had been awake to warn me before I left for work. Even in such a small town as Vairsun, all the gossip skips right over me and my nocturnal life.

A blessing and a curse.

Turning from Ultna, I grab my Guard jacket from the closet, hanging my normal one in its place. I slip my arms into the sleeves, and my thick plait of lavender and mulberry hair falls forward over my shoulder, showing off my mixed blood in its dark and light shades.

I tug at the front of my jacket, adjusting it, and catch my reflection in the windowpane. My pale Light Elf skin nearly glows, drawing attention to the slight upward tilt of my ears' points, marking me as 'other.'

I turn to Ultna, ready for whatever torrent of words he wishes to spout. In not-so-short order, he informs me that a Blood Elf was brought in for robbery.

"He's to be kept until a decision can be made as to his punishment. It may take a while," he says, glowing with pride.

But I only sigh at the lingering prejudice. The Blood War may have gripped our land for 35 years, but all the Masters were cleared out years ago.

They're not Blood Elves anymore. They're not slaves. They're Fox Elves again.

Why can't the Light Elves just move on?

Choosing not to ask, knowing the answer will fall short, I let it drop. Instead, I ask, "What did he steal?"

Ultna drops his gaze, faltering before me.

Did he think I wouldn't ask?

"Bread," he whispers.

My brow furrows. "Just bread? Did he hurt someone when he took it?"

Reflexively, I touch my daggers, one sheathed on either thigh. I cast my mind over my sparring sessions in the training room down the hall with Ultna and Deima, the day guard. My stomach churns uneasily.

Have I prepared enough for a violent prisoner?

Ultna shakes his head, refusing to meet my eyes. "I'm sure he would have, given half a reason," he spits. "As if they *need* reasons. He was probably just planning to hurt the bakers after taking it. The filthy animal didn't realize a patrolman had just come through the door."

A derisive laugh escapes me, and I shake my head. Noticing a single loaf of bread on a table near the desk, I ask, "Is this it?"

"Sure is. Detained as evidence." Ultna smiles again, proudly upholding his duty.

A single loaf of bread, and he's been here all day? That hardly seems fair.

But I know all too well that once a Blood Elf is in jail, Light Elves struggle to let them go. I scoff, chest puffing out with a deep breath.

A sneaking suspicion makes me ask, "When did he last eat?"

It isn't usually up to me to feed anyone here. Prisoners are generally asleep during my shift. But we don't get many Fox Elves in this town, let alone in this jail.

"What could he possibly need? He probably ate whatever he stole before he went into the bakery," Ultna sneers.

"So, he hasn't eaten?" I ask, voice flat.

Ultna sits silently, confirming my suspicion.

Sighing, I ask, "What's his name?"

"Do you really need to know? You're not going to talk to him, are you?"

I stare at Ultna, wondering how he could ever consider himself to be a nice person, which I know he does. Crossing my arms, I wait him out with one brow arched.

He caves under my gaze and utters, "Beluroan."

Beluroan...

My heart flutters at the name. Something stirs within me, buzzing beneath my skin. Not that I'll admit how much I like the sound of it in current company.

As Ultna hangs his Guard jacket and retrieves his normal one, I take a candle and journey down the stairs into the cold storage, only to find the shelves packed to the brim. Deima restocked today, filling the cellar with bread, fresh and dried fruits and vegetables, several varieties of dried meats, and a couple jars of boiled eggs.

Ultna leans down the stairway and calls out a tense goodbye. I wish him a good night, and the front door shuts firmly behind him. I settle the candle on a shelf and climb back up the stairs. Bypassing the desk, I venture down the hall.

Strong, nimble hands stick out between the bars of the closest cell, arms propped on metal as Beluroan leans his weight on them. My gaze lingers on his long, graceful fingers.

I roll my eyes at myself and redirect my gaze to the sconce hanging on the wall between the two empty cells at the back of the room. Entering the cell room, I turn my back on the desk and its brightly burning candelabra to face Beluroan.

And the breath goes out of me.

A lock of dark red hair sweeps across his forehead to hang by his ear, having escaped the tie that holds the rest back. A few strands drape over one shoulder. Tan skin frames dark green eyes, sparkling like gems in a handsome, rugged face. His lips part with a sharp intake of breath when our eyes meet.

He smiles, and warmth flows through me.

Why does he feel… familiar?

My eyes trail over him, over the gaping black leather vest and the toned physique lurking beneath his white shirt, over his rolled-up sleeves and the two undone buttons at his collar.

A scar peeks out, winding and snaking over his collarbone, running across his chest, only to disappear beneath his shirt. The candles cast wavering light and shadows over him, almost disguising the way it branches out from one thin line into many, like roots.

Chills run down my spine.

It's from lightning magic…

I furrow my brows, straining to see it better.

How far down does the scar go?

Delicate heat sweeps through me as I imagine what it might be like to trace it with my fingers. Immediately, I berate myself.

I have to say something to this man. I need to actually make words fall from my lips. I can't just stand here looking like an idiot.

"My name is Elairie," I begin. "I'm the night guard here. Your name is Beluroan, is it not?"

He nods, eyes drifting over my face and hair, then down the length of me.

I can practically feel his gaze as it roams over me, and heat blossoms deep within. Excitement roars freely through me, but I keep my features plain, hiding it as well as I can.

Sizing him up, I pull my aura magic forward to see how he bends the air around him, but what I find makes no sense. He glows with fire and bolts of lightning. Only bits of his personality come through the swirling mass of chaos and heat.

But my mind fills with honor and loyalty.

Confused and overwhelmed by the electrified inferno twisting around him, I fade the aura magic out. Marshalling all of my will, I continue, "I understand you've not been given anything to eat, for which I apologize."

Finally, he speaks. "I've gone hungry for far longer before," he says, deep voice gravelly, yet soft somehow. He raises one eyebrow.

Was that meant to be suggestive? Or am I imagining things?

I swallow.

Which would be worse?

Forging ahead, I ask, "What would you like to eat? We have dried beef and cured ham. Plenty of fruits and vegetables. Bread and eggs."

He cocks his head to the side. "I get a choice? Had I known *this* was what awaited me, I would've gotten arrested a long time ago." He laughs, deep and rich, sending strange shivers down my spine. He shakes his head at the ground and takes a deep breath. "I'll have whatever you're having."

I nod, then quickly leave the room, hoping the chill of the cold storage will chase the fire from my insides. I barely keep myself from running down the stairs.

Of course.

This man, this man who is in jail, this is who I'm attracted to.

Not the men my mother has thrown in my way. Not the ones who jumped there of their own accord, thinking my mixed blood exotic.

It's him.

Of course.

I fight the urge to smack the palm of my hand against my forehead.

If Grandmother were still alive, she'd die. A FULL Blood Elf. And he's in jail. She'd instantly hate him. She'd be terrified of him.

Gods.

Hastily, I fill two cups with water. Placing them on a table in the corner, I snatch up a tray. My mind drifts back to the cell above, wondering if this man was *actually* flirting with me.

Surely not.

It was just my imagination playing me for a fool.

I pile apples, rolls, several pieces of dried beef, and some dried fruit onto the tray, then stop short. Grabbing a second tray, I separate the food.

We're not about to sit down at a table and eat from the same tray.

I roll my eyes and hope the little bit of extra time will help me clear my head. A laugh bursts from me.

I settle the cups on the trays, gather them up, and extinguish the candle. My heart flutters as I try not to skip up the stairs. In the lobby, I take a breath to steel my resolve. Outside the door to our training room, I take a few more breaths.

It doesn't help.

My eyes fixate on the bars, seeking out his arms. But they no longer stick through the bars.

Better get moving.

Before I do something stupid.

I spur my feet to action, dragging myself into the room. Again, my heart falters at the sight of him, at the strange familiarity of him. I barely keep my jaw from falling open.

Leaning back, propped up on one elbow, he sits with one foot drawn up to the edge of the cot. Oh so casually, he examines his nails. His vest gapes, falling open to the side, and his shirt clings to him.

Gods...

But realization dawns on me.

He's messing with me.

His chest rises with a deep breath, and he glances up, rewarding me with a coy smile and confirming my suspicions. I balance the tray in the only horizontal opening in the bars. Without a word, he gets up and slinks toward me with an almost feline grace.

He takes the tray gently and sits back down on his cot.

Settling in at the desk, I take a long drink of the cool water. We eat silently, and I'm thankful for the time it affords me to calm my nerves. But I glance at him too many times as I eat.

And more often than not, his eyes linger on me.

He eats slowly, controlling his pace. But it makes me wonder.

Does he not usually get this much food in one meal?

My heart clenches, though I'm sure he'd bristle at the pity.

Then, it hits me, as if all the stone and earth Luxitore ever created were falling down upon me, as if Jemarie were taking all the wind from my lungs…

Does he have a family?

No necklace of eternal bonds peeks out from the open neckline of his shirt, but given the scar on his chest, it may have broken when the magic hit him. My stomach plummets, and I tell myself it's only out of concern for his possible family. With him here, they may not have food.

It isn't because he's attractive. It's because his family might be starving.

But I know better. It's both. The two concerns mix, curdling in my stomach.

I finish my food shortly after Beluroan. Gathering my tray and cup, I move to take his. "Would you like more food or water?"

The simple question surprises him. After a moment's hesitation, he says, "Just some water, please."

Has no one ever shown him simple kindness?

The lightning scar glares up at me in answer, making my own upbringing seem privileged. People turned their backs on me all the time, but no one turned their magic on me.

He hands me the tray, then drains the remainder of his water in one long pull. My eyes linger on his neck, but I force myself to look away. Reaching through the bars, he passes me the cup. Our fingers brush, and gentle warmth flows between us. His hand lingers, and my breath hitches. Swallowing, I pull away.

But I still feel his touch.

Heat rushes to my face, and he drops his gaze quickly.

I dart from the room, tripping over myself to get to the relative safety of the cold storage. I barely notice when I bump into the desk in the front lobby.

I rush down the stairs and drop everything on the table in the corner. My hands shake, sloshing a few drops of water over the rim of Beluroan's cup as I refill it.

I need to get myself under control.

What is this?

Slowly, I climb the stairs, determined to be calm. Two deep breaths. Another for good measure.

But my heart hammers as I move down the hall.

When I pass him the cup, I keep my hand low, allowing plenty of room above my fingers for his. Minimizing physical contact should make it easier to control… whatever this is.

But he places his hand directly over mine.

Again, that soft, soothing warmth floods into me. He gazes directly into my eyes, smiling, almost smirking. I retreat to relative safety, leaning against the desk.

But I don't tear my eyes from him.

"So, all you had to do to earn this lovely retreat was steal a single loaf of bread?" I ask, keeping my voice light, joking.

Beluroan chuckles as he turns and walks to his cot. He sits down, and though he tries to hide it, a hint of anxiety flickers across his face. "Yeah, well, it isn't nearly as bad as I expected jail to be." Soft as his words may be, worry strains his voice.

"How long will you be staying?"

"Until they decide what to do with me." He shakes his head, sighing. "That's all I was told."

A selfish part of me hopes it takes a while. The sane part of me hopes they get over their prejudice and let him go quickly. He deserves to get back to his life.

"I'm sorry," I blurt. "It really isn't fair to you. It's just… now that they have a 'Blood' Elf behind bars, the townsfolk won't want to let you go. They don't care that the crime you committed was minimal and probably necessary."

I raise my hands in a gesture of helplessness, and shock spreads across his face. "Everyone is still so scared of the Blood Magic. It doesn't even matter that Kaistrum and his ilk have died off, and now, you're all just trying to get by. They can't look at you as a Fox Elf again, not yet. You're still Blood Elves."

Beluroan stares at me, open-mouthed, and heat rushes over me.

After a moment, he says. "I never thought I'd see the day. A Light Elf, not only acknowledging the prejudice, but apologizing for it." His eyes seem to pierce my soul, digging deep into the core of my being. "But you're not just a Light Elf. That's why you see it.

Because they look at you differently too. So, shouldn't you include yourself? 'We' are just trying to get by, right?"

My mouth goes dry, and I wish I had refilled my cup, as well. "I guess I should."

All the reactions I've gotten in the past from new acquaintances flash before my eyes. I watch them process me, trying to assimilate my existence into their cut-and-dry lives.

Tension pulls my lips into a frown as I wonder how much to tell this man. I can't tell him my entire family history. But then again, it's not like he'll shun me.

"I'm a quarter Blood Elf."

"Was that… willingly brought into your family line?" He seems to stumble over the words, struggling to pretty up the subject so as not to offend.

I shake my head. After a moment, I manage, "My grandmother wasn't given much choice."

"For that, I'm sorry." His lips turn downward, and a deep crease etches itself between his brows.

If only my grandmother could have heard his apology. Maybe she heard it from the Valley. Perhaps she can rest a little more peacefully now, knowing that not all Blood Elves are like the one who raped her.

Taking my thoughtful silence as the end of the conversation, Beluroan unlaces his boots and kicks them off. He sheds his vest and lies back on his cot. Pulling the blanket up to his chest, he yawns and says, "Goodnight, Elairie."

"Goodnight. Sleep well, Beluroan." I peel my eyes from the muscles plainly outlined beneath his shirt, looking back to his magnificent eyes. A pang of disappointment shoots through me, but he had to sleep sometime.

He offers up another smile just before he closes his eyes. Sitting behind the desk, I review our conversation at least a hundred times, and yet I am *still* awestruck. I marvel at his perspective, his confidence, his lack of bitterness despite a difficult life.

I glance at him, eager to renew our conversation, but a dreamy smile plays on his lips.

Redirecting my thoughts, I retrieve a book from the drawer, but it does little to occupy my mind. A few thoughts gnaw at me, repeating over and over.

Does he have a family out there wondering where he is? Do they fear for his life? Are they hungry?

What happened to give him that scar?

I swallow hard.

Is his heart already spoken for?

Chapter 2
Beluroan

I wake, sore and stiff, back aching from this damnable cot. But my eyes dart to the desk immediately. Light streams in from the window behind it, landing on an empty chair.

She's gone.

Disappointment rolls through me.

Stretching, I roll onto my back and listen to the gentle male voice drifting through the jail.

Must be the day guard... It certainly isn't the grump that was here last night.

I groan and rub my eyes, chastising myself.

That isn't entirely fair. He must have a reason for hating my kind so much, but Godsdamnit, I'm not the one who hurt him.

I sigh and shake my head.

My eyes drift shut again, forsaking the barren ceiling and painting the backs of my eyelids with breathtaking images of Elairie. Dark, welcoming blue eyes set perfectly against alabaster skin gaze upon me with kindness and curiosity.

My memory lingers over her long, thick hair, shaded with so many different hues of purple I could never hope to count them all. But I'd love to try, to undo that long braid and let my fingers get lost in her hair.

My mind wanders over the image of her, sliding slowly down to her graceful neck and the swell of her breasts. I feel my heartbeat quicken and stop myself before I get wrapped up in these thoughts.

She's one of the guards here.

I'm in jail. Her *jail.*

Though she doesn't agree with them keeping me here, nothing could happen with her.

But... She seemed to like me.

She was kind to me, despite being raised by people who'd probably be terrified of me.

How much have they suffered because of that one man? Did her grandmother ever get over it? Were Elairie or her mother ever accepted here?

So many questions swirl through my head, all centering around this woman I barely know. But in the end, I come back to one.

Will they release me before I see her again?

I *should* be hoping for a quick release. This is jail after all, but I can't lie to myself. I want to see her again.

My sister and my nephews pop into my mind. A deep sigh lifts my chest, pulling in the scent of wood smoke drifting in from the hearth in the front room.

Poor Saerine.

They must be worried sick.

Saerine is no fool. She knows our meager coin isn't enough for what I come home with on market runs. Much as she tries to hide it, I see the worry creasing her brows every time I go.

She knows, deep down, that I'm a thief.

Sure, her healing services are always needed somewhere, but going into the homes of strangers makes her nervous. After what happened to bring the boys into the world, I'm amazed she finds the strength to do it, at all. Every house, every man that needs healing…

I shudder, and the cot creaks beneath me.

Every man she heals could be like the one who tricked her into his home on pretenses of injury, the man who beat and raped her, the man who unintentionally fathered Oran and Kraimin. I remember how she cried that night and many nights after, even flinching away from me for a while.

And yet, she goes out healing, either trusting that most men are good or braving the danger for the sake of feeding her children.

I do what I can, taking any job I'm offered to lessen the strain on her, but my Earth magic isn't as highly demanded as her healing abilities.

Impotent rage builds within my chest, and I struggle to contain it. Instead of screaming or pounding my fists on the wall as I wish to do, I calculate how long I can afford to be away from home. I think back over the state of the pantry, the amount of food we had when I left.

Since I won't be there eating any of the food, I can afford a few days here.

I breathe a sigh of relief, knowing that my slip up won't leave their stomachs empty. Momentarily freed from the worry of feeding them, my heart skips a beat, and I find myself hoping to stay another night.

Not that I can ever tell Saerine.

But I want to see Elairie again, to hear her laugh. I want to touch her hand, even if it's only while passing a cup through the bars.

A smile lifts the corners of my mouth, and I wonder…

Did she feel that strange warmth when our hands brushed? I've never felt anything like it.

Even just the memory sends shivers down my spine. Then, realization dawns on me.

Gods, I even blushed.

Hopefully, she didn't see that.

I think I looked down quickly enough to hide it, but maybe not.

I certainly dropped my gaze fast enough to miss any effect it may have had on her.

The day guard walks into the cell room, surprising me and cutting off my thoughts. Fear lurks in his eyes, slinking around behind a mask of bravery. He doesn't say anything and leaves quickly, quiet footsteps disappearing down the hall. After but a moment, he brings me bread, some cured ham, and dried fruits and vegetables. Another veritable feast.

He even brings me a second cup of water before meandering back to the desk in the front lobby. Aside from peeking in every so often to be sure I'm not up to anything suspicious, he stays out there for the rest of his shift.

***

As the day passes and the shadows undoubtedly make their way around the sundial in the middle of town, someone rings the large bell hanging near it. The sound shatters the still air, mocking me as it marks the high point of the day.

After another eternity, the evening guard comes in to begin his shift, bringing with him the realization that I likely won't eat again, or even see another face, until Elairie comes in. Excitement builds within me at the prospect, and my chest feels too small for my heart.

What magic has she worked on me for even the thought, the hope, of seeing her again to have such an effect?

The guards exchange a few words in the other room, and I listen in. It seems that no decision has been made regarding my fate, either out of hesitation as Elairie supposed or because I'm such a low priority that they need not bother with me.

Either way, I'll be here another night.

I'll see her again.

My heart swells, nearly choking me. A sudden, restless energy fills me, and I feel as though I could run for miles. Except... I can't leave my cell.

Desperate to burn off some energy, I busy myself with whatever kind of exercise I can manage here.

Maybe I'll squeeze a nap into my busy schedule so I can stay up later talking to her.

That is...if she wants to talk to me again.

My poor, stupid heart crumbles at the thought, but it makes no sense.

Why such a maelstrom of emotions, so soon?

Is it simple boredom?

As I lower myself to do some push-ups, I try not to think about it.

***

I wake from my nap at sunset, long before Elairie will be here. Disappointment wells within me, and a soft sigh escapes my lips.

Gods, I hope she doesn't realize I'm adjusting my sleep schedule to fit her work schedule.

It just sounds... pathetic.

Yet, I don't turn over to sleep the night away. Some strange force burns in my heart, compelling me to stay awake.

Lying on my cot, I lazily scratch my chest. My fingers brush the scar, sending my mind back to the day I got it. The Blood Magic was a cruel thing, but the lightning magic was excruciating.

No fourteen-year-old should have to bear it, let alone the sight of their mother dying before their eyes.

I rub my hand over my face, trying desperately to dislodge the sight of her convulsing body, her empty eyes. But I know it won't go away for long. It never does.

Aching for a distraction, I try to think of something else, anything else. But my mind doesn't wander far. It roams through the years since that night, meandering through the dark forest and skirting past hungry wolves.

Has it really been nine years?

And yet, has it only been that long?

With so many years of suffering, so much time on the road, my 23 years have been a blurred eternity. The world was never carefree, not for us.

I open my eyes and roll my head to the side. I look to the hallway, wondering how long it'll be until Elairie comes in.

What would she think of the life I've led? She's a guard at a jail. She surely wouldn't approve of some of the things I've done to get by.

It shouldn't matter, but my heart aches at the idea of being rejected by her. I never cared about being pushed aside or brushed off in the past.

But for some reason, her opinion matters.

Chapter 3
Elairie

My eyes open to the dark ceiling of my bedroom, and for a moment, I listen to the sounds of the house. Silence rules, and disappointment fills me.

Is Mother avoiding me? What's she trying to protect me from this time?

I groan internally, wishing she'd accept that I'm not a child anymore.

Going through the motions, careful to be quiet, I dress for work and braid my hair. I strap each piece of light armor on. A simple, double-layered leather vest with some padding, sheaths that strap around my thighs for my daggers, sturdy leather boots, and fingerless leather gloves.

Not that I'm likely to need it.

Beluroan doesn't seem like the type for escape attempts. He may be a thief, but he's honest. Despite the weird lightning and fire aura, that much was clear.

I sneak down the stairs, taking my candle with me and avoiding the creaky steps. A smile slips onto my face at the food Mother left on the table for me. It goes down smoothly, and I set off for work with my mind on Beluroan. I picture his face and smile again.

The crisp night air chills my bones and turns my breath into clouds. I keep a brisk pace, arms folded in front of me for warmth. Only now do I realize that I left my jacket at home in my haste. The thin blouse beneath my vest does little to warm me. I chide myself, all the while thanking the Gods that I don't live far from the jail.

I pass small cottages, all dark but for the candles flickering in what I assume to be the bedrooms. Cottages become businesses, all of which lie dark and dormant for the evening, except for the tavern.

Forsaking the road, I walk on lush grass interspersed with springy moss. My eyes roam over Vairsun. Moonlight plays in curls of smoke rising from chimneys, carrying my gaze upward. On the north side of town, the Nouvai Forest lies in the shadow of the Cargam Mountains, beautiful and foreboding.

I turn a corner, and the jail springs into view. Candles burn within, casting a warm glow through the windows. I rush toward it, spurred on by the cold air and the butterflies in my stomach.

I burst through the door, and Ultna nearly topples out of his chair. Laughter bubbles up within me and spills over. His face scrunches into a scowl, yet I can't even begin to take him seriously. My nervousness has shattered, and butterflies flutter out through my parted lips.

But my laughter only serves to deepen Ultna's frown.

I quickly rein myself in and rush to the closet, grabbing my guard jacket. I slide it on, desperate to chase the chill from my bones. The hearth lies lifeless and barren, so I hold my hands near the flame of the nearest candle. Unsurprisingly, it does little to warm me.

"Why didn't you have a jacket on? It's not like you were running late." Ultna glances at the clock candle and adds, "You certainly had time to put one on."

I can hardly tell him I was rushing to get here because I wanted to talk to Beluroan. I'd rather not admit just how ridiculous I'm being.

Instead, I say, "I thought I overslept."

He gives me a strange look but says nothing more, opting instead to change the subject. "Our unwelcome guest is still here." His face scrunches up. "I wish they'd just figure out what they're going to do with him, so he can leave. One way or another."

My mouth drops open. "One way or another? His crime is hardly a hanging offense. *That* is just your own hatred speaking."

Ultna recoils as if I slapped him. He jumps up from the chair, face red with anger. "And *that* is simply your *mixed-blood* speaking." He spits the words at me, and one strand of his mint-colored hair falls forward. He stomps to the closet and exchanges his guard jacket for his normal one. Jerking the thing on, he storms out.

For a moment, I can do nothing but stare after him. I raise one eyebrow and clench my jaw. Anger courses through me.

Has he been holding that in this whole time? Was he just waiting for a chance to rub this in my face?

He always treated me fairly, for the most part, but now I wonder if that was just because he was being paid to put up with me. Any time we sparred, I know he took it especially hard that he could never best me.

Why would he even work here if being near me is that terrible for him?

Especially since there are bound to be Fox Elves brought in at some point.

I force down one deep breath after another, slowly pushing the anger out.

It doesn't matter.

He can be as angry as he wants. He's wrong. Sooner or later, he has to face that.

I pace, trying to calm myself down. Pulling in measured breaths, I slow my heart.

My mind drifts into the next room, and I realize that Beluroan heard everything. My face burns, undoubtedly shifting to a deep scarlet as humiliation washes over me.

Wonderful.

Gods, it's been a great night so far.

Desperate for busy work, I decide to feed Beluroan, assuming that Ultna wouldn't have deigned to do so himself. I eye the training room as I pass, tempted to take out my frustrations on the dummy in there. Somehow, it seems more embarrassing to let Beluroan know it bothers me so much.

I push myself down the hall, and slowly, excitement trickles in, replacing the anger and irritation and humiliation. My heart leaps into my throat, and my stomach drops into my shoes. But when I enter the cell room, I find Beluroan red-faced and pacing. Catching sight of me, he stops short.

Is he angry that Ultna spoke to me that way?

My heart soars at the prospect of this man caring what people say to me. But more likely, his anger is a result of being confined here another night. I stifle the wave of disappointment that sweeps through me, chiding myself for being so irrational.

But I want him to want to be here with me, silly as that sounds. I can admit it to myself, at least. No one else will ever know, but I can revel in it here in the safety of my own mind.

Unless Beluroan has empath magic…

My breath catches as the full implications of that possibility slither through me. All the thoughts I had about him last night, all the strange feelings… He'd know them all.

No. I can't think about that.

Emerald eyes soften as he gazes at me, and my insides turn to mush. I barely suppress a grin, passing off my smile as politeness.

Concern smooths the scowl on his face. With slow, measured steps, he approaches the bars. "Are you okay?" he asks.

Such a simple question, but it stirs a dangerous hope within me.

Maybe he does care.

That goofy smile pulls at the corners of my lips, trying desperately to break my control.

"Yes," I say. "It's not the first time I've been spoken to that way, and it certainly won't be the last. I'll be fine." Silently, I applaud my false bravery.

"You shouldn't have to deal with that." His voice barely rises above a whisper. His words reach out to me, pulling me in.

My eyes lock with his, trapped, but I notice an additional button on his shirt hangs open. Though I long to look, to trace that scar with my eyes since I can't do it with my fingertips, his eyes hold my gaze.

I smile at him, and heat builds all around us. The air crackles with electricity.

Words. I need words.

My brain scrambles to come up with something, anything. "Um," I begin, rather eloquently, "I, uh." I stop to clear my throat, then try again. "Have you eaten anything?"

Smooth.

So. Very. Smooth.

He looks down, chuckling. "Not since before the morning guard left." The energy that swirled around us moments ago burns in his voice. His fire and lightning aura springs to mind.

Clearing my throat, I ask, "What would you like?"

After a brief pause and a devilish smile, he says, "Surprise me."

I dip out of the room, hoping to hide the blush creeping over my skin, and rush to the cold cellar. I fill two trays and two cups. I'm not hungry, not with my stomach in knots, but I know the bread I ate at home won't hold me over for long. And surely, this strange feeling will fade.

Yet, my heart thuds hard against my ribs. My head spins with our exchange.

He actually seemed to care about me, about how I was treated.

I try to convince myself that he's just being sympathetic. I repeat it like a mantra as I climb the stairs.

Not that it should matter if he cares or not.

Not that it should matter if he feels the heat that floats around us, the same heat that flowed through my skin when we touched yesterday.

But it does.

Feeling thoroughly pitiful, I walk into the cell room. He stands with his arms braced on the bars, just like before. His hands stick out, clasped on this side of the bars.

But he's untied his hair. It falls freely around his shoulders, looking like he's swept his hand through it a few times. His eyes twinkle with a devilish light that threatens to outshine all the stars in the sky despite the darkness that lounges seductively behind it.

I glance down at the open collar of his shirt and notice that he's undone another button. Shadows play beneath the fabric in the flickering candlelight, showing me more, and then less, of him. My eyes dart back up to his face, and his lips part in a slow, knowing smile.

He's baiting me.

A deep blush spreads over my face, and I hope the shadows hide it.

I hold the tray through the small opening, offering him his meal. He reaches for it with both hands.

And one hand finds mine.

A delicate weight builds in my stomach, burning me from the inside. My lips part in an almost gasp. My skin tingles beneath his touch as he slides his thumb back and forth over the skin of my knuckles, practically setting them on fire. My heart speeds up, and my breath grows shallow as the air around us comes alive with fire and lightning.

His eyes darken, and he glances at my lips.

Does he want to kiss me?

I try to ignore the hopeful tone of my thoughts, try to ignore the fact that, if not for the bars, I'd throw myself at him.

But the bars are most certainly there, and they bring me crashing back to reality. I pull my hand back. It slips so easily from his grasp, but heat lingers on my skin.

Beluroan's eyes burn with the fire that threatened to consume me, *us,* just heartbeats ago, and I find myself wondering if he was as entranced as I was. The image of two moths fluttering toward the same flame flits through my head.

I drop my gaze to the floor as a fresh burst of red erupts over my skin. I retreat to the desk with my tray, but in the back of my mind, a question lingers.

Does he have a family?

Beluroan settles on his cot, and I find myself thankful to whoever made his tight, black pants. Pulling my eyes up, I catch his gaze again. We stare openly as we eat, and the air around us burns. Fire plays inside me, and lightning skips along my skin, a perfect echo of that strange extra aura that swirled around him.

But the idea of a wife cools me off.

Just do it. Ask.

"Was someone waiting for you, or for you to bring them food? Do I need to notify your family that you're here?" For a moment, I applaud my framing of the question.

Beluroan pauses, hand mid-air, then settles his jerky back onto his tray. His head tips to the side as several emotions flicker over his face. But a knowing smile soon spreads itself over his features. He nods, cocking one eyebrow up.

Maybe I didn't hide it as well as I thought I did...

My stomach churns, and I fidget with a piece of bread.

"My sister and my nephews will be waiting, but I can explain it to them later," he says. His lips quirk up into a lopsided grin, and he adds, "No one else."

Relief washes over me like cool spring rain. A smile spreads over my face, and I drop my gaze to my food to hide it. But concern still churns within me.

"Do they need food?" I ask. "I could take them some while you're here."

"We have several days' worth of provisions set back, as long as Saerine keeps the boys reined in." His eyes soften in appreciation. "Thank you, though."

After a moment, he asks about my family.

"It's just my mother and me. My father died in battle when I was two. My grandmother lived with us for a long time, but she died ten years ago."

He hangs on my words, leaving me to wonder if he harbored the same concerns.

"Why have you not married yet?" he asks.

My jaw falls open, and I stare at him, struggling for words. Finally, I say, "No one really drew me in."

Until now.

Until you.

"No one 'drew' you in? Past tense?" He raises one eyebrow and smiles, daring me to admit to these strange feelings.

I blush, stammering, "Well, you know." I shrug as noncommittally as I can manage.

I look at him, and my heart stutters as my eyes rake over the smile on his face.

How is he so relaxed?

Why aren't his insides squirming the way mine are?

Gods, I'm such a fool.

Silence descends on us, and I chew on dried apples to busy myself. Light and shadow chase each other through the room, playing together as the candles flicker.

"So, what were they like?" Beluroan asks, surprising me. "And what about your mother, what's she like?"

I consider him for a moment, wondering what to tell him. My brows furrow, and I tip my head to the side. But he seems genuinely curious, a thing which sends my stomach fluttering.

And what harm could it do to pass the time with conversation?

"My father was a great man, from what I've been told. He didn't care that my mom was half Blood Elf and half Light Elf. He looked past it and fell in love with her almost instantly." With a smirk, I add, "Apparently, he always said he was a goner the moment he saw her."

A wistful smile crosses my face, and I can't help but think of the way I'm drawn to Beluroan.

Is this what my father meant?

"You sound like you never believed that."

I shake my head. "I didn't. I always thought it took a lot of time, and a lot of work, to get to that point."

"Not always." An impish grin raises the corners of Beluroan's mouth. He watches me, gauging my reaction.

For my part, I try not to look like a lovesick youngling. But all my efforts at managing my expression mean that I forget to tell him about my mother and grandmother.

After a moment, he gives up on toying with me, at least for now, and asks, "What about them do you like most?"

His question surprises me, compelling me to answer honestly. "Well, my father could always find a reason to be happy. No matter what storm was rolling in, he always found a silver lining. I don't remember much of him, but what I do remember… He was always smiling." Tears prick at the corners of my eyes.

"My grandmother was stronger than anyone I've ever met. She went through so much and suffered through it all on her own. People around here practically shunned her. And she still managed to raise my mother to be a great woman."

Tears threaten to spill over, so I rush onward to a less painful subject.

"My mother is infinitely compassionate. She helped my grandmother to see that not all Fox Elves are bad and raised me to believe it. Even after what happened to her own mom, and then losing her husband in the Blood War, she saw what was really happening. She looked beyond it."

"They sound amazing," Beluroan whispers. His eyes fall to the floor, staring into some faraway place. A frown tugs at his lips, scrunches his brows.

My hands ache to reach for him, to ease the sadness that so clearly eats at him. And though I know the answer might hurt, I want to know. So, I ask, "What's your family like?"

His eyes find me.

He hesitates.

Voice rough with emotion, he finally says, "My mother and father have been dead for a long time now. My mother traded her life for mine." He looks me over, carefully picking apart my expression before saying, "My father traded his life to kill our Master."

He was a slave…

Sadness wells within me. But bits and pieces fall into place, and I wonder aloud, "Is that where you got the scar on your chest? From your Master?"

He looks at me, really looks, green eyes pensive. Slowly, he nods. "Yeah. It all happened on the same night. My sister, Saerine, pulled me through somehow. Even back then, she was an excellent healer."

He pauses, swallowing thickly before continuing. "She ended up having kids a while after that, but not by choice. Same as your grandmother."

He lets out a long, deep sigh, "I've been helping her however I can. We moved around a lot, but a few years after she had the boys, she wanted to settle down. It isn't always easy, but we get by."

I nod, and silence falls over us. We both finish our food before I get up the nerve to ask my next question. I turn his words back on him, asking, "So why didn't *you* ever get married?"

From his perch on his cot, he slowly looks me up and down, eyes finally coming to rest on mine. A soft smile spreads over his features. "I guess I just hadn't met anyone who drew me in."

He raises one eyebrow at me.

Chapter 4
Beluroan

Gods, am I actually flirting with this woman? And is she really flirting back?

Were my eyes deceiving me, or was she blushing? Surely not.

Elairie picks up her dishes and walks over to my cell. Her hips sway beautifully with each step, hypnotizing me. I swallow hard, pulling my eyes back to her face.

Rising, I approach the bars with my dishes in hand.

With every step, the air grows warmer. My skin tingles, begging me to reach for her. My mouth goes dry, and I swallow again. My mind fills with images of taking her hand and pulling her closer so that I might touch her face. Maybe I could sink my hand into her lush hair.

The bars are far enough apart...

Maybe I could kiss her.

My eyelids droop, and I feel the changes in my body as my mind wanders just a bit further down that path. I take a deep breath to steady myself and clear my mind of thoughts of Elairie and I tangled up together.

If I tried something like that, she'd probably just think I was after her keys.

Offering up my tray, I try to resist the desire to touch her hand. I really do try, but as soon as she takes hold of the tray, my free hand reaches for her. My fingers brush lightly across the back of her hand, up to her wrist. My entire body tenses, and my stomach clenches.

Her scent floats on the air, taking hold of me. Citrus and spice mix together in an alluring blend. And suddenly, the air is scorching. She holds my gaze, and a flicker of something moves in her eyes.

Is she feeling this too? Or am I losing it?

I rest my hand on hers and stroke my thumb over her skin. Fire blazes through me. I take a step forward, wanting so badly to close the distance between us.

But my movement brushes our joined hands against the bars. She looks down in surprise, and I watch reality crash back down upon her features as our surroundings come into focus.

A jail cell.

She's the guard, and I'm the prisoner.

She blinks several times, long lashes fluttering like thick, black fans. She withdraws, and my heart cries out for her touch.

"Do you want more water?" Her smooth, luxurious voice comes out deeper now, throaty.

Not trusting my own voice, I nod.

She turns to leave, walking slowly away. I lean my head against the bars and close my eyes. The feel of her, the look in her eyes, it all lingers, taunting me. I breathe deeply, but it doesn't help. The scent of her dwells here, consuming me.

I recall the widening of her eyes as she took in the undone buttons of my shirt, and my mind wanders, imagining her hands undoing the other buttons, sprawling over my chest. But I redirect my thoughts, drifting back over our conversation.

Her childhood can't have been easy.

Born during the Blood War, she would've been pushed from society, just as her mother and grandmother were.

But what must that have been like? To be accepted, but also shunned.

My place in the world has always been crystal clear.

But hers would have depended on who was around. She must've had to gauge how each person felt about her before she did anything. And she wouldn't have been able to act the same around one person all the time, because they'd act differently around certain people.

My head spins at the idea of trying to determine when to fade into the background and when to exist.

Then, a thought strikes me.

She didn't even flinch when I told her we were slaves. She didn't ask what horrible things I did or look at me like I was a monster. She just asked about my scar.

Does it not matter to her what I may have done?

Does she not care enough to worry or wonder?

Despite our short acquaintance, my heart shrivels in my chest. I tell myself that she cares more about how it affected me, all the while wondering how she can have such power over me already. No one else has ever pulled me in so completely.

Is this what it feels like to fall in love?

The thought comes into my mind unprovoked, shaking me to my core. Desperately, I try to chalk this all up to lust.

But then, why should I care so much about her life?

Why, if it was just lust, would I have been so enraged to hear that damned evening guard speak to her the way he did? If it was only desire, that shouldn't have mattered.

But it did.

My head swirls with how little she cared what he said, trying to discern whether it was an act to appear brave in front of a prisoner. My stomach plummets at the thought of being only a prisoner in her eyes, for surely she feels the sparks between us too.

She must.

Her footsteps in the stairwell put an end to my desperate search for answers. Resolving to resist the urge to touch her hand, determined to talk to her and figure out what this is, I compose myself.

Footsteps sound in the hallway, and my heart skips a beat. When she walks through the door, excitement floods me, and my lips spread in a slow smile.

She holds the cup out through the bars, and though it takes all my willpower, I place my hand below hers, only brushing her skin. I sweep my eyes over her face and find her guarded.

If only I had empath magic…

She retreats to the desk, but the fire of her touch plays along my skin. I chug the water to alleviate my dry mouth and force myself back to the cot, placing far too much distance between us.

I kick off my boots, letting them thud to the floor. I watch Elairie carefully as I pull my vest off, delighting in the sharp rise of her breasts as she pulls in a deep breath. Smiling, I settle the vest on the end of my cot with a soft sigh of relief.

Maybe it isn't just in my head…

Elairie's gaze drops to her hands, hidden by the desk.

"So," I begin, "what do you normally do here? You know… when there are no prisoners."

She shrugs. "Depends on the night. There's a training room down the hall. It has a dummy and some wooden weapons. Sometimes, if one of us stays over a bit when we switch off, we spar in there. I try to practice or use the weights almost every night. Sometimes I read. Sometimes I draw."

"Do you have any drawings here, now? I'd love to see them."

She smiles and shakes her head. A light blush colors her cheeks. "I take them all home. They're not much to look at anyway."

"I'm sure they're wonderful." Even if they weren't, I'd love them because they're hers. "They have to be better than anything I could draw."

"I doubt it." She laughs, and the sound fills me with joy. My heart threatens to burst out of my chest. Her eyes sparkle like sapphires, and I ache for a closer look at them.

Opting to change the subject, I say, "So, you can fight?"

She nods.

"Please, tell me you kick that evening guard's ass on a regular basis." A huge smile threatens to split my face wide open at the thought of her pummeling him.

Again, she laughs, and impossibly, my smile widens.

"I've sparred with him a few times. He has yet to beat me." A laugh interrupts her. "It always makes him mad."

"Good. He deserves it." I chuckle, despite my sincerity.

Concern creases her brow, etching deep lines into her beautiful skin. "Has he been cruel to you?"

"No, just negligent. But he was cruel to you. That was more than enough for me not to like him."

Internally, I freeze, realizing my words.

Please, Gods, don't let her ask why it bothered me so much.

She starts to speak but thinks better of it, closing her mouth. Finally, she says, "It's nothing. I've heard worse. I'm sure you have too." She looks at me intently, then smiles. "I'd be lying if I said I didn't want to go take it out on the dummy in the other room though."

"Ouch. I'm not a dummy." I grin at her.

"Very funny." She shakes her head, but the smile never leaves her face. "I meant the one in the training room."

"There are other, much more enjoyable ways to take out your frustrations, you know," I say. Shock sweeps through me as the words slip past my lips, but I roll with it, giving her a wink.

Calling my bluff, she asks, "What might those be?" Her eyes twinkle with more emotions than I can pin down.

With a smirk, I say, "Well, drawing and reading, of course."

"Ah, yes, of course." She laughs again, warming pieces of my heart that I'd never even realized were cold.

I draw my legs up onto the cot, crossing them beneath me. Leaning forward, I brace my arms on my knees.

She holds my gaze. Slowly, sadness etches into her face as her eyes dive deep into my soul. "What was it like? Being a slave, I mean. How did it work?"

My mind grinds to a halt, and I pull in a deep breath.

"Sorry," she says. Words tumble from her lips, falling over themselves as she adds, "If you don't want to talk about it, that's fine. I'm sure it can't be easy for you, I just… Well, I always wondered what it would've been like, and how anyone could ever get over it afterward. You seem like a wonderful person. It must've taken a lot of strength to get past it."

I take a deep breath, then say, "It's ok. I don't mind telling you. I just don't know how to describe it." I shrug. "When the Master ordered me to do something, I didn't have a choice. My mind rebelled, but my body acted according to his command. My arms and legs moved of their own accord, or his, I guess. I was just along for the ride."

I run a hand through my hair, look down at the floor, and sigh. "If it was more of a passive command, like 'don't leave my land,' I could do what I wanted until I reached the boundary of his land. Then, my body would just… stop. My legs would go no further. I couldn't even reach my hand past the boundary he set."

Shaking my head, I close my eyes for a second. "It was terrible. So many times, I wanted to run away. I wanted out. But I was never strong enough to resist it. I don't even know if it's possible."

I glance up at Elairie. One clenched hand rests over her heart.

A part of me wishes she were reaching for me, wishes her arms were wrapped around my waist to keep me afloat in these memories.

Sighing, I continue, "If we did something the Master didn't like, he used his magic on us. He had several types of elemental magic, so the punishments varied. Pain was the only constant."

"How old were you?" Elairie whispers.

"I was born his slave. Father killed him when I was 14. Saerine was 16. We tried living in the forest for a while, but we could never find enough food. Wolves nearly killed us over scraps… I don't even know how many times."

"I'm sorry," Elairie says, eyes softening.

The words shake me. She doesn't need to apologize. It wasn't her who did these things. But she hates that it happened, that it happened *to me.*

Where has she been all this time? How much easier would things have been with someone to help me through?

Sure, I had Saerine, but I always worried about getting her through it, getting Oran and Kraimin through it. Even just having enough food for them is a challenge. We never get the chance to sit and talk. If Saerine would even want to talk about it.

But with Elairie, I have nothing but time to sit and talk.

Briefly, I wonder if we were supposed to meet this way. Without the bars, we would have crashed together. We would have given in to the heat around us.

Or at least… I would have.

Anything she wanted from me, I'd give.

But like this, we can't go any further than talking.

Is that how it was supposed to be?

Internally, I laugh, chiding myself for thinking this could have been arranged by the Gods. As if anything about me or my life could be so important as to necessitate Godly interference.

Realizing I haven't spoken for a while, I say, "Thank you." She tips her head, surprised, so I continue. "No one ever wants to talk about it. Thank you for letting me. And for caring enough to be sorry for things you didn't do."

She smiles sadly. "It shouldn't be swept under the rug. People need to talk about it. They need to know how terrible it was for the people enslaved. Maybe then they could call you Fox Elves again, instead of Blood Elves."

"Maybe eventually. I don't see it happening any time soon though."

Sighing, she offers up a reluctant nod. "Well, if you want to keep talking about it, go ahead. I'll gladly listen."

"What do you want to know?"

"Well, how did they actually bring people under the spell?"

"Aromatic oils worked on people close by. Same with powders. Potions last longer and don't wear off, no matter how far away you roam. But it's hard to convince someone to drink a random potion." A morbid laugh escapes me. "My Master would douse himself in the oil and go to a village. Once the Fox Elves' wills bent to the oil, he'd command them to drink the potion."

"How long did the potions last?"

"I never saw anyone need a second one."

Her brows furrow.

I hesitate, wondering if I should go on.

She's handled it all fairly well thus far.

"A lot of slaves were sent to battle and never returned. Some were tortured and killed in front of everyone. I was never sure if it was because their potions were going to wear off or if he just thought we were expendable. I think it was just that they weren't needed anymore because some were new recruits. Except for those who were especially skilled in something or those who could use magic, the Master didn't seem to care who died. At least, not toward the end."

Sadly, I add, "Any excuse was a good excuse."

"He didn't worry about running out of slaves?" Incredulity shines on Elairie's face, and rage simmers in her eyes.

I shake my head. "Kaistrum was already dead by then. He knew it wouldn't be long before it was his turn. As long as he had enough to protect him if the Light Elves found him, he didn't care."

Elairie wrings her hands, making me dread the next question.

I know I'll answer her because I want her to know, not that it makes sense. But wanting to tell her doesn't untie the knots in my stomach as I wait for her to speak.

At long last, she begins with, "The night you got that scar…"

My mouth goes dry. I run a hand through my hair and let out a deep breath.

She rushes on, "Did he mean to kill you?"

She looks like her heart might break depending on my answer. Or maybe I just want her to care that someone wanted me dead. I take a deep breath to steady my voice and tell her the only thing I can tell her.

The truth.

"Yes. I can't be sure since he wasn't around to answer any questions when I came around, but with the amount of magic he used…" I nod solemnly. "He meant for me to die. I think he'd given up on escaping the Light Elves, at that point. I can do some Earth magic. It was extremely useful in farming and construction. I could've built fortifications. But he still wanted to kill me."

I nearly choke on the next words. "He almost did, even though Mother…" A lump in my throat chokes my words.

In a small voice, Elairie asks, "What happened?" Then, she quickly adds, "If you don't want to talk about it, that's fine. I understand."

"No, I'll tell you. It might take a bit, though."

"I've got time." She smiles sympathetically.

I sigh, then dive in.

"My parents had been out for a couple weeks on an errand for the Master. Saerine and I never asked what they had to do. They always came back with blood crusted under their nails or on their clothes, but we were still excited to see them." I sigh.

I stare at my hands as that night consumes me, pulls me back in time.

I watch night fall all around me, hear the laughter trickling from our family, broken and beaten, but happy for the shortest moment. I remember hoping they'd get to stay for more than just a couple of days.

The Master approaches, meandering through the slave huts to 'enforce curfew.' All it would take is a simple command, and curfew would be obeyed. But cruelty twists his features.

He leers at Saerine, even as he stomps toward us. I fall silent, patting her arm to shush her.

But it's too late.

Lightning courses through her, dragging screams from her throat. She twists and jerks with it as it moves outward from her shoulder, burning her clothes as it streaks down her back. A macabre dance grips her, and I scream her name.

And the Master turns toward me.

I rush forward, desperate to ease Saerine's fall. My heart pounds in my chest, and impotent rage coils tight in my belly. But lightning bursts through me before I reach her, singeing every fiber of my being.

The Master saunters closer. An eerie smile spreads his lips, haunting in the light of the torches and the moon.

I try to scream, but my throat threatens to rip wide open. I slam my eyes shut, blocking out the world. My skin burns, and my joints ache. Eternity spreads out before me as I shake and twist in an agonizing frenzy. My heart starts to give out, fluttering weakly as spasms rock my body.

And then, the lightning stops.

I fall to the ground, and all I see is my mother. She stands between me and the Master, flailing and writhing in pain.

My eyes fade in and out as darkness slowly consumes my vision.

Mother falls, landing so close.

I reach for her, crying as I try to hold her hand. The life starts to fade from her eyes as an errant twitch jerks my hand closer to hers.

Gripping her hand, holding on for dear life, I beg, "Stay with me. Please."

I shake my head, forcing myself out of the memory. I relay the details to Elairie, trying to keep my voice level but failing.

"We tried so hard to stay there, with each other. But we couldn't. We held on for dear life. Until we didn't."

I rub a hand over my face. "I was scared. Scared of death. Scared that I'd never see her again if I closed my eyes. But I still do. Her face haunts my dreams, even more than the Master's. Her beautiful green eyes with streaks of blue, so frail, focused on nothing but me. Then, focused on nothing…" My voice breaks over the words, cracking painfully. I blink back tears, refusing to cry in front of Elairie.

I clear my throat. "Saerine saved me. She healed me. When I woke up the next day, she told me what happened. Mother died, still clutching my hand. She saved me. Father had found a big stick or a piece of lumber. Something. He'd slammed it into the Master's head. Saerine says she still hears the sick thud of it sometimes, still sees his nearly bashed in head. Master still got him though, and far faster. He was in survival mode at that point. Torture was out of the question. He unleashed a terrible amount of magic on Father. He had to have died instantly. I hope so anyway. I can't imagine what that much magic would have *felt* like."

I hear a sniffle and look up to see tears falling down Elairie's beautiful face. My mouth drops open. Standing, I rush to the bars. "I'm sorry," I tell her, my heart twisting with new pain. "I didn't mean to make you cry."

"It's ok." She shakes her head. "You don't need to be sorry. I knew it wasn't going to be a happy story." She looks at me earnestly. "What happened to your Master?" As her mouth forms the word 'Master,' her face shifts into an expression of disgust.

"That's the only good part of the story. I can't even lie and say I feel bad for him, or for being glad that he died the way he did. He suffered for a week. For a few days, he still had enough control over the slaves to keep the healers trying to save him. But as his spirit faded, his control slipped. And since they all wanted him to die, as his control slipped, they fought him. Each and every second he moved closer to death, they got stronger. They stopped trying to help him. Stopped cleaning him up. Infection set in, and he grew weaker. Eventually, they stopped trying altogether. He died in a pool of his own blood. I don't envy him his death."

After a brief hesitation, I admit, "I wouldn't change it though. He deserved every bit of the pain he felt."

Silence falls between us as Elairie wipes the tears from her face.

"I hope you don't think less of me for that," I whisper.

She looks up at me, surprised, and quickly shakes her head. "No, of course not."

Relief floods through me.

"What was his name? Your Master, I mean."

"Traimon. We never called him that though. We weren't allowed to. Sometimes we forgot he even had a name other than Master," I scoff.

"Well, with a name like Master, who needs a normal name?"

"It does roll off the tongue easier than Traimon." A small smile creeps onto my face as the tension breaks. I lean against the bars, bracing my weight on my arms again.

Clamoring for a happier topic, I say, "Your name is nice though."

And just like that, we're flirting again. But this time, she knows some of the darkness in my heart. She knows, and she didn't turn away. She didn't even flinch.

When the conversation shifts to magic, she says that her mother is a fortune teller and an empath. "I can sense auras. That's how I know you're not a terrible person," she says with a laugh.

"Not completely, anyway."

We laugh, and her eyes sparkle like gems.

"How does it work?" I ask. "How much can you learn about someone that way?"

"You can get an overview of their personality. I've practiced quite a bit, so I can get some finer details too. Like, I know that you're a good person, but you'll break the law or fight to protect someone you love. I know you have a strong sense of honor."

Her fingers move, worrying at the bottom seam of her shirt. She stills them, clasping her hands together on her lap, and looks down. "Sorry. I check all the people they bring in here. Kind of a self-preservation thing."

"Don't be sorry. It's smart," I say. "I wouldn't want you to get hurt."

It's bordering on an admission of my feelings for her, but I can't let her keep feeling bad for protecting herself. Self-consciousness stills my tongue, and I sit, wondering what's going through her head. Eventually, I stammer out a lame question, but it's enough to start the conversation up again.

Time moves far too quickly, pulling the morning toward us. My eyelids droop as my nap wears off. I try to fight it, but a yawn escapes. I slouch on the cot, and

Elairie teases me for it. By the time her shift ends, I'm nearly horizontal.

Sadness falls over me, and I wonder if they'll release me today. I should be excited at the thought, but it would mean not seeing her again. I want to figure something out, just in case, but I can't exactly ask her if I'll ever see her again or make plans for if they release me. I have no right to ask her something like that.

So, as she gets up to leave, all I say is, "Goodnight, Elairie."

"Sweet dreams, Beluroan." Her smooth voice follows me into sleep.

Chapter 5
Elairie

I float home, marveling at the strange connection between Beluroan and I. Our conversation sparkles in my mind, a gleaming beacon of hope and promise.

But why should it?

I try to talk myself out of my delusion, telling myself that I have no reason to hope. After all, Beluroan made no declarations of his feelings, if he feels anything for me at all.

And why should he?

We've only known each other for a couple of days.

And yet, my heart flutters.

My home comes into view, the tiny cottage peeking out behind our old fence. My mother stands near the kitchen window, eyes blank, held firm in the grips of a vision. Her eyes slowly refocus, and a smile spreads across her face.

At least it was a good vision.

I smile and quickly cover the remaining distance to the door.

Maybe she'll stop avoiding me, now.

The exhilarating smell of freshly brewed mint tea greets me as I step through the door. Two cups wait on the table with a jar of honey between them. My eyes drift to a plate of bread and a jar of strawberry jam.

I hope it's one of the jars she made.

I don't know what she does differently, but hers always turns out better.

Mother turns to greet me. A hint of sadness strains her eyes, but a warm smile plays on her lips. We sit together, drinking tea and talking.

She asks about work, and I blush. I hold back the details, telling her the bare minimum about Beluroan.

But how much does she intuit?

She opens her mouth to speak but thinks better of it. She smiles into her tea, taking a long sip. For a single heartbeat, I wonder if she'll induce a vision to learn more, but I know better.

"How did Ultna take having him there?" she asks with a raised brow.

I relay the details, and anger simmers in her eyes. But only briefly. Some errant thought claims her, and whatever has been keeping her away from me lately lurks in the depths of her eyes.

Just tell me…

But she says nothing.

She finishes her last bite of bread and jam as I drink the remnants of my tea. Mother glances at me with a sad smile.

"Well," she begins, "I suppose I should head off to work. I'm sure many people will want to see me today." She chuckles.

She moves to clear away the dishes, but I tell her not to worry about it. She glances at me as she heads for the door, and I can almost see the words hovering on the tip of her tongue.

But she stops herself.

I'm struck yet again with a sense of something lost within her, something forlorn. And this time, I feel it. Deep concern and anxiety twist my stomach.

But it doesn't make sense.

Normally, I can only get a clear idea of what type of person someone is. I've never been able to see into the depths of someone's eyes and feel their emotions.

Don't be silly, Elairie.

It's not like I have empath magic.

She must be more worried than I thought if I could see it that clearly.

But somehow it seems like more than that.

She was trying to hide it. I just saw through it.

A yawn bubbles up within me. My eyelids droop as I clean our dishes. Exhaustion dogs my heels as I climb the stairs and slip into bed. My eyes fall shut before I can puzzle out the odd sensation from downstairs.

***

I wake with my stomach in knots, wondering if Beluroan will still be at the jail. For the sake of his sister and nephews, I hope not.

But for my sake, I hope he's there.

My mind whirls with the impossibility of finding him if he's been released, even in a town this small. Of course, he'd know how to find me. He could drop by the jail to see me some night.

But would he?

I stretch, and my toes peek out from under the blankets into cold air. Shivering, I roll over, curling up beneath the blankets and resolving not to rush out without a jacket tonight. Dread fills me at the prospect of seeing Ultna again.

And I'm not getting there early. He will finish his shift this time.

To the Abyss with him.

Immediately, I regret wishing such a terrible fate upon him, jerk or not. I sigh, wondering why I can't use the term lightly, as so many others do.

My stomach clenches as a strange feeling wells up within me, separating from the guilt of casual condemnation. Worry tightens my chest, and thoughts of the food supplies at Beluroan's home fill my head.

But the feelings aren't mine.

They're separate somehow, distant.

They're Beluroan's.

Just like with Mother at the table, I just know the feelings are his.

I rise from my bed and cross the room, head and heart full of the tension that floods him.

No. That isn't how this works. I just know how much food they have left.

He told me, didn't he?

I scour my memory, trying to pick out the details of our conversation about their food. But it doesn't explain it.

This isn't just me worrying. An odd second feeling, an extra set of emotions lurks within me, like a thought in the back of my mind. There, but not there. Just separate enough to recognize it as not being my own.

Just like Mother used to describe empath magic.

My hands still on the door of my wardrobe.

But this isn't how magic works. I've never been able to do this before. I can sense auras. I'm good at that. But I'm not an Empath.

Magic doesn't develop. It's either there or it isn't.

My feelings are just... confused.

Maybe I'm coming down with something.

And yet, just as I know new types of magic don't develop out of nowhere, I know this is an exception. Some way, somehow, it's happening.

Just ignore it. There's something more important at hand, right now. I need to get food to Saerine, Oran, and Kraimin.

Then it hits me. Panic trickles down my spine.

Did Beluroan tell me his nephews' names?

He told me Saerine's name, but theirs? He must have. How else could I have known? I don't have Fortune Magic.

My heart stutters, sinking at a different rate than that second set of emotions.

I'm not an Empath either, but what is this? I feel his emotions. I felt Mother's.

I shake my head to dislodge the nonsense and focus on getting ready for work. Trousers, on. Short-sleeved blouse, on. I tug on my light armor and gloves.

I rush through the rest of my preparations, trying to keep my mind on only the things I'm doing, the motions of my hands as I lace my boots, the feel of the buttons and buckles of my vest.

Braiding my hair in a new way, I tell myself that it's not for Beluroan. I put it up in a bun with small braids wrapped throughout. I smile briefly into the one mirror in our house, silently pleased with what I've done.

I put my jacket on and meander out the door, focusing on my footsteps. But as I walk, that same distant worry creeps into my heart. My palms sweat with it. Desperate to ease the tension, I decide to offer again to take them food.

It helps, easing my own worries. But that separate little nagging in the back of my mind persists, fraying my nerves.

Because Beluroan doesn't know I plan to offer food again.

His stress sinks into my stomach like a rock, bringing with it the certainty that this, somehow, is empath magic. His emotions, not mine, grip my heart and squeeze it tight.

Maybe Mother has heard of this before… Maybe it was mentioned in those old scrolls she and Grandmother used to read all the time.

I shiver, though whether from the brisk air or the icy maelstrom inside me, I can't be sure. Taking a deep breath, I resolve to ask her tomorrow.

Beluroan's emotions fade as I approach the jail, and uncertainty settles in the pit of my stomach.

Was that real? Or did I imagine it?

Either way, relief floods me now that I have my mind and my heart to myself.

I rush into the jail, desperate for the warmth it offers. Ultna stands, ready to leave with his guard jacket already hanging near Deima's. He says nothing, scowling when he bothers to look at me. He disappears out the door before I even switch into my guard jacket. The black fabric hugs me, warm and snug.

Silence rings out from the cell room, and my heart beats unsteadily as I wonder if he's quiet, or asleep, or… gone.

He has to be here. He wouldn't have been worrying about Saerine and the kids otherwise.

Maybe he's asleep. That'd explain why his feelings just faded out.

I wish for them to come back, but without any mastery of Empath, that lies beyond my control.

I chuckle, chiding myself for wanting this thing I doubted and hated mere moments ago.

Anticipation and hope build in my chest as I venture toward the cell room. My feet beg to speed up, to match the hammering pace of my heart. Heat and lightning build around me, tugging at my aura magic, flowing through my veins. They dance along my skin, and I know that only one thing could satisfy them.

Beluroan's touch.

I force myself to slow down, lest my too quick footsteps give me away. I can't let him know how worked up I am.

Because he probably isn't.

I clear the threshold, and my gaze seeks him out.

Lounging on his cot, he glances up. Roguish stubble decorates his chin. His hair cascades around his shoulders, and the top buttons of his shirt hang open. A warm smile spreads across his face when our eyes meet, sending my heart soaring.

I try to use empath magic, hoping to discern some clue about his emotions. But I fail.

Was it even real?

I stuff it away and smile back. "Any requests for dinner tonight?"

"My requests aren't exactly on the menu, so whatever you want to bring me is fine," he says with a raised eyebrow, stoking the fire that burns around us.

I almost ask what he means, just to be coy, but fear stills my tongue. If he only wants to go home, a completely reasonable wish, my heart would crumble.

He may as well tell me these feelings are mine and mine alone.

"I'll be right back," I say.

This time, as I meander down the hall, the flames and bolts of electricity don't subside. Not immediately.

They follow me to the front desk and into the stairwell. Only when I reach the cold storage room does the air around me return to normal. The fire and sparks disappear, and a chill settles over me, taking their place.

I gather our food in a rush and hurry up the stairs. As soon as my feet hit the landing, the air ignites around me, chasing the chill from my bones.

A glance at the unlit fireplace sparks an idea.

Walking into the cell room, I ask, "Would you like the fireplace lit? It's all the way in the other room, but after a while, it warms this room too."

He considers me carefully, choosing his words. With a guarded expression, he says, "I really don't need it, but if you'd like it lit, that's fine."

Does he feel this?

Or is he just one of those people who never gets cold?

My mind spins as the fire around us threatens to consume me.

"I don't need it either," I say.

Raising the stakes, I set the trays on the desk. Reconsidering it the entire time, I remove my jacket and add, "I'm actually a bit warm."

I drape it over the back of the chair and pick up Beluroan's tray. Turning around, I find him searching my face in earnest.

I've given him a hint. I've acknowledged this strange, heated aura.

Now, it's his turn.

Watching him closely, I implore him to say something, anything. His gaze drops to my lips for a single heartbeat before he closes his eyes.

A second set of emotions bursts across my awareness, too quick and too complex for me to disentangle. I struggle to bring them back, but it's no use. My mind reels with my own emotions, the fire and lightning aura, and the mysterious new magic. Harnessing it, using that new skill for all it's worth is beyond me.

Giving up, I slide Beluroan's tray through the bars. Metal grates on metal, and he opens his eyes. Dark mystery shines in his gaze.

He rises, watching me carefully as he walks toward the bars. Not bothering with the tray, he sets my skin on fire, laying his hand directly on mine. He slides his thumb over my knuckles, and it takes everything I have to keep my hand firmly on the tray. I ache to drop it, to let it fall so that I might explore his hand, his wrist.

My gaze drifts over his features, coming to rest on full lips, and I wonder what they'd feel like pressed against my own.

My mind fills with images of Beluroan pressed against me, hands grasping my waist and lips caressing my neck. I see him kissing just below my ear, and my skin pricks, aching for his touch.

Whirling from the scene in my mind, I pull myself back to reality. Beluroan traces patterns on my wrist with fingers made of lightning. A sharp intake of breath pulls heat into my lungs.

A quiet voice in the back of my mind, a voice that sounds a lot like my mother's warnings when I first got this job, tells me to be careful. He could be planning to pull me up against the bars and steal my keys.

But thanks to my aura magic, I know him better than that.

So, I shove that little voice away as Beluroan moves closer, bridging the gap that separates us. His hand deserts my wrist, and he reaches between the bars to touch my face, making my skin burn. His fingers spread over my cheek, and his lips part, drawing in shallow breaths. He searches my eyes.

His hand skims across my skin, sliding down to my neck and sending a flock of butterflies fluttering through me. He caresses my jaw with his thumb, melting me as a pleasant weight builds in my stomach.

My fingers tighten, fighting to hold on to the tray, determined not to let it fall to the ground. But I don't remember why.

He reaches out with his other hand, placing it on the bars.

And the moment breaks.

The bars.

My eyes focus on them, reminding me that nothing can happen. I close my eyes, lowering my head as reality sinks in. I wrap a hand around Beluroan's on the bars, and he sighs.

Flames play along my skin, burning everywhere we touch. Lightning spreads through me. I open my eyes, searching his gaze for answers.

But his eyes are closed, head resting against the bars.

I clamor for something to say, something to do. We can't stay like this all night. Reluctant to leave his touch, I say, "We should probably eat." The words hurt as they drag their way up my throat.

Our eyes meet, and a deep sadness passes between us. Beluroan drops his gaze, nodding. As he pulls his hand from my face to take the tray, my heart fills with ice.

Though our feet drag in protest, we draw apart, settling into our normal seats and eating silently. Yet, my giddy heart gallops, and my mind spins.

It isn't just me. He feels whatever this is. He has to.

Why else would he have touched me like that?

I reach up to touch my cheek, recalling his gentle touch. I can almost feel his skin on mine. And that look in his eyes.

What was he searching for?

Did he want me to tell him how I felt? Did he see how much I wanted those bars to disappear? How badly I wanted to wrap myself up in his arms?

The suddenness of all this unsettles me. But something about it feels right. Somehow, I know I couldn't escape the bond forming between us, even if I wanted to.

And I definitely don't want to.

I take a slow sip of water, buying myself time to think. I ache to use empath magic to gain some sort of understanding, but it's too new. I can't use it at will. Not to mention how invasive that would be.

And then, I wonder.

Did I have a vision?

Heat stirs within me at the prospect of us tangled together, him pressed against me, and I find myself hoping it was a vision. But how many new types of magic can I hope to develop?

The normal answer would be none.

But I felt his emotions, felt Mother's emotions. That's Empath Magic.

But knowing the names of his nephews isn't. Random insights, visions… That's Fortune Magic.

I sigh, then drain the last of my water. Turning to face him, I find him watching me, empty tray sitting beside him. A smile tugs at one corner of his lips.

I don't dare ask why.

Instead, I opt for an easier subject. "There's something I wanted to talk to you about." Beluroan sits forward in his seat, and I go on, "Saerine and your nephews, do they still have enough food?"

Brows knitting together, he asks, "That's what you want to talk to me about?"

His eyes cloud over with…

Is that disappointment?

Still cautious, with frayed nerves, I say, "For now, yes. There are other things too, but I need to get this out of the way first."

Reluctantly, he answers, "No, they probably don't anymore." He rubs a hand over his face. "Not unless they were strict with rationing."

Before he continues, I let the words tumble out, trying to ease his worries.

"Would you like me to take them some food in the morning? Just in case they don't let you go tomorrow. Mother and I always have a big garden. There are plenty of fruits and vegetables left that we can't hope to preserve before winter. Lots of bread and some cheeses. It wouldn't be any trouble."

Surprise rings in his tone as he asks, "It really concerns you that much?"

I nod, not daring to admit how much I've been thinking about it. Or that I felt his worry for their growling stomachs.

"Are you sure it wouldn't be any trouble? And that you and your mother would have enough to get through the winter?"

"I'm sure."

Beluroan nods. "Please, take them what you can spare."

"I will after my shift. If you want, you can write them a letter."

"Thank you." Shaking his head, he continues, "I can't even begin to tell you how much this means to me."

A smile spreads over my face. "I'm just glad I can help."

Silence falls over us. I want to ask about what happened between us just moments ago, but I don't know how to start. Questions spin through my mind.

But outside, someone shouts, dragging my attention away.

Chapter 6
Beluroan

"Looks like we'll have to talk more later," Elairie says, rising from her chair. She leaves me, venturing to the front lobby and taking part of this intense heat with her.

The shouting outside intensifies, coming closer and closer. My stomach ties itself in knots.

The front door opens, and Elairie calls out to someone, asking if they need help. The reply eludes me, but the yelling gets louder.

Whoever the patrolman has in tow screams, "Get your damn hands off me," and, "To the Abyss with you."

Not exactly the smartest things to say to a patrolman.

I move closer to the bars, straining my ears, but they breech the lobby, bringing the man's words within earshot.

"The lass had it comin' to her. Did you not see how she was dressed? She may as well have put up a sign advertising her goods. She certainly had enough hanging out of her dress."

Cold fury rushes through me. My hands start to tingle, just like earlier. Sparks fly from my fingertips again, existing where they shouldn't.

This doesn't make sense. I don't have fire magic.

"Shut up, you miserable creature," the patrolman hisses in the lobby.

Elairie asks, "So, I assume he tried to force himself on some poor woman?"

"After mugging her, yes," the patrolman says. "She was only visible through her dress because he ripped it when he tore her necklace off."

Cold and to the point, Elairie's voice comes out low as she hisses, "Let's get him in a cell." Powerful undercurrents seethe beneath her words.

She passes me, eyes locked on the two cells at the back. She picks through her keys at the cell diagonal from mine as the patrolman drags the new prisoner in. They notice me, but only barely, neither seeing my sparking hands.

Both men look like they could snap a tree in half with one hand. But the prisoner is a Blood Elf. Unkempt hair, black as ink, reaches halfway down his back. Eyes the color of old blood glare at the world around him, framed by skin barely darker than mine.

Chills run down my spine at the sight of him. Hatred fills me knowing that there are men like this out in the world.

He looks at me with malice in his eyes and jerks his head in Elairie's direction. "At least there's some pretty company here."

A sickening sneer paints his face, and he dares to wink.

My fists clench, and the sparks dissipate. Gritting my teeth, trembling with rage, I say, "You rotting piece of filth."

Laughing, he says, "Thanks."

Elairie finds the right key and unlocks the cell. But the patrolman moves too quickly, already unlocking the prisoner's cuffs.

Shouldn't he get the bastard into the cell first?

"You know," the patrolman says, "I could get someone to cover my area if you want me to stay here with you. Two prisoners at one time could be a lot to handle."

One wrist free. The prisoner doesn't move, but fear trickles through me.

Surely, they've done this before. The patrolman must know what he's doing. Besides, the man wouldn't dare try anything with a patrolman and a guard right there.

Would he?

The patrolman continues, barely paying attention. "I could stick around, help you out. Then, once these two fall asleep, we could talk or something."

Realization washes over me.

He likes her.

He's not paying attention to the prisoner because he likes Elairie.

Jealousy and anger hit me hard. "Pay attention to what you're doing, not on attempting to flirt."

But it's too late.

The patrolman turns to me as the other cuff unlocks. The prisoner throws a wild elbow into the patrolman's jaw and knocks him out cold. He falls to the stone floor, limp. Blood gushes from his nose and mouth.

Before I can even blink, the new prisoner wraps his arm around Elairie's throat, pulling her back against him. Her keys fall to the floor with a loud clank.

"No!" I scream. I thrash against the bars like an animal in a cage, desperate to reach them, but the prisoner skips out of reach.

Elairie claws at his arm and kicks at his legs, but the behemoth barely notices. Using his other hand to pull his arm tighter against her neck, he squeezes the air from her.

As Elairie's beautiful face turns red, panic builds within me. I grab the bars of my cell, trying to wrench them apart. My earth magic flows through me, so natural, like an extension of myself. My hands warm up, heating the metal they hold and snagging my attention for a heartbeat.

I can think about fire magic later.
For now, I'll use it.

I let the fire move through me, let it heat the bars in hopes of bending them. Gritting my teeth, I scream out, hoping the Gods will send someone in to stop him.

Elairie's face turns a terrible shade of red. She claws at his arm, but her movements slow. Sensing the fight leaving his victim, the vile man loosens his grip, keeping her conscious. She takes a deep breath and closes her beautiful, dark blue eyes.

Oh, Gods. He wants her to keep fighting.

Vomit rushes up my throat, but I force it down.

Arm still around Elairie's neck, the man uses his other hand to undo his belt.

My insides boil, and my hands ignite. The metal bars glow within my fiery grip, and I pull as hard as I can.

I scream out as her head lolls forward.

But then, her eyes flash open, and she slams her head back into the prisoner's face. His nose shatters with a terrible, satisfying crunch, and he howls in pain as blood pours down his face. She does it again, and this time, there's more squish than crunch.

But she's not done.

Elairie slams her elbow into his stomach, a solid hit, and he releases her. The man doubles over with a gulp of air and blood, clutching his stomach. She turns toward him, places her hands on his shoulders and drives her knees into his groin.

He falls over, bloody and whimpering.

Shock overtakes me, quickly followed by relief.

Elairie drags him into his cell, barely struggling to move the giant, and slams the door shut. He lies motionless on the floor. Her right hand moves to the dagger strapped to her thigh. She grasps it, chest heaving, then releases the hilt.

Snatching up her keys from the floor, she locks the cell and backs away from him. Bending at the waist, hand trembling, she checks the patrolman's neck for a pulse. Her hand comes away bloody, but she nods.

Slowly, she crosses the room and sits between my cell and the empty one, drawing her knees up to her chest. Her head falls forward into her hands, streaking the patrolman's blood over her face as she cries into her palms. Tears roll down her wrists.

I kneel beside the bars, putting a gentle hand on her knee.

Her head jerks up, eyes darting to the new prisoner, but he lies motionless in his cell. Her gaze falls upon my hand, then lifts to me.

Tears stain her face, and red streaks color her eyes. Blood shines in her hair and on her face, and strands of lavender hang loose from her bun.

I stare at her, marveling at her strength, even as my heart breaks for what she's just endured. She's beautiful, despite the blood and the tears.

She scoots closer, leaning against the bars of my cell. Reaching through, I wrap my arms around her shoulders. They shake as she sobs, and I stroke her hair, oblivious to the blood that comes away on my hands.

Slowly, her tears subside, and she gazes up at me. "Thank you," she whispers. Her eyes drift upward to the bars around me, and she smiles. "I'm glad he isn't as strong as you."

Confused, I ask, "What do you mean?" After all, the new prisoner is clearly stronger than me.

She points up near the corner of my cell, right where I strained to get through. "You bent the bars," she says.

I look again and find a curve. "I cheated," I laugh. "I used earth magic."

A soft laugh escapes her, and relief flows through me like a warm river.

"These are strong bars," I say. "Even with magic, I didn't get them very far apart."

"That you moved them at all is impressive. They have wards on them to guard against earth magic." She laughs again but seems genuinely impressed.

"I needed to help you. You obviously didn't need my help, but I needed to help you. More than I've ever needed anything before in my life."

Elairie's eyes fall to her lap. She opens her mouth to speak, but the patrolman moves, moaning in pain.

With one last look into my eyes, she pulls herself from my arms and goes to him. Lightly patting his face, she brushes short strands of flaxen hair off his forehead.

"Kaimaer, can you hear me?"

Sharp pangs of jealousy stab through me, and I wonder if she cares for him. Just because they haven't vowed themselves to each other doesn't mean there's nothing between them.

Why does it matter so much to me already?

"Kaimaer?" Concern creeps into her voice. "I need you to answer me if you can."

The man mumbles, gradually opening his eyes. Elairie and I wait as a tense silence unfolds around us.

But the man's eyes focus on her, and a smile parts his lips. "Hi," he says. "I take it you made me look bad?"

A sigh of relief slips through Elairie's lips. Laughing, she says, "Well, someone had to get him into his cell."

She rubs a hand over her face, then helps Kaimaer sit up, leaning him against the desk. "Sit here. I'll call for another patrolman and a healer." She looks at me and adds, "I'll only be gone a moment."

Kaimaer laughs, and I wonder if maybe that sound is how earthquakes start. The giant seems to shake the ground beneath him.

Looking at me, he says, "Don't get any ideas while she's gone. I can only take so much humiliation."

Despite myself, the corners of my mouth turn upward.

Charismatic. Funny. Ridiculously muscular. Humble. I have no doubt he could beat me to a pulp if it came to it. Had he and the brute in the other cell actually fought, the entire jail may have crumbled around them.

I don't stand a chance.

Why would Elairie want me when a man like this obviously wants her attention?

After a few moments, Elairie returns. "The signals are lit."

Kaimaer nods and leans his head against the desk.

Elairie stands in the doorway to the hall, eyes darting from the other prisoner to Kaimaer, then to me. Her gaze lingers on me, taking in my face before sweeping over me.

A thrill shivers over my spine in the wake of her gaze.

A million words die on my lips thanks to Kaimaer's presence, and silence fills the cell room. Elairie makes no move to get closer to him. But she doesn't move closer to me either.

In no time, a patrolwoman strolls in with impeccable posture. Hair like a robin's egg sticks out in short spikes, and eyes the color of faded amber rake over the scene.

Where do they get these people for the patrols?
She may actually be stronger than Kaimaer.

A willowy man follows in her wake, looking like he might blow away in a light spring breeze. His long hair has faded to white, and his beard reaches nearly to his navel.

Setting straight to work, the patrolwoman disappears into the lobby. The hearth crackles to life, and she returns with two metal bowls.

The healer, apparently named Geeran, treats Kaimaer first. Nearly silent, he removes a small waterskin from the largest pocket of the sash draped across his body. He pours some of the contents out, filling a bowl with water that dances with its own light.

Listening to Elairie's account of the attack, he reaches into his sash, pulling bits of plants from one pocket, then another, and sprinkling them into the bowl.

When he finishes his work, he hands the bowl to the patrolwoman, who disappears into the lobby. A soft clink reaches through the hall as she settles the metal bowl on the stone hearth before returning.

Geeran looks at me appraisingly, then at the other prisoner.

"Whenever you're ready, Jaym," the healer says.

The patrolwoman looks to the man in the other cell and nods. Elairie approaches the door, fiddling with her keys for the barest instant before unlocking it. Jaym moves through the door first, but Elairie follows quickly.

My heart pounds in my chest at the sight of her so close to that beast of a man, but she and Jaym work quickly, turning the unconscious man onto his back. Geeran enters the cell, leaning over the man's inert form. He pulls something from his sash, and puts it in the man's mouth.

"He won't be any trouble for several hours, now," the healer breathes.

And the tension goes out of the room.

As Geeran pours some of his blessed water into the bowl, he tells us that the man's name is Courg.

So, Geeran is a healer and *a fortune teller. Useful combination.*

No wonder he didn't have to ask Kaimaer what hurt.

He cleans the prisoner's face and prepares another tonic. Jaym takes it to the fire in the other room, bringing the first bowl back with her when she returns.

She hands it to Kaimaer, and he drinks slowly. He makes a face but drains the bowl quickly. Setting it aside, he wipes his bloody face on a handkerchief.

Finally, Geeran turns his attention to me. He comes to the bars, sky-blue eyes diving into my soul. I fight the urge to take a step back, surprised by this frail man's power to intimidate.

He nods, then looks to the bent bars of my cell. With a wave of his hand, the bars bend themselves back into place. Another wave, and a shimmer cascades over all the bars of the cell. After a few seconds, it fades.

A new ward.

He has earth magic too?

My mind reels, trying to decide if I broke the old ward or if it was just weak. After all, I'm skilled with earth magic, but not that skilled.

Turning to Elairie, Geeran says, "In the morning, I'll make a formal statement to the Commander regarding my assessment of these men. I've seen all I need to make my recommendations and condemnations."

Jaym fetches the other tonic, and Geeran administers it to the unconscious man, using some sort of magic, I think, to keep him from choking on it. Then, they leave his cell, and Elairie locks it.

And finally, I take an easy breath.

Geeran turns those wise old eyes on Elairie. "Now, it is your turn, dear." He seems a bit sad. "I can't make a tonic for your emotions, but for your neck and your head, I can mix something."

Elairie seems ready to protest, but one raised hand from Geeran stops her.

"It's no trouble. I insist."

Jaym hurries to the lobby and returns with another bowl. Geeran pours some of his shining water into it, adds a few herbs, and lets Jaym take it to the fire. This time, she waits by the hearth.

"They will likely hang him," Geeran says, voice emotionless. "The list of crimes he committed, tonight and on previous nights, is too great for them to let him off with anything less than that."

"And Beluroan?" Elairie asks. Her words come out weighted, but I can't place the emotion hanging on them.

"Most have forgotten that a thief was arrested. After word of tonight's events gets out, the rest will forget too. It will give the Patrol Commander the opportunity he's been waiting for to release him without causing an uproar."

Elairie's face wars with itself, displaying too many emotions for me to piece together.

A deep quiet settles over Geeran, chilling me to my core. His next words do little to ease the feeling. "You have a long journey ahead of you." The words are a whisper, meant only for Elairie and me, and I wonder if maybe he can somehow prevent others from hearing him. Kaimaer doesn't even look up.

Geeran glances my way. "The Gods will provide."

Jaym returns with the tonic, an additional bowl of water, and a rag. But that cryptic, ominous warning hangs in the air.

Elairie drinks the warm liquid quickly, but she doesn't make a face like Kaimaer did. I can only hope she doesn't need them often, that hers simply tastes better. My insides squirm at the thought of her needing a healer often enough to grow accustomed to the taste.

She dips the rag in the water and wipes the blood from her face and hands. Releasing her beautiful hair from its bun, sending waves of lilac and mulberry swirling about her face, she cleans the blood from her hair, as well. Once done, she pins it back up quickly.

As they move to leave, Jaym finally speaks, but her voice comes out too high for her muscular frame. "Are you fit to return to your patrols?"

Kaimaer nods. "Of course. Geeran is an excellent healer. I'm as good as new." As if to demonstrate, he pulls himself up from the floor easily.

"Good. I need you back out there, then."

Jaym and Geeran sweep out of the jail, both surprisingly agile. With one last lingering look at Elairie, Kaimaer departs.

The door shuts behind them, leaving Elairie in the middle of the room with her eyes closed. She barely moves, barely breathes. My arms ache to reach out to her, but too much space separates us. I move forward, getting as close as possible.

My shuffling feet draw her attention, and she opens her eyes. Stepping closer, Elairie takes my hands in hers, leaning her head against the bars. My skin burns at her touch, making me wish for more. Despite the circumstances, my body tenses.

But the image of her leaning over Kaimaer's inert form flashes before my eyes, sobering me immediately. Clenching my jaw, I force myself to ask. "Would you have asked Kaimaer to stay?"

My heart stops, and my lungs refuse to take in air as I wait.

When she finally answers, it's not quite what I hoped for. "If I'd been given the chance to answer, I would've considered it."

My lungs shrivel in my chest.

Somehow, I choke out the words, "So, when you said no one had drawn you in before, did you mean before him?" My voice breaks, and heat blossoms over my skin.

I'm such a fool.

"No," she answers softly. "Definitely not. I wouldn't have asked him to stay for his company. I knew there was going to be trouble. It just came much sooner than I thought."

My knees nearly buckle as the weight lifts from my shoulders. My head falls against the bars. "I imagine his aura is terrible."

"It wasn't even—" she begins but cuts herself short.

"It wasn't even… what?"

"It wasn't just his aura. Something weird is happening." Her eyes move back and forth between mine, considering, searching for something.

Finally, she says, "I felt your worry for Saerine and the boys earlier, just before work. Before we ate, when I had the tray, but you hadn't taken it, I got a burst of emotions from you. It was so quick and there were so many mixed together that I had no idea what you were feeling, but I felt them. I felt my mother's feelings this morning. Each time, it was like I had two sets of emotions."

Before she can think her way out of telling me, she hurries onward.

"But I've never had empath magic before. I've never had any of my mother's divining ability either, but I knew your nephews' names."

So, it's happening to her too?

I stare, openmouthed, struggling to wrap my head around this revelation.

"I know," she continues, "it sounds crazy. Magic doesn't just appear out of nowhere."

"Except for today, apparently," I say.

She doesn't move as she waits for me to go on. Her hands hold mine so tightly that I fear for the safety of my fingers.

"I guess you didn't see the sparks shooting out of my hands when that bastard made the comment about having 'pleasant company in here.' Or that I heated the bars to help bend them." I take a deep breath. "You were a little busy, at that point."

"You're getting new magic too?"

I nod but say nothing, reaching up to caress her face. She leans into my touch, mumbling something about asking her mom about our new magic.

But her words run together and trail off toward the end.

The air ignites, and my hand slides down to her neck. She looks up at me through her lashes, and I'm gripped by the urge to grab her waist and pull her to me, to crush our lips together.

Damn these bars…

She wraps her hand around mine, and her touch is gentle, tantalizing.

The front door opens and closes and Elairie jerks away, leaving me bereft at the loss of her touch. In the lobby, the morning guard prepares himself for the day, unaware that there are now two prisoners instead of one.

"I have to tell him about what happened," Elairie whispers.

She searches my face, starts to reach for me, but a quick glance down the hall finds the morning guard coming our way. So, she draws back into herself.

It cuts me to the quick knowing she won't reach for me in his presence. Despite all reason, despite my place behind bars, it hurts.

"I'll be right back with some paper for you to write a letter to Saerine."

"Thank you," I say.

Turning, Elairie says, "Deima, good morning. I hope you're prepared for an eventful day or two." She spares one last glance for me, then meets Deima in the hall.

My gaze drifts to Courg's unconscious form. Rage fills me, and tiny arcs of electricity shoot between my fingers. Briefly, I wonder about the new magic, about all the pain it could inflict upon Courg.

Not that I could hurt him while he lies unconscious and defenseless.

Besides, if Elairie can resist the temptation, I have to.

In the lobby, someone shuffles things about. All the while, Elairie relays the events of last night to Deima.

When she finishes, he says, "Oh, Elairie, you should've sent for me. I would've come in early. You should've gone home."

"I'll not be responsible for dragging you away from your family any sooner than necessary," she says.

A brief pause, a heavy silence.

"Besides," she continues, "I'm fine. Geeran gave me a tonic and gave Courg something to keep him asleep. Actually, he's still out cold on his cell floor."

Deima sighs. "I guess I can't change it now, so there's no use arguing."

The drawers of the front desk close, and Elairie says, "I'll be right back. Beluroan has requested that a letter be sent to his sister, explaining why he hasn't come home."

I hear the chair creak as Deima sits down in the other room, then Elairie appears before me. I pull in a deep breath at the sight of her. The air crackles with electricity.

Would Deima notice it if he came in here?

Did Geeran or Jaym or even Courg notice it last night?

Or maybe the Gods have given this gift only to us, to show us the way, to make sure we never overlook this connection.

I scoff at such fanciful thoughts.

Elairie hands me the paper, quill, and ink. Safe from prying eyes, she reaches through the bars to touch my face. My heart skips a few beats, and my stomach leaps into my throat.

She pulls her hand back, a smile playing across her face, and says, "I'll give you some privacy to write." Then, she returns to the lobby.

I sit on my cot, but it's too soft for writing. Settling on the floor with the paper spread out before me, I write.

I fill several pages, telling her of my time here and of the strange connection with Elairie. The events of last night come out, and the quill scratches the paper as I tell her how desperately I needed to break out of the cell to help Elairie.

I look over the letter when I finish, face flushing as I realize just how much I've revealed. Briefly, I consider crumbling it up and starting over, but I shake my head.

Maybe it'll convince Saerine that she can trust Elairie.

The door to the lobby opens and closes again, piquing my curiosity. The chair scoots across the floor, and I hear Deima get to his feet.

Elairie speaks first, saying only, "Good morning, Commander."

He's here already?

"Good morning. Geeran has just been to see me." His deep voice softens with concern as he asks, "Are you alright?"

"Yes, I'm alright," Elairie says. "Geeran is an excellent healer."

"He is, but we both know he can only treat physical wounds."

"I know," she whispers. "I'll be alright, though. In time."

A sad hush falls over the jail, broken only by a rasping snore from Courg.

I scowl at him.

"Well, he'll pay for his deeds. His crimes are great, and they are many." The Commander clears his throat. "He'll hang this afternoon."

Good riddance.

The Commander continues, "Then, there is the matter of the other man being kept here."

I stop breathing, waiting for him to say what they plan to do with me.

"I hated keeping him here. His family must be worried, but I didn't know how to release him without causing an uproar. Terrible as this situation is, it means I can make this right."

The deep voice of the Commander resonates through me, filling me with hope.

"Release him this afternoon, secretly, after the hanging. Word of last night's events are already circulating, and people have moved on from the thief in the bakery. Take food from the cold storage below to his family and replenish the stores as necessary."

My shoulders fall as I blow out a breath.

The lobby floor groans, and the deep voice echoes down the hall once more. "Elairie, I've got a patrolman coming for guard duty tonight. You take the night off."

"Yes, sir. Thank you," she says, and the words border on a whisper.

The floorboards in the hall creak loudly beneath the Patrol Commander.

I close the inkpot and fold my letter to Saerine. Scrambling to my feet, I gather everything up and set it on the cot. I repress the silly notion of saluting this man, not wanting him to mistake it for mockery.

He ducks through the doorway, showing white hair cropped short. He straightens, standing more than a head taller than me. His pale green eyes pierce mine as he stares down at me, muscles straining at the seams of his clothing.

Gods, I hope he knows which prisoner I am.

His eyes dart to the other cell, narrowing at the sight of Courg. Distaste distorts his strong features. Geeran must've told him who was who.

Thank the Gods.

He turns back to me. "My name is Pakaibra," he begins. "I'm sorry you've been held here so long. I hope you can forgive me for that. I wanted to avoid chaos. Gods know what an angry town might've done to you."

"It's alright." My throat goes dry. I swallow, wishing for water. "I understand. You walk a fine line of balance in your position."

He lifts his brows, surprised by my response, surprised by *me*.

"I'll do what I can to set this right. Geeran tells me you're quite gifted with earth magic." He smiles wryly, glancing at the newly repaired bars of my cell.

My eyes go wide.

"I assure you, that was only to help Elairie. I didn't want him to hurt her. I'd never try to escape my cell otherwise," I stammer, making a fool of myself with every word.

Pakaibra holds up a hand, stilling my babbling tongue. "I know." He nods sagely. "Geeran told me his opinion of you. He's never led me astray, and I trust he never will. That he thinks highly of you speaks volumes. And I can tell a little about you, myself."

Shocked, I wait for him to continue.

He doesn't keep me in suspense for long. "I see no reason to waste your gifts. I'll find a position for you with either the construction or farming teams for the city. Of course, where you end up also depends on your preference. And that of the Vairsun Representative."

I nod, dumbfounded.

The Patrol Commander and the Representative are going to discuss me? They're going to find me a job? I must be dreaming.

"Would that be amenable to you?"

"Very much so," I manage.

"I'll find a few options, discuss it with our Representative, and send word to you." He pauses, then, with curiosity sparkling in his eyes, he adds, "Geeran said that you and Elairie will soon be invaluable to us. He wouldn't say more, but I look forward to finding out."

"So do I," I say.

"It was a pleasure to meet you, Beluroan. I'll be in touch." And with that, he leaves with a quick goodbye to Elairie and Deima.

Elairie enters the cell room with Deima on her heels. My arms try to reach for her, but I fight the urge.

Deima stands in the corner, staring at Courg with a scowl wrinkling his pale face.

"I'll still deliver your letter with the food, if you'd like," Elairie offers. "I'll explain that you'll be released this afternoon."

"Thank you." I gather the writing instruments and hand them to her. I give her the letter last, and fear trickles over my spine.

Will she read it?

My heart pounds at the thought of her seeing my feelings laid out, bare and unfiltered.

Before releasing the letter, I dare to run my thumb over hers, one last touch before she leaves.

"Where shall I take this?"

I give her directions to my house, wondering why I hadn't thought to do that before now.

"Alright. I'll take it there straight away." Then, she mouths, "See you soon."

Turning to Deima, she says, "I'll be back after lunch. Better to eat first. These things make me lose my appetite." She turns to leave, taking our fire and lightning with her.

Chapter 7
Evaerga

Evaerga's heart pounds, and the room drifts away as a vision closes in on her. The scents and sounds of the cottage become those of another world as her spirit journeys to the caves of Mount Hybar in the Cargam Mountains.

Gourmaht and Waergou sit, talking in a small cave two tunnels from the command room. Looking pleased with himself, Gourmaht leans back in his chair and listens to his second-in-command.

"We just need to gather more subjects for another attempt. We have all the ingredients in abundance."

"So, begin gathering," Gourmaht says with a sinister smile. The candles on the table glow brighter as rage mingles with his fire magic. "Start by finding whoever is watching us."

Waergou closes his eyes in concentration for a long moment, then smiles when he opens them. "She's in Vairsun."

Gourmaht's eyes shine, and the candles burn brighter.

Realization dawns on Evaerga as the vision ends and her spirit tumbles back into her body.

"They sensed me last time…" she breathes out, pressing a hand to her stomach. Her heart drops. "But if they traced my spirit back, if they initiated this vision and found out where I am…"

Dread fills her, and her mouth goes dry. Her hands tremble, and her knees wobble beneath her.

"They're more powerful than I thought."

She closes her eyes, trying to gain control of herself. Pulling in slow, measured breaths, she reminds herself, "Elairie will be home soon. I can't let her see me like this."

Evaerga brews chamomile tea, hoping to soothe her nerves. Staring into the fireplace, her mind lingers on her daughter.

But another vision begins, cutting off her thoughts.

The face of a Blood Elf swims into focus. Dark red hair and eyes that shine like emeralds. A scar from lightning magic sprawls across his chest.

Beluroan.

He lies on a cot, thinking of Elairie. A bond grows between them, and the strength of it frightens him.

As this brief vision draws to a close, Evaerga feels her shattered nerves gradually piece themselves back together.

Maybe he can care for Elairie.

After they come for me.

Her stomach clenches at the thought, pushing a sob from her.

But the bond she sensed in the vision was more than everyday attraction. There was something deeper to it. It swirled on the air around him, moving through every bit of his being. For a single heartbeat, she wonders if it was an aura. Then, a thought strikes her.

Could it be?

Some of Mother's old scrolls spoke of it…

Rushing to her late mother's room, Evaerga searches vigorously. Dust wafts into the air as she rifles through the wardrobe and all the many chests. Clothes and trinkets spill over the floor as she upends trunks.

Eventually, she finds a chest full of scrolls. Some hold devotions to the Gods, others detail the forms of magic, their uses, and various spells.

At long last, she finds what she seeks. A scroll about Blessed Ones. She casts her eyes over it, devouring the words on the page.

Before she finishes, another vision claims her, pulling her away to a lush valley. A pristine river runs through the middle, and every plant glistens.

Dense grass cradles her feet, begging her to lie down. In the distance, flowering vines wind up the trunks of mature trees.

Evaerga spins in place, marveling at the mountains which scrape the sky on three sides of the valley. But the remaining side holds only a cliff's edge, sending the river toppling down to the world below.

Clouds drift beneath the cliff, floating along in thick groups.

And suddenly, Evaerga knows where she is, knows that if she dared to peer over that edge, her entire world would lie beneath.

This is the Great Valley.

She steps back from the cliff and turns to face the mountains. Her heart falters as she takes in the five beings gathered before her.

It can't be.

Her mind spins, and her breath catches.

The Gods.

Doorma, a black and white marbled fox with five tails, stands as high as the roof of Evaerga's cottage. The magnificent being speaks, voice a beguiling whisper floating through Evaerga's thoughts.

"It is as you surmised. Elairie and Beluroan are Blessed Ones. We granted you the power to sense it for yourself in that vision, that you might believe it more easily. Together, they have the potential to achieve great things. Their magic will become ever more powerful as their bond grows."

Her amber eyes glow, illuminated from within.

Evaerga stares at her, openmouthed.

But the Gods have no time for mortal awe.

Baereen, a wondrous blue and green sea dragon, speaks, filling Evaerga's mind with a loud, crisp voice. "Provided they rise to the challenge, they can do a great service for all the creatures of our creation. Fox and Light could live in harmony once more."

A deep sigh puffs out his chest. "But if they fail, a darkness more terrible than you can imagine will fall over the land."

Further down the line, an enormous stone golem towers over Doorma and Baereen. Vines twine throughout Luxitore's massive frame, clinging to mineral deposits.

His voice booms, rumbling the earth beneath them as he says, "They will face a great many hardships along the way."

But Luxitore says nothing more, tells Evaerga nothing of the challenges her daughter must face.

Nepiter, the six-winged bird made of fire, considers her, and Evaerga's brows draw together, huddling in concern. Bursts of lightning arc from one wing to another, and flames drip from his mouth, defying natural law.

"As they battle their way through the dark," he says, voice crackling with electricity, "they will face many sacrifices."

"As will you," he adds, burning Evaerga with his words. Eyes as black as soot stare into her soul.

Her heart clenches.

One God has yet to speak, and Evaerga turns to her, expectantly, hoping for something good, something better than what the others have said.

Jemarie floats on the air, watching. Inky black skin shines in the sunlight. White eyes glow, illuminating the air around them.

She lifts one arm, and the iridescent feathers which extend from it shift from blue to purple to white as the light moves over them.

"Fret not," she breathes, voice light and airy.

The powerful tail that coils beneath her Elven torso shines with scales of the same shimmering, changing colors as her feathered arms. Hair the color of deep waters hangs down to cover bare breasts.

"The trouble is well worth it," Jemarie continues. "And they will have each other."

Waves of fear wash through Evaerga, cold and clammy despite the warm air of the Great Valley.

Doorma whispers into Evaerga's mind. "You can help them now, but only this once. Hide all of your mother's scrolls within Elairie's belongings."

I can only help them once?

Baereen's long tail swipes through the air. Webbed spines decorate his back, all the way down to the tip of his tail, and they glisten in the sun.

His voice floods out of him. "We have hidden Elairie's existence from Gourmaht thus far, and since the two of you have lived modestly enough, they will not feel a need to search your house once they find you. Beluroan has already encountered Gourmaht, but his involvement has also been veiled."

Jemarie reaches out, sending the feathers of her arm through a flurry of colors. She breathes, "Place the scroll about the Blessed Ones on top. Fill a new scroll with everything you know of Gourmaht and his plans and place that alongside the scroll of the Blessed Ones."

"Even now," Doorma says softly, "they ride against you. Gourmaht's minions will find you after sunrise. Write everything down. Leave the scrolls where Elairie will notice them, but not in plain sight. Arrange them as Jemarie bade you." Her glowing eyes soften. "When they find you, go easily. It will lessen their cruelty."

Evaerga's stomach plummets.

The great fox sighs before continuing. "We know you have many questions. Hold onto them just a little longer. We shall see you again soon."

All five Gods incline their heads, and Evaerga slips back through the darkness and into her cottage in Vairsun.

A sick feeling creeps into her, and she tries not to think about the Gods or how soon she'll see them. Blinking back tears, she finds a quill, an inkpot, and parchment.

Despite her efforts, tears roll down her cheeks as she writes the things the Gods bade her to write. Sobs choke her as she struggles to add a final goodbye.

"Be careful, my dear."

But the words don't feel right. She tries again.

"Great things lie ahead for you, but also great peril."

No, that can't be the last thing I say to my daughter.

Heart twisting in her chest, she presses her hands over her eyes. Tears seep out, rolling down her palms to her wrists.

It can't be. So soon?

After such a short, hard life, can it really be the end?

She looks back on a childhood spent mostly at home, ridiculed by the village children. Her mind fills with the struggle of resisting the Blood Magic, relying on the Light Elf blood from her mother to get her through.

She sees Journai, the first Light Elf aside from her mother who looked at her with anything other than contempt or fear, sees the budding romance they shared and how quickly she fell in love with him.

Their wedding and Elairie's birth flow through her mind, bright spots in a dark life that grew darker when Journai went to fight in the Blood War.

Her heart clenches, and she reaches for her necklace of eternal bonds. Journai wears his even now, deep in his grave, the simple silver chain with small emeralds set throughout a perfect match for hers.

I'll see him again soon, though. And Mother.

But who will comfort Elairie? Who will tell her stories or put on a pot of tea to cheer her up after a nightmare? Or dry her tears when society leaves her out in some new way?

She's a grown woman, now.

And she'll have Beluroan.

Evaerga's heart tears itself apart as she finally writes, "I shall see you in the Valley. I love you, Elairie."

But that isn't enough.

Retrieving another sheaf, she writes a scroll for Beluroan, imploring him to go on this journey with Elairie. As an emissary from the Gods and a representative of their people, she asks him to help Elairie rid the world of the Blood Magic, once and for all.

As a mother, she begs that he take care of her daughter.

"I know it is a lot to ask of a person, but it is necessary."

"You will know Gourmaht. The Gods said you have already encountered him."

Unsure how to end this letter to the person she must trust with her daughter's fate, a man whom she's never met, she simply says, "Be safe. You can do great things."

She places the trunk of scrolls at the foot of Elairie's bed. It looks innocent enough. Many such chests rest at the foot of beds in other homes. But Elairie has a wardrobe, and so has no need of one. It will stand out to her.

Evaerga places her handwritten scrolls and the scroll of the Blessed Ones atop the stack, turning them perpendicular to the rest. Tears cascade over her cheeks as she wanders back downstairs.

She stows her writing equipment away, then pieces her mother's room back together, pausing here and there to indulge a cherished memory.

Shuddering as sobs wrack her body, she sits at her kitchen table and pours herself some chamomile tea.

She watches through the kitchen window as the sun rises, casting a warm amber light over everything.

Elairie's favorite light. Too bad we couldn't see it together one last time.

But she can't be here for this.

The beating of hooves sounds in the distance, growing ever closer.

Chapter 8
Elairie

I pick up a few items in the cold cellar, wondering what Saerine and the boys like to eat. The strange new divination abilities guide me to beef jerky, and I snag every bit of it from the shelves.

Hoping to avoid suspicion, I deny myself another goodbye to Beluroan. Stowing his letter in the basket, I step into the fresh morning air. Warm amber light slants sideways through town as the sun rises.

I walk quickly, following Beluroan's directions. I pass my own cottage on the way and consider stopping to speak with Mother.

But the need to get food to Saerine keeps me moving.

At their quaint home, I knock gently. Only a moment passes before the door opens a crack. Large fuchsia eyes peer out at me beneath locks of hair nearly the same color. A warm tan caresses soft features with delicate shadows.

So, this is Saerine.

"Hello," I begin lamely. "My name is Elairie. You don't know me, and I hope this isn't awkward for you, but I have word for you from Beluroan." The words fall out in a tumble, and I cringe at the impression I must be making.

She opens the door a bit further, revealing a dramatic hourglass figure. She eyes me warily, one hand clutching the door.

Shuffling the basket into one hand, I retrieve the letter and offer it to her. As she unfolds it, I say, "The food in the basket is for you and your sons."

"Did you read this?"

I shake my head, but suspicion furrows her brow.

She casts her eyes over the page. Gradually, her shoulders relax, and her eyes soften. "You really didn't read this, did you?"

I shake my head, again. "It wasn't written for me."

She looks me over, then nods. "Come in."

She steps aside to let me pass, then leads me down a short hallway into a cozy kitchen. Setting the letter on the table, she gently takes the basket from me and begins unloading it onto a large wooden counter.

"Make yourself comfortable," she says without turning.

I settle into the closest chair, determined to keep my eyes from drifting to Beluroan's letter. But my thoughts don't stray from it. "How did you know I hadn't read Beluroan's letter?"

"Because a good portion of it was about you." She keeps moving as she says it, sparing me only a glance over her shoulder. "You would've either felt awkward, or been overjoyed, or relieved. Maybe embarrassed."

She grabs the beef jerky I packed and sets it down beside the basket. Finally turning to face me, she leans back against the counter. "But you just seemed nervous."

Embarrassed?

My mouth goes dry.

What's in that letter?

I fiddle with the buttons on my jacket, mind awash with the million things Beluroan could have said about me.

I'm certainly embarrassed now.

"You're good at reading people," I say.

"I've had to be."

I nod, desperate for something to say but coming up with nothing. I fidget beneath the intense scrutiny of her gaze.

Pulling my eyes up to meet hers, I decide to get the official stuff out of the way.

"Well, Beluroan was arrested for theft. The Commander didn't want to stir everyone up. He should've released Beluroan, used it as an opportunity to quell the prejudice, but he didn't. I don't know why. I offered to bring you food sooner, but he said you had enough to last a few days."

Saerine watches me. I squirm beneath her stare, wondering what she's searching for.

"But I was getting worried, so last night, I offered again. It didn't seem like they were going to let him out anytime soon… So I'm here. But…"

I swallow the lump building in my throat. My eyes fall to my lap. "There was a Blood Elf brought in last night. He was…"

My mouth goes dry, and I struggle for words. I drop my gaze to my hands, balled into fists in my lap. Silence screams through the house.

"He was terrible. He tried to... He was going to…"

The vision of what he would've done flits through my mind again, just as it did when I dragged him into his cell. My mind fills with the sounds of his labored breathing, the feel of his filthy hands.

Saerine's soft voice floats toward me. "I know… It was in the letter." She sits down across from me. "You don't have to talk about it if you don't want to. But I'll listen if you do."

I shake my head. "I'm not sure I can yet. I won't have a choice at his tribunal this afternoon though."

A few heartbeats pass as I try to keep from crying. The vision of what he wanted of me, of that horrible man pushing me against the bars and violating me, flashes before my eyes. I try to blink it away but fail.

Desperate to get my mind on something else, I say, "Well, the Patrol Commander and the Representative have decided his fate. He'll hang this afternoon, and Beluroan will be released."

After a brief pause, I continue, "The Commander told me to bring you food from the stores at the jail. I was just going to bring some from my house, but he wants to make things right. The healer who came in last night told the Commander that Beluroan is gifted with earth magic. The Commander promised to find a job for him. Things should be much easier for you after that."

Saerine considers my words before speaking. Cautious hope peeks out through her eyes. "So, he'll be out today?"

"This afternoon."

"What do you think of him?"

The question moves so far from the previous topic that I stammer.

What do I think of him?

I want his arms around me. I want to feel his hands, his lips. I need to learn about him and tell him everything.

A smile spreads across my face, and I blush.

Saerine's sweet voice brings me out of my reverie, "So, you like him?"

My cheeks burn.

Saerine takes my hand and says, "Your secret's safe with me." With a quick wink, she goes on, "He's a good man. Don't worry."

I can't bring myself to meet her gaze. Instead, I nod. "He really is."

My mind returns to those bent bars and their broken wards. Many prisoners before him tried to break them and failed horribly. Some even hurt themselves in the process.

"Well, I don't know if he's told you this, or if he'd want *me* to tell you, but I'm his sister, so I can say what I want." She laughs, a deep infectious laugh, and I join her in it.

"He thinks very highly of you," she says. "He sent you here. That says a lot."

I blush, hoping she's right.

I glance at the window and see the sun moving up into the sky. "I wish I could stay and talk a while longer, but I need to get back. I'll have to be present at the hanging."

"I'm sorry you have to see him again. At least you get justice though."

I nod briefly. "Thank you. For talking to me."

As I rise to leave, Saerine fetches the basket from the counter and hands it to me. She folds the letter and presses it into my hands.

"Tell Beluroan he should let you read this."

She walks me to the door and says, "I'm sure I'll see you again."

We say goodbye at the door, and I wave to her as I walk away. We both smile warmly.

I breathe a sigh of relief as I glance back over my shoulder. Two tiny, sleepy faces look out at me from an upstairs window.

***

Geeran, Jaym, and Kaimaer wait outside the jail, all smiling sympathetically as I approach. The woman I assume was to be Courg's first victim lingers nearby, eyes downcast.

Commander Pakaibra and a few other patrolmen and patrolwomen squeeze out the door. Courg walks in their midst, chained and dragging his feet.

My stomach turns at the sight of him, but I fall in line with everyone else as we march to the gallows. Only two stay behind in the jail.

Deima, doing his duty.

And Beluroan waiting patiently for release.

People gawk at us as we pass, pointing and sneering at Courg. They follow us through town, joining the crowd when we reach the gallows. More and more people file in until nearly the entire village stares up at us.

The boards creak beneath my feet, and the sun beats down on me. Sweat rolls down my back in tiny rivulets, and I gulp back a breath, trying to decide if it's the sun… or my nerves.

Geeran and the other woman speak first, and I close my eyes, trying to hold myself together.

My heart pounds and my stomach churns as I give my statement, stammering through the events of last night. Nerves fraying, I clasp my shaking hands behind my back.

And finally, Courg gets his chance to speak. Bile rises in my throat as he spits, "They practically begged for it."

The crowd shouts and snarls, but only for a moment. Commander Pakaibra quiets them quickly.

"I've consulted with our Representative," he says, "and we are of one mind. We move to hang this man."

My heart stops as the crowd murmurs, and I wait for them to object, to overturn the decision.

To doubt me.

But they agree, voting unanimously against Courg, and I breathe a sigh of relief.

"Have you any last words?" the Vairsun Representative asks. Her bright white hair sways serenely in the gentle breeze, far too calm for such circumstances.

"You'll all be sorry," Courg hisses. "You'll pay."

And though his angry words aren't surprising, they strike a strange chord within me, chilling me with an icy prophecy of dark times ahead.

The hangman slips the noose around Courg's neck and without hesitation, pulls the lever. My breath catches as the boards beneath him drop, and he swings, kicking frantically.

But his eyes never leave mine, and I hear him leering, "Save them if you can." His voice seems to float through my mind, but it can't be.

His face turns red, then purple, and all the while, that same sentence repeats in my mind. Over and again, I hear him snickering.

His movements slow, but still, he stares at me. Blank eyes taunt me as his body sways.

***

Unlocking Beluroan's cell, I return his letter. "Saerine apparently wants you to let me read it."

He smirks, blushing. "Maybe someday," he says, tucking it in the inner pocket of his vest.

We leave the jail behind, venturing past market stalls and skirting through back alleys. My hand aches to reach for him now that nothing separates us. My feet drag, begging me to draw out this time with him.

I tell him about the strange warning from the dying criminal and the final insult launched directly into my thoughts. Something eerily reminiscent of some advanced fortune magic Mother once told me about.

"I'm going to ask my mother about this and the new magic. Would you like to come with?"

My frantic nerves tie themselves in knots.

"I just thought you'd want to know about the magic too," I hurry to add. "If not, that's fine. You don't have to come with."

Beluroan wraps his hand around mine, and my breath rushes out. Our fingers intertwine, burning pleasantly, melting together.

"Of course, I'll go with. I want to know what's going on. Besides, you met my family. It's only right that I get to meet yours," he says with a smile.

"Well, Mother should be at home eating lunch. If she isn't there, we can check the stall she rents."

Beluroan says nothing, sending my nerves into a tailspin.

I cast a nervous glance his way.

He smiles, and my insides squirm delicately. Images of us tangled together float through my mind.

Maybe after Mother goes back to work...

I shake my head.

No. We've only known each other a few days.

It doesn't matter that it feels like we've always known each other, that we seem tailored to fit together.

Taking a deep breath, I struggle to ignore the storm of desire raging inside me and the inferno that threatens to consume the two of us from all sides. But Beluroan squeezes my hand, sending electricity surging through me.

Gods, how am I going to handle myself if Mother isn't home? We'd be alone together, with no bars to separate us... with a bed just upstairs...

I shake my head to clear the too-pleasant images that rise to claim me.

The cottage crawls into sight, and a strange force pulls me toward it. A slimy feeling slithers into my heart, quenching my frantic desire and twisting my stomach into knots. I walk faster, desperate to close the distance.

The faint smell of tea long since brewed wafts to my nose as I open the front door. The kettle still hangs over the hearth, and a cup rests on the table.

Mother must still be home. She would've put those away.

But a quick search of the first floor finds her missing.

I rush up creaking wooden stairs with Beluroan trailing along behind me. Pungent aromas greet me as I pass one drying bundle of herbs after another.

I check her room but find it empty. I head to my own room. Nothing. Confused, I venture into my grandmother's room, but no one waits for me there either.

Panic builds within me. A strange, terrible premonition swirls in my gut.

Peering into my room one last time, my eyes land on a chest at the foot of my bed, exactly where it shouldn't be. The sick feeling in my stomach builds to a crescendo as my feet drag me forward.

I leave Beluroan in the doorway and collapse before my grandmother's chest, buckling beneath the weight of dread. I touch the lid, hesitant, but I know what I'll find within it. I recognize the scuff on the side, the tarnish on the latch. I know what chest this is.

But why is it in here?

And where is Mother?

My heart doesn't want the answers, but my hand moves of its own accord, lifting the lid. My grandmother's scrolls lay before me, waiting to teach me about the Gods.

And magic.

I swallow, gathering my courage, as Beluroan comes to kneel beside me. He rubs a gentle hand on my back.

Three scrolls sit atop the rows, turned perpendicular to the rest. I lift them gently, afraid to break them.

Afraid that they may break me.

My mother's gentle, sloping handwriting labels one with my name and one with Beluroan's name. The third has never been touched by her pen.

"What's going on?" Beluroan asks, deep voice laced with concern.

"These are my Grandmother's scrolls. It's her trunk." Pausing, I try to get my head around everything this could mean. "These aren't normally in my room. And there was never one with my name, or yours."

I hand Beluroan the one addressed to him and place the unlabeled one between us on the floor. Dread unfurls within me as I unroll mine. Beluroan's sits in his lap as he watches me, waiting while I read.

Elairie,

My time is brief, and I have so much to tell you. I've had several visions these past few minutes, the last of which was an audience with the Gods, but their message is grave.

A man named Gourmaht seeks to recreate the Blood Magic. He and his followers labor in a cave system in Mount Hybar, deep in the Cargam Mountains. The willing recruits search for potential slaves, kidnapping Elves and bringing them back to test the potions.

So far, everyone they've tried to enslave died. But if they succeed... Gourmaht is of mixed blood. He'll enslave all Elves.

Oh, Elairie, I wish this didn't have to fall on your shoulders, but the Gods decided long ago that it must. You and Beluroan were created the moment the world found this path.

The two of you are Blessed Ones. The other scroll explains what that means, but... I'm afraid it's up to the two of you to stop Gourmaht. The Gods said Beluroan would know him, that he met the vile man at some point. Maybe that'll help you.

You have to find him and defeat him. You have to destroy everything that has to do with the Blood Magic. Their writings, their potions, their recipes... Destroy it all.

I wish I could help you, but his followers are coming for me. They ride for Vairsun already. The Gods have hidden the two of you so far, but my purpose was only to raise you, to warn you.

And that's done now.

Be careful, my dear.

Great things lie ahead for you, but also great peril.

I shall see you in the Valley.

I love you, Elairie.

I couldn't have asked for a better daughter.

My tears splash onto a scroll already stained with my mother's tears. Beluroan's arms slide around me, pulling me close. He cradles my head against his shoulder, and a torrent of sobs bursts from me at the loss of the last of my family.

My hands tremble, and tears flow over my cheeks. The floor seems to drop out from under me, and my stomach falls with it. A shudder of horror sweeps through me. Sobs shake my frame, and Beluroan tightens his arms around me.

If the Blood Magic is renewed, I'll lose him too…

A chill sweeps through my heart, and my lungs hitch and heave. Sobs rack my body as my mind fills with dark images.

Because somehow, I know that Gourmaht intends this Blood Magic to be used more cruelly than the first.

And no one will be able to fight him.

I choke back a sob, but only barely.

He has Mother…

Darkness closes in around me, and the cottage drifts far away. A brief vision of her flashes before my eyes, and I see her bound and laid out on a cart, pulled by fast horses to a faraway place. Blood runs from a wound on the side of her head, and my heart breaks.

Have they already killed her?

They ride north for their camp, fearlessly making their way through the darkest parts of the Nouvai Forest. The cart bounces as they hit a bump in the path.

Mother moans but doesn't wake.

Relief sweeps through me, and my heart rejoices just knowing that she yet lives.

I watch as they ride off into the distance, leaving me behind on the path, alone with the trees and the shadows. Then, the darkness of the forest becomes all-consuming, pushing me back to the cottage, back to my room and Beluroan's arms.

"Elairie?" he asks, voice high with panic. He searches my face frantically. "Elairie, what's wrong? What just happened?"

My eyes focus on his. I wrap my arms around his neck, pulling myself closer to him. My heart hammers in my chest, and my mind races, desperate for a way to save my mother.

He holds me tightly, and though my ribs ache, I don't protest. "They took Mother, but she's alive."

"Who took her? And what happened just now? You were crying, then you just went still. You looked right through me. What was that?" Fear coats his words, pushing them from his lips far too quickly. He pulls back and grips my shoulders, searching my gaze intently.

"I had a vision. Mother's unconscious, tied up in a horse cart. They're taking her to a camp on the way to the mountains," I say. "I have to save her. I can't let them kill her."

Then, the letter comes back to me, and I gasp. "We have to stop them. We can't let them renew the Blood Magic."

The color drains from Beluroan's face. "Renew the Blood Magic?" His eyes pierce my soul. Voice low and serious, he asks, "What are you talking about?"

"Mother knew. She had visions of them. They found out about her somehow and took her. I have to get her back. I have to stop this."

"What?" Beluroan looks at me like I'm mad. "We can't go to them if that's what they're doing. We need to run, far and fast. We can't be anywhere near them. We certainly can't run straight toward them."

I stare at him, openmouthed. Anger fills me, and I pull away. "I can't let them kill my Mother!"

He flinches, and a twinge of guilt twists within me.

"Besides, there's nowhere we could run. Where would we go? If they use the Blood Magic, they'll build an army. They'll overrun the Cargam Mountains, the Nouvai. They'll take all the villages in the forest, killing or making slaves of everyone in them. They'll spread out across the entire country. We can't let them have all of Avaencery."

Beluroan gapes at me. "How could we ever hope to stop them? That's a job for the Commanders and the Representatives. Not us."

Hoping Mother wrote something that might inspire him, I ask, "Have you read the scroll she wrote for you?"

"What?" Completely thrown off, he shakes his head. "No. I was trying to calm you down."

"Read it. Please."

Beluroan rubs a hand across his beautiful face, then grabs the scroll from the floor. He reads it once, quickly. His expression changes several times as he does. With a brief glance at me, he reads it again.

Finally, he speaks. "Elairie, they won't keep her…" He drops his head, staring at his hand and the scroll it contains. Sighing, he says instead, "What are Blessed Ones?"

"I don't know." Fighting hard to believe I can somehow save Mother, denying the fear that claws at my heart, I unfurl the last scroll.

It details the Abyss the Gods existed in before they made the Great Valley for themselves and the boredom that pushed them to create the world. I skim through tales of drought before Jemarie made water and air, skip past tales of the world being overrun by Luxitore's plants before Nepiter made fire and lightning.

My eyes roam over paragraphs of Baereen's fish and animals for the water, of Doorma's animals for the land. I remember well the stories my mother told me of the predictability of animals, and how it drove the Gods to make sentient life.

Humans who forsook the Gods and honor for bloodshed. Dwarves who turned their back on the surface world for caves. Elves who held true to the Gods.

Mother never mentioned the Sirens or their predilection for cruelty, nor the Fairies and their fondness for pranks.

She told me often how the Gods mourned our losses when war broke out, but she never mentioned the next part.

One day, they made a single being, a single soul, of unfathomable proportions. Then, they split it in two, and those new beings were eternally bound. Hearts forged from the same inferno and electricity, bodies carved of the same clay, minds of the same water and air. Life and thought blown in on the same breath.

An aura of fire and lightning would always surround them when near each other, guiding them closer.

On finding each other, they would be drawn together, and as their bond grew, they would gain more and more magical abilities until they became more powerful than any others on Earth.

Protected by the faith of the Gods, they could accomplish what the Gods themselves could not. And so, the Gods leave the fate of the world they love so much in the hands of Blessed Ones.

Beluroan and I sit quietly, staring at the scroll. But it explains everything.

"Is this real?" I whisper.

I glance at him, eyes raking over his features before falling to my own hands. I turn them over, analyzing every scar, every imperfection.

But Blessed Ones? Accomplishing things the Gods can't? There's no way.

Courg's last words come to me, "You'll be sorry. You'll all pay."

Then, his thought in my mind, "Save them, if you can."

Did he know?

My mind whirls with thoughts of that vile man sensing us, having visions about us, and reporting back to Gourmaht somehow.

I shake my head.

The Gods would have mentioned that to Mother. She certainly would have put it in the letter.

My eyes seek Beluroan. His jaw hangs slack, and he stares into space.

Could I stand to see him turned to a slave?

The answer comes easily.

No.

I reach up to touch his face, and that wonderful heat greets my skin. Finally, his eyes focus on mine. Desperate to comfort him, I say, "We were made for this. Surely the Gods made us equal to the task."

"And if they didn't?"

I consider this for a moment, hating that the scroll didn't say Blessed Ones always succeed. A chill sweeps through me.

"I don't know. But I know we'll fail if we don't try."

Reluctantly, Beluroan nods. "Where do we even start? We can't just go to the mountains and walk right in."

"Well," I think for a moment, "Mother said you encountered Gourmaht before. Where did you meet him?"

"I don't know. I don't recognize the name." At a loss, Beluroan wipes a hand over his face.

"Maybe you'll know him when you see him." I lean my head on his shoulder and wrap my arms around his waist. Every inch of my body tingles with electricity, yearning to melt into him.

Beluroan leans his head on mine, slowly moving one hand over my back. He nuzzles into my hair, and the fiery aura that surrounds us burns hotter.

A small sigh escapes my lips.

Gently, he touches my neck. Tilting my head back, he gazes into my eyes, and fire burns through me as his thumb caresses my jaw.

My breathing hitches as his eyes drop to my lips. An irresistible gravity draws us together. Sliding his hand to the back of my neck, Beluroan pulls me in, brushing his parted lips over mine.

My breath comes in gasps, and I crush myself to him, surprising us both. He recovers quickly, pulling me hard against him and deepening our kiss. We fuse together, mouths dancing intimately.

I slip a hand over his chest, luxuriating in the feel of his strong figure. I trail my hand up to his neck, into his hair.

But he isn't close enough.

My body screams for more, burning for his touch.

The air around us disappears, replaced by the heat of Nepiter's forge. I gasp, desperate for air, but I don't want to pull my lips from his to let it through.

A distant noise pulls at my attention, but I ignore it, greedy for more of him. Beluroan pulls back, holding my gaze with eyes darkened by lust. He brushes his lips against mine, then across my cheek, moving to my ear. Hot breath dances on my skin.

A shiver runs down my spine, and I melt in his embrace. My head falls back, and Beluroan's hungry mouth finds my collarbone.

Again, that faraway sound comes echoing through the house. This time, I hear it for what it is. A knock. It speeds up, growing insistent, getting louder.

Why is someone visiting now?

Reluctantly, I pull back, hoping the feeling of his lips on my skin will linger. Taking a deep breath, I try to steady myself.

Beluroan breathes fire across my skin and leans his head on my shoulder. A deep, shuddering breath rocks him. Lifting his head, he gazes into my eyes.

Again, the knocking sounds downstairs.

"I should probably get the door," I say.

I touch his cheek one last time, then rise to my feet. At the door to the hall, I glance at him, sprawled out on the floor. With eyes closed, he shakes his head and chuckles quietly. After another deep breath, he gets up and follows me down the stairs.

The air still crackles around us, but I drag my feet from one wooden step to another.

Chapter 9
Beluroan

Fear courses through me as I follow Elairie to the door of her cottage. I shudder at thoughts of Gourmaht's mixed blood and the power it would grant his Blood Magic.

Fox and Light would finally be united… as Blood Elves.

Elairie and I would be slaves.

Or would they kill us, kill her, for rising against them?

My heart falters, stopping me in my tracks.

I lift my gaze to her as she walks to the door. My eyes trace the strands of purple winding together in her hair, shimmering in the light. My breath catches when I imagine her at the hands of a Master.

Sighing, I try to focus on the good in this. At least I know the force between us is real.

Her scent wafts back to me as we walk, orange and cinnamon. Helplessly, I take in a deep breath. The strange combination has always been my favorite, and I never questioned it.

Is it because it's the scent of my other half?

My mind drifts back up the stairs to Elairie's bedroom. The feel of her on my lap, that intoxicating scent, her lips on mine.

I wanted to keep her in my arms for the rest of my life. I wanted to drink her in so deeply that I wouldn't have room for anything else within me.

And suddenly, all I can think of are the things I wanted to do upstairs, all the ways I wanted to hold her, to touch her. My head swirls with the thought of her lips on my skin, the memory of her breath, hot and quick.

I clear my throat, trying to redirect my thoughts. She looks at me over her shoulder, smiling beautifully, and my heart flutters in my chest.

Will I ever get used to this?

Will I even get the chance?

A trill of fear plays along my spine as Elairie opens the door. A stray bout of paranoia makes me wonder if it's the people who took her mother.

But Elairie greets the visitor, soothing my nerves.

"Geeran," she says with a warm smile. "What a pleasant surprise. Come in."

She steps back to let him pass, shutting the door with a brief glance outside. Moving to clear the table, Elairie gathers up the teacup her mother used. But she stops, turning it in her hands and staring at it as if it might tell her how to proceed.

Geeran sits at the table, struggling for words. Finally, he says, "I'm so sorry, Elairie."

The delicate cup slips from her hands only to shatter on the floor, and she stares down at the pieces, unblinking.

I step past Geeran and put a gentle hand on her arm.

She looks up at me, lip trembling. In her eyes, darkness builds, and I can't help but wonder if Geeran's words broke through her denial.

I pull her close, and she leans into me, cradling her arms against her chest. The warmth of her flows through me, and I almost forget the terrible future that awaits us.

Drawing back, she covers herself in the armor of denial again. It slips over her like a second skin. Her posture shifts, and she lifts her chin.

"Sorry for what? Mother's still alive," she says.

"I don't know these men who've taken her, but I saw enough of their spirits to know they won't keep her alive long," Geeran says. His voice is soft, but his words hit like hammers. "She knows something, something they won't let get out. If she's alive, the risk is there."

Elairie shakes with the impact of his words. I pull her to me. She shuffles closer, and the remnants of the teacup crunch beneath her feet. She devolves into a sobbing mess, wrapping her arms tightly around me.

I rub her back, moving my hand in small circles. Tears soak into my shirt, but I don't move, don't pull away.

Slowly, she steadies herself. With a deep breath, she wipes the tears from her face.

Without releasing me, she looks at Geeran and says, "I want to try to save her."

"I fear you won't make it in time, dear girl."

His lack of tact borders on criminal, pulling my jaw open.

"I don't know your quest," he begins, "but I know what the two of you are. You will need to learn how to use your new magics as they develop. I volunteer to teach you what I can."

Sighing, I say, "We can't ask you to put yourself in danger. Besides, you're needed here."

"You don't have to ask." Geeran assures us. "As for my duties here, I'll speak with Pakaibra about employing your sister in my stead. She's one of the best healers in town. He intended to find work for you, but it seems you'll be absent. I can do far more good for many more people in aiding you than I ever could if I stayed."

"He's right," Elairie says, barely audible.

Silent reflection creases Geeran's face, digging ditches in frail skin and making him appear even older.

Could he survive the trip? Would he survive Gourmaht and his followers?

We don't even know what kind of forces they've gathered.

The range of possibilities spreads out before me like a chasm, and despair pulls me toward the edge. We might face a bunch of aging magic users with no skill for battle. Or we might arrive in the mountains to find an army of vital young Elves, warriors trained to fight with and without magic.

Geeran's voice tugs at my attention. "What exactly is the quest the Gods have set for you? Do you know yet?"

Elairie nods.

I glance down at her, then say, "A man named Gourmaht seeks to renew the Blood Magic. We must stop him. Elairie's mother had visions about it. The Gods told her to leave a message in Elairie's room."

One eyebrow raises on that ancient face, and I see him piece together that I was in Elairie's room.

Does he think that we…?

But we didn't. Blessed Ones or not, it's far too soon.

I shake my head to clear away images of Elairie's soft skin, warm beneath my touch, her eyes dark with need.

"I just don't understand why they couldn't have warned her sooner," Elairie says. Bitterness envelops her words, and she drops her gaze to the floor, balling her hands into fists.

"I can't speak for the Gods, but I'm sure they had reason for their actions," Geeran says.

Lifting Elairie's chin so that she looks into my eyes, I tell her, "Maybe if you hone your fortune magic, they might speak with you. You could ask them yourself."

Elairie nods and whispers, "Okay." Turning her gaze on Geeran, she asks, "How can I learn to use it faster?"

"Practice is the best method for most people. In this case, the two of you will benefit from practicing together. The bond between you is your strongest weapon."

He looks us over briefly, then continues, "You're off to a good start." He smiles, even chuckles, but the deep, warm sound holds an undertone of sadness.

I blush. "We need to start practicing as soon as possible. Have you read anything about how long it takes for each power to develop?"

He shakes his head. "There are very few writings on Blessed Ones. The Gods rarely see fit to create a pair, and most of what we knew of the last pair was destroyed in the Blood War. We know so little of your kind."

"Can we practice on the way there?" Elairie asks.

"We're not ready to leave yet," I say. "I know you want to save your Mother, but we have no gear for a trip like this. We're certainly not ready for any battle once we get there."

"So, we get our gear together and leave tonight. I'm not sure where their camp is, but it's several weeks' journey to the mountains on foot. We can practice as we go."

Sighing, I give in.

Partially.

"We'll gather our gear tonight. We need to speak with the Commander. I need to tell Saerine… *something*." I sigh again, trying to think of some way to explain this to her without endangering her.

My eyes rake over Elairie, take in the dark circles forming beneath her eyes.

I add, "And you need rest. You haven't slept since before you came to work last night, and you've been through a lot since then. This is far too dangerous for you to be tired."

The mention of sleep draws a yawn from her.

"My point exactly." I smile reassuringly. "We'll leave as soon as we're ready, I promise."

She falls against my chest, giving in for the time being. "Shall we go get supplies?"

Geeran clears his throat. "I'll take care of that. The two of you sleep. I'll bring the Commander back here to speak with you tonight."

Elairie yawns again, leaning her head on my shoulder.

Geeran rises and heads to the door. "I'll be back in a few hours with the Commander. Rest up." He smiles, and his wispy frame floats across the floor.

As the door closes behind him, Elairie nuzzles her face against my chest. My knees tremble, and sparks shoot through me.

"Let's get you up to bed," I say.

I tell myself to let her go up alone, to go home and talk to Saerine.

But Elairie presses against me, tightening her arms around me.

I'll tuck her in and leave.

That's all.

I turn her around. My hands rest on her shoulders as I walk her to the stairs, trying to keep enough distance between us to maintain some semblance of self-control. Yet, my hands burn from even that minimal contact.

I'll tuck her in, say goodnight, and go home.

But my eyes roam over her figure as she climbs the stairs ahead of me. Her swaying hips hold my attention, and I swallow hard. I drop my arms, but it doesn't help.

At the top of the stairs, she meanders into her room. After unbuckling the daggers from her thighs, she sits on her bed and tugs her boots off. She shrugs out of her vest, tossing it onto a small table.

My heart pounds in my chest.

How much is she going to take off?

I drop my gaze, wondering if I should leave. But she stops and falls back on her bed. I stand near the door, awkward and at a loss for words.

My mind fills with thoughts of peeling her clothes away, running my hands over her skin. I just want to forget everything for a little while.

I swallow again, then open my mouth to say that I'm going home.

But before I speak, Elairie sits up.

Pulling the pins from her hair, she says, "You don't think we can save my mother either... Do you?"

Silent tears roll down her cheeks.

I cross the room quickly and kneel before her.

But I don't know what to say, where to begin.

I don't know how to tell her that she's right, that I don't think we can save her mother.

"We'll do everything we possibly can," I say, hating the way her face falls. "We just can't run in there blind, that's all."

The tears don't stop, so I move up to the bed, sitting beside her. I pull her into my arms and say, "Us dying won't help her."

She relents and wraps her arms around me. She cries silent rivers down my leather vest, shoulders shaking all the while.

I hold her until her tears subside and her breathing evens out. Leaning back, I find her asleep in my arms. Peace smooths her beautiful features.

I slip my arms beneath her and maneuver her into bed. I pull the blanket up over her, but I can't just leave. With a gentle hand on her cheek, I kiss her forehead. My lips burn.

And I burn for more.

Her eyes flutter open, and she takes my hand in hers. "Do you have to go?"

My heart melts, and my breath deserts me. The fire around us roars.

"Lay down," she says. "You have to sleep too. We can talk to Saerine together before we set off."

I freeze, wondering at her motives, wondering if she's just stressed and exhausted. "Are you sure?"

She nods and pulls the blanket back for me.

"Really?"

She looks up at me as she says, "I don't want to be alone."

I'm helpless.

I pull my boots off and let them thud to the floor. I take my vest off, dropping it beside the bed. My heart beats a frantic pace, rattling violently in my chest.

I untuck my shirt out of habit, but I catch myself before I pull it over my head. Taking a deep breath, I crawl into bed. Elairie smiles and nestles in close. I pull the blanket up, another habit carried over from nights sleeping alone.

But I certainly don't need it.

Our fiery aura heats my veins, threatening to burn me alive.

Wrapping my arms around her, I pull her as close as I can. Her arms slip around my waist, and our legs entwine.

I lay motionless, desperate not to make her change her mind about this. My senses heighten, savoring the scent of her, the feel of her, and I wonder if I'll ever fall asleep.

But slowly, the fire surrounding us gentles to a blissful warmth, and the lightning settles to a soothing buzz. Elairie's slow, even breathing hypnotizes me.

My guard drops, and I pull her tighter against me. She nuzzles her face into my neck, and a soft, guttural sound eases past my lips. My eyelids droop, then close completely.

In the back of my mind, I know I should go home. I should talk to Saerine.

But it's so warm and comfortable here with Elairie melting into me.

And my eyes are just so good at being closed. Surely, they'd be disappointed if I forced them to open.

***

I wake to find that darkness has fallen beyond the window, but Elairie still sleeps in my arms. I inhale deeply, filling myself with the scent of her.

I lie still, trying not to wake her, trying to draw out this peaceful moment.

Elairie slides her leg between mine, and shivers run down my spine. Her soft white skin stands out in the darkness, and long lashes fan out over her cheeks.

Gently, I caress her ear, tracing the outer edge of its tip with one finger. Dark eyelashes flutter, opening onto the world. Her dark blue eyes sparkle in the scant moonlight. She smiles, stealing my breath away.

Scooting closer, she runs her hand through my hair. Her nails brush across my scalp sending shivers down my spine, and my eyes close.

My hand moves to the back of her neck, pulling her in. Our lips come together, softly at first, but we ignite quickly. Her arms tighten around me, and she throws one leg over mine, electrifying me, incinerating my inhibitions.

I roll her onto her back, move between her shapely legs, tense with desire. Elairie's hand slips down to my lower back, and she pulls me against her. My lips find their way to her neck and ravage it.

My mouth trails along her skin, dropping kisses along the way from her jaw down to her collar bone, eliciting a soft moan from perfect, full lips. Bracing myself on one arm, I grab her hip and press myself against her. Her hands tighten, one wrapping in my hair and the other clutching at my back.

I nearly fall to pieces.

Leaning my head against her shoulder, I try to steady myself. Citrus and spice fill my nose, and the thrill of it makes me dizzy.

But the pause gives me clarity.

We can't do this.

I *can't do this.*

Everything that's happened flashes through my mind, from Courg's attack last night to Elairie's missing mother. Not to mention the weight that's been dropped on our shoulders.

I can't do this.

If this happens between us, I want it to be under better circumstances than this. I want to know it's not just because she needed comfort.

Taking a deep breath, I lay down beside her.

Silence descends on us, and Elairie goes still.

I turn to face her, rising onto my elbow. "I'm sorry," I say. But how can I explain myself? "I shouldn't have done that, I know. It wasn't right."

"What?" Her lips curve into a delicate frown, and her brows reach for each other. "What do you mean it wasn't right?"

"I just mean that… with all of this going on… I don't want to take advantage."

"Take advantage?" Anger wages war across her features. "Who said you were taking advantage of anything?"

"I just wouldn't feel right," I add, but the frown on her face only deepens. I open my mouth to speak, to fix this, but a knock at the front door interrupts me.

Geeran's here…

But I can't leave it like this with Elairie.

She sits up, ready to climb from the bed. I rise to my knees on the mattress and put a hand on her shoulder. "Wait, please."

What can I possibly say to make this better?

I take her hands in mine. "With everything that's happened, I just wouldn't feel right about it. I can't do this."

The anger fades from Elairie's face, but a frown still tugs at her lips. "We should go talk to Geeran."

My heart drops.

Downstairs, Geeran's knocking grows more insistent.

Elairie rises, and I follow. We grab our things and descend the stairs in silence. I ache to reach for her, to fix this, but a chasm lies between us.

The fire around us merely simmers.

Chapter 10
Elairie

We settle in at the table. Beluroan watches me carefully as we repeat everything we've learned, but a cool river tempers the inferno that normally surrounds us.

His rejection repeats in my mind, sours my stomach.

What would he have been taking advantage of? That we're Blessed Ones?

Is that all it was for him?

Strengthening our bond for our magic, then thinking better of it?

The thought tears through my heart. I shake my head, turning my focus back to the conversation around me.

"I've found a position for Saerine," the Commander says to Beluroan. "And I'll keep an eye on her and her children in your absence."

A sigh of relief eases past my lips.

Beluroan nods, but worry still creases his brows. My eyes trace the lines of his face, and he meets my gaze.

Darkness seeps in around the edges of my vision, slowly pulling my spirit from the room. He comes to kneel beside me, taking my hand as Pakaibra's voice fades.

The vision whisks us away from the cottage, and our spirits fly to a tiny camp deep in the forest. We stand with hands joined, staring at four Elves gathered around a campfire.

Fortune magic whispers through my mind, telling me these are the Elves who took my mother. My blood boils, and I grit my teeth.

One of them, a young woman with a shaved head, has the faraway look of someone in the grip of a vision. The others wait, staring into the flames.

When her eyes focus on the world before her, she hisses, "Fetch her."

A form beside her separates from the shadows. A malicious smile spreads over his features, but darkness hides sunken eyes. He disappears into a tent only to return, dragging my mother along behind him.

My heart twists in my chest.

Dirty ropes bind her hands. A gash on the side of her face sucks in the light, and dried blood coats her skin.

"Mother!" I scream, voice breaking.

But she doesn't hear me.

The woman with the shaved head steps closer to her. "What do you know, and who did you tell?"

"All I know is that Gourmaht wants to renew the Blood Magic, and he's somewhere in the Cargam Mountains. That's it."

The bald woman looms over my mother, leaning close. "Who did you tell?"

"No one."

The woman steps back and motions to the shadowy man. His hand flies out, slamming into my mother's face.

She stumbles backward, nearly toppling into the flames, and I gasp. Cold horror sweeps through me.

But my mother doesn't make a sound.

She squares her shoulders, lifts her chin. A single tear trickles over her cheek, and blood flows from the gash on her face, now weeping once more, cascading to her tattered shirt.

The bald woman shouts, "Who did you tell?"

Mother's words come out a whisper, "No one. I told no one. I couldn't bear to speak of it."

Finally, this satisfies them. The bald woman enters another vision. But fortune magic tells me it isn't by choice, tells me that Waergou triggered it. The same man who traced Mother's location.

When she snaps out of it, she says, "Gourmaht believes that she told no one. She *has* no one, after all, so who would she tell? Such a pitiful, lonely existence."

Turning to the remaining two figures, she says, "Make it look like an animal attack. Provoke one if you can."

Then, she vanishes into the tent behind her.

The shadow man shoves Mother to the ground, and my mouth falls open. Beluroan's grip on my hand tightens.

Don't let them do this.

The remaining Elves, two faceless figures, drag her to the edge of the firelight. Shadow wraps around them, hiding their faces.

I reach for a stick, anything to use as a weapon, but my hand passes through. Only my spirit stands here.

The Elves pull knives from within their cloaks and slash my mother's arms, her stomach, her legs. A terrible scream erupts from me, but they hear nothing.

Mother bites her lip, silent and still. Blood trickles from her mouth where teeth pierce flesh.

I tug at Beluroan's arm, desperate to go to her, to save her, but he pulls me into his arms.

"Elairie, we can't do anything," he gasps, voice cracking as he tucks my head against his chest.

They drag her past us, leaving a trail of blood glistening on leaves and broken twigs. Far from their camp, they drop her to the ground.

They cut her legs, slash the backs of her ankles. They take turns, moving in perfect synchrony. A well-honed team.

Violent sobs rack my body, shaking Beluroan.

They untie her binds, and for a moment, I think they may leave her, be done with this mess.

But they grip her hands, then slam her forearms down over their bent knees. The bones snap, and my stomach lurches.

Only then do they turn, sauntering away from the carnage they wrought. The air around their camp glimmers for an instant as they throw a ward up.

Twigs snap behind me as wildlife moves in, sniffing out freshly spilled blood. I turn to stare into the darkness, heart in my throat.

No… Please, no.

Slowly, beasts close in, circling in the underbrush. The distant fire shines in the wolves' eyes. Dread builds in my chest, and I struggle forward, desperate to scare the animals away.

But after only a few tentative steps, they set upon her.

I scream, begging for mercy, demanding their retreat. But only Beluroan hears my cries.

Teeth sink into her stomach, and the wolf shakes its head. Her body jerks with the movement, and blood pours from the wounds. Another beast tears at her legs, leaving strips of flesh hanging from the bone.

And finally, Mother screams.

A deep, bone-chilling sound that I know will haunt me.

My heart twists, and tears prick at the corners of my eyes.

Two more wolves appear, stepping free of the shadows to tear into Mother's arms. Bitter sorrow rips through me as I stare at the shining liquid on my mother's face.

She screams once more, and another wolf appears, this one far larger than the others. Its yellow eyes glow as it approaches. Leaping upon her, its teeth clamp onto Mother's neck, cutting off her scream. Her last breath comes out a sickening gurgle, bubbling through bloody holes in her neck.

Sobs rattle through me, and I fall to my knees. My throat tears open with a scream, and Beluroan kneels beside me, pulling me into his arms. He holds me tightly, whispering soft words of comfort as he turns my head away from the scene before us.

I scrunch my eyes, desperate to block it out.

But I hear them.

Ripping into her flesh. Snarling at each other in their frenzy.

A single tear falls from Beluroan's face onto mine. He covers my ear with one hand, pressing my head against his chest to cover the other.

My arms tighten around him. I open my eyes briefly, staring at the monsters' camp. Two figures stand, silhouetted by the fire. They watch, taking joy from her death, and waves of sickness roll through me.

Merciful darkness sets in again, pulling Beluroan and me away. Our spirits settle back into our bodies in my kitchen.

Geeran and Pakaibra wait for me to speak, but I can't. My mouth falls open in the taut silence. I gape at Beluroan, kneeling beside my chair with my hand in his.

And I break.

Leaping from my chair, I land in Beluroan's arms, nearly knocking him over. My tears soak into his shirt, and my breath comes in sharp gasps.

Beluroan sits, drawing his knees up on either side of me. I press into him, burying my face in his shoulder, and his embrace tightens.

I cry until my eyes dry up and burn with the effort. My lungs rake in great shuddering breaths, as if trying to break my body apart. Exhaustion washes through me, and I still.

"I'm so sorry, Elairie," Beluroan whispers against my ear.

I glance up at him to find tears on his cheeks. Dark red hair clings to them, stuck to his skin.

He touches my cheek and says, "I'm so sorry. That it happened… and that you had to see it." He shakes his head.

I cup his face, leaning my forehead against his. Soothing warmth seeps through me, emanating from every point of contact.

"Thank you," I croak. "For being there with me. And for being with me now."

Beautiful emerald eyes stare into mine. "I will always be there for you." He places a gentle kiss on the tip of my nose, then brushes his lips over mine. "Never forget that."

My eyes prick with the promise of tears, but I blink to dissuade them. I nod, not trusting my voice.

And yet, his words warm my cold, battered heart.

Nearby, a throat clears.

Beluroan tells them, "They killed Evaerga."

The words hit me like a charging bull.

Geeran and Pakaibra express their sorrow, and I acknowledge them with all the politeness I can muster. But I don't get up, don't leave the safety of Beluroan's arms just yet.

Revising our plans, Beluroan says, "We'll leave tomorrow, not tonight. Geeran, I hate to impose, but would you mind going to Saerine? Please tell her that I'm alright, and I'll stop by in the morning. Tell her only what she *needs* to know. I don't want to endanger her, as well."

Pakaibra assures us that he'll send a patrolman to stand watch at the door here and at Beluroan and Saerine's house. He and Geeran excuse themselves, leaving us alone.

But we don't move.

For a long time, we sit on the floor as my lungs heave, wrestling air inward.

Eventually, Beluroan speaks. "Let's go upstairs. You should rest."

Words stick in my throat, so I nod.

As we pull ourselves up from the floor, I wonder if he'll refuse to lay next to me after what happened earlier. My heart aches at the thought, desperate for the comfort of his touch.

We climb the stairs, hands linked, and I wish for the sweet embrace of unconsciousness. But fear slinks through me, promising nightmares will plague my sleep.

What if I dream she's alive and wake to find that she's not? Would that be worse?

We crest the stairs and slip into my bedroom. The blankets lay in a tangled heap, and the scene flashes before my eyes. I see him atop me, see our lips fused and his hands all over me. Heat floods me, pools in my stomach.

But my cheeks burn with humiliation.

One more thing gone wrong...

I crawl over to the far side of my bed, allowing some small hope that maybe, just maybe, he'll want to lay next to me.

But I force myself to say, "If you don't want to stay, you don't have to."

The words cut me to the bone, and I turn away, facing the wall with a blanket over my head. I don't want to see his face if he leaves.

His footsteps thud across the floor, and my heart stops, waiting. The mattress settles beneath his weight.

I freeze as he lays down. My heart beats faster and faster as he scoots closer, pressing against me. He slides one arm beneath my head and wraps the other around my waist. My skin sizzles everywhere we touch, and a comforting warmth seeps through me.

Nuzzling his face into my hair, Beluroan draws in a deep breath, and his arms tighten around me.

My heart splinters, and tears cascade over my cheeks, drenching my pillow.

"Shh..." Beluroan gentles, his lips brushing my ear. "Come here." He rolls me to face him and cradles my head against his shoulder.

"You stayed..." I choke the words out, barely coherent.

"Of course, I did," he says, rubbing my back. "I'm not going anywhere."

Beluroan touches the side of my face. Pulling back to look at me, he asks, "Unless… you want me to go?"

I shake my head and bury my face in his chest. My tears fall with renewed fervor.

I choke out a string of sounds, trying to say, "Don't go." Then, another attempt, "Mother's gone… I don't want you gone too."

"I'm not going anywhere." He pulls me closer.

My mind fills with the wolves. The sight of them tearing into Mother sears itself onto the backs of my eyelids. The two Elves and their knives stand permanently silhouetted against the fire in my mind.

But the soothing movement of Beluroan's hand on my back and the warmth of his touch slowly push the thoughts from my mind, sending me into a deep, dark nothingness.

The last thing I hear as I fall asleep is Beluroan's voice, "I will *always* be there for you."

Chapter 11

Beluroan

I wake in darkness, limbs tangled with Elairie's. She gazes at me with a single unshed tear glistening on her lashes. My heart twists in my chest.

Gently, I stroke her cheek. "Did you sleep alright?"

Her voice catches as she says, "Better than I expected."

I nod, hoping she didn't have nightmares. "Do you need more rest?"

She shrugs, so I suggest getting some food.

Maybe the distraction will help her.

Relief and anxiety war within me as we force ourselves out of bed. I ache to crawl back under the blankets, but with so much at stake, we can't lie around much longer.

A solemn silence dogs our heels all the way downstairs. Elairie disappears into the root cellar, and in her absence, I clean up the broken fragments of the cup her mother used.

Not that we can escape reminders of Evaerga in this house.

Traces of her linger in every corner. Herbs hang to dry for various spells used to strengthen and direct divination. A sweater lies, not quite complete, with all her knitting materials beside her favorite chair. Slippers rest before it.

Wait. Her favorite chair? How could I know it's her favorite?

Then, as if I needed a reminder of the horrifying scene of her death, I remind myself.

Was.

It was *her favorite chair.*

Pouring water into cups, I wonder where that knowledge came from.

Is this how fortune magic develops? Random insight?

Elairie re-enters the room, and my breath catches at the sight of her. Strands of lilac and mulberry curl around her face, tousled from sleep, and a few buttons on her shirt hang undone. Red streaks rim her eyes, yet it does nothing to diminish her beauty or the gravity that pulls me toward her.

We sit together, eating quietly. Fresh bread coated with the best jam I've ever had in my life, hard-boiled eggs, beef jerky, all washed down by crisp, cool water.

Yet, Elairie doesn't seem to notice any of it. She stares at the table, chewing methodically.

I wrap her hand in mine. Bringing it to my lips, I kiss her soft skin. She lifts one corner of her mouth in a sad smile.

After eating, Elairie finds two backpacks. She hands one to me, and I venture into the root cellar, packing everything I can fit while she goes up to her room.

With my pack full, I ascend the stairs. She sits on the edge of her bed, strapping daggers onto her thighs. Tight black pants with many pockets cling to her. A white shirt with thin straps hangs loosely on her frame.

She leans forward, strapping another, much smaller knife to her ankle. Without sitting up, she looks up at me. Her shirt hangs loose, but I diligently keep my eyes above the gaping neckline. A smile spreads over her face, melting my heart.

Clearing my throat, I ask, "Do you need any help?"

"Can you grab the healing stuff from the wardrobe? It's just basic stuff, but we should probably take it."

Turning, I pull the wardrobe doors open and find a couple of wraps, a few jars of herbs, and a poultice. I open the latter and sniff it gingerly. Saerine has a few jars of this around the house for little scrapes and cuts.

Was she wounded recently?

The thought makes me queasy.

Elairie rises from the bed, grabbing a dark long-sleeved shirt from behind her and pulling it on over the little strappy one. The neckline scoops every bit as low as the undershirt, tempting my gaze.

But she shrugs into a black jacket and heads to the hallway.

Closing the backpack as I go, I follow her into the next room. Evaerga's room.

I sling the backpack over my shoulders, waiting in the doorway. My hands hang limp at my sides.

She spins in place, gazing at the simple furnishings. A bed, a wardrobe, a washstand.

With a sigh, she opens the wardrobe and retrieves a small, many-pocketed bag. She grabs a black pair of walking boots and a folded blanket, then looks around her mother's room one last time.

She hands the blanket to me, and our fingers brush, shooting sparks through my entire body. She settles on her mother's bed, tears splashing onto the floor as she pulls on Evaerga's boots.

We move downstairs, and Elairie retrieves a pair of black gloves from her grandmother's room. She slides them on and wiggles her bare fingers where they peek out the ends. Her chest rises and falls with a deep breath before she turns toward me.

"I packed the scrolls Mother left for us, but…" She gulps down a breath. "Should we look through the rest? Maybe there's something else that could help us."

"Sure. What are we looking for?"

"I don't know," she mumbles.

"Maybe we'll know it when we see it."

I retrieve the trunk and settle it on the kitchen table. The sun rises beyond the windows, casting golden rays of light through the windows to dance atop its wooden surface.

The sound of a horse and carriage makes my heart stop. A knock at the door freezes my blood. I glance out the window, leaning over the small countertop to get close, and sigh with relief as Geeran raises a hand to knock again.

How did he afford a horse and buggy?

The symbol of the Vairsun Guard shines on the side, and I nod my understanding.

I guess we can just bring all the scrolls.

Daggers slice easily through twine, and the bundles of dried herbs fall into waiting palms. We stow them in Evaerga's sash, and Elairie takes one last look at her home before we step out, her eyes brimming with tears. Her hand lingers on the doorknob as she shuts the door behind us, and my heart twists in my chest.

We wave to Pakaibra's patrolman as we pass him, and I take Elairie's hand. Leaden feet drag me to the cart.

But warmth seeps into me from her touch.

My stomach churns as we load our things. I grip the wooden sides with sweaty palms, climbing in with wobbly knees.

Settling down between crates and sacks, I close my eyes. The cart shifts as Geeran hauls his light frame up and sets the horse moving.

I put an arm around Elairie, trying not to think of the looming goodbye as we roll toward my home.

"Would you mind telling me of your vision last night?" Geeran asks, offering a different distraction altogether.

I wince, wishing he would leave Elairie in peace, but he specifies.

"How did the vision happen?"

I purse my lips. "Don't you have fortune magic?"

"I do," he says. "But what was it like to experience the vision together? Could you interact with each other?"

"Yeah…Why?" I ask.

"I didn't know joining someone on a vision was possible," Geeran answers. "But then, I've never been around Blessed Ones."

Elairie surprises me and joins the conversation. "So, people don't normally do that?"

"I've never heard of it before."

"It didn't happen with the vision yesterday morning though," I say.

"Your bond must have strengthened between visions."

Elairie and I both go quiet. My mind fills with our kiss, and my skin warms.

We roll on in thoughtful silence, bumping along the cobbled road. We pull up alongside the fence at my cottage, and Saerine bursts through the door immediately.

Geeran stays with the cart, but I look to Elairie as I climb out, offering her a hand. She leaps down after me, and Saerine throws her arms around us, fuchsia hair tickling my neck.

My heart warms, and I breathe a sigh of relief, relishing this peaceful moment.

"We probably shouldn't be out here," Elairie hedges.

"Of course," Saerine says, releasing us. Color blooms over her cheeks, and she leads us in.

As soon as we cross the threshold, the boys bound down the stairs. They leap onto me, nearly knocking me over with the force of their hug-charge. Shouts of "Where have you been?" and "What took you so long?" and "What did you bring us?" fill the room.

Laughter overwhelms me, and I hug Oran and Kraimin tightly. Excited giggling bursts from them.

I search for a way to answer their question but think better of it. They don't need to know I was in jail. With one of them balanced on each hip, I turn and say, "This is Elairie. She's very special to me."

A sharp intake of breath lifts her chest, and a warm smile spreads over her face.

My heart flutters.

Clearing my throat, I tell the boys, "I have to go away for a while. She's going with to keep me out of trouble.

"Why do you have to go?" Oran asks.

But Kraimin whispers, "Can I hug her?"

Nodding, I set him down and watch with a smile as he latches onto her. She wastes no time, scooping him up. His tiny arms wrap around her neck.

"You're really pretty," he says, staring her full in the face. "How many purples are in your hair?"

She laughs, and my heart warms.

Raising one eyebrow, I say, "Maybe I'll get a chance to count the colors while we're gone."

She meets my gaze, cheeks turning a lovely shade of scarlet.

"Okay, boys," Saerine says. "Go play for a little while."

Reluctantly, they slip from the room, and Elairie and I go upstairs. From the trunk at the foot of my bed, I dig out a backpack I haven't used since we settled here. Taking a deep breath, I pack only the essentials.

An old habit.

One I'd hoped never to indulge again.

Elairie stands near the bed, eyes roaming over my room. I wish this place were cozier, that it looked more like a home. With her here, I suddenly want things that I've held onto forever, just because I could, so I might have something to show her of my life.

But I don't have that.

"Do you need me to help with anything?" Elairie asks, voice sweet and gentle.

I shake my head. "It's alright. I've got it. You can sit down if you want." I gesture to the bed.

Tentatively, she sits, and my head fills with thoughts of laying her back, kissing every bit of exposed skin, removing clothes so I can kiss more of her. I want to hear that soft moan again.

I swallow hard and try to clear my head. Rather than reach for her, I force myself to pack.

But I stop short as I begin packing clothes.

I may not have done much to get dirty in jail, but I've worn these clothes long enough. And there's no telling how long it'll be before I can wash after we set out.

Holding up my clothes like an idiot, I say, "I, uh, should probably change."

Elairie blushes, and her skin burns almost the color of my hair. Dropping her gaze to her lap, she mumbles, "I'll give you some privacy," then rushes from the room.

But a hint of sadness lingers in her eyes.

Too late, I realize I should've kept packing, throwing in random junk to stall if necessary. I should've used the time to explain what I meant about not wanting to take advantage.

Does she really think I'm only with her because the Gods forced this on us?

I clean up quickly, hoping for some alone time with Elairie to explain soon. But we'll have Geeran with us throughout our trip.

Gods, did I mess this up?

Does she think I don't feel right about being with her?

I stop midway through pulling my shirt on, horrified at my own mistake.

But it was just the circumstances. Abyss below, she'd been through more than enough for one day.

But if she thought the one person made to be with her didn't want her...

My heart sinks. Yanking my shirt down, I grab my pack and rush out of my room.

I'll just have to show her how I feel if I don't get the chance to tell her.

Steadying myself, I descend the stairs and find Elairie and Saerine sitting at the table, talking about the boys. I take the seat next to Elairie, mind reeling at the conversation I know must come.

After a deep breath, I ask, "What did Geeran tell you last night?"

"He said you were Blessed Ones, and your time has come." She looks back and forth between us. "I don't know what that means though. I've heard of Blessed Ones, but…"

"But… what?"

"It scares me." She glances at her folded hands. "If the Gods made you this way, something really bad must be happening. You'll be in a lot of danger." Looking at Elairie, she says, "Geeran said… Well, it already got your Mother killed. I'm just worried."

She opens her mouth to say more but goes silent instead.

My chest collapses as I exhale.

"Well, I'm not sure what I can tell you without risking your safety," I begin. "We know what we're supposed to do, just… not how to do it. Not yet."

She purses her lips, eyes strained with fear.

The journey ahead flashes through my mind. The trek north, the hike through the mountains, the countless dangers along the way.

I add, "We'll be gone a long time."

"Where do you have to go?" Saerine's voice comes out quiet.

A deep sigh leaves me, and I close my eyes.

Nearly whispering, Elairie says, "I'm not sure we should tell you. If they thought for a second that you knew anything, they'd come after you too." She shudders.

I rub Elairie's hand, sending my own temperature soaring.

Saerine relents and nods silently.

Feeling the weight of time, knowing Geeran waits for us, I say, "Pakaibra spoke of employing you in Geeran's place. He said he'd watch over you and the boys."

A small scrap of the burden she'll carry in days to come breaks away, chipping off the huge stone lain across her shoulders. She nods, and I watch relief wash over her in bittersweet waves.

I want so desperately to stay, to linger here with her. But time tugs at me, urging me to move.

I squeeze Elairie's hand and force myself to rise. She follows suit and embraces Saerine. The gesture surprises me, but I smile. Saerine calls the boys down to say goodbye, then throws her arms around me, squeezing until I fear my bones will shatter.

"Be careful," I tell her.

"You too." She draws back, staring into my eyes. "Don't forget that this power comes with a lot of responsibility."

Stunned, I nod.

Oran and Kraimin come running down the stairs at full tilt. Crouching down, I hug them as tightly as Saerine hugged me, only stopping when they protest.

I look them over one last time, taking in every detail. Their ruddy complexions, their dark red hair like mine, their eyes, so much like Saerine's. Desperately, I try to commit everything about them to memory.

Even the smudges of dirt they already wear on their faces despite having been awake such a short time.

I look to Saerine. Worry clouds her tan face, and her magenta hair is tousled from running her hands through it over and again, a nervous habit we share.

I want to remember it all.

I spare no glances for the rooms around me. She and the boys are what matter, not these walls and ceilings.

Rising, I take Elairie's hand as we walk to the door. Oran and Kraimin run up the stairs, and Saerine drops into a chair in the kitchen. Her sobs assault my ears until we cross the threshold.

With my heart twisting in my chest, I pull the door shut behind us.

Chapter 12

Elairie

Crammed in the back of the cart with our provisions, Beluroan and I sit in silence, despairing all we leave behind. The future, more uncertain now than ever before, looms over us.

But Beluroan grips my hand, and heat dances through me.

The clopping of hooves on hard-packed soil makes this whole mess far too real. The Nouvai Forest closes in around us, wrapping us in shadows. The underbrush shudders, and my heart stops. But a rabbit bursts forth.

My mind paints the forest around us with menacing silhouettes. Over and again, I see the treacherous Elves who cut up my mother and left her for the wolves.

Will we even make it to the mountains?

Pushing the images away, I drop my gaze to my hand, held firm in Beluroan's grasp. His nimble fingers interweave with mine, sun-tanned and glorious next to my pale skin. A single scratch runs across the back of his hand.

My eyes trace that little line, and the skin slowly stitches itself back together. I gasp, blinking to clear my vision.

But it doesn't change.

Concentrating, I will the scratch to heal, and the process accelerates. It smooths over, gradually blending into that lovely tan.

Beluroan stares at his newly mended hand. He runs a finger over the tiny scar left behind

"How…?" he whispers.

My new fortune magic whispers through my mind, telling me that a poultice of calendula would have done just as well. If used together, there'd be no scar, even if the scratch were much larger.

"Did you feel it?"

Nodding, Beluroan says, "It tingled, just like when Saerine does it."

Glancing over his shoulder, Geeran asks, "What happened?"

"I think I have healing magic now." Awe fills me, and my heart swells. Turning to Beluroan, I ask, "Do you have any other injuries?"

Rolling up his sleeve, he shows me a scrape on his arm. I try desperately to heal it, focusing intently. But nothing happens.

Frustration bubbles up within me, and I mumble, "Damn it all."

Beluroan chuckles, and I blush. I drop my gaze, but he pulls me into his arms.

"Don't be embarrassed. It's fine," he says. "It won't come to us *that* quickly."

He nuzzles his face into my hair, and my spine melts.

And though I wonder if he's always this affectionate or if this is just obligatory, a product of what we are, my heart flutters. I shiver as electricity surges through me.

Aching for a distraction, I ask Geeran if healing magic is always so effective on its own.

He fills us in on the intricate details of healing, careful to tell us that severe injuries require both magical and herbal remedies. After a brief pause, he says,

"Though with the two of you, I have no idea if those restrictions will apply."

Marveling at how little is truly known about Blessed Ones, I change tact, asking about fortune magic instead. "How do you use divination to find out something specific? Like when Waergou found Mother by triggering and tracing a vision."

"It can be tricky. Divination is easier if you know something about that which you seek. Think of it like fishing with a net," Geeran says. "If you want a certain type of fish, but you cast your net out at random, you're not likely to find it. You might come up with nothing, or you might come up with fish you care naught for and scattered bits of plants."

"However," he continues, "if you know something about the fish, what types of places it prefers to live in, for instance, you can cast your net there. Your chances greatly improve."

Geeran falls silent, leaving us to process his words.

But Beluroan runs his fingers up and down my arm, pulling my mind away from the matter at hand. He leans his head against the wall of the cart and closes his eyes.

Fighting to keep my mind on track, I ask, "So if he knew nothing about Mother, was it blind luck?"

"Not quite. Advanced magic users can sense when they're being watched. As I'm sure you've experienced, divination magic heightens the senses. Some things simply come to you," Geeran says.

I nod, though he can't see me do so.

"Waergou likely sensed her watching him during her first vision and gained some scrap of information about her. Then, he used that to find her, triggered the vision to learn more about her, and closed in upon her whereabouts."

"How do you trigger a vision in someone else though?" I ask, mind whirling.

Geeran looks over his shoulder at us for a moment, then says, "Again, that's something only the most advanced among us can do. For now, we should focus on things closer to the skill level at which you currently find yourself."

"Oh." I don't quite manage to keep the disappointment from my voice.

For several hours, we ride on, learning how to "cast out a net" for specific information or visions. As the sun moves higher in the sky, Geeran tells us of the magical shields that could stand between us and the knowledge we seek.

"They can be placed on certain people or locations but it's tiresome work, leaving the caster vulnerable," he says. "Most who need a shield can't take the risk of maintaining one, so they go without. Unless they recruit someone else to cast it in exchange for protection."

Eventually, Geeran gives me topics to search for. "Imagine darkness closing in around the edges of your sight. Focus only on the topic at hand. Visualize it in the center of the darkness and send your mind out after it."

As we bump and clatter over the road, I try to find Deima. I imagine him sitting in the jail, likely alone. I picture darkness with only him.

But I find nothing.

Despite the familiar topic, despite knowing that jail like the back of my hand, despite knowing his eyes, his smile, I fail.

"Should I search for something else?" I ask, groaning with frustration.

"No, keep trying. You can do this," Geeran assures me.

Beside me, Beluroan sits still. His hand rests on mine, burning my skin with a delectable heat. I rip my mind away from it.

I stare at the wood of the cart and focus on Deima.

He would've had breakfast by now. He's probably sitting at the front desk. The cells are empty, so he won't need to check on anyone.

Does he have a fire in the hearth, or is he wearing his guard jacket, braving the chill?

The world around me fades, and black edges my sight.

Holding tightly to my hand, Beluroan comes with me as magic pulls me from the cart, sending my spirit all the way back to Vairsun.

We stand in the lobby of the jail, staring at a warm fire crackling in the hearth. Turning, we face Deima, sitting at the desk, like I knew he would be.

His jacket hangs over the back of his chair, and he leans forward, staring down at the papers before him. A lock of pale blue hair hangs down, tickling his jaw and blocking part of his face from view.

He's working on the budget.

We did go through more food over the past few days than usual... Maybe he'll go shopping again tomorrow.

And just like that, we're pulled to another location, another time, following Deima through the market tomorrow morning. He picks up fresh apples, but not as many as he normally would.

I'm not there to eat them.

A pang of sadness sweeps through me.

Pakaibra told him I was visiting family in Kaern.

Deima wanders through the market, and I feel his worries that the patrolman covering my shifts won't like the food he normally buys. He picks up a few extra things here and there, getting a wide variety, and resolves to ask the patrolman what he likes before he shops again.

All this information drifts into my mind, just another part of the vision.

With no warning, our spirits soar back to the cart, bumping along the uneven path through the Nouvai. "It worked," I breathe out.

Beluroan squeezes my hand. "Deima's going to miss you."

"Did you both experience the vision, again?" Geeran asks.

Beluroan simply says, "We did."

"You should try to trigger a vision yourself to see if you developed divination as well or if it was simply the contact with Elairie."

Beluroan tries to induce a vision of his sister, to no avail. His new magic still dwells within the elemental realm, while mine has yet to stray from life magic.

When we all finally give up, Geeran asks what happened in the vision. I relay the details, then ask, "Are visions of the future changeable?"

A shrill wind blows, and Geeran pulls his jacket tight around him. Beluroan and I huddle closer together, and the heat between us grows.

"The short answer is no," Geeran answers. "Clear visions are set in stone. There are infinite paths that the world can travel, but if you have an unclouded vision of an event yet to come, all the pieces have fallen into place. Visions of a changeable future show many different possibilities within the same vision, or sometimes, they're foggy."

I yawn, and exhaustion tugs at me, urging me to recline, to take a nap. Beluroan offers to take over, practicing his lightning magic.

"Hold your hands out, palms up, and imagine electricity surging through your body," Geeran says. "Channel it to your hands, arcing between your fingertips."

The horse tugs the cart along. The rocking motion pulls my eyelids low as sleep reaches for me. I force myself to sit up straight, battling the weariness of learning new magic.

Beluroan does as Geeran instructed, conjuring a few small sparks. Gradually, the sparks multiply until continuous streams of electricity flow freely between his fingertips. They crackle and sizzle, and the hairs stand up on my arms

***

Winter comes to bite us as we make camp for the night. Exhaustion rises up to claim Beluroan and me. Our excitement to learn and our looming duty pushed us too hard today, and a trickle of fear creeps in.

What if something, or someone, finds our camp? Will we be able to fight them?

Geeran insists that a ward of protection around our camp will suffice, but I glance nervously at Beluroan.

The sun casts its last rays out across the sky as I move through the forest in search of kindling. Deep, ominous shadows play on all sides, gathering on the forest floor.

I finger the dagger on my thigh with my free hand. Despite the birds singing overhead and the fireflies flitting about, a chill enters my heart.

The terrible vision from last night fills my mind. *Was Mother awake for her last sunset?*

The shadows morph into the silhouettes of those two Elves from the vision. My heart hammers against my ribs, and I decide that the sticks I've gathered will be enough to start our fire. I rush back to camp, desperate not to be alone with the shadows in my mind.

Trees become blurs, and roots threaten to pull my feet out from under me. As camp comes into view, I see Beluroan dropping a few branches onto a small stack. The sight of him comforts me.

I slow my pace to avoid startling him or Geeran. Glancing around, I find only bedrolls arranged around a small depression in the earth. No tents. I arrange my sticks in a cone within the depression.

"Geeran," I begin, meaning to ask for flint but change my mind. Instead, I turn to Beluroan. "Want to try your hand at this?"

Beluroan saunters toward me, jacket hanging open. His shirt clings to the muscles beneath. I swallow hard as he kneels beside me, and the heat between us blazes, keeping the chill air at bay.

How does it not ignite everything near us?

Holding out one hand, Beluroan focuses. Slowly, his hand begins to glow, and smoke rises from his fingertips. Tiny flames appear, growing until they consume his hand. He reaches for the cone of sticks, and they ignite.

He lets out a laugh, and the flames on his hand extinguish.

We feed more sticks into the flames, and their leaves crackle, sending tendrils of heat and embers skyward. Geeran comes close to warm his creaking joints.

"Since we don't have tents, could either you or Beluroan use your earth magic to make a small shelter?" I ask.

A blush creeps over my skin as I consider requesting two shelters, one for us and one for Geeran.

But instead, I say, "Getting caught out in the rain doesn't seem very pleasant."

Geeran chuckles. "Well, it isn't going to rain tonight. I've already looked ahead for a few days." Glancing at me, he adds, "You can do that now too."

"I guess I can," I whisper.

Mother used to do it all the time…

"As for shelter," Geeran continues, "we should conserve our strength. The two of you need to practice as much as possible. By all accounts, you should be so tired by the time we make camp that a shelter *can't* be made. And I must conserve my energy in case any creatures or bandits find their way to our camp."

I relent, deserting my hopes of finishing what we started in my room.

Not that he wanted to finish it then.

Why would he want to finish it now?

Chapter 13

Beluroan

I rub Elairie's back as we share a modest meal near the fire. She eats quietly, brows furrowed. Her fingers trace the top of her boots, her mother's boots, every so often.

"I think I'm going to lay down," Elairie whispers shortly after finishing her food. Exhaustion tugs at her eyelids, but I know it's more than that.

I move my bedroll over near hers, watching carefully to see if she objects. When she doesn't, I settle in. Sliding into her own bedroll, Elairie takes my hand. Warmth sweeps through me and builds in the air around us.

Silence falls, broken only by the delicate shuffling of Geeran's footsteps and the crackle of the fire. He puts up a ward around camp, and cloth rustles as he settles in for the night. Within moments, his snores shake my bones.

Tears glisten on Elairie's cheeks, shining in the soft firelight. Her shoulders shake. I wipe the tears away with my thumb, but new ones fall to take their place. I scoot closer, folding her against my chest. She cries in earnest, shuddering with harsh breaths.

Despair washes over me, but from a distance, like something stuck in the back of my mind, the back of my heart. Had Elairie not described it to me, I might not recognize it for what it is.

This isn't my emotion.

It's hers.

Elairie's grief floods through me, overwhelming in its intensity even at a distance. As it seeps into my bones, I hold her tighter, needing the closeness as much for myself as for her.

Gradually, her sadness slips from my grasp, but I find no relief in its wake. My brows furrow.

I actually miss feeling her pain?

How lost am I?

After fighting so hard for my independence, could I truly offer it up willingly? Shock blooms through me for just an instant, but I shake my head.

Because this isn't slavery.

This is right.

This is who we are.

Elairie's sobs become a painful whimpering, then soften further as sleep comes for her. Soft, even breaths break against my neck, but I'm left wondering how many of our nights together will end in tears that only end with sleep.

Then, the enormity of what just happened dawns on me.

Empath...

I've crossed into life magic.

The stark difference between the two disciplines stuns me. Elemental magic is a thing to harness. But life magic, at least empath magic, takes over.

I shudder.

Surely, it can be controlled and honed. Sharpened.

The fear of being completely saturated with someone else's emotions at any point rattles me to my core. I only hope it was so strong because it was Elairie's feelings. To feel someone else's heart so clearly within me seems wrong.

She curls into me, burrowing into my chest, and tries to lace her legs with mine. Our bedrolls block her efforts, and she groans in frustration.

Stifling a tired chuckle, I kiss the top of her head.

Slowly, the fire burns down, and sleep rises to claim me amidst the soft sounds of Elairie's breathing and the riot of Geeran's snores.

***

Morning comes all too soon for my taste. My brief stint with nocturnality in the jail has ruined the daylight. Elairie buries her head in my chest.

Nearby, Geeran stirs, and we force ourselves to rise for the day.

After a lean breakfast, we set out again. A chill pierces the air, and I offer to take the reins to spare Geeran.

He grabs a blanket, wrapping it tightly around himself as he climbs onto the bench. "Your time should be spent practicing, not navigating."

Taking a deep breath, I nod.

Elairie and I huddle up with a blanket to ease Geeran's concerns, but the heat of her presence chases the winter air away just fine. We spend the day practicing and discussing my new empath magic.

"You should practice that today," Geeran insists. "Search with your heart."

I scrunch my brows.

What does that even mean?

But I try.

Beside me, Elairie progresses with her fortune magic, learning quickly. A spark of hope floats through me, letting me believe, at least for a moment, that we might be equal to the task the Gods have set for us.

175

But so much lies ahead.

Flashes of Dwarves in the mountains, burly and war-torn, flicker through my mind. The thought of Elairie coming to harm turns my stomach.

We eat our lunch as we ride, and I figure distances in my head. At this rate, we'll reach Banrould tomorrow.

Hopefully, they'll have tents for sale.

The deep vulnerability of sleeping in the open settles over me, but Geeran speaks, pulling me from my reverie.

"Have you rested enough to try again?"

"Yes," I say.

"Good," Geeran says. "Then, let's give it another shot. Don't be discouraged, though. Empath is the hardest to learn. People guard their hearts."

After yet another failure at seeking out Elairie's emotions, I believe him. Each botched attempt is a chasm between us, like she's on the other side of Avaencery, the other side of the Romai Caldera.

Tightening my arm around her shoulders, I close my eyes and concentrate. Finally, I feel the walls around her heart and begin scaling them.

But...

Should there be walls here?

Shouldn't our hearts be open to each other?

We were made for each other, after all.

Nevertheless, I climb, and understanding blooms within me. Anxiety twists in my gut, but not my own.

Hers.

I focus on it, trying to find its root. The feeling of a missed step when climbing the stairs, the feeling of too many heartbeats skipped, comes to mind, and it makes sense.

She fears rejection, a blow she isn't certain she could handle if delivered by her Blessed counterpart. Knowing that I have no intention of pushing her away, a path opens before me.

Footholds in the walls, grips for my hands.

I scale the wall easily.

That strange feeling of possessing two hearts, two sets of emotions, comes over me again. I traverse fields of frustration, simmering with failed attempts to master our new magic. Pools of anxiety swirl around my feet, desperate to move faster, but not so fast that we reach Mount Hybar before we're ready.

Echoes of my own feelings, almost exactly.

Delving deeper, I find more walls. They seem to have been put up for the same reason, but they're stronger, taller.

Even knowing that I won't reject her doesn't help me overcome these.

My heart aches.

Mine, not hers.

I lose control of the magic, and her feelings slide out of me, wisps of her burdens trail along my skin like fingers before deserting me entirely.

What other secrets does her heart hold?

A pang of sadness expands within me, filling the space left behind by her emotions. The sudden aloneness takes a toll, as does the exertion.

I rub my eyes, whispering, "I could use a nap."

Elairie watches me, wondering if I was successful, no doubt.

Is she worried I saw too much?

"We'll be ready by the time we get there. Don't worry." I pat her knee reassuringly, letting my hand linger for only a second.

She relaxes, perhaps assuming that was all I saw or felt of her heart.

With a smile, I say, "You could practice empath now. Maybe that'll help you feel better."

Maybe if she sees how I feel…

But exhaustion tugs at her eyelids. She's been practicing divination magic for hours, making massive strides.

I nod, giving up for the time being.

I'll just have her practice it tomorrow.

"Should we set up camp soon?" I ask.

My suggestion finds Geeran amenable. He shivers beneath his blanket on the bench, teeth chattering lightly and reins shaking in his hands.

We stop at the first clearing we come to, and Elairie goes in search of kindling. I walk with her, seeking larger sticks as we trudge through the undergrowth.

Almost of its own accord, my hand reaches for hers, twining our fingers together. My heart skips a beat.

We walk in amiable silence, enjoying our first bit of alone time since leaving Vairsun. But the sun takes its heat as it sets. The forest around us turns a wintery grey, and chills sink into my bones despite our Blessed heat.

We gather wood for the fire, and each stick is like a grain of sand through an hourglass, our alone time slipping away.

I ache to tell her how I feel, but the words elude me. All too soon, we have enough sticks to maintain our fire through the night.

Elairie shivers beside me, and the sticks in her arms clatter together.

I blow out a breath as we trek back to camp, Elairie none the wiser to my feelings.

Chapter 14

Elairie

I soak up the heat of the fire as we eat. I bite my apple with a crunch, and an odd thought strikes me. "Geeran?" I begin.

"Hm?" His eyes lift from the apple cradled in his thin hands.

"Can only people with aura sensing tell what we are? Or is there another way?"

"People with aura sensing will know when they see you, but only if they know about Blessed Ones. If they don't, they'll have no idea what they're looking at. People with divination might know it if it comes to them in a vision. Aside from that, your existence should be protected."

"Should we shield ourselves? Maybe we won't have to fight until we find Gourmaht."

"We might have to fight, no matter what," Beluroan says, and I deflate. "There are vagabonds and outlaws everywhere, not to mention the wild…"

He stops himself, but I know what he was going to say.

Wild animals.

Like the wolves that tore my mother apart.

I take a deep breath, swallowing hard. But I force myself onward. "I'll put up a ward of protection on our camp each night, Geeran says. "Through the day, we'll just have to keep our wits about us."

Then, he adds, "Evaerga's note said you've been hidden thus far. Once you can practice without exhausting yourselves, I'll feel safer using my energy for a shield."

A pang of loss shoots through me at the mention of Mother, and my throat grows tight. I blink away tears and switch topics. "So, why is our aura fire and lightning? Why only Nepiter's elements?"

"Astute observation," Geeran answers.

A rush a pride sweeps through me, and I smile.

"They're the elements of the heart," Geeran says, voice wistful. "Of all the pieces of sentient beings, the heart is by far the strongest and the purest. Emotions can cause us bodily distress. They can change our thoughts and decisions. Yet, we cannot think our way out of our emotions, nor can we decide our feelings."

He looks us over and continues. "The heart overwhelms, so its elements come to the forefront. For Blessed Ones, the need to be near the other half is so strong that the heart creates its own aura, as a sort of beacon. Air and water, that of the mind, keep you in each other's thoughts. Earth drives a desire to join physically."

I blush, all too aware of that drive. The firelight flickers over my skin, and I hope it hides the color in my cheeks. I want to look up, to see if heat simmers over Beluroan's features, but my eyes fix on my boots.

Geeran continues, unaware of the effect his words or choosing not to pry.

"Doorma and Baereen gave us free will. Powerful and destructive as that can be, especially regarding Blessed Ones, it's influenced by the other elements. Even if it weren't, you were granted the exact same breath of will. The two of you would always want each other. No one else."

"So, how is that free will?" My voice comes out harsh.

"You can choose to be with someone else and stay apart. You just won't be as happy."

Is Beluroan only with me to avoid being miserable?

"You really aren't much for pep talks, are you, Geeran?" Beluroan says with a chuckle, softening the comment. But his hands fidget nervously.

"I suppose not," Geeran answers with a quiet smile.

We finish our food, and Geeran puts up the promised ward of protection. Beluroan drags his bedroll over next to mine, almost touching. My heart pounds as we lie down, facing each other.

Geeran's snores batter the air, and I know I'll never have a better chance. I can't rid myself of the pain of losing Mother, but I can clear this up.

"You know, Beluroan, if all of this is just because of what we are…" I hesitate, stomach churning. "You don't have to. If it'll make you feel better, we can just be friends."

My insides twist. My breath catches in my chest, and my heart falters.

He stares into my eyes, mouth working silently. Shadows flicker over his face as tendrils of flame lick the air behind me. His brows furrow, and he touches my face.

I brace myself for whatever he may say, brows reaching for each other.

Inching closer, he brushes his lips against mine, burning me with his touch. My brain shuts down, and I struggle to understand this as an answer. It seems too good to be true.

Resting his forehead against mine, Beluroan says, "I'm sorry about the other night…"

He pauses, searching for words. His mouth forms a few silent sentences, moving against mine.

After a small shrug, he says, "You'd already been through so much, and there's no way you were thinking straight after your mother… I couldn't take advantage of that. I'm not sure I could've forgiven myself."

Shock spreads through me, and I go still.

"Elairie…" His voice quivers as my name crosses his lips, sending shivers down my spine. His fingers trace my jaw, and sparks shoot through me. "Believe me," he says firmly, "it isn't because I just want to be friends. I want a lot more than that."

Heat pools within me. My heart expands, and I press my lips to his.

Lightning cracks through me like a whip, and I push hard against him, rolling him onto his back, tangling my fingers in his hair.

His hands roam over my back, pulling me tighter to him. Our legs entwine, as much as they can through the bedrolls. My breath comes in gasps, and my heart threatens to explode.

Beluroan pushes me back, slipping his arm into my bedroll, nudging a leg between mine. Heat bursts through me.

His hand finds my hip, one thumb sliding back and forth, slipping beneath my shirt to glide over bare skin. Fiery kisses burn my neck, and I moan softly.

Geeran's snores stutter, then come to a coughing halt, and I freeze.

Beluroan lets out a long, controlled breath.

I touch his neck, feel his heart beating hard beneath my fingers. With one long, last kiss, my world burns to the ground, and he lays down beside me.

Snaking his arm around me, he pulls me to him. Our fiery aura intensifies, nearly burning me alive, yet somehow, the bedrolls don't burn away.

Geeran sits up on the other side of the fire and whispers, "Is everything ok?"

With a sigh, I say, "Yes. Everything's fine."

Beluroan smiles wickedly.

I nestle in as close as possible with two bedrolls and a third wheel separating us. Guilt rolls through me, and I chastise myself for thinking so unkindly of Geeran after all he's doing to help us.

But some alone time with Beluroan would be… very nice.

I shiver at the thought.

Wrapped in his arms, snug in a cocoon of fire, I kiss Beluroan's neck one last time. The fire around us simmers to a smoldering warmth, and I drift off to sleep.

***

I wake with my arms slipped between the buttons of Beluroan's bedroll. Warmth flows between us. I slip one hand free and push a few wild strands of hair out of his face, delighting in the heat that seeps into my fingers at the small contact.

His eyes flutter open, and a dreamy smile spreads over his face. My heart skips a beat as his hand snakes under my bedroll to grasp my hip. He pulls me close, pressing me to him. Nuzzling his face into my hair, he breathes deeply, then exhales in a half-moan, half-sigh.

I shudder.

I slip my hand beneath his shirt, skin burning at the direct contact as I trail my fingers up and down his spine. He rewards me with a soft groan.

Behind me, Geeran pokes around camp, knocking a few things around in the cart, feet dragging the ground as he walks around. I glance at him over my shoulder.

He pats the horse on the back before, smiling, before meandering back to the fire. I take a deep breath, readying myself to meet the day.

But Beluroan brushes his lips against my ear. Hot breath caresses my skin, and my eyes close. His lips part, and he nibbles gently at my earlobe.

I stifle a gasp. My blood rushes and my heart hammers vigorously.

Barely audible, Geeran's voice drifts toward me from beyond the horse. "Did you say something, Elairie? Are you awake?"

Beluroan moves his lips to my neck, dropping a sensuous kiss on my flushed skin.

My voice cracks, breathy as I say, "Yes, we're awake."

Beluroan kisses my neck again, and I wonder if he's doing this on purpose, trying to get me riled up. Even so, my body reacts.

My nails dig into his back, and I crush my hips forward against his. Beluroan gasps quietly, and satisfaction bubbles up within me.

Geeran calls out, "Breakfast is ready when you are."

"We should probably get up," I whisper, staring into magnificent emerald eyes.

"Well," Beluroan begins softly, "I, uh…" He clears his throat. "I think I'll need a moment." He takes a deep breath, blushing.

I smile at him coyly, knowing full well why he doesn't want Geeran to see him stand up. I chuckle inwardly. "I'll bring you some food. I'll be right back."

Planting one last kiss on Beluroan's cheek, lips tingling from the contact, I fetch our breakfast. We sit in charged silence as we eat, and I hardly notice my food. My mind lingers, tangled in the bedrolls.

***

Beluroan's hand rests on my leg beneath our blanket, just above my knee, heating my flesh. Yet even now, he practices. As the horse pulls us along the bumpy road, he tries to feel Geeran's emotions.

As we pass another cart going in the opposite direction, Beluroan turns to me with a deep sadness in his eyes.

Of Geeran, he asks, "How long has it been since he passed?"

Geeran sits quietly. Eventually, he answers, "Four years." With a sigh, he says, "You got much further into my heart than I expected."

I nestle in against Beluroan's side as he says, "You never got to grieve for him, did you? You can tell us about him."

We ride on in silence, but eventually, he tells us about a man named Jaetus.

"We grew up together, practiced our magic together." Geeran's voice takes on a wistful quality as he adds, "We were inseparable."

My heart aches for him.

"As we grew older and became men, friendly pats on the back began to linger. I was so nervous," he says, voice going quiet on the last words. "I didn't want to mess up the friendship I'd always had with Jaetus, but… I couldn't hide my feelings from him, either."

He sighs, and my heart twists.

"Then, one day, we were mixing up a poultice. Our hands brushed… And he didn't pull away. I looked up at him, and one strand of his soft, black hair had fallen into his face, just like it always did. Gods, I love how it always did that," Geeran's voice catches. "I couldn't just let the moment pass. His hand was still on mine, those warm amber eyes of his seemed to be glowing, and I… I had to."

He chuckles. "I was so nervous. My heart nearly burst out of my chest. I'd never kissed anyone. Jaetus sort of had. Well, someone had kissed him once, but he said he wasn't interested. When he told me about it, he said he'd already found someone special. I just sat there, listening, hoping he meant me. I thought maybe he did, but that didn't make it easy to get up the courage to actually kiss him when the time came."

Geeran laughs, and I join him.

"I was such a mess," he says, "but it didn't matter when our lips touched." He sighs and falls silent.

Bouncing along, we pass yet another cart.

We must be getting close to Banrould.

Once it passes, Geeran continues.

"When Kaistrum started taking slaves, we panicked. He came through Vairsun with the aromatic oil on, shouting commands… We locked ourselves in our bedroom, and I had to restrain Jaetus."

I sit up straighter, never having wondered about Geeran's time during the Blood War.

"He fought me. He didn't want to, but the Blood Magic forced him. He apologized the whole time. But it was worse *after*. Watching his family turn from proud Fox Elves to slaves, to Blood Elves… And he couldn't save them, couldn't fight in the war. He would've been turned into a slave himself."

My mouth goes dry, but now that Geeran's started speaking, the words tumble out.

"He was a prisoner in our home. He couldn't risk being seen by anyone who might turn him in to save themselves. We kept the windows shut, sealed off the chimney so none of the aromatic oil could get in."

"We went through so much, and we were so good together. Despite it all, we had a great life. But in the end, there's only so much that healing can do. It was his time to go. I couldn't help him…" Geeran's voice trembles. "I can't believe it's been four years since I held him in my arms. Four miserable years."

My stomach flips.

Beluroan wraps an arm around my shoulder and pulls me to his side, holding me close in the silence that follows Geeran's story.

***

People fill the streets of Banrould, milling about busily, and my nerves tie themselves into knots. Beluroan and I duck out of view.

"How are we going to stay hidden?" I whisper.

"Saerine and I lived here for a while. I know somewhere we can go while Geeran gets supplies." Beluroan looks at me with mischief in his eyes. "Are we staying in Banrould for the night, Geeran?"

"I guess that depends on how long this takes. I need to check in with Pakaibra, as well."

"Geeran?" I ask. "Could you pick up some paper and a pencil or pen?"

Beluroan looks at me with furrowed brows.

"Sure," Geeran answers. "But why?"

"Well, I didn't expect the cart. I was trying to pack light, so I didn't bring anything to draw. But it's not like I need to worry about carrying it around, and it might be nice when I'm not practicing."

"I'll find some. It'll be good to refresh your mind." Geeran pauses for a second. "Shall I pick anything up for you Beluroan?"

"An instrument?"

"Anything in particular?"

"No. Whatever you can find without spending much."

I look him over, surprised.

"Can you stay hidden for a couple of hours?" Geeran asks.

"That shouldn't be a problem." Beluroan says with a smirk.

He points out an alley, and Geeran drops us off. As soon as we leave the cart, our hands entwine, and Geeran rides deeper into town.

We wander between buildings, turning to follow another alley. A tiny gap too narrow to walk side by side leads us further, bricks catching my clothes.

The little shop building ends, and the tiny channel opens up, depositing us into a curious little dead end. Four buildings butt up against each other with just enough space for a large cart, not that you could ever get one back here.

I peer down every alley that leads here, but they all end in walls, blocking the view from the streets around us. No windows face us. Tall grass surrounds us, and white flowers huddle in the corners.

"It's magnificent," I whisper.

"I used to hide out here after stealing food." Beluroan turns to me, trailing a hand over my arm. "Any time we got to a new place, I always mapped it out, found all the little hidey holes and escape routes I could."

He sits down, back against a wall, and tugs me down beside him. "I used them a lot. I was only seen stealing twice before Vairsun. Once here, and once in Aivrard. Thanks to little spots like this, Vairsun is the only time they caught me. I'd just hide out in little forgotten places until dark, and we'd leave that night."

My mind whirls, wondering if he would've slipped away if the Patrol hadn't caught him.

"Every town has little nooks and crannies that no one thinks about, spaces left empty because of land disputes or a shortage of funds to do anything with them," Beluroan says.

"This was always my favorite one." He pats the ground beside him. "The grass is always soft and springy, perfect for a nap. And unless it's the dead of winter, there are always flowers of some sort."

He leans his head against the wall, sighing contentedly. Taking my hand in both of his, he strokes his fingers over the back of my hand. My skin crackles at his touch.

"Sometimes I used to come back here just to relax. I'd buy whatever instrument I could find for as little money as possible and just play. Even if I'd never played it before, it was fun to try." His face brightens in a smile.

"And these walls are so thick, no one hears it. Or if they do, they just assume it's their neighbor," he adds with a chuckle.

"If we make it back to Vairsun, you should show me the little places you found there," I say.

He looks over at me, eyes pinched.

"First, the hideouts in Vairsun aren't very good. They're just crawl spaces under the backs of buildings that are butted up against each other. I can still show them to you, but they're nowhere near as good as this one."

Beluroan pauses, staring intently into my eyes. "Second, and more importantly… Why *if* we make it back to Vairsun? What happened to, 'Surely the Gods made us equal to the task?'"

I falter, dropping my gaze to our hands. He reaches up, lifting my chin so I'll meet his soft gaze.

But my eyes brim with tears as I say, "That was before they…"

The words stick in my throat, but I force them out.

"Before they killed Mother. If I couldn't even save her, how can I hope to save all of Avaencery?"

Flood gates open, sending tears cascading over my cheeks.

Without missing a beat, Beluroan scoops me up and pulls me onto his lap. I lean into him, weeping against his shirt.

His lips brush my ear as he whispers, "There was nothing we could've done. Even if we'd set off as soon as we found those scrolls, as soon as you had your vision, they had so much of a head start, we never could've caught up to them in time."

His hands slowly rub my back. Placing a kiss atop my head, he says, "Don't blame yourself or question your abilities. There's *nothing* you could've done."

His words have a certain buoyancy to them, helping me float on my sadness, rather than sink and drown.

I stare up at him. "Thank you," I say. Leaning my forehead against his, I breathe deeply.

I can't let him down. I can't lose faith in us. Not when he believes so strongly.

Beluroan caresses the side of my face. "You don't have to thank me." A smile lifts the corners of his mouth. "I worry about it too. This is a big responsibility… But look at how far we've come already. We'll be okay."

Our eyes lock, and his words pull me in. My heart hammers in my chest.

I lift my lips to his, and electricity shoots through me. I try to restrain myself at first, keeping the kiss gentle. Our lips brush together tenderly, and I lose my breath.

I pull back for an instant, gazing into lush green eyes. But the gravity between us beckons, and I fall. Our mouths meet again, so sweetly that my heart aches.

My lips brush over his, back and forth, then dip to kiss his neck. He gasps, eyes closed, and I place one hand on his neck. I brush my lips against his ear, and he rewards me with a moan.

Beluroan snakes one hand from my knee up the outside of my leg. He lets it rest just where my thigh becomes my backside, sending sparks skipping across every inch of my skin.

I nip his ear, and his hand grasps my thigh. My breath catches, and my heart nearly gives out on me.

I slide my hands beneath his jacket and push it back over his shoulders. The neck of his shirt scoops down in a slight v, and my lips seek out his exposed collarbone.

He slips my jacket off, and a deep hunger takes over me, pushing me to kiss his lips. He cups my cheeks, pulling me in. Our mouths dance, sending my head spinning.

I bite gently at his lower lip, earning a guttural moan. His hands tangle in my hair, and the touch burns me alive. His lips leave trails of fire on my neck.

Beluroan lays me down on soft grass. He ravages my neck, my collarbone, lips moving down, all the way to the low collar of my shirt.

My heart hammers, and heat bursts through me. I pull at the bottom of his shirt, sliding it up his muscled torso. I rip the fabric up over his head, staring up at him, eyes roaming over him.

My fingers trace the lightning magic scar from his collarbone over his chest and stomach, fingers trailing all the way down just below his belly button.

Beluroan leans his head on my shoulder, breathing raggedly. One hand clenches my hip.

I move his hair to the side, kiss the top of his shoulder, press my hips up against him. He showers my neck with kisses.

My skin burns as he pushes my shirts up, sliding his hand over my stomach. Electricity moves through me, and my insides clench.

A soft voice draws my attention, but still, his teeth nip at my neck. My stomach flips.

Someone clears their throat, and Beluroan rests his head on my shoulder. He growls through clenched teeth. His nails dig in as he clenches my hip.

I lift my head to look over at the intruder, and then drop back onto the ground. I roll my eyes and close them, drawing in deep, steadying breaths.

Some kid, maybe seventeen years old, stands there. She pointedly averts her gaze, wavy silver hair hanging about her alabaster face as a shield.

Beluroan struggles to get his body under control, at least enough to stand up without giving this girl a show. His tight black pants don't hide much.

The kid pipes up again. "I was starting to worry you weren't going to stop. It took a long time for you to hear me."

"And yet, you stayed?" Beluroan's voice comes out strained. After a deep breath, he rises and sits back on his haunches. "Sorry."

I prop myself up on my elbows, looking at his bare chest, reveling in the heat that courses through me.

"No worries," the girl says. "It obviously wasn't a good time for me to show up. I kind of need to be here for a while though."

For the first time, Beluroan actually looks at her. "Laying low, huh?"

He settles against the wall. Much to my disappointment, he reaches for his shirt. He starts to put it on but thinks better of it, dropping it in his lap. Looking at me, he chuckles and says, "I don't think I need this just yet."

Speechless, I sit up, pulling my shirts back down over my stomach. I scoot over to sit next to him and whisper in his ear, "If only I could have mine off."

A blush spreads over him, and I smile. The girl in the corner also blushes, though that isn't what I was going for.

Turning to face her, I ask, "What's your name?"

"Vourneima."

Beside me, Beluroan responds, "I'm Beluroan, and this is Elairie. Now, what did you do that you need to hide out for?"

Vourneima looks down sheepishly, "I… sort of… stole some stuff."

"Why? And why actually tell us that?" Beluroan asks.

"Well, my boyfriend needed food. He doesn't make much money, and I don't make enough for both of us. So…" She holds up a bag.

"His parents were slaves," the girl says. "They died in the Blood War, so they can't help him. My parents *fought* in the Blood War for 20 years, and even though, once they joined the fight, they saw it through to the end, they're still afraid there's another one out there, controlling people."

She purses her lips, then continues in a huff, "They don't want me with him, let alone helping him or stealing food for him."

She sits down at the wall across from us. "As for why I told you… This isn't exactly a place most people seek out, not unless they need to hide. I assume you're not going to be telling people about your time here."

Clever girl.

Beluroan shakes his head. "Well, I'm sure your boyfriend appreciates everything you do for him." After a brief pause, he adds, "It's certainly not an easy life."

"You were a slave too, weren't you?"

Her bold question catches me off guard. I thought her more reserved than that. After all, she has yet to stop blushing.

Beluroan seems to take pity on her and puts his shirt back on before nodding. "Yeah, I was."

"So… What was it like?" Looking down, she adds, "My boyfriend doesn't like to talk about it."

"I can't say I blame him," Beluroan says. After a deep sigh, he continues, "It's hard to describe."

He pauses, considering his hands. Eventually, he meets her gaze, saying, "You know, when you touch something hot and your hand jerks back of its own accord? You don't think about it. It just happens. You want your hand to jerk back, of course, but it just happens."

"Yeah…" she says, drawing the word out, brows furrowed.

"Now, imagine if, instead, your hand reached out and grabbed that really hot thing, and you had no control over it. It just happens, without your say-so, against your will, even. That's what it's like."

His eyes drop to his lap once more. "No matter how much you scream, in your head or out loud, you can't stop your body from doing whatever you've been told to do. You could be told to murder the one person closest to you, and your body would do it, regardless of what you want."

I lay my hand on his arm, trying to offer whatever comfort I can.

It must've been terrible…

Creeping in around the edges of my sight, darkness overtakes me, whisking me away to the place where Beluroan grew up, his family's hut on his Master's land. Somewhere in the Cargam Mountains, between the Vendaela River and the Draecon River, it huddles far from Mount Hybar.

But this vision is different.

I don't stand on the outside, viewing from afar. This time, I watch through Beluroan's eyes, feeling everything he felt that night.

The Master looms behind 9-year-old Beluroan.

Me.

Us.

Dread seeps in, and panic sends his heart racing. One thought fills his head, screaming over and over.

NO! Gods, please…No…

But the command has already been issued.

Beluroan's mother sits in the corner, huddled in a little wooden chair. Someone else's blood coats her hands, left over from her last mission. But while she was out, she said something she shouldn't have. Now, it's up to Beluroan to administer the punishment.

Beluroan screams, and the hoarse cry rips through my throat.

His feet drag him across the worn wooden floor, and Mother cowers.

Fear. Hatred for Master. Pain.

It all hits me like solid stone, and it's too much. Just like it was too much for him all those years ago. His emotions are mine, and mine are gone. I'm him now, and I'm screaming.

Our hands fly out to beat her, slamming into her stomach, and she does her best to hide her pain, trying not to make it harder for us.

"Let him see your pain!" Master bellows, sending spit flying from his mouth.

Instantly, Mother begins weeping, whimpering. Fear and agony shine in the sweat on her face. Her features contort into an unrecognizable mask.

My, his, *our* fists keep swinging, despite the biggest struggle of will I've ever felt.

Our hands bleed from the impacts with Mother's face, knuckles split open, and her features blur together in all the crimson splattered over her.

Ours and hers.

My heart shrivels in my chest.

Please, no… Stop, hands! Please stop…

Whimpering fills the hut, ours and hers.

Tears fall, and noses run. Ours and hers.

She falls from her chair. But our body shows no mercy, straddling her. Our fists continue to fly. Blood and tears and snot matte her luscious fuchsia hair.

Only 9 years old, but strong from all the farming and construction work, each punch carries too much force for such a small boy. The rotting boards beneath us creak with every impact.

Her dark green eyes flutter closed. Shallow breaths struggle to lift her chest. Our heart clenches painfully, but our body doesn't relent.

Our fists fly, striking fast. Agony spears our knuckles. Tears pour from our eyes.

"Please," we whisper, choking on agony and exhaustion.

Two more punches.

"Enough." Master's voice is a cruel hiss, and we fall limp beside Mother as His command deserts us.

Master leaves, boots loud on the old wood.

Rising to our knees, we hold Mother's face in our hands. She still breathes, but only just. Blood flows freely from her busted lip, her swollen eyes, her broken nose.

Saerine and Father rush in. Fighting back tears of her own, Saerine works to heal Mother.

Darkness floods in around my periphery, mercifully ending the vision.

But the sight sears itself into my memory.

My spirit slams back into my body, knocking the wind out of me. Beluroan gasps beside me.

I climb onto his lap, straddling him, and throw my arms around his neck. His arms wrap around my waist, constricting my breathing. His head drops onto my shoulder, and I cradle his head, fingers tangling in his hair.

A single silent tear drops from each of his eyes to land upon my chest, but countless tears fall from mine.

Vourneima makes a sound of discomfort and asks, "Is everything ok?"

But we don't answer. We sit, wrapped around each other, sizzling with electricity and run through with agony.

Chapter 15
Beluroan

My heart pounds against my ribs. My hands shake at the horror of reliving it, and I wish Elairie could've been spared that trauma.

But she saw it.

She saw it all.

My Mother's bloody face flashes before my eyes, and I squeeze them shut. I burrow my head into Elairie's shoulder, and her arms tighten around me.

Everywhere we touch sizzles with the bond that grows between us, offering a comforting warmth. It flows through me, slowly chasing the fear and pain from my bones.

Vourneima mumbles something, but I don't catch it.

More important matters draw my attention. Because I can't just ignore this. I can't pretend Elairie doesn't have to deal with this now too.

I raise my head and look up into dark blue eyes. Tears glisten on her lashes, and her bottom lip trembles softly.

"I'm sorry you had to see that," I whisper.

Leaning her forehead against mine, she says, "Don't worry about me. Are you ok?"

A sad smile tugs at my lips, then slips away. "Did you… Was that vision… *different* for you?"

Because it was different for me. But maybe that was just because it was my memory.

I cling to a scrap of hope that she watched from the outside, that it was just a normal vision for her.

But a voice in the back of my head tells me that I would have sensed her, would have felt her near.

She nods. "I wasn't an outsider. I was… you. Or at least, I saw it from your eyes. I *felt* what you felt."

A cold wave washes over me, and I close my eyes with a sigh. "I was afraid of that."

"Hey," she says. With a gentle touch, she lifts my head and gazes into my eyes. "It's ok. We'll get through it."

I stare into those deep, dark pools of blue. A cool river flows through me, whispering softly, soothing my heart.

Across this tiny expanse, Vourneima clears her throat.

I guess we can't ignore her anymore.

Lifting one corner of my mouth sadly, I nod in her direction, indicating to Elairie that I'm ready to talk to this girl.

She moves off my lap, settling beside me and leaving me cold at the loss of contact. I reach for my jacket and pull it on.

Elairie does the same.

"Sorry, Vourneima," I say.

She stares at us, eyes narrowed with suspicion. "What just happened?"

"We had a vision, that's all."

"Uh huh. And I'm a Representative."

I chuckle at her skepticism, but I can't tell her more than that. I look up at the sky, judging the position of the sun.

"Well," I begin, "It's time we got going. If you don't tell anyone about our time here, we won't. Deal?"

A million questions seem to perch on her lips, begging her to speak. After all, people don't usually share visions.

Butterflies riot in my stomach as I wait for her to agree. The fate of our world depends on her silence, not that she knows that.

But she knows what's at stake for her.

She nods. "The two of you are very peculiar. You know that, right?"

Elairie laughs. "Yes, we know."

"Thank you, Vourneima." I rise to my feet and offer a hand to Elairie.

She takes it and stands, telling the girl, "It was very nice to meet you."

"Nice to meet you too," Vourneima answers.

Our footsteps echo off the close walls as we traverse the alleyways. My past hangs over me, and I take Elairie's hand, hoping to stave off the chill the memory put in my veins. Heat buzzes through me at her touch, just as I knew it would, and I take a deep breath.

But Elairie's feet drag the ground, boots scuffing at the rocks, the dirt.

"Sorry," she whispers. "I think… I might have accidentally triggered that vision."

I stop in my tracks, arm pulled forward as she takes another step. I stare at her.

"Why? Why would you *want* to see that?"

She turns to me, eyes pained. "I didn't mean to. I was just thinking that it must've been terrible, and that no matter how you described it, I'd never really understand. Then, the vision started."

Her gaze falters, falling to the ground, but more words tumble out of her, "I really didn't mean for the vision to happen. I'm so sorry. I didn't want to put you through it again."

I take a deep breath, steadying myself, and pull her into my arms. "It's ok. More practice with fortune magic, and you'll be able to control it better."

Elairie nods. She gives me a quick kiss, and the taste of her lingers on my lips as we walk on.

"I'll try really hard," she promises. "I don't want to put you through that, again."

"Thank you. Try not to worry about me though. I've had years to deal with it."

Not that those years have been enough.

I kick at a rock, sending it skipping on down ahead of us. I kick it again when we reach it. "Should we tell Geeran about it?"

"We don't have to tell him what the vision was about, but we should probably tell him that we *lived* your memory. I don't think that's quite… normal."

I nod, sucking my lips in.

We continue down the alleys, arriving at the main road mere moments before Geeran. We settle into the back of the cart with a blanket thrown over us, and Elairie nestles in close. Her hand rests on my thigh, and heat surges through me.

***

Nahkie Lake glistens a perfect blue in the early evening light. Trees cling to the water's edge, huddling close, leaving only a few gaps.

Exhausted from hours of practicing, we pick a clearing with a slope leading to the water and set up camp quickly. Geeran procured a single large canvas tarp that we fashion into a lean-to. He tucks his bedroll in at the far edge, allowing us all the privacy he can.

Unbuttoning the sides of our bedrolls, Elairie unrolls them and places them one atop the other. All the air rushes out of me, and my heart beats frantically. I imagine how close we'll be, imagine the feel of her pressed against me, and my blood roars through my veins.

Stop it. Geeran will be right there.
Nothing's going to happen.

I fight off images of my hand sliding beneath her shirt, touching her bare skin.

Desperate for busy work, I stack sticks for a fire. Imagining flames coursing through the sticks before me, I pull the energy forth. I concentrate harder, picturing tendrils of smoke rising from them.

Slowly, the magic builds within me, and I focus on it, nurturing it. Within moments, smoke sprouts from the sticks, followed by tongues of flames. The fire grows, taking root and sustaining itself without my aid.

A burst of pride shoots through me, and though I hate myself for it, I hope Elairie saw this minor triumph. A glance finds her unpacking food from the cart, and I stuff down my disappointment. She and Geeran carry our dinner over, and Elairie nestles up close to me.

"Oh," Geeran begins, "I got the items you wanted."

He rises, old bones creaking, and goes to the cart. He digs through crates and returns with a small book of paper, a pen, a bottle of ink, and what appears to be a mandolin.

I laugh. "Where did you stash those? We sat in that cart all afternoon and didn't see them."

"They were in the storage under my bench. I didn't have time to move anything else to make room for them."

"Thank you." Elairie says, taking the things Geeran offers her.

"Really, thank you. How did you even find this? Mandolins are human instruments." I look it over, surprised by the condition of it. I strum it lightly, and my jaw drops.

It's in tune.

"How much did it cost?" I ask. "I hope you didn't spend too much."

"The merchant had been hanging onto it for a while. He said it intimidated everyone in town. Too exotic. He threw it in for almost nothing."

A burst of excitement flows through me as my fingers pluck the strings, getting acquainted with the instrument. I glance at Geeran and ask, "How did things go with Pakaibra?"

"He's spoken with the Vairsun Representative. The Elders have been consulted, as has the General."

"Pakaibra works quickly," I say, blowing the words out on a breath of admiration.

Geeran nods. "General Haedra will meet us in Kaern, with as many troops as can be surreptitiously gathered. Unless something happens before then, we'll decide our next move with her guidance."

We finish eating and inform Geeran of today's strange vision. At first, he wants to know what we lived out, but he relents.

Geeran sits silently, chewing over what we've told him.

"It's just us, isn't it?" Elairie asks. "No one else does that?"

"It's just you," he says with a slow nod, brows furrowed. He stares into the fire, head tilted.

Elairie's gaze drifts to the lake, hands fidgeting in her lap. After a moment, she says, "Shall we swim before the sun sets?" She makes a show of sniffing her shirt and grimacing.

Geeran chuckles, a rare sound. "I wouldn't mind cleaning up."

With blankets under our arms and hands linked, Elairie and I make for the water. My skin sizzles where we touch, and a chill sweeps over me when we separate at the bank to disrobe. I cast my jacket and vest to the ground, and she does the same.

She blushes, turning her back to me as she tugs her long-sleeved shirt off. That little white shirt with thin straps clings to her form, and I swallow.

My heart rate speeds up, and I turn away, trying to control myself. After all, Geeran is right there. A small part of me wonders if that's the cause of her bashfulness, given what she said in the alley about wanting her shirt off.

Though I guess that was a different situation.

Pulling my shirt over my head, I wonder why it was ok with Vourneima around, but not with Geeran. Unless it's a consideration for his broken heart.

The sound of cloth falling behind me catches my attention, but I don't look. In my periphery, she walks to the water wearing naught but her white shirt and black underwear. I close my eyes, pulling in deep breaths.

I kick my boots off, fingers fumbling with the buttons of my pants. They fall, taking my daggers with them and hitting the ground with a solid thunk. The chill air does its best to cool me, but it's no match for the heat of Elairie's presence.

I take another deep breath and turn to the lake. Water reaches up to Elairie's waist. She looks back at me, glancing over her shoulder with a sweet smile playing on her lips, dancing in her eyes.

I sprint for the lake, kicking up a spray of water on entry. She squeals as it splatters over her, and I laugh, deep and hearty, a laugh I haven't known for a long time.

A mischievous smile decorates her face, and she splashes back at me. For a few blissful moments, we forget everything and play at water wars. Just like all those couples I used to make fun of.

I didn't get it.

I do now.

She splashes me repeatedly, but one splash from me is bigger than five of hers.

I rush her, arms sliding around her waist, and tackle her. We go under for an instant, and when we come back up, her arms have wrapped themselves around me.

Peering through a wash of red hair, delighting in the sound of her laughter, I brush the loose strands of lilac from her eyes. She smooths my hair back in turn.

Her eyes fall to my lips, and I tip my head, aching to accept any invitation she might extend. But she takes a deep breath, eyes darting toward the bank. Toward Geeran. Her gaze softens, but he isn't looking. She looks back at me, and that mischievous glint returns to her eyes.

She really is worried about hurting him.

I nod, glad to just be near her.

She pulls back, managing only a pitiful attempt at a splash, and I completely drench her with one move. The sunlight slants through the air, casting warm yellow light over her, sparkling in every drop of water that clings to her skin.

My eyes wander over her. Two dark circles hide, just barely concealed, beneath her soaked top, and I wonder if she really thought about this white shirt.

I pretend not to notice, but I've already lost the war. A massive wave of water surges forth and bowls me over. My knees buckle, and I topple backward.

Surfacing, brushing the hair from my face, I splutter, "What just happened?"

Elairie stares at me, openmouthed. She looks down at her hand, cups water in her palm, and lifts it. After only a moment's concentration, the water in her hand swirls. Slowly, the miniature whirlwind rises, looking more like a tornado than a little pool of water.

A surge of wind comes out of nowhere, whipping the tiny vortex into the air and spinning it into individual drops that fly around us.

My jaw drops as the setting sun catches each droplet, sending out millions of rainbows. The air swirls and rushes at me, splashing the water droplets all over my face. Then, in an instant, it all dissipates.

I wipe my face and stare at Elairie.

Her eyes have yet to leave her open palm.

"That was amazing." My words come out quiet, reverent. "How did you do that? How did you control it so fast?"

"I don't know." Finally, she looks up at me. "The wave was an accident, just like the vision…" She trails off with a shrug.

Clearing her throat, she says, "I felt the magic though. I felt the force in the wave, and I just thought, why not take hold of it? So, I did, I tried." She smiles, incredulous. "And it worked."

Can it really be that easy?

I know our willpower is all it comes down to anyway. That's the basic gist of controlling all our magic.

But it was so quick.

I look back up to the shore. Geeran sits by the fire, watching us, and I thank the Gods that we won't have to explain this.

I look back at Elairie. "Can you try to do it again?"

She glances at her hands, then closes her eyes. Gradually, the air begins to spin around us, whipping the water into a frenzy. We stand in the eye of the storm, shielded from view of anyone beyond the vortex. Sunlight slants through water droplets, sending rainbows flashing about.

Elairie's eyes spring open, lit up with joy, and she rises onto tiptoes to kiss me. Our lips meet softly, and her arms tangle around my neck. My arms slide easily around her waist, and I pull her close.

We fall deeper into the kiss, mouths dancing together. My hand slips down to her hip.

And all the swirling water falls around us.

We jump, startled by the noise of it.

Laughing, Elairie says, "I guess I wasn't focusing enough."

Giddy with this sign of progress, we head ashore and wrap ourselves in layers of blankets. We clean our clothes in the water, all but the leather garments, then tote them along to dry by the fire.

Geeran puts up a ward around camp as soon as we get close enough, and we all sit, wrapped in blanket cocoons. The sun dips below the tree line, blocking a good portion of the light.

"So," Geeran begins, "air and water at the same time?"

Elairie nods. "Why do you think I got them together?"

He shrugs. "It's hard to say." The crackle of the fire nearly swallows Geeran's soft voice.

"Hazard a guess?" I ask.

"It has been a little while since any new magic presented itself for her," Geeran says. Turning to Elairie, he adds, "Or perhaps the bond between the two of you strengthened enough to garner that kind of progress."

For perhaps the second or third time since I've known him, Geeran smiles. "That would explain how you controlled it so quickly."

A thoughtful moment passes, then Elairie asks me, "Is your magic stronger?"

I hesitate, unsure which kind to try, and finally decide on fire. Staring into the flames, I coax magic through my body and watch as fire flows out through my fingertips. It swirls outward, circling the campfire.

I weave the flames into a lattice surrounding our campfire. Lifting my other hand, I send forth streams of lightning to sprawl throughout the latticework inferno, branching into millions of tiny electrical fingers.

I let the fire sputter out, gradually turning to a fence of smoke that floats away. Then, I transform the streams of electricity into uncountable sparks, crackling out of existence.

A deep well of pride bubbles up within me. I try to hide it, but a huge grin slips onto my face.

"That was beautiful," Elairie whispers.

She leans against me, resting her head on my shoulder. A pleasant warmth spreads through me.

But today's magical exertions have taken their toll, and exhaustion settles over us. Her eyes droop, and so do mine.

Since we're mostly dry, I say, "Shall we go to bed?"

Elairie manages a small nod, and Geeran says, "We can talk more about water magic, tomorrow."

Elairie and I curl up together in our combined bedroll. Limbs tangle, and our bodies try desperately to melt together in the heat between us. It quickly simmers to a warm fuzzy feeling, and we drift into a peaceful sleep.

***

The sun comes back around, and I struggle to keep it at bay, burying my face in Elairie's hair. But my movement wakes her. She turns and looks into my eyes, blinking away sleep. My heart skips a beat as her long lashes flutter.

Will I ever get used to her?

Fear wells up within me.

Will I even get the chance?

My heart twists in my chest, and I pull her closer.

Chapter 16
Elairie

My hands busy themselves, unpacking to set up camp for another night on the road, but my mind wanders far from this task. Our lessons on water magic, the most powerful and diverse of all magic, consume me.

How long will it take to master all three forms? And the conversions between them?

Too long…

My heart drops into my boots. So many forms of magic yet lie beyond my grasp. So many obstacles lie between us and Gourmaht. My mouth goes dry, and my hands shake.

To hide my trembling fingers, I lift a bag of food from the cart. My feet lead me to Beluroan and the fire that crackles to life at his insistence. The sun descends quickly, and only a few rays of light meander through the trees to find our camp.

Somewhere in the shadows, leaves rustle. A low rumble reaches out of the underbrush, and my heart stops. A chill seeps into my bones.

It was just my imagination…

It had to be.

But growls ooze from the shadows.

Wolves.

My breath catches in my throat, and our horse whinnies nervously.

Spinning to face the hidden beasts, I say, "Beluroan…"

He rises but stops cold, staring into the trees. And then, I see them.

The flickering fire and the fading sun cast eerie shadows over their figures as they prowl through thickets and bushes. My mind flits back to the vision of Mother, and I can almost see them tearing into me. Their lithe forms slink through the shadows, and my heart stutters.

Beluroan slowly makes his way to me, eyes never leaving the beasts in the undergrowth.

"I guess this is our first test," he whispers, more to himself than anyone.

Taking his words to heart, I tell Geeran, "Only interfere if it looks like we really need it."

Silence greets my request, punctuated only by the soft footsteps of seven wolves. They slide through the forest on the edge of camp, edging ever closer.

"Magic first," I whisper, but my heart beats my lungs, chopping my words up and tainting my bravado. "Keep them at a distance as long as possible."

A lanky grey and white wolf steps forward with teeth bared. Firelight glints in its eyes.

Panic surges through me, and all I can hear is the sound of teeth sinking into Mother's flesh, the gurgling screams as her life finally faded. I force the memory from my mind, struggling to keep calm.

Swallowing, I pull forth my newest magic. I whip the air around this brave wolf into a frenzy, pulling the air from its lungs. I can almost feel them collapse. The wolf falls over, unconscious, but I keep pulling, pursuing death, not unconsciousness.

Blood seeps from its nostrils, from its mouth, and sickness coils in my gut.

It would've killed me. Or Beluroan.

With that thought, I shove my regrets and sorrows away.

Another wolf slinks free of the underbrush, eyeing Beluroan. A sinister growl erupts from the tawny beast, but Beluroan greets it with streams of purple and white lightning. They reach out, wrapping around the wolf, surging through it. The smell of burnt hair and roasting flesh fills my nose.

I gag as it falls, convulsing.

Beluroan recoils, and horror plays over his features. He reaches for the lightning scar on his chest, and his emotions burst through me.

Disgust at using magic to kill. Fear of being like Traimon. Fear that he'll lose me. It all floods my senses, disorienting me. My hands tremble, and my stomach roils.

A heartbeat more, and I see how much I mean to him, how deeply he fears losing me. My heart skips a beat.

And just as quickly as they came, his emotions desert me.

On the edges of camp, the wolves pace, considering us and the two fallen beasts.

I use their hesitation, whispering to Beluroan, "It's not the same thing." I ache to look at him, to see the effect my words have on him, but dare not tear my eyes from the wolves. "What Traimon did was torture. This is self-defense. You're nothing like him."

Before he can respond, the remaining wolves move in, howling eerily. Three set their sights on Beluroan, and the other two stare me down. They edge closer, pulling my nerves taut.

All at once, they pounce. My heart freezes, and instinct guides my hands to my daggers. I slash out, landing a glancing blow. Precious drops of blood spill from the female alpha, and she yelps.

My attackers fall back, regrouping.

I strain my ears, trying to pick detail from the chaos of Beluroan's struggle, for I dare not tear my eyes from my own attackers.

And then, inspiration strikes.

Using empath magic, I feel my way into the alpha's heart. Pure savagery reigns, burying a familial bond beneath the drive to kill us, to eat us. Vicious fury pours into me from the wolf's heart, and I struggle against it, even with the distance of empath.

I have to do this quick.

Carefully, I pluck a kernel of fear from my own heart, planting it within the wolf.

But nothing happens.

The wolves lunge at me, jaws snapping. I slash desperately, narrowly avoiding a bite on the arm, another on the leg.

Finally, the magic takes root. The alpha eyes me warily. Her attacks grow hesitant, and she leaps away from my blade.

A trickle of hope seeps into me, and I feed the magic I've planted in her. The seed grows, and I can see it, see the dark red vines spreading through her, the black leaves expanding to fill her heart.

She whimpers, retreating into the trees, melting into the shadows. Sharp barks call out, beckoning for the other wolves to join her.

But they refuse.

Teeth latch onto my arm, and I cry out. My flesh tears as my other attacker jerks its head, back and forth.

Pain sears my veins, and fury guides my hand, driving my dagger into the beast. But it doesn't let go, doesn't relent.

I bring my blade down again. Desperation grips me, and blood drips over my skin.

But the beast yelps, loosens its grip.

I jerk my arm free.

From the shadows, the female alpha barks, beckons to her pack mates. Finally, my attacker joins her, and I turn to find chaos.

A wolf sets off at a sprint through camp, fire blazing along its entire body. My eyes seek Beluroan, and ice washes over me.

A wolf hangs from his arm, jaw locked. Another snarls at his feet. It leaps for his neck, but his blade finds flesh, driving deep into the beast's side.

My heart clenches, and I scramble for something to do to help him.

I can't lose him.

I'd never get to tell him that I... love him.

Reining in my thoughts, I feed the other wolf's fire with my wind, and the flames double in size. It yowls in pain, and my heart twists. I give it more air, trying to put the thing out of its misery.

The fire builds to a crescendo, filling the air with the odor of singed fur. With a few whimpers, the wolf falls over, dead but still burning.

I turn on the remaining alpha, focusing on the water in its skin. Frost appears on its back legs at my urging. I send it creeping up the wolf's haunches.

The creature yips, turning to snarl at whatever might be attacking its legs. Finding nothing but its own crystallizing skin, it turns back on Beluroan.

I let the frost progress, up its back, down its tail. The creature panics, half-running, half-dragging itself away and howling for the other wolf to join it. After only a few snarled commands, the remainder follows.

Relief washes over me, and my shoulders droop.

As they sprint through the woods, I seek out the female alpha, pulling the false fear from her heart. True fear grows alongside it, and I know she'll stay away. Reaching further, I thaw the male, forcing the water back into the tissue.

With a sigh, I turn to the burning wolf in camp. Pulling water from the air around us, I extinguish the flames. The sizzle sickens me.

Beluroan surveys the damage, the three fallen wolves, but abandons his assessment quickly. Crossing the distance, he wraps his arms around me. He flinches, and I pull away, eyes dropping to his arm.

I gasp at the tattered sleeve, the blood weeping from his flesh. "Beluroan!"

"It doesn't matter," he says, voice a hoarse whisper. He wraps his arms around me again.

I throw my arms around him, and a lance of pain reminds me of my own injury. Yet, we cling to each other, aching to be close.

"I was so afraid I'd lose you…" he whispers into my neck. He smooths my hair, adding, "There were just so many of them."

"Shhh…" I whisper, holding both sides of his face. "It's ok."

Our lips meet, soft and tender.

Beluroan cradles my hand in his, eyes dropping to the ragged tears in my flesh, the blood staining my shirt. "Can you heal yourself?" he asks, voice thick with emotion. "Or do we need Geeran to look at it?"

But the gaping slashes and punctures in his arm bleed far worse than mine. My stomach turns as I stare. Tattered leather and cloth hang from his arm, soaked through and dripping.

"Let's take care of you first," I say. "You're in far worse shape."

Geeran appears beside us, beckoning us to safety. "I have tonics waiting. Come."

He ushers us toward the fire, gently helps us free of our jackets. Frail hands prove stronger than they look as Geeran tears my sleeve off at the elbow, tears Beluroan's at the shoulder.

If we're ever apart, if our aura dims, we're going to be cold.

The thought of being separated from him sends a shiver over my spine.

Geeran hands us tonics, and I cradle the warm bowl in my hands for a heartbeat before downing the bitter mixture. Beluroan sniffs his and pulls a sour face.

I laugh. "Your sister's a healer. How are you not used to these?"

He rewards me with a rueful smile, then drinks his tonic. Wiping a stray droplet from his lips, he says, "I tried not to get hurt just so I wouldn't have to drink these things."

Geeran chuckles quietly, looking over our injuries. With a smile, he says, "I never realized tonics had preventative qualities."

Concentration draws his brows together as he pulls the healing properties of the tonics to our arms, letting them aid his magic to stitch our bodies back together.

A delicate tingle spreads over my skin. Gashes narrow as raw skin reaches out, trying to reunite with itself. A thin sheen of clear liquid trickles from the barely-open wounds.

Retrieving a jar of salve, Geeran applies generous globs to Beluroan's wounds, now reduced to narrow slashes in muscled arms. Where punctures once glared at us, only little pink circles remain. With deft, practiced movements, Geeran wraps a long strip of clean linen around Beluroan's arm and ties it off.

With the worst injuries taken care of, he turns to me. The magic and tonic left only thin, bloodless cuts adorning my forearm. Geeran applies a thin layer of salve and wraps my arm.

But the high of battle is fading, sapping my strength. The toll of so much magic, of fighting for my life, pulls my eyelids low. My shoulder slump, and a yawn erupts from me.

Geeran nods, satisfied with his work. "Now," he says, voice soft and caring, "off to bed with you both."

He'll hear no protest from me.

***

I stretch in our bedroll pallet, feeling every bit of our fight with the wolves last night. My body aches, muscles groaning with yesterday's exertion, reminding me just how little I've exercised since meeting Beluroan a week ago.

Has it really only been a week?

Beluroan stirs, and his hold tightens around me. I curl into him, nestling into the warm shelter of his muscular arms.

If only I could have slept like this every night of my life...

Taking a deep breath, I open my eyes. The sun glares down at us, much higher than I expected. I turn toward the fire and find Geeran sitting with the trunk of scrolls open before him. He looks up, smiles at me.

Beluroan slowly wakes, whispering in my ear, "Good morning." The smooth rumble of his voice sends shivers down my spine.

His hand slides under my shirt to rest on the small of my back, electrifying me with his touch. My insides squirm pleasantly, and a sigh crosses my lips.

Still foggy with sleep, my mind wanders as freely as I wish Beluroan's hands would. Images of him kissing me paint themselves across my imagination. I see my hands pulling his clothes off, tearing at my own. In my mind, I kiss every inch of his beautiful, tan skin, then he rolls me onto my back to ravage my neck.

Beluroan nibbles softly at my ear, and I melt. My hands grasp his back, clawing at his shirt.

Gods, this is killing me.

With a sigh, I mumble, "We should really get up."

A small moan of disappointment preludes Beluroan's answer. "I guess." He laughs, then releases me.

After breakfast, Beluroan and I skin the wolves we killed, minus the burnt one. Confident that the meat won't have spoiled in the cold night air, we save on rations and roast what we can over the fire.

At our mention of trading the pelts, Geeran assures us not to worry about money. "Pakaibra has arranged it all. Our expenses are covered."

But the idea of wasting doesn't sit well with me. Or with Beluroan.

Once we've eaten and packed, we set off for Aivrard. Geeran tells us to take the day off from practicing, insisting on a day of rest. I say a silent thank you, surprised by my own eagerness.

Despite the occasional bump in the road, I decide to draw. Hiding my paper from Beluroan's view, I draw him.

Or at least, I attempt to. I can't capture that little smirk that hides in his eyes when he teases me. The angle of his solitary raised eyebrow when he flirts eludes me.

Beluroan familiarizes himself with the mandolin, strumming through the notes. He quickly pieces together a melody, surprising us all.

The road we travel upon meanders into Aivrard after only a few hours, snaking through thick trees. Tight knit roots weave in and out of the earth, and I marvel that they built anything here without extensive earth magic. But a few buildings dot the ground, regardless.

Homes adorn the trees, nestled into branches, hugging the trunks. Wrapped in balconies, they perch high above us. Rope bridges connect them to each other, to the center of town. Moss and vines hang from every surface, vibrant and lush.

Our horse pulls us along, and I gaze up, jaw slack with awe. Homes and shops tuck into every available nook and cranny.

Elves meander over bridges, perfectly in tune with the sway of the ropes and the creaking of the boards they trod upon. They climb staircases wrapped around tree trunks, stepping aside to let each other pass. A few lean on delicately carved wooden rails, speaking with friends or lovers on balconies.

The bustle of the market grows louder with each of the horse's steps, and I stare up, eyes tracing every bit of the place. I try to memorize the treehouses, the smiling faces, the laughter.

In an instant, I hope for a home here with Beluroan, hope for a treehouse with our children playing on balconies.

But it's so far from Vairsun.

Would the distance be too great? Would Saerine and the boys want to move here?

I shake my head, shocked at my boldness, and return my attention to the town around us. Fox and Light Elves abound, mingling to a degree. High in the trees, I see several shops run by Elves with mixed blood.

Divination tells me that they buy from the Light Elves at a marked-up rate, still paying less than someone of full Fox Elf blood would. Then, they sell to the Fox Elves. Theft is only an occasional necessity here.

As we ride through the market, Geeran calls out to the shopkeepers on the ground level, asking after a tailor. But the attention makes me nervous.

Suddenly, I stare up at the people above us with fear in my heart. I slink down into the cart, hoping to pass unnoticed.

And somehow, only a few people spare us a glance.

A Light Elf on a balcony scrutinizes us with furrowed brows and a tipped head. His child tugs at his shirt, drawing his attention away, and he quickly gives up on us. He shakes his head, then turns his focus to the young one urgently begging his attention.

Beside me, Beluroan relaxes, letting out a breath. He sits up straighter, throws his arm around me.

Beyond the walls of our cart, a Fox Elf wearing many skirts tells Geeran of a tailor on the first tree level, just a few tree trunks away. She even points it out, shaking dark brown hair from her face.

At the next staircase, Geeran slows the horse to a stop, saying, "I'll stay with the cart."

He reaches into a pouch concealed beneath his sash and pulls out a few coins. He hands them to us, but I stare at his outstretched hand.

"You'll have to be measured or pick clothes that will fit you," he says. "You'll be fine here."

Taking a deep breath, I nod. He drops the coins into my hand, and I curl my fingers around them. My stomach fills with butterflies at the prospect of venturing out amongst the people.

Beluroan takes my hand as we climb the winding staircase, ascending into town. Another Elf comes down, and I follow behind Beluroan, keeping my eyes above his waist, where they belong. At the top of the stairs, we turn down a surprisingly sturdy bridge, venturing toward the tailor's shop.

Dotted with small, circular windows, the multilevel treehouse wraps around the trunk. The arched door hangs open, welcoming us.

Inside, we find a small woman perched at a table, busily stitching a pair of pants. Her mulberry hair sweeps back into a bun, pulling sandy skin taut.

I breathe a sigh of relief.

She's a Fox Elf. She'll serve us, even without Geeran here.

"What can I help you with?" She asks, squinting up at us. Then, she sees our jackets and beneath them, the sleeves of our shirts. She smiles. "Do you need a repair or new garments altogether?"

"I guess that depends on if you have anything that will fit us." I shrug. "We're pressed for time, so if you already have something, that would be better."

Nodding, the woman says, "Feel free to look around. Everything I have for sale is on the first floor."

After a few minutes, I find a pale green button-down shirt and a tight, black leather jacket. When I try them on, Beluroan stares. Heat crawls up my neck, over my cheeks, and I smile.

We find a form-fitting black shirt and jacket for Beluroan, and it's my turn to stare. I blush, and Beluroan pulls me into his arms.

"So, you like them?" he whispers.

His eyes dart to the front of the store, and I look, as well. But the massive tree trunk blocks our view of the tailor.

Beluroan tightens his grip on my waist, and my heart races. His lips find my neck, and he pushes me up against the tree.

His eyes shine like emeralds when our gazes meet, and his breathing accelerates. He presses up against me, hand gentle on my neck. I slide a hand up his chest, letting the other rest on his stomach. His thumb pushes my chin up, tilting my head back.

Despite my parted lips and the invitation they extend, he stares into my eyes. Tension builds between us, pulls us together. His chest rises and falls quickly beneath my palm, but still he waits.

In a hoarse whisper, he says, "You're magnificent."

I move my hand beneath the hem of his shirt, running my fingers over his lean, muscular stomach. He closes his eyes, and a shudder rolls through him. A deep breath fills his chest, presses it to mine. His eyes open, darkened by lust, promising to swallow me whole, and he moves closer.

Our lips meet, and we ignite.

The aura around us burns as his hands sweep down to my backside, lifting me up. I wrap my legs around his waist, throw my arms around his neck. Our mouths dance, and he presses hard against me. My entire body tingles, aching for his touch.

One hand grips my waist, the other my thigh.

"Oh, Gods…" I mumble against his lips.

Beluroan nips at my lower lip, sighing deeply.

He pulls his hand from my waist, placing it firmly on the tree trunk behind me. He takes a deep breath. Staring into my soul through hooded eyes, he says something about another customer in the store.

Only then do I hear the voices at the front.

Beluroan sets me down, giving me one last kiss on the neck. "Let's go pay for these," he says, voice still heavy with our kiss. Retrieving our old jackets and shirts, he drapes them in front of himself.

A devious giggle sweeps through me.

We pay the tailor, receiving only a single sideways glance for our flushed faces and disheveled hair. The other customer, a man of mixed blood, glances at me.

A sheen of blue glistens in his near-black hair. Set perfectly against richly tanned skin, pale green eyes shine as they slide over me.

"Hi," he says with a smile, gaze trailing over me again.

I put a hand on Beluroan's lower back and return a polite, "Hello."

He nods, and though his smile changes, it doesn't fade. With a pleasant goodbye, we leave the tailor's shop. We climb to the upper levels to sell the wolf pelts and restock our supplies, delighting in the freedom of moving about in a town that doesn't care about us.

If only we could stay here for the night... We could stay at an inn. Maybe Beluroan and I could actually have some privacy.

And maybe I wouldn't ruin it with tears or terrible memories.

As we leave Aivrard, Beluroan picks up the mandolin again, and I put pen to paper, trying to capture the idyllic nature of the treehouses. I even draw a house with a glorious view, one I could share with Beluroan.

Chapter 17
Beluroan

Geeran's ward goes up as soon as we stop for the night, just like last night. My eyes search the shadows lurking beneath the trees, and I shudder at what might hide in the darkness.

This deep in the forest, wolves are the least of our concerns.

Taking a deep breath, I glance upward. The sky peeks down at us through gaps in the canopy. Stars play coy, hiding from view in the sun's fading rays.

Maybe Elairie and I can stay up late and watch the stars…

"Might we set up camp slightly differently?" Geeran says behind me.

He suggests assembling the canvas tarp in the shape of a "V," separating us from him. My heart races at the thought of even that semblance of privacy, and I hurry to do his bidding.

My mind drifts while I work, landing upon Elairie's drawings. She only got a few sketches in between practice sessions today, but my mind boggled at her skill when I caught a glimpse.

She wasn't hiding them today. Not like yesterday morning.

She didn't mind me seeing the sketches of the treehouses of Aivrard.

She seems rather taken with the quaint little town, and as I drive another pole into the ground, I admit that I was too. Saerine and I only ever passed through. We tried to live there, but the very things that make it so idyllic also make it hard to hide after stealing something.

Narrow staircases and rope bridges, close-quarter balconies… All the little hideouts I could exploit in other towns are just open air there. I didn't need to steal as much, but when I did, my only hope was to move stealthily or leave quickly.

Driving another pole into the ground, I briefly entertain the idea of settling there with Elairie with our own treehouse and a family.

We'll have more than enough magic by then to make a living. We won't have to steal.

After securing the canvas to the poles, I unpack our food for the evening, imagining a future with Elairie, the woman I was made to be with, all the while. A smile tugs at the corners of my lips.

Until realization dawns, and I chide myself.

We've only known each other a short time. I doubt she's even considered this.

My hands still on the pouch of jerky I was about to lift from the cart.

Does time matter, considering what we are?

Or am I just rationalizing now?

I sigh and leave that topic for another day.

We gather around the fire to eat. Geeran sits close to the flames, soaking in the warmth with his long white hair tied back. The sun sets, and the stars blink into existence. Geeran nestles into his bedroll soon after eating, and thunderous snores rumble from his side of our lean-to.

Finally alone with Elairie, I struggle for words. After throwing a few logs on the fire, I take her hand and lead her to our little bed.

Stammering, I say, "I don't know if you're tired or not, but… we don't have to go to sleep right away."

Color blooms over her pale skin, visible even in the flickering light of the fire. "But," she begins, "Geeran is right there on the other side of the canvas."

"Oh. No," I say, realizing how I sounded. "I mean, that would be nice…"

Oh, Gods, I'm making it worse.

The fire swirling on the air around us intensifies, and color spreads over my cheeks. "I just meant… maybe we could watch the stars."

"That sounds nice," Elairie says.

Though I stare at my feet, hiding the heat in my face, I hear the smile in her voice.

We shed our boots and jackets, then our gloves and vests. Elairie removes her new green shirt, down to just that little strappy shirt and her pants.

My lungs forget how to breathe, stuttering wildly. The air around us scorches.

With a grin, I pull my shirt over my head, reveling in the way her eyes roam over me. Her breathing speeds up, but so does mine. I can practically feel her gaze, caressing my skin.

A dark whisper glides past my lips, "Shall we?"

I peel back the top bedroll, and we climb in together. I stare out at the stars, but she faces me, head on my shoulder, as I pull the bedroll up over us. I wrap an arm around Elairie.

Her hand moves playfully over me, drifting from my chest to my stomach in sweet, torturous moves.

And I forget the stars.

My hand slides to her hip, and I hook a thumb under her shirt, tracing elaborate patterns on her skin. Elairie lifts a leg up over mine, tangling hers with mine and pressing against my side.

Deep breaths.

I stare up at the sky, trying to calm myself. A cluster of stars shoots across the night, illuminating the dark expanse for a single heartbeat.

Clearing my throat, I whisper, "Did you see that?"

Elairie nods, moving her head against my chest. "It was amazing." Her voice comes out breathy with desire, scorching my skin.

I swallow hard as she slides her hand up my chest and trails her fingers over my collarbone. I close my eyes.

Did she decide the canvas allows enough privacy, after all?

She caresses my neck, and my body tenses. My hand roams beneath her shirt, gliding up her back. Fingers like feathers move down her spine. She shivers, chasing the rest of the world from my thoughts and shattering the last of my control.

My lips seek hers, hungry for the taste of her. My hand moves to her stomach, then slowly upwards, past her navel, over her ribs. As my hand slides up to cup her breast, Elairie gasps.

My lungs struggle for air. My heart races.

She deserts my lips, raises herself up onto one elbow, and kisses my neck. Then, my shoulder, my chest. As my hand slides to her back, then lower to her bottom, her lips roam over my stomach.

My heart might actually explode.

Abyss below, I *might explode.*

Her hand grips my hip, then my butt. I grit my teeth against a moan. Elairie straddles me, and her hand wraps in my hair.

Our lips lock together, and I grasp her hips, pressing her down against me. Our bodies grind together, and she whimpers softly.

But I want to make her do more than that.

So much more.

Just as I'm about to roll her onto her back, to peel off her clothes and kiss and taste every bit of her, she pulls back.

"What was that?" she asks, peering into the darkness.

"What?"

What was what? What's she talking about?

And then, I hear it.

Heavy footsteps.

I sit up as a tremendous screech splits the air. Firelight outlines the enormous beast against the shadows, orange glow sparking hungrily in its black eyes. Standing on its back legs, it towers over us, at least twice my height.

Horror holds my gaze steady upon the nightmarish creature before me. My eyes trace the wings folded against its back, then linger on its front legs, clawing greedily at Geeran's ward. Amber light dances on the mahogany feathers that coat its entire body.

"Is that what I think it is?" Elairie asks, voice trembling.

I nod. "An owlbear."

Another blood-curdling screech shatters the night on the other side of camp, and my heart sinks.

"Not just one," Elairie whispers. She swallows hard. "Can the ward hold back two of them?"

Desire spoils in my gut, replaced by cold dread.

I shake my head. "It'll hurt them, but they'll get through." I shudder, then add, "With two of them absorbing the damage… They'll still be in good enough shape to hurt us, maybe even kill us."

Elairie stares at the feathered beast towering over us, clawing at the invisible ward. Its ears lay back against its head, and its beak shines in the firelight.

"We have time, right?" she asks.

The beast answers for me, growling and screeching, clawing at the barrier which holds it back. Each attack on the ward elicits another pained snarl. On the other side of camp, its partner shrieks, just as desperate to claw its way through to a meal.

"Some time. Not much," I finally manage.

"Much as I hate to say it, get dressed." Elairie's eyes trace my form, sending heat fluttering through me. But she pulls on her overshirt and rises. "I need to talk to Geeran. I have an idea."

In a daze, I put my boots on, wondering how she got control of herself so quickly.

Does this not feel the same for her?

My heart falters, but I keep moving, pulling my shirt on. I grab my vest and jacket and stand, despite the wobble in my knees.

Elairie leans over to pull a boot on, glancing nervously at the owlbears every few heartbeats. "I'm sorry," she mumbles, not quite looking at me. "I should've paid closer attention. I just got so swept up. When I heard it…"

She tugs her other boot on, hiding her face behind a curtain of her hair as she laces it up. "I thought I'd gotten us all killed. I forgot all about the ward."

She pulls in a deep breath, then finally meets my gaze. Her hands never stop moving, tying her boot laces as she whispers, "I can't lose you."

Her voice breaks, and my hands freeze halfway through pulling my jacket on.

That's what shook her out of it?

I pull her to me, wrapping her in my arms. She lays her head on my chest. The owlbears screech and growl, but I say, "I don't want to lose you either. At least you heard them. I didn't."

I kiss the top of her head, and we scramble into the rest of our gear. Daggers sheathed, we rush to Geeran's side of the lean-to. His snores grow louder as we approach, and my jaw drops.

"How? How has he not woken up?" I exclaim.

Elairie nudges his shoulder until he stirs, but it takes far too long. My mind flickers back to tangled limbs and heavy breathing just before the owlbears appeared, and I make a mental note of just how much it takes to wake him.

Once awake, he hears the racket and sits up straight.

"They'll be through the ward soon," I tell him.

"I have an idea though," Elairie pipes up. "If Beluroan and I each put up another ward, inside yours, can we maybe lace each of those with some empath magic?" Her words come out rushed. "Could we do that?"

We stare at her, surprised. I've been using wards since I learned to use my magic, and I never thought of that.

Granted, I've never had two owlbears tearing into my ward, so I never needed anything stronger.

But what would she do with empath magic?

"Perhaps, but to what end?" Geeran asks, glancing at the owlbears.

"I just thought I could weave in a bit of fear to chase them off. It worked with the wolf," she says.

"We didn't have a ward up when the wolves came," I mumble, eyeing the beasts outside camp.

"No, I planted it in the wolf's heart."

"You went into the wolf's heart?" Geeran asks, shocked and appalled. But curiosity wins. "What was it like?"

"Pure savagery. It was terrible," she answers, voice a whisper. She shakes her head. "Would it work? Could we incorporate it into a ward?"

Glancing back and forth between the owlbears, Geeran says, "It's worth a shot." A thoughtful pause, then he asks, "What did you do to the wolf you killed?"

"Wind magic. I took the air from its lungs."

Geeran nods.

Looking at me, Elairie says, "Let's get started." She stands and closes her eyes.

As she visualizes the area she wants to include in her ward, she tells me the scope of it so I can put up another within it. She tucks hers within Geeran's, condensing it, making it stronger.

But a third ward couldn't hurt.

Despite the immense pain a ward can inflict, the monstrous owlbears slash, peck, and snap at it. Beaks and claws work ferociously.

Envisioning a spider web in the shape of a dome, I weave smaller webs in to strengthen it. Thinking back on Elairie's idea, I pull forth some empath magic.

But how did she do it? How did she put fear into the wolf's heart?

She said she planted it. Did she mean that literally?

In my head, I picture a small seed, planting it under the wall of my ward. It doesn't take root at first, and I feel silly for taking her words at face value.

But slowly, a crimson vine rises, unfurling black leaves.

Encouraging it, I feed it thoughts of death and pain, watching as it grows. The slender plant takes root, curling throughout the webs. For the sake of caution, I plant a few more seeds around the edge of the ward, sending out tendrils of fear.

Once the ward is complete, I open my eyes. Elairie stands nearby, already done with hers.

One of the owlbears screeches, and we jump, gathering as close to the fire as we can stand to be. Even the horse draws closer, panic plain on its face.

Elairie approaches the poor beast, pats its mane, and closes her eyes. Within seconds, its manic whinnies quiet and the fearful expression leaves its eyes.

I've severely underestimated empath magic…

But I get no further time to consider it.

Geeran's ward breaks with an audible snap, and the owlbears cry out in triumph. A ward that would have stopped all seven of those wolves barely dulled these beasts' feathers.

Small, bald patches adorn their massive paws. They kick the air, and the firelight licks the blood seeping from the spot where a claw used to be.

Dropping down to all fours, they charge. Though a limp slows one of them, they cover the distance quickly, slamming headlong into Elairie's ward. Roars of pain erupt into the night, shaking the birds from the treetops.

But the savage beasts persist, sending black leaves and flowers flying everywhere. Shrieking and howling, they tear into her ward.

We huddle closer, waiting with bated breath. Heart pounding, I focus on my ward, still perfectly intact, wondering how long it'll stay that way. My hand finds my dagger, just in case.

Elairie grabs my free hand, gripping tight. My eyes trace her ward, and then, it hits me.

I can see it? How can I see her ward?

And how is it so similar to mine?

Small webs woven in and out of a single, massive domed web. She has fewer small webs, but they're laced in almost exactly like mine. Her abundant vines of fear wind in a much more intricate pattern. Black leaves and flowers aplenty bloom on shining crimson vines.

The owlbears slash at the ward, at the tendrils of terror, sending leaves and small bits of web falling to the ground. The fallen magic disperses at their feet.

But exhaustion and agony weigh down their cries.

A spark of hope burns to life within me.

The closer one hoots, calling to its partner, then spreads its dark wings. Clumps of feathers litter the ground around the animals, and patches of skin show through.

Carrying on noisily, it tries to dissuade its mate, but to no avail. The other owlbear slashes away, losing yet another claw, still more feathers. A great many leaves and strands of spider silk fly through the air, disintegrating as they go.

The beast slashes the main stalk of one of the vines, and the entire plant falls away, leaving a huge gap in the latticework.

But the owlbear shrieks, flapping its wings frantically.

Finally, it gives in, answering its mate's call. They take to the air in a flurry of swirling feathers, and I make a mental note to gather some for Oran and Kraimin.

Elairie's ward still stands with half of the webs intact and a quarter of the vines. Mine stands sentry over our inner sanctum, unscathed.

I drop forward, hands braced on my knees. "We should be safe for the night."

Elairie lets out a breath of relief, but my heart won't slow down. My mind races, full of all the different ways things could have gone wrong.

If Elairie hadn't thought to infuse the wards with fear, would they have left so soon? Would they have broken through hers entirely? Or mine?

Geeran turns toward the horse and pats it gently. "We should try to get some sleep."

Elairie laughs quietly. "I'm not sure I can."

"Let's at least lay back down," I whisper.

Pulling her along, I meander to our bed. After stripping down to pants and undershirts, we curl up. Our legs entwine and we wrap our arms around each other.

Gentle warmth spreads through me as Elairie kisses my collarbone. She whispers against my chest, breath caressing my skin, "I can't lose you."

"I'm not going anywhere." My hand slides into her beautiful, wavy hair. Citrus and spice fill my nose, and I kiss her forehead. I hesitate, but the words slip past my lips, "Just don't leave me, ok?"

Again, her words whisper over my skin. "I won't." She smiles. "I promise."

"I'll hold you to that, you know," I say, pulling her closer.

Our lips meet, lingering.

"I'm counting on it," she says.

Chapter 18
Elairie

Exhaustion weighs me down after a day spent practicing, so I take a break, pulling Grandmother's trunk toward me. I run a hand over the old wood, feeling the scuffs and scrapes, and smile.

Picking up a random scroll, I unfurl it and let my eyes drift over the words. It details the failings of the humans on the far continent.

I lean back, resting my head on Beluroan's shoulder as I learn how they forsook the Gods and their ways, and in turn, were forsaken. My jaw drops at the prospect of the Gods abandoning them, only checking on them to make sure they didn't endanger the rest of the planet.

For a moment, I read it aloud, whispering under my breath, "Their earthen desecration and vile acts against one another, the destruction of entire species and the constant wars deemed them a lost cause in the Gods' eyes."

With brows raised, I blow out a breath and return it to the trunk. Selecting another, I try not to think of Mother digging through these same scrolls just before they took her.

Unfurling a new one, I find recipes. My Grandmother's looping handwriting reveals the inner workings of a healing salve and a salve for divination. Every ingredient lies among Mother's dried bundles, tucked in the sash.

Maybe I'll try my hand at these later.
But for now, more practice.

"Let's check on Saerine," I say. "We can see if physical contact is the only way to share a vision."

He nods, scooting away from me. The loss of his touch chills me, far more than it should.

Settling in, I imagine darkness creeping in at the edges of my sight with Saerine in the center. I trace a lock of fuchsia hair, crossing tan skin to drape over eyes of the same shade. I imagine her smiling in her kitchen, and then, the vision begins.

My spirit glides over the land to find her sitting at her table with Pakaibra. Beluroan stays behind, and suddenly, I wish he'd come with, if only to spare me the task of explaining this sight.

Two plates rest on the table, dotted with crumbs. Half-empty teacups hold the last of a full kettle. Their hands rest upon the table, so close, but not quite touching.

Saerine's eyes sparkle as she glances at their hands. Pakaibra laughs heartily at a joke I only just missed, throwing his head back.

The wonders of divination tell me that they've been talking quite a bit since we left. At first, he merely checked in on her, like he said, but there was a spark. Their conversations stretched into hours, and he paid more visits than necessary.

She even invited him to have lunch with her a couple days in a row.

And the boys love him.

But the boys are at school now.

I smile, and my heart warms at the thought of her finding happiness.

Pakaibra's laughter quiets, and he pulls in a deep breath. His fingers fidget on the table, curling into his palm and fanning out again. He swallows and reaches out, placing his hand over Saerine's.

Color warms her cheeks, and a smile crinkles his pale green eyes. Pakaibra lifts her hand to his lips, kissing it far more gently than I would expect from a man his size.

And suddenly I'm not sure I should be here.

His deep voice rumbles out as his lips brush Saerine's knuckles, "I should really get back to work."

Thank the Gods.

But I'm the only one who feels relief. Saerine's features shift from exhilaration to disappointment.

"I suppose," she says, nodding her resignation.

Opening Saerine's hand, Pakaibra kisses her palm. "Believe me, I don't want to. I have so much to do though." He shakes his head and sighs.

"I'll walk you out," Saerine answers.

They hold hands as they meander toward the door, casting sidelong smiles at each other. I give them privacy to say goodbye, calling my spirit back to my body.

How am I going to explain that to Beluroan?
He's going to ask. Or Geeran will.

Before I can find words, Geeran asks, "Were both of you along for the vision?"

"No," Beluroan answers. "I guess it's only when we're touching."

"Well," Geeran begins, "what was it about?"

"I just checked in on Saerine." I aim for nonchalance, but my voice falters, betraying me.

On edge, Beluroan asks, "What happened? Is something wrong?"

"No, no," I rush, hating that I couldn't control my tone. "Nothing's wrong. It just wasn't the best time to check on her."

His brows furrow, and he stares at me. "Why?"

"She… wasn't alone."

Confusion spreads over Beluroan's face, but only briefly. "You mean…?"

Rather than finish the sentence, he raises one eyebrow.

When I nod, he asks, "Who was there? She wasn't seeing anyone when we left."

"Well…" I try to stall, but I know it's useless. "It seems that she and Pakaibra…"

Beluroan shakes his head. "Are you sure?"

Again, I nod. "They haven't… done anything, yet."

My words bring a sigh of relief, but I can't help recall the blush on her cheeks and the smiles they shared. I laugh. "Is that really so bad? He's a good man."

"I guess not." Beluroan pulls me into his arms. "It's time she found someone. But I don't get to give him the 'Don't hurt my sister' speech."

Laughing quietly, he continues, "Not that I could intimidate Pakaibra. The man's the size of an owlbear."

"He most certainly is not," I chide him, but our heads fall back as we laugh.

***

As we set off for another day on the road, I find myself hoping we'll reach Daenor at night fall. Given how important it is to stop Gourmaht before it's too late, we can't justify stopping early. The timing will have to be perfect.

244

I busy myself with practicing water and air magic to keep my mind off our accommodations for the evening.

As the sun moves up into the sky, Beluroan runs a finger over a scratch on my ankle from an errant stick last night. My skin tingles at his touch, but when he withdraws his hand, the tingling remains.

I watch, heart in my throat, as the scratch heals and disappears, then lift my gaze to him. He stares, marveling at his new magic.

Then, he sets to work, stopping only when he runs out of bruises and scrapes to heal.

We eat on the road, then work on manipulating multiple forms of magic simultaneously, but our practice is cut short.

Darkness creeps in around the edges of my vision, stealing Beluroan and me away to a wondrous valley.

Luscious grass cradles our feet. The nearby river sparkles as it flows over the edge of this strange, earthen platform, tumbling to the oceans of our world. Mountains reach into the sky around the perimeter, enclosing this little haven in their embrace.

Five beings stand before us, and I stare, openmouthed.

The Gods.

Doorma stands in the center with all five tails swirling gracefully in the air behind her. The marbled fox whispers directly into our minds, "You may soon need to forsake stealth. Gourmaht nears success."

My stomach drops, and a wave of dread washes over me, incongruous with this place.

Doorma's glowing amber eyes dance, and she adds, "The path the world has taken brooks no possibility of stopping him before he recreates the Blood Magic."

On the far right, Nepiter perches. Bright red flames drip from his mouth, defying the natural order of the mortal world as he says, "Fear will fall like rain."

Lightning shoots from one of six fiery wings to another, and my eyes do their best to follow. My heart races, and my mind whirls.

But the Gods do not wait for mortals.

He carries on, saying, "The people need faith to band them together lest they splinter and turn against each other."

Glistening as though slick with water, Jemarie breathes, "Cling to anonymity as long as possible."

Her inky black skin seems even darker next to the shining blue and purple scales of her tail. Iridescent wings and glowing white eyes only add to the contrast. Though her voice is the only wind in the Valley, her dark blue hair flutters softly as she looks between us.

"Only reveal yourselves when absolutely necessary to keep the peace. Trust your instincts."

Standing sentinel between Doorma and Nepiter, Luxitore looms. The massive golem speaks, shaking the ground with his words. "Make haste," he says.

I stare at the moss and flowering vines wrapped around and throughout his body, wondering what it would feel like to have something growing on me.

On Doorma's other side, a brilliant blue-green sea dragon waits. Spines rise from his back, joined to each other by a thin membrane. His sharp voice snaps into my mind, sudden and far too crisp. "Your magic needs strengthening. You have a great deal of work to do before you're ready to face an army of thralls. But you have certain advantages."

Doorma's whisper floats through my mind, "The two of you will be immune to this Blood Magic. Your Blessed blood will keep you safe." Her five tails flicker softly, and she continues, "Use that knowledge wisely. Until we meet again."

Their words slam into me, and I scramble to assimilate them, to move past the wonder of seeing the Gods before death, the wonder of speaking to them.

Darkness closes in, and my body calls for my spirit as the vision draws to a close.

But this can't be the end.

"Wait, please," I blurt out.

Doorma cocks her head to the side, but they let us stay for the time being. The darkness recedes.

"Before you send us back, can I ask a couple of questions?"

Jemarie breathes out, "Go ahead."

"Why…" I trail off, wasting my chance.

Just say it.

"Why didn't you warn my mother sooner? Maybe it would've done her some good… Maybe it would've saved her."

Baereen shifts, spines glistening in the sunlight, and he tells me, "There are so many paths the world can travel. There were yet a great deal that would have kept Evaerga from harm."

His voice rings loudly in my mind, startling compared to Doorma's soft tones. "That morning, certain events happened throughout Avaencery which eliminated all other paths."

Doorma whispers into our heads, "We told her as soon as we knew it would happen. If we told her any sooner than was strictly necessary, the consequences could have been terrible."

Gruff and few of words, Luxitore shakes the ground beneath my feet as he asks, "Anything else?"

I don't know if Beluroan has any questions for them, but I certainly do. So, I speed along. "What would've happened if Beluroan hadn't been caught by the Vairsun Patrol? Would he have skipped town?"

Jemarie whispers, "Saerine would have convinced him to stay and lay low for a while." Her words seem almost conciliatory. "She and her kids are settled in. Oran and Kraimin have even made a couple of friends."

Nepiter electrifies the air with a few words of his own. "There were paths yet to be eliminated in which the two of you wouldn't have met for days or weeks. Some few of those still allowed for success on your quest."

Finally, Beluroan speaks. "Is…" He hesitates, wiping his free hand on his pants. "Is there still a chance we could fail?"

"Of course," Luxitore says. The flowers on his many vines quiver with the rumbling of his voice.

Doorma seems to sigh, then says, "There are yet infinite paths for the world. Each decision made eliminates a few. Yet, each decision opens new paths which wouldn't have been available to the world if any other path were travelled."

Her tails swish softly in the air behind her, and her head tips to the side. Amber eyes grow distant, as if looking into the future.

And maybe she is.

"In many of these," Doorma says, "the outcome of your journey is positive. Conversely, just as many have a negative outcome. In a great deal more, your mission is met with mixed results."

"That is why," Jemarie begins, "it is paramount that you master your new magic and maintain your skills for battle. Strengthen your bond. That will be your greatest weapon."

"Have you any further questions?" Baereen asks.

Beluroan and I glance at each other.

We can't squander this opportunity, but for the life of me, I can't find any more words in my brain. I shake my head, and Beluroan does the same.

"Well, then," Doorma says. "Until we meet again."

We soar back to our bodies. The trees around us seem lackluster compared to those of the Great Valley. The birds sing beautifully, but they pale in comparison to the voices of the Gods still ringing in my mind.

Was that real?

I glance at Beluroan. Surprise and confusion war on his face, and I'm sure I wear a similar expression. We sit in somber silence until Geeran's curiosity forces us to speak.

On hearing that it was an audience with the Gods, he overflows with questions. We tell him everything we can remember, thinking it might satiate his curiosity, but the well of questions within him runs deep.

When we tell him what they said, the questions we asked, and the answers they gave, his eyes scrunch together. He falls silent. The horse's hooves beat a steady rhythm, but they do nothing to chase away our fears.

Finally, Geeran says, "The two of you should get back to work. I'll save the rest of my questions for another time."

And so, we do. We practice until we're exhausted, then we practice some more. Not until hours later does it dawn on me that the Gods said we would be immune to *this* Blood Magic.

What's the difference between this Blood Magic and the old?

How many ways are there to make this stuff?

My blood runs cold at the thought.

***

We venture over wooded hills, reaching Daenor in the middle of the afternoon. We restock as we pass through town, and my nerves wind tight. But few notice us.

On all sides, the townspeople eye each other suspiciously. The rift between Light Elves and Blood Elves deepens, reopening old wounds.

Near the tailor, a Light Elf murmurs to his fellows, "They were all gone… or dead."

One of them stares openly at Beluroan and me.

Geeran, much to my displeasure, stops the cart and calls out to them. Only then do they notice him.

"What are you talking about?" Geeran asks calmly. "We've been on the road for days and have heard little news."

"Have you heard of a town called Douhaen?" a man with pale yellow hair asks. "The whole town is gone. All the Elves that lived there have either disappeared or they've been killed. All that's left is empty houses… and bodies."

Fear trickles through me, and I freeze.

The other two, a silver-eyed woman of middling age with light brown hair and a woman slightly older than her with silver hair and light brown eyes, whisper back and forth. I catch only bits and slivers.

"It's happening," one says.

"It has to be. They're using the Blood Magic again," says the other.

If Fox Elves were using Blood Magic, why would the whole town be gone? Only Fox Elves would've been enslaved.

My stomach plummets.

This is it.

This is when we must announce ourselves.

Geeran seems to have overheard them, as well, for he says, "Are the dead of both Light and Fox blood?"

"Yes." The man hedges, reluctant to say more.

"And are the missing both Light and Fox Elves?"

The man merely nods, suddenly sheepish. The two women fall silent. The crowd around us watches, motionless and quiet.

Geeran continues, "Then does it not seem odd? Surely, the Fox Elves are not responsible. Has the Patrol been dispatched?"

All three nod in unison.

Speaking in that peculiar tone of disappointment that cuts to the bone, Geeran says, "Then, wouldn't it be prudent to wait for their investigations before jumping to conclusions?"

Dropping his gaze to the ground, the man says, "I suppose."

Geeran's words placate the crowd, and we leave town with our anonymity intact, though only just. The breath rushes out of me when the trees swallow the small town.

***

The sun still shines far above the horizon when Geeran insists on making camp. "We can use the caves off the road for shelter."

My heart beats rapidly, wondering why we need a shelter now. "What's wrong?"

"A storm is coming. The horse and cart won't fit in the caves, so we'll need to build a shelter."

I breathe a sigh of relief, having forgotten that divination could be used for weather prediction.

Mother did it all the time.

My mind wanders, recalling other things she used divination for. Checking in to see if I was safe at work, looking ahead for a good harvest, staying home a little longer to talk if she knew I had a rough night at work.

Tears well up, and I practice magic to distract myself, letting the exhaustion keep my mind off her.

I pull water from the air, letting it pool in my hand. I focus intently, freezing it, then melting it. With each transformation, I feel sleep reaching for me, begging for my company. I push air beneath the water, letting it hover above my palm before boiling it.

I move through one magical feat after another, saving only enough energy for a fear-laced ward.

We leave the path, venturing into the woods. The cart rattles and shakes over bumps, and I question this campsite, pitying our poor horse.

Once out of sight of the road, Geeran and Beluroan weave their magic, burying roots that might trip the horse and moving stones from our path. The horse pulls us along easily after that.

A steep hill comes into view through the trees, pocked by several small caves. Most are too small for even a single person to lie in, but two large caves wait to accommodate us.

Geeran and Beluroan set to work, building a shelter for the horse and cart. They lace branches overhead, weaving them into a ceiling. Saplings spring up, twining into walls which butt up against the hill.

They leave an opening just large enough for the horse. Unhooking the cart, I lead the beast in.

Then, they raise a small ledge around the bottom to keep the coming flood waters out. They do the same at the foot of the caves and create overhangs at the openings. They even hollow the caves out and shift the rock to narrow the entrances.

My heart flutters at the thought of sharing such privacy with Beluroan.

Will it matter how tired we are once we're curled up together?

I glance at him, bubbling with excitement despite all my efforts today. But his eyelids droop, and his movements slow. Disappointment settles over me.

Or maybe we'll just fall asleep.

As they finish up, I set up a ward, using the cave-pocked hill as one side. I weave a dome of webs around our camp and plant vines of fear along the base, anchoring several into the hillside. After unpacking and covering the horse with a few blankets, I put another ward over the horse's shelter.

Geeran deposits two bedrolls and blankets in the bigger of the two caves. Then, he disappears into the small one with his own bedding.

My heart beats feverishly as I approach our cave. Beluroan bends to spread our bedrolls, and my eyes trail over him. Gulping in a breath of air, I force myself to focus and seal our cave entrance with another fear-laced ward.

We eat a small meal, watching the world beyond our cave turn grey as the storm moves in. The temperature drops, and the rain transforms into slush.

I hope Geeran is warm enough...

I lean against Beluroan, curling into his side, and the fire around us burns hotter than ever.

"So, you were afraid I would've left Vairsun?" Beluroan's tone is light, almost teasing.

He wraps an arm around me, and my heart skips a beat. My breath catches.

"Well, yeah." I try to play it off. "Things would've gotten a lot worse if you left. It was so close. Doesn't that scare you?"

"I try not to worry over things that didn't happen," he says, smiling broadly. "Besides," he adds, nuzzling my hair, "Saerine isn't the only one who'd grown attached to Vairsun."

"Really?" I look up into his eyes, shining like emeralds despite the dim light.

"Really. Plus, there's no way I could've dragged Oran and Kraimin from another house, from friends." He brushes his nose against mine, chuckling. "Even if I hadn't been caught, it wouldn't have been long before we met."

His words send his lips whispering over mine.

We brush together, desire tempered by exhaustion, but our weariness quickly evaporates in the heat of our aura. Lips crush together hungrily. Our hands grasp at clothing, nearly ripping the fabric.

I climb atop his lap, and our jackets fall away. My hands tremble as I tug his shirt upwards, off. Dim light traces his muscles, and shadows play on the lightning scar that branches over his chest. My fingers trail over it, tracing his lean form in winding patterns.

His hand twines into my hair, and he pulls me in, pressing his lips to mine. Heat pools within me, searing and desperate. He slips a hand beneath my shirts, fingers leaving trails of fire in their wake.

But it isn't enough.

I tear off my shirts, tossing them aside. He cups my breasts, ravages my neck, and I breathe deeply to steady myself.

My lips roam over him, nipping at his neck, his shoulder. He grasps my bottom, and I moan against his bare skin.

He flips me to my back, kneeling between my legs. He explores my bare torso, kissing my neck, my chest, my navel. Butterflies move within me, and my lungs struggle to keep up. He rises, taking my mouth with his, and I groan, aching for more.

My hands find the button of his pants, and he goes still, breathing fast. I slide my hands into the back of his pants, grasping his firm buttocks and pulling him against me. Our bodies press together, but it isn't enough.

I slide his pants down, and he kicks them away, poised above me in only his underwear. I trail my fingers up his back, relishing the shudder that moves through him.

He undoes my buttons, sliding my pants down and taking my underwear with them. His fingers trail over my thighs, burning me alive.

Our mouths meet, dancing together, and he moves against me.

My body aches, begging, arching. And he obliges. His hand slides down my stomach, gliding between my legs. His fingers play over me, sending my heart galloping. His teeth close over my shoulder, tugging a deep sigh from my lips.

His touch grows demanding, moving faster, slipping inside, and I writhe beneath him. Gasping, I arch my back, pressing my breasts to his bare chest.

I push his underwear away, hands quickly deserting the cloth in favor of him. He gasps when I take him in my grasp, resting his forehead against mine and breathing heavily.

Our mouths meld together, and he eases into me. A short burst of pain gives way to ecstasy, and I clutch his back. We move together, holding tightly to each other. Beluroan slides an arm beneath me, grasping my hip with his free hand.

I tangle fingers into his hair, pulling him in for a kiss, gasping against his lips. My other hand grasps his backside, pulling him deeper, and a wild sound bursts from me.

My body burns for release, and heat flows through me. I arch my back, pressing myself to him. He kisses my neck, nips at my shoulder, and I tumble over the edge, crying out.

My nails dig into his back, and he finds his release, body shuddering as he whispers my name.

He touches my neck, eyes locked on mine in the near darkness.

"How can you mean so much to me already?" he whispers.

I stare up at him, wondering just what I mean to him. I know what he means to me. I know that, even after such a short time, I'd rather die than live another day without him.

Shock spreads through me as the implications settle over me.

"Well," I say. "I guess when you're Blessed, you just know it, right?"

Regret washes over me the instant the words leave me.

But Beluroan chuckles. "I guess so."

He kisses my lips, slowly, as if savoring me. He rolls onto his side, pulling me with him, and says, "Even if we weren't Blessed Ones, I'd still love you."

I stare at him, shocked into silence. He stills, pulling in short, controlled breaths.

"Really?" I ask.

He swallows, nods. "Yeah." After a pause, he stammers, "But if… If you don't feel that way…"

"No, no, I do," I say, rushing to reassure him. Smiling, I say, "I love you."

He kisses me, pulling me tight against him. Our legs entwine, and our kiss deepens.

A delicate ache builds within me, and I roll him onto his back. His hands explore me, and we join again, moving slower, softer.

We shatter, falling to lie in each other's arms. Clothes lie strewn about, forsaken. Ensconced in his arms, I pull a blanket over us just before sleep claims me. In case Geeran wakes first.

Chapter 19
Beluroan

Elairie nestles between my legs in the cart, leaning against me. The scent of cinnamon and citrus wafts up to me. Her soft backside presses against me, even more alluring after what we shared last night.

I breathe deeply, steeling myself.

Mud clings to the wheels of the cart as the horse pulls us back to the road, and I focus on the path, reaching out with my magic to flatten the earth the horse will trod upon, burying roots to ease the beast's burden.

Once back on the road, the trees fly by. The well-worn bridge over the Draecon River finds us quickly, and I reach out once more, using my magic to shift a few loose stones in the railings, fitting them back into place as we cross.

The waters below rage with the recent influx of water, rushing past. Elairie plays with it, exercising her water magic, slowing certain spots, speeding up other places. She creates a sheet of ice over a small section, then melts it.

I marvel at how easily she manipulates it already.

The wind blows, harsh and chilly, telling us that it won't be long before the river freezes of its own accord. Geeran huddles on the bench, bundled up in blankets and hunched against winter's assault.

I close my eyes as we approach Booran, listening to the wind. It ebbs and flows, swirling around us.

Is Elairie doing this too?

But the magic that flows within the breeze emanates from me. My eyes snap open, and I take control, whipping it around faster. I condense the wind, turning the air to a thick fog, then thin it out once more.

Elairie looks at me over her shoulder, smiling beautifully. She laces our fingers together, and my hand grows warm. I drop my gaze, only to find tiny flames sparkling on her fingertips.

But I feel no pain.

My jaw drops. "Shouldn't your magic hurt me?"

She shrugs. "I don't know."

"Make the flames bigger?"

She hesitates, so I say, "You can heal me if it hurts me."

She relents, and her brows crease in concentration. The tiny flames grow, but I feel only warmth.

"Is this like the fortune magic? Is it only like this if we're touching?" I ask.

Reluctantly, Elairie releases my hand and scoots away from me. I shiver in her absence, stunned at the difference.

She lifts her hand and summons a flame on one finger. I swallow nervously as she feeds it, building a small inferno.

I lift my hand, hesitant. Every instinct tells me not to touch fire, but I force myself to move. My fingers warm as tongues of flame lick my skin.

But nothing more happens.

I breathe a sigh of relief.

Watching me carefully, Elairie stokes the fire. It turns from red to blue to white, yet I feel only warmth.

I shake my head, marveling at the oddity for a moment longer before pulling her back into my arms.

The flame extinguishes as her concentration wavers, and she falls against me with a giggle. "I guess when the Gods made us of the same stuff, we got the same magic." Her words come out soft, filled with wonder.

"I guess so."

"You could ask them about that sometime," Geeran says. After a brief pause, he adds, "There is one other thing I'm curious about, if you wouldn't mind asking."

"Sure," I say. "What is it?"

"If you had a child, what magical abilities would pass on? It seems to me that would be a very powerful being."

Elairie and I look at each other, stunned.

"I hadn't even thought about that…" I whisper.

"We'll ask if we speak with them again," Elairie says.

"Once you improve your divination, you could try initiating a vision with them. Normal Elves can't do it, but you two are far from normal. It would be worth a try."

"I'm glad you're with us, Geeran." I shake my head, stunned. "I wouldn't have thought that possible. I certainly wouldn't have dared to try."

Booran appears in the distance, barely visible through the trees, and all talk of Blessed Ones and our magic ceases. We shroud ourselves in silence and crates of supplies.

The horse carries us toward the town center, complete with a massive ornate sundial, looming over the town like a sentinel. But today, it serves as a divider.

Light Elves stand to one side. Fox Elves on the other side.

And everywhere, shouts fill the air.

Geeran steers our horse right through the crowd of onlookers toward the angry center. People whisper as they move out of our way, and their words shake me to my core.

Another town in the mountains, empty. As with Douhean, most vanished. Only bodies were left behind. And apparently, more died this time.

They must've heard about Douhaen and fought back.

"You damned Blood Elves! We'll find *these* Masters too!"

"Tell them we're coming for them!"

From the other side of the sundial, the Fox Elves shout back.

"There are no Masters!"

"Please, we're not doing this!"

My stomach plummets. Somehow, I don't think a few calm words from Geeran will sooth this crowd.

Chaos fills the air, a raucous mixture of anger and fear assaulting my ears. I peer through the slats of the cart at faces contorted with rage.

"You damn scum..." someone hisses, and everyone goes quiet. A tall, wiry Elf moves through the crowd, and people part to let him pass. "It wasn't enough for the lot of you to kill my wife and my son. Are you coming back for me now?"

He takes a step toward a burly Fox Elf with curly black hair and says, "Well, just like last time, I'm not going down easy."

A chorus of "Fight!" erupts from the mob surrounding us.

As the Light Elf pulls his arm back to throw a punch, Elairie stands up beside me and shouts, "WAIT!"

The group spins to look at us. The Light Elf stops mid-punch, a few strands of light brown hair slipping free of their tie. Elairie reaches down and hauls me up to stand beside her.

"Don't do this," she says, shaking her head. The crowd stares.

"The Fox Elves aren't the ones doing this."

A young Elf whispers, "Fox Elves?"

Have they never heard our true name?

"Blood Elves," another answers.

But Elairie isn't done. "There's a man in the Cargam Mountains trying to renew the Blood Magic," she says. "But he's not a Fox Elf. And he's not a Light Elf. He's mixed."

Jaws drop, and a collective gasp rolls through the crowd.

I take a deep breath and say, "We're on our way to take care of it though."

I put my arm around Elairie's shoulder, and she wraps hers around my waist.

"This might be hard to believe for those of you who know what this is," I say, pausing to gather my nerve, "but we're Blessed Ones. Any of you with aura or fortune magic can confirm it. The Gods made us so we can try to prevent the darkness this man could bring to Avaencery."

They look at each other, then back up at us. Silence rings in my ears.

Geeran speaks up, unafraid to be the bearer of bad news. "His blood would allow him to control Elves of either race."

Shock spreads over the people before us, slow and poisonous.

"The disappearances are his way of gathering subjects to test his potions," Geeran continues. "He has yet to successfully recreate the Blood Magic, and we aim to prevent it if we can."

Trying to save them from panic, Elairie says, "We're going to try to find a way to immunize people against it in case he succeeds. For now, stay as calm as possible. He hasn't ventured far for… 'recruits,' and all his attempts have failed. Remember that."

Alarm shows clearly on their faces, but we can't stay much longer. We need to be on the road. My stomach flips, and my eyes drift up to the mountains, desperate to be on our way.

"But we can't afford to fight amongst ourselves," I say. "We've been in contact with the Patrol, the General, and the Representatives. Once we tell them that we've revealed ourselves, I'm sure they'll give you more information."

I take Elairie's hand and say, "For now, we need to be on our way. We have a long way to travel."

We sit back down, and Geeran flicks the reins on the horse's back. The crowd parts before us, silent and staring.

Whispering to Elairie, I voice the only bright side. "Maybe this will pull everyone together. Maybe, just maybe, we'll be Foxes again when this is over."

***

"Word will travel quickly," Pakaibra tells us. "I'm sure the Gods were right in counseling you to reveal yourselves, but it seems…" He runs a hand through his hair. "I worry too much, I'm afraid."

The corners of his lips lift into a smile, and I wonder if Saerine told him that. The magic of this modified vision confirms that suspicion.

He huffs a deep breath, then says, "There's so much on your shoulders. It seems dangerous to risk Gourmaht learning of your location."

"Geeran already agreed to shield our whereabouts from him," Elairie says. "It's a risk, but it's necessary."

Pakaibra nods, staring at the papers on his desk thoughtfully.

Tugged along on Elairie's first attempt at using a vision for communication, I glance around his office. He sits alone, with countless papers scattered across his desk. I raise a brow.

I thought he'd be more organized.

The magic of divination tells me that he normally is, but we've caught him at a bad time. Vairsun fares no better than Booran, with Elves acting out against their neighbors. Now that he's calmed everyone, he's left with reports to fill out.

I hope word of our existence will stop this mess…

"Will the three of you be alright without guards?"

Elairie and I glance at each other.

"Gourmaht has outposts throughout Avaencery, but they're not very big," she says.

Does she get different information from the visions?

"Up until now, they were meant for…" Elairie trails off before adding, "maintaining secrecy. The people manning those outposts are brutal, terrible people, but… We can handle them if it comes to that."

I squeeze her hand.

"The Gods said we'd be immune to this Blood Magic. We might be able to spread that immunity to others," I say. "We just have to figure out how."

"Work quickly." Pakaibra's voice rumbles in my chest, despite the distance that separates our physical bodies. "Is there anything I can do to help?"

"I don't know." Elairie whispers.

She straightens and says, "Maybe organize some sort of statement to be given by the Patrol. Rumors are already getting out of hand. Maybe giving people the facts will stop them from panicking."

"I can handle that," Pakaibra says with a nod, relaxing now that he has a task.

"How are Saerine and the boys?" I ask.

The big man's mouth opens, and he drops his gaze for a moment.

I swallow, remembering that he and Saerine are… involved.

"They're well," he says. "I wanted to talk to you about something though."

Do I tell him that I know?

Or just wait for him to tell me?

My stomach flips in the awkward silence, and my palms sweat.

"Saerine and I…" Pakaibra trails off, struggling for words.

Elairie saves us the trouble. "The two of you are seeing each other, are you not?"

We startle at her words. Our eyes meet, and he scrubs a hand at the back of his neck.

Elairie continues, "I checked on her a few days ago and saw the two of you talking in her kitchen. You were both so happy." She smiles warmly.

The wonders of this fortune magic reveal many long nights in Pakaibra's past, most spent hunched over this very desk. I see his dedication.

And his loneliness.

Empath magic kicks in, and his emotions sweep through me, sweet and shockingly tender.

If I'm honest with myself, he's exactly what I would've picked for Saerine. Strong enough to protect her if need be, because she's definitely not a fighter, and kind enough that I know he'd never hurt her or the boys.

But I'm still her brother.

So I say, "I'm happy for you two. But, so help me Gods, if you ever hurt her…"

"I assure you," Pakaibra says, "you needn't worry over that. I could never hurt her." Sadness fills his eyes as he adds, "She's been through more than enough for many lifetimes already."

How much did she tell him?

"Take care of her," I say.

While I'm gone.

If I don't make it back.

"I'll do everything I can for her," he says.

I nod and clear my throat. "Well… If we think of anything else you need to know, or if anything else happens, we'll contact you."

"Yes," he answers, clearly more comfortable talking to me, the Blessed One, than me, Saerine's brother. "I'll prepare a statement and speak with the General and the other Commanders."

"Until we meet again," Elairie says before pulling us back to our little cart.

We bump along on the uneven dirt road, rattling over roots that stick up in the path, and try desperately to think of a way to protect others from Gourmaht.

***

We make camp just off the road with fear-laced wards up. Despite all that protection, my stomach turns.

Because now, we're hunted.

We discuss alternate routes over dinner, but thanks to our meeting with General Haedra in Kaern and the bridge crossing the Stravic River in Eadaion, we have one option.

The path we already travel.

My eyes dart to Elairie, and I find her fiddling with her gloves and boots, remnants of her mother and grandmother. Tears pool at the corners of her eyes, and I take her hand in mine.

After dinner, we curl up on our side of the lean-to. I pull her tightly against me, trying desperately to suppress my desires. But the air around us charges with electricity, and my body burns for more.

I kiss her forehead, breathing deeply to take in the scent of her. Elairie wraps her arms around me, nestling in close.

Gradually, we drift off to sleep. As my eyes close, I wonder if I've ever felt so at peace and know that the answer, despite everything that's going on, is no.

Chapter 20
Elairie

The trees thin as we ride, replaced by open fields. Farmers toil, rushing to harvest before it's too late.

Kaern sits in the distance, awaiting our arrival with the Patrol Outpost perched in the town center. Taller than anything around it, the great stone building stares out at the world around it, standing sentinel in what would otherwise be a small farm town.

My eyes drift to Beluroan. Briefly, I wonder how he feels approaching the second largest Outpost in Avaencery, having spent half his life outside the law.

Upon arrival, a guard ushers us inside to a large room full of lavish furniture. Luxuriously upholstered chairs dot the room in little clusters, nestled between white stone columns.

A desk waits at the back of the room, dark wood shining in the warm light as it guards a single door. Two grand staircases frame the desk, curving up to a balcony.

I stare at the ornately appointed room, shocked that an Outpost would possess such elegance. The guard speaks, drawing my attention as he tells the wispy man at the desk our names. His clean-shaven head shines in the light of the high windows as he nods, indicating one of the staircases.

Our guard leads us up the stairs quickly, then through a large door to a wide hallway. A maze of halls and doors awaits, and suddenly I'm thankful for the escort. I wrap my hand around Beluroan's as we follow him through the labyrinth.

Finally, we step through a door into a small room with comfortable chairs in the corners. Doors on either side lead to changing rooms.

"Wash and change clothes," the guard says, dark eyes expressionless. "General Haedra wishes to discuss matters over lunch. Your clothes will be washed while you eat, and you'll get your new armor after your meeting with the General."

He turns to leave us, and I cast a glance at Beluroan before stepping into the women's changing room. A chill follows me, filling the space between me and Beluroan.

I strip quickly, dropping my clothes in a heap. My eyes trace my form in the mirror, and I cringe.

The dirt and sweat of travel, the mud of the cave… it all clings to me, heavy and stifling.

Taking up a clean cloth, I dip it into the water and scrub it all away.

Finally clean, I sift through racks, shelves, and drawers full to the brim with armor and clothing, searching for something to wear. Everything is on offer, from full plate armor to formal dresses, though I can't imagine a need for the latter in an Outpost.

Though we are dining with the General…
Maybe it wouldn't hurt to look nice.

Moving to the formal clothes, I pick out a slender black dress and step into it. The high collar rises to the neck, but the shoulders and back lie open. It scoops down to rest just above my buttocks, and a slit reaches from the floor all the way up to my thigh.

My hair falls in tangles about my face, and I pale at the idea of sitting to eat with the General with this mane. Butterflies fill my stomach.

Approaching the small mirror over the washstand, I stare at the mess of lilac and mulberry left to its own devices on the road. Toying with the end of a wavy strand of lavender, I try to tame the beast.

Beyond the door, footsteps ring out as Beluroan and Geeran reenter the sitting room.

"Come with me," the guard says. "I'll see you to the dining room."

I comb my fingers through my hair, listening as Beluroan says, "Shouldn't we wait for Elairie?"

"I'll come back for her. Don't worry. There's another guard posted outside the door."

Geeran says, "She'll be alright, I promise."

As I work my hair into something reminiscent of elegant, they leave, and I feel every step Beluroan takes away from me. My heart reaches for him, but he walks further still. The aura that swirls around us stretches thin, trying to cover the gap.

The door opens and closes behind me, and the mirror reveals a woman in full regalia, armor gleaming in the light. She pulls her gloves off, tossing them onto a shelf.

I clear my throat, and she turns to face me, pulling off her helmet and placing it on an armor rack.

The insignia on her chest gleams, denoting her rank.

General Haedra.

She shakes out her long, white hair, standing with her chest thrust out and her shoulders back. Her gaze sweeps over me, analyzing.

Should I salute her? Or curtsy?

Her mint eyes scan the length of me, and I blush before her scrutiny. She unbuckles her chest plate, depositing it onto the rack with her helmet. The top buttons of her blouse hang open.

Her hips sway as she takes a few steps toward me, gaze sweltering. "You're stunning."

I swallow, blushing.

My hands fall from my hair to hang limp at my sides. She takes a few more steps toward me, almost toe to toe, and touches my face.

Does she know who I am?

Surely, she wouldn't be this forward if she knew…

"My name is Haedra," she says, stepping closer.

The knot in my stomach ties itself tighter. Beluroan's absence cuts me from the inside, and her presence, so close, standing where he should stand, makes it worse.

I take a step back. "I'm Elairie."

Her hand leaves my face, and she cocks her head. "As in, Elairie Jooncourgahmas?"

I jolt at the mention of my formal name, having gone years without hearing it spoken aloud. I've certainly never heard it used to clarify whether I should be flirted with or not.

Silently, I wonder if Haedra does stuff like this often.

But I simply say, "Yes, that's me."

Eyebrows raise, and she takes a step back. "I wasn't expecting you for at least another day." Smiling, she adds, "Well, I apologize. It's great to meet you."

Haedra extends her hand, and with that, she shifts seamlessly from shameless flirt to General.

We make conversation about the trip here, and Haedra surveys the dress I've chosen before selecting a royal blue gown for herself. I turn to the mirror to finish my hair, allowing her privacy to change. Not that she seems to care.

All the better. I'll get to Beluroan faster if she dresses quickly.

Once finished, I turn to face her. The neckline of Haedra's dress plunges between her breasts. It hugs her hips tightly, only to become fluid and loose below her thighs. She leaves her hair down, letting it frame her striking face.

A guard awaits us outside, prepared to take us to the dining room, another thing I didn't expect this place to have.

"This place has everything," I whisper.

Haedra smiles, and says, "During the Dwarven War and then the Blood War, this outpost was used for strategic meetings more than the one in Adalheid."

The guard leads us through another hallway, booted feet clomping on the wooden floor.

"The primary battlefields in those conflicts were too far north for Adalheid to be effective from a strategic standpoint," Haedra says. "Adjustments were made to accommodate the needs that came along with that. The building was enlarged to include a dining hall, additional meeting rooms, changing rooms, and even sleeping quarters."

But I barely pay attention.

Every step we take brings me closer to Beluroan, and my heart slowly pieces itself back together. The air around me grows warmer.

We reach the cozy dining room, and my heart skips. Beluroan and Geeran sit at one end of a massive table, chatting away.

Beluroan turns his gaze upon me, and his lips part to draw in a breath. His eyebrows raise as he looks me over, and a blush crawls up my neck.

He rises to greet me, and my eyes dance over his frame. A dark grey suit clings to him, hugging his figure as if it were made for him. My eyes linger on his broad shoulders, plainly visible with his hair tied back.

I ache at the sight of him. Even such a short separation was too long. My skin burns for his touch, and desire pools within me.

I wonder if we could sneak off to the sleeping quarters...

I rush to his side, barely able to stop myself from tackling him. Our hands lace together, and my world shifts back into place.

Geeran smiles at us, wrapping a dark cloak tighter around himself.

Surveying us, Haedra says, "I love seeing everyone dressed up." She smiles warmly. "If only every meeting could be conducted in such finery and over a nice meal."

General Haedra dismisses the guard and takes her place at the head of the table. We sit, and guards carry in trays of decadent food.

As we eat, we recount everything for Haedra. We tell her which types of magic we've gained and the various things we've learned from the Gods.

Though Haedra clearly has questions, she waits, focusing intently on our words. But on hearing that there's a chance we could protect others from the Blood Magic, her curiosity outweighs her patience.

"So, if it comes to war, Gods forbid," she begins, "our troops could be granted immunity?"

"Potentially." Geeran tells her. "The exact method still eludes us."

The room falls silent. Lost in thought, I eat without tasting anything, a true shame.

"I can't say for sure whether this would help," Geeran eventually says, "but surely it can't hurt. Perhaps the two of you should look for the recipe of the Blood Magic. Maybe you could divine an antidote of sorts from that? Treating poison always starts with careful study of the infernal stuff."

"It's as good a place to start as any," I tell him.

But Haedra shifts uncomfortably in her seat. "Now," she begins, changing the topic, "what kind of progress has been made toward mastering your new magic?"

Beluroan finally speaks up, "A fair amount of progress."

With a soft laugh, Geeran adds, "More than a fair amount. You sell yourself short, Beluroan." A genuine smile lights up his face.

The rare sight warms my heart.

"They seem to skip the initial phase of learning altogether. The magic appears at random only once, the first time. After that, they can beckon it at will. They begin not with calling the magic forth, but with shaping it, controlling it."

"Interesting." Haedra sits forward in her seat, tipping her head to the side as she considers us.

"There have been a couple times when their life magic came forth without their willing it to do so, but not often. Certainly no more than still happens to anyone gifted with life magic, even long after mastering it," Geeran says.

Haedra hangs on his every word.

He continues, "Conventional limits don't seem to apply to them in a few ways."

"How so?" Looking back and forth between the three of us, intrigue shows clearly on the General's face.

"Well," I say, running a finger along the edge of my plate, "we aren't hurt by each other's magic."

The General nods, and I decide to get the next part out of the way.

"One of the times the life magic came forth… unbidden, we were sent on a vision into Beluroan's past." I search his face, hating that I must say it at all.

"We relived one of his memories, rather than watching from the outside. And since we were touching when the vision came over me, we both experienced it, even though Beluroan doesn't have fortune—" I glance at Geeran, then correct myself, "I mean, divination, yet."

"And you *accidentally* went into the past?"

"Ah, yes," Geeran remarks. "That's what I forgot to have you test out."

"What do you mean?" Beluroan asks, voice tight.

Surely, Geeran doesn't want us to relive more of Beluroan's memories.

"Well, generally, looking back is more difficult in divination than sifting through the present or future. The past gets buried beneath the present and all the things that could've been. I meant to have the two of you try to find something in the past. Maybe it's easier for you."

"It might be," I say. "After all, the one time we did it was an accident."

"Yes," Geeran states. "But that was a memory, and Beluroan was involved in finding it amongst the rubble of the past. That may have made it more accessible."

"Rather unfortunate, given the nature of the memory," Beluroan mumbles, just loud enough for me to hear. Beneath the table, I squeeze his hand.

"Perhaps," I suggest, "we could try finding the original recipe for the Blood Magic. Maybe we can find out why we're immune to this kind, but not the first."

Beluroan nods. Geeran agrees readily, but Haedra hesitates.

Reluctantly, she says, "That might be for the best." Her beautiful face becomes serious. "If there are differences in the recipes, yet they yield the same results, there may be even more ways to make this damnable stuff."

"I hope to the Gods there are no other ways," I whisper, more to myself than anyone else.

"Looking back that far though…" Geeran hedges. "No normal Elf could do that. The two of you *might* be able to, but it could be a long shot."

As we finish our meal, Haedra makes arrangements to send jars and potion materials with us.

She meets my gaze, then Beluroan's, and says, "If you find a recipe for the antidote, make what you can and leave it at an Outpost for me. I'll have more made and distribute it."

We choose a location to assemble troops just south of Mount Hybar, but I wonder how much of this will change.

So much depends on what Gourmaht does, and I hate how much control he has.

But General Haedra calmly plans our next move. Despite the blocked trade routes with the Dwarves, despite the danger. Somehow, she makes it all seem less daunting, almost setting me at ease.

With our meal complete, we venture back to the dressing rooms. Beluroan and I lead the way, recalling the few turns we made earlier. Haedra and Geeran follow behind.

"They do bleed, do they not? They're still mortal?" Haedra asks quietly, with fear and reverence lurking in her words.

Have we intimidated this unshakable woman?

The thought makes me strangely uneasy.

"Only just," Geeran answers, voice soft.

In the dressing room, a full set of armor awaits me. Lightweight leather pieces promise freedom of movement, but the metal reinforcements promise safety.

Haedra helps me put it all on over my freshly washed clothes, buckling clasps and holding pieces in place while I fasten others. She hands me new boots and gloves, but I shake my head.

"Yours look worn," she says, and the condescension in her voice hurts.

But the scuffs on the leather, the softness inside the gloves, are marks of my mother and grandmother.

A tear pricks at the corner of my eyes, and I whisper, "These were my mother's, my grandmother's. I won't replace them."

Though clearly unhappy about my decision, Haedra relents.

Finally dressed, we rejoin Beluroan and Geeran in the sitting room. Immediately, I lace my fingers through Beluroan's, reveling in the warmth of our aura. I rake my eyes over him, smiling.

Beneath his open jacket, a chest piece like my own shines. Similar pieces of armor adorn his frame. But he's traded in his boots and gloves, free of sentimentality. Metal gleams on every surface of his new boots that would accommodate it, and the leather of his gloves looks supple and smooth.

My mouth goes dry as I take him in.

Despite the layers of leather between our hands, the contact sends heat seeping into me. My lips spread in a grin just being beside him again.

How did I exist before him?

Tearing my eyes from him, I look to Geeran. His attire remains largely unchanged, except his cloak. The new one burns a vibrant crimson which shimmers with a delicate light of its own.

What enchantment did they put on it?

Haedra escorts us out, still draped in that devastating dress, and wishes us all the speed and luck we could possibly need. "I'd wish the blessing of the Gods upon you, but it seems you already have it," she says with a coy smile.

We load ourselves back into the cart, and the guard at the Outpost door offers a solemn nod as we ride away. I cast a glance back at Haedra, only to find her smile gone, replaced by concern.

***

As the day wears on and our practice grows easier, we turn our attention to the antidote. I cast my mind out, searching for Gourmaht's recipe.

In no time, darkness reaches for me, creeping in at the edges of my vision. I pull Beluroan along with me, and our spirits sail to the Cargam Mountains. The craggy behemoths spread out before me, but their edges blur.

I wipe at my eyes, trying to clear them. But my eyes are fine. The *vision* itself is hazy.

What is this?

Divination supplies the answer. What I seek has been blocked.

He's shielding himself.

Or having someone else do it.

I push harder, forcing my way into Mount Hybar.

If nothing else, we now know exactly where he is. That has to count for something.

Shrouded by a thick fog, the rock face shows no detail. Snow falls around us, further obscuring my view, but I keep pushing.

Blurry figures fill the cave. Mixed bloods work alongside Fox and Light Elves. All around the cave, they repair armor and sharpen blades of varying sizes. A few sit at tables, eating meals I can't make out.

I let my aura magic come forth, and disgust courses through me. Every Elf in sight simmers within blood red swirls or clouds as black as coal. Every aura in the cave swells with hatred and aggression, but their details elude me.

Hands trembling, I approach the Elf nearest me. His face remains a blur, a splotch of colors and vague shapes, even at arms' length, but I don't dare get closer.

From somewhere deep in the caves, we hear him. Gourmaht yells angrily, but the echoes and the shield garble his words. Two openings await at the back of the cave, but our spirits gravitate toward the larger one. Drifting down the tunnel, we pass cave after cave.

Moisture lingers in the air, rank and musty. Torches dot the walls, but the space between them lets shadows gather.

The tunnel dumps us into a small cave, confronting us with four openings in the far wall. My spirit drifts forward, leaning toward the second from the right, dragging us down deep into the mountain. The steep decline twists and winds through the rock, and finally, opens onto a massive cave filled with Elves.

But only a few spirits linger.

The darkest auras I've ever seen float around the living as they busily gather herbs and scrolls around the edges of the cave.

Bodies lie strewn about the floor, recently deserted with no auras to speak of.

A man whose name I can't quite grasp says something to Gourmaht. The shield transforms his words, slurring them and twisting them beyond recognition.

But the glare Gourmaht gives him is unmistakable.

Beluroan steers us closer, staring intently at Gourmaht's face. It shimmers like a reflection on water, wavering before our eyes, but slowly, it swims into focus.

A few strands of dark blue hair hang loose, having fallen from their tie in a fit of rage. Ivory skin glistens with a thin layer of sweat, and his black eyes match his aura. A massive earth scar barely holds his face together, and his jawline promises to cut glass.

Beluroan gasps beside me, shaking his head as if to deny this new development. Gourmaht stands there, red-faced and shouting gibberish at the man before him.

And then, he stops, mid-sentence.

All around, his companions stare at the mass of dead Elves on the cave floor. Three bodies, three people, try to pull themselves free of the pile. They move slowly, groaning with every agonized movement.

But eventually, they sit up.

I thought them dead. Apparently, so had everyone else. Open mouths make black holes in blurred faces, chilling me to my core.

The three living Elves on the cave floor shiver, blurred bodies quaking. They survey their surroundings and the bloody eyes and ears of the bodies tangled into their limbs.

Their auras, one lilac, one royal blue, and one orange, seem normal enough in and of themselves. But angry clouds whirl around them, so thick that I can but glimpse the auras and people within.

My blood runs cold, and I grip Beluroan's hand.

Gourmaht speaks, and for the first time, I understand his words. Perhaps a dip in his shield caster's focus. But I don't need these words. I know them before they leave his lips.

"It worked on them." He looks around at all the fallen. "We're almost there." He steps closer to his new slaves, speaking to the man who bore the brunt of his anger just a moment ago. "When will the next group be here?"

Three slaves…

And how many dead?

My heart aches, grieving the lost lives and what the survivors mean for the rest of us.

Darkness closes in on us as we're whisked back to our little cart, wheeling along between farms.

"Gods," I whisper.

Beluroan runs a hand through his hair, pulling me closer to him with his other arm. "We don't have much time."

We fill Geeran in, words tumbling from us, and he sits quietly on the bench for a moment, eyes fixed on the horizon.

Eventually, he says, "You're sure it was shielded? It wasn't actually foggy? Or a vision of an unclear future? That would appear foggy."

"No," Beluroan says, confidently. "Once I saw Gourmaht's face, a few details got clearer. It wasn't the future. His second-in-command, Waergou, is shielding them. I didn't see his face, but I know the point of one of his ears got lopped off in battle."

"I was just asking, because…" Geeran blows out a breath. "Shields usually keep others out completely. Since you knew Gourmaht, you might have seen him, and only him, surrounded by complete darkness, but…"

Geeran pauses, then asks, "Did you actually steer the vision, Beluroan? Do you have divination now, or was it just because you were with Elairie?"

We look at each other and shrug. "Only one way to find out," I say.

We scoot apart, and he stills. Slowly, his eyes glaze over, and that faraway look creeps onto his face, just as it always came over Mother's. When he comes back to us, a smile lights his features.

I curl into his arms. "What are you smiling about?" I ask, craving a bright spot in this shadowed day.

"I checked on Oran and Kraimin. They were helping Saerine put away clothes." He tips his head to the side and says, "Sort of. They weren't much help." He chuckles.

Geeran allows a few moments of happiness before asking, "How did you know Gourmaht?"

Beluroan stills beside me, quiet and tense. "He was my Master's son."

"You didn't recognize his name?" Geeran asks.

Beluroan shakes his head. "I never learned his name. We were told to call him 'Sir.'"

My nose wrinkles.

They certainly were an entitled bunch.

"What was he like?" Geeran asks, far calmer than I feel.

"Terrible." Beluroan shakes his head again, running a hand through his hair. After a deep breath, he drops his head back against the wall of the cart.

"Master— I mean, Traimon, took a Light Elf mistress. She wanted better treatment for her two children, so she laid with Traimon, carried his child."

Beluroan's brows furrow before he goes on.

"Gourmaht lived in the big house, taught all his life that only strength and power mattered. How you got them, what you did with them, were insignificant details. He was praised for cruelty, punished for kindness."

A deep sigh lifts his shoulders.

"I mean serious punishment, not just the time-out's that Saerine uses for the boys. Abyss below, the huge scar on his face is because he started to feel bad for someone he was tormenting. Making someone cry out for their mother in front of their own kids… I guess it got to him."

I cringe at the thought, and Mother's still face and silence as the Elves slashed her body flashes through my mind.

"So Traimon showed him what happens to weaklings. He unleashed nearly the full force of his magic on Gourmaht. I think he was about 18, maybe. I was seven or eight. He learned quickly. He was terrible before, but… He was never the same after that. Harder. Crueler."

My stomach turns.

Beluroan shrugs, shakes his head. "Gourmaht's mother thought it was deplorable, but he was treated by all the best healers. He was set to take over for Traimon, after all."

"But Master never offered her other kids a better life like she thought he would. She still put up with it, for Gourmaht. Until Traimon nearly killed one of her other kids. She had the gall to say something to him about it."

Beluroan pauses, closing his eyes. My heart twists, dreading his next words.

"Traimon had a lot of mistresses. Losing one was no big deal. And she certainly wasn't his favorite. His favorite lover was another Master, actually. She had her own little 'kingdom' set up on a hill north of us."

"Anyway," Beluroan says. "Master was starting to spiral, so he didn't just use his magic on her. He beat her, first. Forced Gourmaht to help, told him that he had to prove he wasn't weak like her, actually had him finish her off. By that point, Gourmaht was so far gone that he got into it. He went into a rage and nearly killed someone else, as well."

Beluroan sighs deeply. A heavy silence descends over us, and I wonder if Gourmaht would've been different if he hadn't been raised to be a monster.

Maybe if he'd been raised the way his siblings were? A terrible existence, to be sure, but maybe he wouldn't be recreating the Blood Magic.

I turn to Geeran. "Can we initiate an audience with the Gods?"

"If it were anyone else, I'd say no. The two of you…shield breaking Blessed Ones…" Geeran goes quiet on the last few words, then says, "I'm not sure. Why?"

"I just have a question… Well, a lot actually. We could ask what you wanted to know too, about if we had a child."

"We may as well try," Beluroan says.

We sit side-by-side, fingers laced together, and concentrate on the Great Valley and the Gods. The horse plods along, tugging the cart over bumps and dips in the road. After a while, I consider giving up, but Beluroan convinces me to keep trying.

Slowly, darkness creeps in at the edges, inching into our view. Our spirits separate from our bodies, and we soar far above Avaencery, ascending at a dizzying rate.

The Gods wait for us, assembled in all their splendor. I stare at them, mind awash with their glory.

Doorma's voice whispers through our minds, "You have questions?"

"Yes, we do." Beluroan confirms.

"Would things have been different if Gourmaht had grown up differently or was this going to happen, no matter what?" I blurt out.

Jemarie's white eyes glow brighter as she speaks. "We created you when it was guaranteed that he would try to recreate the Blood Magic. He was never going to be a good person, but he didn't have to be this awful."

"Next question?" Luxitore says, voice echoing and rumbling through the ground beneath our feet, brusque words pushing us forward.

Beluroan asks, "What would happen if we had a child? What magic would that kid have?"

A collective gasp breaks loose from the Gods. They all turn to Luxitore.

The lightning arcing across Nepiter's wings accelerates, and he asks, "Did we miss a path?"

Baereen speaks at the same time, running over Nepiter's words. "Was there another path we overlooked?"

Voice laced with concern, maybe even fear, Doorma asks, "They're not going to have a child, are they?"

My head spins, and a deep sickness seeps into my stomach as the Gods panic before me.

Luxitore shakes his head. "No child. They can't. I remember their making."

They consult each other as if we're no longer here, and impatience unfurls within me, expanding, itching beneath my skin.

The world can't possibly be so precariously balanced that this could scare even the Gods…

Could it?

My voice comes out weak, barely audible, but I ask, "What's going on? I don't understand."

They look back and forth amongst themselves, then Jemarie speaks again. "Luxitore, you're sure?"

He nods solemnly. The flowers and vines throughout his body flutter softly with the movement.

The Gods breathe a collective sigh of relief, and Nepiter says, "You can't have a child."

But his words don't sink in immediately.

"Do you mean that we shouldn't?" I whisper. "Or that we can't?"

Luxitore says, "Both."

My heart tears into pieces, and my stomach drops.

Beluroan slips an arm around my waist, and I lean my head against his shoulder. My eyes prick with tears.

With a sigh that fills my entire mind, Doorma says, "Blessed Ones cannot have children. All the darkest paths the world could ever travel start with the child of Blessed Ones. There are a few times when that child would send the world down a good path, but they are woefully outnumbered."

Baereen tells us, "From early childhood, the child would be more powerful than the two of you combined. It would have no frame of reference to temper its powers, no sense of right or wrong. Nor would that child have the balance that comes from splitting such power between two beings."

The webbed spines that run along his back sparkle beguilingly in the sunlight as he goes on, "To prevent this, Luxitore makes the bodies of all Blessed Ones infertile."

I stare at them, mouth agape with horror.

"In any other being," Doorma says, "it would be a flaw. In Blessed Ones, it is necessary for the survival of the world. The first pair of Blessed Ones we ever made nearly had a child, and we had to interfere. We convinced them not to. Thinking it a fluke, we made the next pair fertile, but it was the same. Luckily, they died before having a child, and we vowed never to risk it again."

Shock sets in, and silence falls. The Gods don't interrupt our devastation, and my mind spirals through all my daydreams of raising a family with Beluroan.

But even if we survive…

Tears fill my eyes, but I blink them away, refusing to cry before the Gods. I take a deep breath, pulling away from Beluroan. He looks every bit as disappointed as I feel, and fresh tears prick at my eyes.

Placing a hand on the side of my face, Beluroan says, "We can still have a family. We'll just take in a child that doesn't have a home."

I consider his plan, consider the life we could have if we survive. I chew at the inside of my lip. Breathing deeply, I nod.

"Was there anything else?" Doorma asks.

There were other things, I know there were, but my mind is blank now.

All I can think of is the family we could have had, the type of family we could still have, and the fact that he must want it too in order to have come up with the idea of adopting so quickly.

I shake my head, and Beluroan does too.

Jemarie says, "Until we meet again."

They all bow their heads to us, and our spirits descend to our bodies. On our return, Geeran marvels at our abilities.

But we curl into each other, weeping quietly.

***

Night approaches, as does the bridge over the Stravic River. An Inn nestled in the little town of Utmaer offers shelter.

Geeran sees us to our room, then disappears, seeking warm food from the tavern on the corner. Beluroan and I shed our jackets and armor, settling on our bed.

Sighing, I drop my head onto his shoulder. "How difficult do you think it'll be to find a child to adopt?"

Wrapping his arms around me, Beluroan says, "Well, we're on the brink of war. There might be a lot of kids without homes by the time this is all finished."

"That's not quite the bright side I was looking for," I tell him with a morbid chuckle.

"I know." Squeezing my shoulders, he leans his head on mine. "We'll figure it out though. One way or another, we'll have a family."

Chapter 21
Beluroan

Geeran returns with fresh water and hot stew in lidded bowls. He retreats to his room, and we eat on the bed, quietly stealing glances at each other.

I scarf my food down, and my eyes trail over Elairie. Warm candlelight flickers over her ivory skin, lending her a gentle glow. Shadows swim in her eyes, and locks of lavender and aubergine frame her soft face.

She glances up at me, blushing beneath my gaze. Her hair falls into her face, and a single strand catches on full lips.

My heart melts. Chuckling, I reach out and smooth that solitary curl behind her ear.

My hand lingers.

She smiles, lifting a hand to hold mine to her cheek. My blood burns for her, racing through my veins, and her eyes drop to my lips for the barest moment.

I swallow hard.

Gathering our bowls, I lean past her to deposit them on the nightstand. Her hand slides over my ribs, achingly delicate, and electricity shoots through me. Yet, the touch tickles, eliciting an embarrassing giggle.

I sit up straight, pinning my arms to my side.

A devilish gleam shines in her eyes as she asks, "Oh, I'm sorry… Did that tickle?"

"Maybe…" I raise one eyebrow, grinning wickedly.

She reaches out, but I catch her hand easily. She tries to pull it back, tries to tickle me with her other hand. I catch that one too. She struggles, laughing brightly.

I hold both her wrists in one hand and pull her close. My free hand moves over her ribs, tickling her frantically.

She squirms, laughing and squealing with delight. But I'm stronger than her. She scoots back on the bed, laughing as she tries to escape. I follow, hand dancing over her ribs all the while.

She falls back onto the bed, giggling madly, musically, and I fall with her.

She wriggles beneath me, wrests one hand from mine. Her hand moves to my side, attempting to turn the tables. I grab her hand, pinning it to the bed.

She stares up into my eyes, all mischief and smiles. Our breaths come in gasps, and her breasts press against my chest with every inhalation. Perched between her legs, kneeling so close I could count the striations in her eyes, my stomach flutters.

I could kiss her…

My entire body aches for it, and I don't bother to resist. My lips find hers, soft and warm and full. She parts them, inviting me in, and I crush my lips to hers. Pressing myself against her, I revel in her warmth. She squirms, moaning softly.

I release one of her hands, sliding my fingers into her hair and pulling her into our kiss. She wraps her arm around me, pressing her hips upward.

We tear free of our shirts, and I bow my head to her breasts, eliciting yet another soft moan. Ragged breaths shake her frame as she rolls me to my back. Straddling me, she kisses my neck, my chest, my stomach.

The air around us shimmers with heat, and her hands fly over the buttons of my pants. She pulls them down quickly, freeing me of all my layers. Her lips find my stomach, slowly moving lower, dropping kisses along the way.

She finds her mark, and I gasp.

A raspy, guttural sound rips free of me, and I tremble beneath her.

But this can't end yet.

I pull her up for a kiss, and she kicks off her boots as I undo her pants. Sliding them down over her hips, I grasp her firm buttocks.

She frees herself of the cumbersome fabric, and my hand slips down between her legs, moving over her, dipping inward. I work my fingers faster, and she collapses atop my chest, moaning and whimpering.

She sits up, taking me inside her, and I gasp. Hips writhing, she bends to kiss my neck. She moves gracefully, working us both to a fever pitch. I grasp her hips, pulling her down over me, driving deeper. Her eyes close, and her back arches.

Voice breaking, she whispers my name.

Aching and about to explode, I flip her onto her back. We descend into a frenzy, moving faster and faster. A sweet ache builds within me, and I kiss her lips, her neck, the tip of her ear. She grasps my hips, pulling me deeper.

We burn together, and with one final movement, we fall to pieces. Her lips find mine, and she arches her back, pressing her chest to mine. Sparks shoot through the room, and my brain goes fuzzy.

The only thought in my mind, the only thing I say is "Gods, Elairie."

As I fall to lay beside her, pulling her into my arms, she whispers, "I love you, Beluroan."

My heart flutters. "I love you too."

We don't bother with a blanket, still burning with the heat of our aura. I use the last of my energy to put a ward over the room. Elairie kisses my neck one last time, and we drift off to sleep.

***

A cloud hangs over us as we make our way to the river, and a deep sense of unease builds in my stomach. I glance upstream at old bridges, crumbled in the Blood War and left in pieces.

Beyond the river, a hill blocks Eadaion from view, and off to the north, hills become mountains. With every step our horse takes, the terrain grows rougher, as our journey surely will.

The Stravic River rushes beneath our bridge, pounding against ancient stonework. But Elairie and I ignore it.

We send our minds out to sift through the rubble of the past for Kaistrum's Blood Magic recipe. Decades of events lie atop it, not to mention the plethora of paths that could have been, all of which collapsed, disused and abandoned as the world chose its true path.

The horse pulls us along, moving slowly toward the hill which blocks Eadaion from our sight. Yet, we keep searching. Finally, as we round the hill, darkness encroaches, and our spirits soar away from here.

Kaistrum stands in a damp cave, locked away from everyone. Tattered pants hang from him, and filth coats his muscular torso. Bile rises in my throat at the sight of him, and my hands curl into fists.

My head fills with terrible names for him, the first Master.

Candles perch upon a table, but beyond their light, I see nothing. I move toward the boundary, but nothing appears.

It must be blocked.

And apparently, by someone stronger than Gourmaht.

Stronger than us.

I turn back to find Kaistrum leaning over three jars on the table. Various pieces of plants lie discarded on the old wood and on the floor at his feet.

Scars decorate his torso, hands, and arms, terrible trophies from fighting in the Dwarven War. But this revelation shocks me.

My teachers never said he fought the Dwarves…

Long, dark brown hair hangs, stringy and unwashed, blocking most of his face from view. He bows deeper over a single jar, staring into its burgundy contents intently. His face goes slack, eyes unfocused.

A vision.

Is he checking the future to see if this one will work?

He reaches beyond the scope of our allowed view and retrieves a quill. It scratches at the surface of his paper as he takes notes.

Kaistrum's olive skin shines with sweat. He glances back over what he's written, then stands up straight. His dark green eyes sparkle as he smiles, but chills run down my spine.

In a hoarse whisper, voice raw from disuse, he says, "It's done."

He almost sounds surprised.

But something snaps behind his eyes.

He screams at the top of his lungs, voice breaking. Elairie jumps. His hands shoot out, grabbing the other jars from the table. Cloudy red liquid swirls in one. Thick black liquid shimmers in the other.

He throws them across the cave with all his might, and they shatter on impact. The sound reaches me, but I don't see the glass break. The potion sizzles on the stone.

Kaistrum flies into a fit of rage, breaking glass, scattering leaves and flowers, shredding papers with failed recipes scrawled across them. He destroys everything but the Blood Magic potion and its recipe.

Creeping toward the table, we commit his notes to memory. Most of the ingredients are common enough. But a few are dangerous if consumed in improper quantities, prepared incorrectly, or if the wrong part of the plant is eaten. Like Aubergine.

Others are pure poison.

Belladonna and hemlock?

If Gourmaht is using the same recipe, it's no wonder his victims keep dying.

I try to memorize how much of each ingredient is used, but another shout from Kaistrum draws my attention.

"They'll pay!" he roars. His composure slips further, and his hands rake across his face, up into his hair. His voice grates through the air as he screams, "They'll pay for what they did to her!"

He falls to his knees, and sobs overtake him.

I pause, staring at him with my mouth hanging open.

The man who enslaved an entire race, the man who tortured and murdered and assaulted… kneels before us, weeping openly. His pain finds its way into my heart, unbidden, echoing through me.

My heart tears in half, and my mind splinters. In this moment, loss is all I know.

Then, Elairie and I are ripped from this place, and the last thing I see is this broken man whimpering a single word, a name, over and over into his hands, "Vaerlin."

Thrust through utter blackness, our spirits slam back into our bodies. Tears pour over Elairie's cheeks as she reaches for her book of drawing paper.

She flips through the pages, and I see the drawings she'd hidden. They're of me. A flash of warmth creeps through the agony left in the wake of that damned vision.

But it doesn't erase the pain completely.

She turns page after page, past quick sketches of cottages and animals we passed along the way, until she finds a blank page. She writes furiously, recounting the recipe as best she can.

She recalls a few ingredients I forgot, and I remember some she missed. But together, we have the full recipe.

We'll have to burn this after we figure out an antidote.

She casts the book and pen aside. Throwing her arms around me, she holds me so tightly I can barely breathe. My heart aches with Kaistrum's pain and insanity, but her embrace pries icy hands from my spirit. I lift her chin, and my lips find hers. We crush together, chasing that rending feeling from our memories.

But even when we've pieced ourselves back together, the feeling of something terrible lying just around the bend lingers.

And suddenly, I realize we're not moving.

Stopped in the middle of the road, Geeran stares straight ahead. The awful feeling intensifies, swelling to fill my chest.

Elairie pulls back, looking into my eyes, and I know she feels it too.

I force myself to look beyond the walls of the cart, beyond her, but see only the hill, only a few trees. We rise to our knees and look past Geeran and his slack-jawed expression.

Eadaion lies ahead, a smoldering ruin. Scorched and salted.

Bodies lie strewn about, burnt and bloody, scarred from magic. Buildings rest in heaps of rubble and ash, smoke still rising from their bones.

My insides churn.

"They did this last night," Elairie whispers. "We were almost here… We could've saved them." Fresh tears roll down her face. "If we'd just moved a little faster…"

"If we'd travelled any faster, we would've needed a new horse," Geeran says. "There's nothing we could've done."

But his voice is hollow.

Elairie and I climb out of the cart. Geeran ties the horse to a tree, and we set off into the rubble of Eadaion.

I reach out, running a hand over blackened stone, the corner of a home I helped construct when Saerine and I lived here. The ornately carved wooden beam that rested atop it now lies in a smoking heap on the ground. Its carvings left no trace in the ash.

A body lies in the collapsed frame, burned beyond recognition, but I remember the people who lived here, remember the smiles that shone on their faces when we finished their home. The woman rubbed her bulging belly often, giddy over the room for the coming baby.

My stomach lurches. My eyes search the rubble, and I hope not to see a tiny body buried within. I turn away, unable to face it if I were to find their child here.

But I find no relief elsewhere.

The market, the homes, the sundial in the center of town, all lie broken and burnt. Bodies litter the ground, alone and in heaps. Smoke still rises from their charred remains.

Bile rises in my throat, and I choke it back.

A little trinket lies in the middle of the road, abandoned in the slaughter. My feet drag me to it, and Elairie clings to my hand, following in my wake. My heart drops as I approach, and my steps slow.

Kneeling, I pick up the baby toy, listen to the comforting whisper of the dried seeds sealed within the nutshell. I turn it over in my hands as tears roll down my cheeks.

But I see no children among the bodies here.

They must've taken them…

My blood runs cold. A sickening lump forms in my throat at the thought of so many child slaves, and my stomach sours.

I set the rattle down where it was. Somehow, it seems wrong to desecrate this place any further. Rising, I take another look around this ruined place.

Elairie releases my hand and moves to the nearest bodies. She reaches out to close their eyes, mourning silently.

But even the small distance between us is agonizing, one more unbearable thing in a town full of pain. My spirit reaches for her, but I join in her efforts, moving from one pile of bodies to the next.

We'll have to check every street, search the rubble of every home…

The task spreads out before me, overwhelming me. Bodies fill my mind just as they fill the streets.

"What you're doing…" Geeran begins, "it's useless. This act, closing their eyes, is a comfort for you, not for them. If you want to honor them, do so by gaining the freedom of their families."

My heart clenches painfully, and a burst of anger surges through me.

Must he always be so harsh?

Was he kinder when Jaetus was around?

My curiosity is rewarded with a vision, of sorts. My spirit never leaves my body, yet it's there, painted clearly in my mind.

I see Geeran helping Jaetus mourn the loss of a parent. His arm drapes lovingly across Jaetus' shoulder as they sit on their bed. Jaetus turns, folding against Geeran's chest, weeping openly. Geeran places a tender kiss atop his partner's head.

The scene ends, and I struggle to piece that younger, compassionate Geeran together with the embittered result standing before me.

Nodding reluctantly, I sigh and stop seeking out the lost.

Elairie comes to stand at my side, closing the small rift between us. Her fingers lace through mine, and her touch fills me with confidence, making me think we might actually be able to do this.

"Ok. Let's stop here for a while," Elairie says. "Somewhere outside of town. We need to figure out this antidote. Geeran, when we do, you can deliver it back to Haedra. We probably shouldn't use the roads anymore, so we won't be able to take the cart anyway."

I consider her words, realizing that she means to travel straight through the forest and up the mountain. Working through what needs done, I say, "While we're trying to figure it out, would you mind packing bags for us? Only the essentials. We need to travel light."

He agrees, and we set to work.

Elairie and I recline against a large tree outside of town, letting the hill block the charred rubble and bodies from view. Smoke swirls overhead, drifting on a wayward breeze.

But it doesn't sweep down to torment us.

Inspired by Kaistrum, of all people, we use divination to check the effectiveness of each recipe we formulate. On paper, we combine healing herbs to combat the poisons and quicken the spirit against the sedatives. We add various plant and animal components with defensive natures.

And for hours, failure is all our visions show us.

We alter amounts of various herbs, take some away altogether. Our minds cast themselves into the futures that could be, traveling the paths of each recipe.

We see people swallow our potion and fall to their knees, eyes bleeding. We watch them wither slowly in their beds. We see them continue as Slaves, slaughtering their families and friends at their Master's bidding regardless of our potions.

But then, we formulate a recipe that calls for our blood. Just as the Blood Magic calls for the Master's blood.

And finally, with half the day gone, that recipe shows promise.

Divination reveals an Elf taking a few steps past the boundary set forth by their Master, nose bleeding and body trembling the whole way.

But they defy the Blood Magic.

We break from the vision, and Elairie circles that recipe. The wind slips through the branches overhead, bringing waves of smoke drifting down to us.

We push further into our visions, adjusting the recipe and retesting, recording every change.

But eventually, we perfect it.

The sun hangs on the horizon, casting long shadows across the world. Geeran sits near the fire at the center of our camp, and our bags perch near our bedrolls, ready for the morning.

A shiver of fear slips through me.

We'll be alone tomorrow…

I remind myself that we have a recipe, a potion that can guard against the Blood Magic.

Even if we fail, even if Gourmaht kills us and raises an army, General Haedra can use this to protect her soldiers and take him down.

I blow out a long breath.

Exhaustion falls upon me, tugging at my eyelids, weighing my arms down.

For half a heartbeat, I allow myself to marvel at the effort and endurance it must have taken Kaistrum to build the Blood Magic from scratch. Even with a starting point, it took us a full day to come up with an antidote.

My mind sags beneath the weight of all I've seen. The paths of the future blur together, an amorphous mass of people and death and blood.

But we have the recipe.

We just have to get our blood to Haedra. And maybe prevent another Blood War.

Gathering the last of my strength, I turn to Elairie. She nods, and we strip off our armor and jackets.

"Geeran?" I ask. "Could you bring us as many jars as you can carry?"

"Sure," he answers, but his brows knit themselves together.

I pull in a deep breath, heart galloping madly.

Elairie takes my hand as Geeran settles the jars on the ground beside us.

"Ready?" she asks.

I nod and release her hand.

She places a jar in the grass between us, and we take up our daggers.

The lines in Geeran's face carve themselves deeper. His lips part, but he doesn't question us. He merely stares in horror.

I turn from him, locking eyes with Elairie. She pulls in a deep, steadying breath. We place the points of our daggers on our wrists, and I nod.

Pain bursts through me as my blade cuts deep.

Even the wind quiets, and all I hear is my own teeth grinding together, my breaths hissing out between them. Taking Elairie's hand in mine, we press our wounds together, holding them over the open jar.

And our blood falls.

It gushes from us, filling the jar more quickly than I would have guessed.

Our blood mixes, swirling within the glass, and the fire and lightning aura around us burns brighter, sparks hotter. The jar glows between us with sparks and tongues of flame rising from it.

I gasp at the sight of it.

"It's beautiful…" Elairie whispers.

I look up to find her eyes shining, glowing with awe.

But Geeran stares on, face a mask of concern. He sees only blood, only deep gashes on our arms.

Deftly, he switches the full jar for an empty one, not letting a single drop go to waste. But even this won't be enough.

With my free hand, I motion for him to prepare a third jar.

He caps the first, shaking his head. "That's a lot of blood. Shouldn't you pace yourselves? Rest. Give it a day and do more then?"

I shake my head. "There's no time. This has to be done now."

Reluctantly, he switches the jar for a new one, and we dig our daggers deeper, renewing the wounds to get this over with.

Geeran gasps, then rushes to the cart for salves and clean linens, already preparing to heal us.

We'll certainly need it.

We fill the third jar, then switch it for a fourth.

I grow dizzy, barely hearing Geeran's protests. But this is the last jar we need. Sweat beads on my forehead as crimson flows from us, filling the glass to the brim.

My head lolls against the tree trunk as I disentangle my arm from Elairie's. I grab a cloth from Geeran, pressing it against my wrist, and she does the same, bumping my arm in the process. I glance at her and find her far paler than usual.

Testing my limits, I concentrate on the cut on my arm, push healing energy toward the gash as Geeran opens salves. My skin tingles, pricking as it tries to close. Blood stops soaking through the cloth.

Maybe I'm healing...

Or maybe I'm out of blood.

I chuckle drowsily, and Geeran stares at me, eyes wide.

He nods at my arm, and I pull the linen free. A single rivulet of blood drips from my wrist, but the cut has mostly closed.

Geeran's mouth falls open. "But you're so weak now..."

Elairie pulls the cloth from her arm only to find the deep gash no longer weeps. Not a single drop of blood falls from her wound, and the edges of her skin meet, though not fully stitched back together.

Fog fills my mind, and the world grows dark as my eyes fall shut. I force them open, and the stunned expression on Geeran's face reminds me of something.

"I had a vision without leaving," I say.

"What?" Geeran's brows come together. "How?"

"Don't know. Just happened," I say.

My words feel off-kilter, slanted somehow. They droop under their own weight as they drag themselves across my lips. "I could still see everything here. Just played out... in my mind."

I shrug, head falling back against the tree.

Elairie drops her head to my shoulder. "Hm," is all she says as she tears the antidote recipe from her drawing book. She hands it to Geeran, saying, "This one."

Then, she rips out the Blood Magic recipe and holds it up, out of Geeran's view. She sets the paper ablaze, and we watch it burn.

I reach out to the flames, fingers dancing in their warmth. The ashes fall around us, then drift away on a gentle breeze.

Quietly, Geeran spreads salve over our arms and wraps them. He takes the book, the blood, and the salves, casting nervous glances over his shoulder as he loads them into the cart. His eyes stray toward us often as he makes dinner, as he stacks our morning rations and a tonic by our packs.

"Can you walk to the fire?" he asks. "Can you eat?"

He rushes over, offering Elairie a hand to pull her up. She leans but doesn't fall. Geeran pulls me to my feet and guides us to sit near the fire.

He shoves food into our hands, and we eat in silence. Afterward, I pull Elairie against me, letting our aura fend off the chills that the fire just can't chase away.

Sleep tries to claim me, tries to pull my eyelids low.

But Elairie speaks, and I force my eyes open.

"Kaistrum's aura was strange," she mumbles. "It was like… the darkest water I've ever seen. And it had crystals of black ice floating in it. Not just a color haze, like most auras."

We sit quietly, and my muddled mind tries to make sense of all we saw in that cave.

"You know," Elairie whispers, "even his Generals were slaves."

Geeran leans forward, intrigued.

"Really?" I ask. The word comes out whole, and I realize it's the first thing I've said that wasn't slurred.

Elairie nods. "Didn't trust *anyone*. He made them drink the potion first and commanded them to never betray him."

My blood runs cold, but I wonder.

What made him so paranoid?

"He made more Blood Magic after that, and they added some of their blood as well. Each General had their own potion for their own slaves." Elairie's thumb moves back and forth over my forearm as she speaks. "But there was more of his blood in it than theirs. Every slave answered to him, first and foremost."

"Did you know that?" Geeran asks me.

I shake my head. "I never met Kaistrum. I didn't know he'd be able to command me too. Traimon gave me the potion when I was a baby, so I don't really remember it."

Pulling in a deep breath, Elairie tells us more of what she learned in our vision, today. "Each General had their own second-in-command too. That's why there were so many Masters, why it was so hard to eradicate them all. It was a whole hierarchy. But *all* would answer to Kaistrum."

I shudder.

I was more of a slave than I ever realized. How many people could have controlled me?

After a burdensome silence, Geeran sets up a ward, then another smaller one inside it.

Though sluggish, Elairie and I put up wards of our own within Geeran's, lacing them with fear for good measure. We crawl into our little bed as Geeran stokes the fire and throws a blanket over the horse.

"Why didn't we bring pillows?" I mumble.

Elairie snuggles into my arms, pressing against me. The ground beneath the head of our bedrolls slowly sprouts more and more grass, growing comfortable.

But I'm not doing it.

My brows furrow.

I mutter, "Earth magic, huh?"

"Guess so," she answers.

And my eyes fall shut for the night.

***

The diluted sunlight of early winter fills the camp as we eat our breakfast. Geeran teaches us to shield ourselves from visions, but we say little else. Looming goodbyes stifle the conversations we might have had.

I hardly notice what I eat, mind awash with all that lies ahead. Alone time with Elairie. Prying eyes. Hills and mountains and charred ghost towns.

My nerves wind tight, and my stomach drops. Swallowing back the last bites of my food, I marvel at how easy our journey has been thus far.

With a sigh, I look to Geeran. He and Elairie have already finished their food. They sit, waiting for me.

I nod slowly, trying to come to terms with it all.

We rise, and Elairie and I pull on our packs.

Geeran approaches, eyes soft and brows carving deep lines in his forehead. He cups my cheek with one hand, cups Elairie's with his other hand. "Be cautious," he says. "In everything you do."

A tear glimmers at the corner of his eye, trembling in the sunlight. "Scavenge everything you can and keep a shield up. Hide whenever possible and don't overexert yourselves."

We nod, and a tear slides over Elairie's cheek.

My throat grows tight.

"There are some feathers and claws from the Owlbears in one of the packs," I say, forcing the words out. "Could you give them to Oran and Kraimin for me?"

In case I don't make it back...

I try to swallow the lump in my throat, but it sticks in place.

"Of course," Geeran answers.

He pulls us into an embrace. My heart threatens to shatter, and Elairie chokes out a sob.

Gods... What if I never see him again?

The thought hits just a little too hard. I start to crack and crumble, but Geeran pulls away.

"Avaencery is depending on you two, but I have faith in you," he says, and though his voice is quiet, I feel his words in my bones.

He turns from us, and Elairie wraps her arms around my waist. I can almost hear his old bones creaking as he climbs up onto the bench of the cart. He rides back in the direction from whence we came, frightening a flock of blackbirds from their treetop perches.

Elairie and I turn to face the mountains, spread out in the distance like menacing sentinels. I take her hand as we plunge into the cold forest.

***

Twigs crunch and pebbles shift beneath my feet as we walk in the shadow of a cliff. The trees atop it loom over us, and darkness plays beneath their boughs. The wind whips through them, screaming, laughing.

But at the foot of the cliff, an injured rabbit lies. My heart twists at the sight of its mangled legs, and I lift it from the rocky ground.

"Sorry, little buddy," I whisper.

And I snap its neck.

Elairie doesn't flinch, just offers to clean it while I make a fire. We stop to eat, savoring the meat we can pick from the tiny creature. We save some for dinner, stowing it in our packs and trusting the cold air to keep it good for us.

The shadows shift as the sun dips in the sky, and our trek wears on us. Every step is too loud. Every breath too large a cloud. Every twig snapping underfoot seems to scream out, to call Gourmaht down upon us.

My heart pounds, and my eyes dart from one shadow to another, certain that I'll find someone, some dark figure, lurking, waiting to kill us. My skin prickles with anticipation, and my stomach churns.

As the darkness builds, we push through thorn bushes laden with berries into a clearing at the base of a hill. Heads turning, seeking a threat, we fill our bellies with berries and the remainder of our rabbit.

Without batting an eye, Elairie carves a hollow in the side of the hill. My jaw drops at her mastery of Earth Magic, so deft, so soon.

The hairs on the back of my neck stand on end as we climb inside, turning our backs on the outside world. I spin back around, certain someone will be there, ready to attack.

But I find no one.

Before anyone can stumble upon us, we put up wards and lace them with fear. I pull Elairie into my arms, hoping my heart will slow soon.

Chapter 22
Elairie

My body aches from another day's hike, and the chill of winter settles into my bones. Viatlow's Pass looms ahead, with sheer cliffs rising on either side.

Darkness dances in the pass, but the screaming winds don't reach us in the depths. The first snow of the season descends, and night threatens to consume us.

"Should we stop for the night?" I shout.

But the winds screech high above, drowning out my words.

I reach out to the magic around me, carving a small depression in the rocky cliff to one side, then draw Beluroan's attention with a gesture.

He nods, and we carve the hollow deeper. I tunnel inward, and he shores it up with columns when I widen the cave. We set out our bedding, divvy up the remnants of our berries and a couple of squirrels we snared last night.

I stare out at the falling snow, shivering, wishing we had something to burn. But we'll have no fire tonight, only our aura.

My thoughts turn bleak as I realize that we'll have no snares out tonight either. Already, the snow is piling up, and we've seen no trails since lunch. I swallow a bite of squirrel, and my stomach drops.

We'll have to break into our dried rations, tomorrow.

I try to keep myself from counting out our rations, from counting out the days we can survive on them. There's nothing for it now.

Beluroan and I sit on our makeshift bed, and I nibble at my food, trying to make it last. I close my eyes, savoring the taste.

A terrible screech echoes through the pass, jolting me. It reverberates through the stone, batters my ears.

Somewhere out there, just above the pass, a griffin soars, defying the storm.

A chill sweeps through me.

They don't hurt Elves…

Usually.

It's probably fine.

But my thoughts do little to reassure me.

I finish my last bite and press myself to Beluroan's side. He wraps an arm around me, and darkness rims my vision. In an instant, our spirits desert our bodies, soaring across Avaencery, all the way back to Kaern.

Blurred people sit before us, gathered at a large round table in the Patrol Outpost. Haedra and Daercaht, the Vairsun Representative, shine in crystal clear detail.

Did Beluroan push through their shield? Or is this another accident?

Briefly, I marvel at just how deeply I've underestimated us.

A thick fog swirls around the room, and all the faces I don't know seem to float beneath murky water. I see the colors of their hair, all shades of pastel, see where every feature on their face is, but the definite shape eludes me.

Words fly around me, garbled and slurred, but their tones are clear enough. Anger simmers just beneath the surface, and when it ebbs, desperation lingers in its wake.

I strain to pick order from the chaos, to shift the sounds into words. Slowly, they pull themselves together, and I catch a phrase here, a word there.

The Elf next to Daercaht is the first to speak intelligibly, "What are we to do then? We've been here most of the day and have yet to come to a decision."

Someone next to Haedra speaks up. "We could *use* their abilities. Blessed Ones can accomplish things we could never even imagine. Abyss below, they gave us an antidote for the Blood Magic. *In one day.*"

My stomach drops, and Beluroan's hand tightens on mine.

They're deciding what to do… about us?

We're helping them. What else is there to do?

Across from Haedra, someone snarls, "Yes, but to do that, they had to find the recipe for the Blood Magic. They know how to make it."

My stomach drops.

We do. We wouldn't make it, but we do know how…

In my mind, I can see that paper burning, see the ink upon the page curling and turning to ash.

But I know the words it held.

"And we all know what happened with Kaistrum," Haedra says. The flickering candlelight sends shadows darting across her pale green eyes.

I shiver, remembering the insanity that danced in his eyes.

But we're not like Kaistrum. We won't make the Blood Magic.

"When that fool of a fortune teller killed Vaerlin," she says, "Kaistrum lost it. Sure, Blessed Ones are great. *When they're together.* If one of them dies, there's no way to know what the other would do. We can't trust them."

Silence falls on the room and fills my heart. Realization settles over me, heavy and stifling.

Kaistrum was a Blessed One? He was… like us?

"And they're even more powerful than Kaistrum and Vaerlin ever were," Haedra says, voice cold as ice. With a scowl, she adds, "And if they ever make their own Blood Magic, we'd need the blood of the Gods to make an antidote for theirs."

A woman with blurry robin's egg hair whispers, "She's right." Her voice wavers as she admits, "We checked."

Another voice assaults my ears, but I don't look at them, can't look at them. I stare at the blurred table as they carry on around me.

"Then, we protect them. Make sure what happened with Kaistrum and Vaerlin doesn't happen to them. Simple enough."

Another voice. "We could still reap the benefits of their powers… with limited risk."

So, they want to lock us away and use us?

"But there would still be risk. Accidents happen," another says.

"Well, yes, there would be risk involved. But we could manage it, surely. How hard could it possibly be to keep two Elves alive?" comes the reply.

"What happens when they get old? One could die far earlier than the other. There's no preventing that."

Haedra stands and slams her hands down on the table, and I jump. Strands of her white hair fall forward over her beautiful face. They almost hide the darkness twisting her features.

"You didn't see what Kaistrum could do!" she yells, voice shaking with fear and fury.

Silence rings in my ears, and my stomach roils.

Voice dropping to a sinister whisper, she says, "It took nine of us to bring him down. Even then, only two of us survived. We were the best of the best. General Droucair led us, his eight strongest warriors and casters, to Kaistrum's doorstep. And we *barely* succeeded."

She slams one fist on the table, making me jump again, and drops her voice lower. "Barely."

The scene plays out in my mind, though my spirit never leaves Kaern, a vision within a vision.

They snuck into Kaistrum's stolen Patrol Outpost at night, killing anyone they came across, slave and Master alike. The Blood War demanded it if there was to be an end.

The nine of them started on the lower floor, quiet as death as they explored each and every room.

Hunting.

At long last, they found their quarry, lying in bed on the third floor. They encountered no wards, and their nerves told them it was a trap.

But it didn't matter.

Out of options, they had to try. And surely, nine of them could handle him.

They approached his bed, and he turned to face them, sitting up. Three candles guttering on the nightstand cast tricky shadows over the room. An eerie smile crossed his rugged face.

I shudder at the sight of it.

In an instant, chaos ensued.

Haedra narrates this vision for us, explaining to the Representatives exactly what happened.

Because they don't see it like we do.

"He looked at us, really looked, and his eyes chilled me to the bone," she says, and I feel the shiver that rolls down her spine.

And in my head, I see it all.

Eyes like the darkest depths of the most ominous forest wrap tendrils of wicked vines around me, threatening to hold me down until the earth consumes me, piece by piece.

"We rushed him, even as he rose from his bed. We knocked him down, all nine of us." Even in the retelling, Haedra's fear reaches out to the Representatives.

"We fell with him… though only a couple of us were still alive. It happened so fast… I don't even know what he did first," she says.

But I know.

Divination tells me *exactly* how he killed them. He pulled the water from their bodies, dried them out and turned their blood to stone. He pulled the air from their lungs until they collapsed.

I shudder. When we faced the wolves, I did all of that except for turning blood to stone.

Could I do that? Am I capable?

The answer comes to me immediately.

Yes.

I can do that and more.

My mind wanders over what I can do, and divination informs me that Beluroan and I have already gained the remaining forms of magic. We just haven't accidentally used them.

In my mind, I see the bodies of Haedra's comrades lying atop Kaistrum. He struggles to push them off, but the stone in their veins made them heavy. He hadn't accounted for that. Nor had he realized he wouldn't be able to target all nine of his adversaries at one time.

Severed from Vaerlin, he was no more powerful than he was the day she died. He was stagnant.

Haedra's sole surviving ally held Kaistrum's head back on the pillow, fighting searing pain as Kaistrum set the man's hands ablaze. Haedra reached down to her side, drew her dagger, and slit Kaistrum's throat. He held her gaze as the life left him.

"Thank you," he whispered, barely audible, and she shivered atop him.

The mini-vision ends, but Haedra continues speaking.

"I tended Raetor's hands as well as I could, but…" she trails off, eyes unfocused. "He still only has minimal use of his fingers. He's covered in scars. The rest of them…"

A few tears fall down her face, dripping onto the table before her. She hangs her head before continuing. "Their skin was so dry and brittle, stretched taut across their bones. Their veins were full of rock. You could see every single one, like gnarled tree branches. They bled through their noses, but it turned to little pebbles."

Her voice falls to a whisper. "I couldn't even close their eyelids. They were so dry… They just flaked off at my touch."

A wave of revulsion moves through me.

Every time she pauses, silence rings through the room. No one else dares to speak, to breathe.

"And he did all of that… In an instant. I don't scare easily, but I was terrified of him. No one else has *ever* scared me like that. Until I met Elairie and Beluroan, until Geeran told me all they can do."

My mouth hangs open.

But she goes on, "*Already*, they're more powerful than Kaistrum and Vaerlin ever were. They can do everything he could *at his peak*. They just don't realize it yet."

Finally, someone else speaks up. "But why?"

Slumping back down into her seat, Haedra says, "It took me a while to figure it out." She shakes her head.

"My best guess is that Kaistrum and Vaerlin were accepted by others before they met. Elairie and Beluroan weren't, so when they finally found someone, they latched on. And the thing with Blessed Ones is, the stronger their bond, the more they give themselves over to it, the more powerful they are."

She takes a deep breath.

"So if one of them dies… The loss would devastate them far more than it did him."

Another long hush falls over the room. Snakes wind and coil in my belly. Beluroan squeezes my hand as we wait for them to decide our fate.

Daercaht breaks the silence, clearing his throat. "Well, no matter what, if one of them dies, we kill the other. We'll have to. I just can't imagine how."

Another voice says, "And if they survive this battle with Gourmaht?"

A collective sigh fills the room. A few blurred faces seem to look out the nearby window. The sun is long gone, and the moon rises higher and higher.

My stomach clenches.

But Daercaht says, "Shall we table the discussion for another day? It may prove invaluable to clear our heads. This is a difficult subject, after all."

Nods all around the table. The Representatives rise and file out. But Haedra lingers. She leans forward, elbows on the table, and drops her head into her hands. Strands of white spill out between her fingers.

Beluroan and I soar back to our little cave in Viatlow's Pass, stunned silent. Staring out at the snowflakes that drift ever downward, I try to piece my thoughts together, but they slip through my hands.

Eventually, Beluroan says, "I'm not sure if it's good that we saw that or bad. I hadn't even meant for the vision to happen. I was just wondering if anything else was going to mess us up."

"And then, the vision inside it, seeing them kill Kaistrum…" I shudder as it washes over me again. Dumbfounded, I say, "He was a Blessed One. He was like us."

Silence falls over us again. Outside, owls hoot and the griffin screeches again. But Beluroan and I merely sigh.

"Why do the Gods keep creating us, if *that's* what we're capable of?" Beluroan asks.

"I don't know." Shrugging, I say, "Maybe we should ask them."

The moment we agree, our spirits soar up to the Great Valley. No effort required, no concentration.

My heart falters.

Are we as dangerous as Haedra says?

The Gods wait for us, lined up in the Valley. They greet us with solemn nods.

"Now that you know," Jemarie begins, "are you happier for it?"

In a whisper, Beluroan says, "I wouldn't quite put it that way."

"Do you regret this knowledge? We did try to protect you from this. Distractions will only hinder you now."

So they're the ones that blocked everything around Kaistrum.

"I think I'm glad," I say. "We know exactly what's at stake now. We know just how careful we have to be."

"So," Doorma says, amber eyes aglow. "You had a question for us?"

After a moment of hesitation, Beluroan asks, "Why? If you know the devastation we can cause, and you clearly do, why keep making Blessed Ones?"

Again, it's Doorma who answers, whispering softly into our minds, "Because without you and other Blessed Ones, the world is doomed. Pairs like you offer at least some glimmer of hope." Her five tails swish sadly through the air. "Without you, there would be no chance of defeating Gourmaht. At the absolute least, the Dwarves would be killed."

Nepiter's voice crackles out at us, "Then, under the rule of Gourmaht's daughter, either the Elves or Humans would die out. She would lead the Elves to the far continent, and one way or another, a species would perish."

"Just like the Sirens and Fairies," Luxitore whispers mournfully, and despite the low volume, it sends shivers through the earth.

The flowering vines that twine throughout his stone body ripple, and the blossoms shift from bright, warm colors to ice blue and purple, crisp mint green and even white.

"Sirens and Fairies?" I ask, recalling the mention of them in a scroll.

With a great sigh that fills my head, Doorma says, "We may as well tell you. Keeping information from Blessed Ones has rarely aided us in the past."

Nodding sagely, Jemarie breathes out. "Long ago, well before the Humans found Avaencery and made themselves known to the Elves and the Dwarves, there were two additional species. The Sirens and the Fairies."

"The Sirens," she continues, "enjoyed luring the Humans from the shorelines and ships, down to the watery depths of the ocean. The Humans grew tired of the Sirens' attacks. So many drowned…"

And I see them, dragged beneath the water, sucking in water and flailing. Held under by the Sirens.

A hush falls over the Great Valley. The Gods' expressions turn dour, and horror shines in their eyes.

Baereen picks up where Jemarie left off. "The Humans fashioned special devices to shield their ears from the Sirens' songs. They hunted the Sirens and hauled them up from the ocean but didn't dare go near their catch. They hung the Sirens in nets until they dried out."

Barely audible, Doorma and Jemarie both say, "It was awful."

Luxitore says, "They killed them all." My bones shake with his anger.

My mind fills with images of the Sirens, beings which look a great deal like Jemarie. Long, shining tails and slick black skin over their Elven torsos. Luminescent eyes and flowing hair. Their ears are different, though. The points extend further, rather like fins.

I see them strung up by their tails alone or crowded in large nets, dying. Webbed fingers claw out, reaching for water. Gills flap futilely on their ribs.

Hesitant, Beluroan asks, "What about the Fairies?"

"Their end was less dramatic," Doorma tells us. "A whisper rather than a scream."

In a soft voice befitting the tale, Jemarie says, "The Fairies skittered to the edges of human society. Each advancement the humans made took them further from the world of magic the Fairies loved so much."

I try to keep my mind from wandering into another vision. I can't bear to witness another extinction, but little images flicker through my mind, regardless.

Small, flying beings, which otherwise look exactly like the humans, huddle in groups wearing tattered rags. They beg for scraps as the humans walk by, unflinching, or ride past in carts which move without horses.

"The Fairies slowly died off. Most starved. Some tricked the wrong Humans and were killed for it. A few were captured, kept in cages as pets. Robbed of their dignity and desire to live, they stopped reproducing. They gave up." Jemarie's words fade in intensity, until they disappear completely.

"We couldn't lose anymore." Doorma says. "Kaistrum and Vaerlin were supposed to make the Blood Magic to—"

"You *wanted* the Blood Magic?" Beluroan cuts her off, outraged. "Why?!"

"It was meant to heal the rift forming in the Elven people and prevent a second Dwarven War. Neither species would have survived," Baereen says, matter-of-factly.

"Decades of enslavement… so much bloodshed, so many deaths… All of that… And you wanted it?" Beluroan asks, bewildered.

I squeeze his hand.

"That wasn't how it was supposed to go," Doorma says, voice pleading as it floods our minds. "The odds of the world following that path were astronomical. Taenram was so inept in every way, there were only seven possible paths, out of millions, in which he would have decided to try to kill them, and only three where he actually killed one or both of them."

"Who?" Beluroan asks.

And then we see him. Yet again, a scene we shouldn't be able to see plays out in our heads.

A 15-year-old Elf of mixed blood creeps into their bedroom. Kaistrum and Vaerlin sleep soundly, curled tightly against one another.

Taenram's dark purple hair looks almost black, casting strange shadows over his face in the guttering candlelight. He sneaks up to the bed, dagger drawn. His pale skin shines with sweat. At the side of the bed, he hesitates, even brushes Vaerlin's soft yellow hair out of her face.

She seems to glow, white skin glistening in the moonlight that reaches through the window. Kaistrum looks clean and healthy, a far cry from the shattered man we saw create the Blood Magic.

A smile spreads across his sleeping face as he tightens his arm around Vaerlin's waist. Their aura matches the one that surrounds Beluroan and me.

Taenram gets closer, pushing past the fear that held him captive. In a quick fluid movement, he slices Vaerlin's throat. Her huge baby blue eyes spring open in shock and pain, slowly letting go of life.

Behind her, Kaistrum sits straight up and looks from Taenram to Vaerlin, taking in the blood gushing from his beloved.

"No. No, no, no…" he whispers. Frantically, he turns Vaerlin onto her back, tries to hold the blood in, tries to heal her.

But it's too late.

She lost so much blood, so quickly.

Vaerlin tries to speak, but only gurgles.

Kaistrum leans over her, kisses her lips softly. "You can't go," he mutters against her lips, voice cracking. "I love you. Please… don't leave me."

But she's nearly gone.

Her body hangs limp in his arms. Sobs shake him, and his agony reaches out, seeping into my heart.

I nearly double over beneath its weight. I feel the moment Vaerlin's soul departs, feel the ripping sensation within Kaistrum. His mind shatters as death tears her away.

Kaistrum turns his attention on Taenram. In a split second, Taenram bursts into flames. White and purple lightning arcs over his skin, and he becomes the personification of the aura of Blessed Ones.

He screams, spins, bats at his clothes, his hair. The young Elf falls to the floor, writhing in pain.

And then, slowly, he goes still.

I shudder and look to Kaistrum, only to find him changed. Gone are the lightning and fire of his Blessed aura, replaced by dark water and black chunks of ice swirling on the air around him.

His expression darkens.

Guards rush into the room, alerted by the screams, and one by one, Kaistrum takes them down. Rage fills him, flowing out in his magic.

They don't stand a chance.

I watch in horror, shaking my head, desperate for it to end. My heart twists as another guard falls.

I can't watch any more.

And with that, the vision closes.

Gasping, breaths rough and ragged, I ask, "Why didn't you tell Taenram what would happen?"

Nepiter answers, "He hadn't strengthened his magic enough to hold a connection with us. He was young, and he hadn't worked at his gift. He saw the potential for darkness in their hearts but didn't look further. He didn't realize *he* was the catalyst."

"Had he not done it," Baereen says, "the world would be a very different place. There would have been no Blood War. The Blood Magic would have been created but would have only been used to prevent the second Dwarven War. Kaistrum and Vaerlin weren't fond of it. They were only making it out of necessity."

"What if he'd killed Kaistrum instead?" I ask.

The Gods pause, glancing back and forth amongst themselves.

Luxitore finally answers, saying only, "It would have been far worse."

"Not as bad as the second Dwarven War would have been, but far worse than the Blood War." Flames drip from Nepiter's mouth as he speaks. "We were all relieved that, if one of them was going to die, it was Vaerlin."

"Why not warn them? Surely they were strong enough to host a vision," I say, daring to accuse the Gods of negligence.

"Yes," Jemarie begins, "but they would have been even more reluctant to make the Blood Magic. One way or another, it had to be made and employed. And it is always so difficult for mortals to see the bigger picture."

Jemarie's tone is compassionate, but with each word, she loses patience. "Many died, but a great deal more would have perished without the intervention offered by the Blood Magic."

"The *intervention* offered by the Blood Magic? It offered slaughter!" Beluroan shouts, red-faced. He steps forward, motioning angrily with his free hand.

To my surprise, the Gods jump, shaken by his fury.

Voice dropping to a sinister whisper, he continues, "It offered torture and mayhem and bloodshed to the sickest, most depraved Elves in existence."

The terrible memory vision of Beluroan being forced to beat his own Mother senseless fills my mind, quickly followed by images of the night his parents were killed.

His Mother lying there, holding his hand as they both faded, he into unconsciousness and her into the bittersweet embrace of death.

The snarl on his Master's face.

"You have to understand," Doorma pleads, "this was a worst-case scenario. It had only the slimmest chance of becoming a reality."

Stepping forward, Nepiter says, "In any case, it had to be done. Whether you like the life you've been given or the world you were born into, it is still better than that which you could have had. True, it is messier than we would have liked. Optimistically, it wouldn't have been necessary to create the two of you, at all. There are risks associated with *your* creation, as well. That you never thought to look into it does not make it less so."

I recoil from his words with a gasp, and my heart falters.

Of course, they didn't want us.

It means the world was about to fall apart. No one wants that.

But my heart still twists painfully.

Even the Gods didn't want us.

Lightning arcs from Nepiter's wings to the ground, burning the grass beneath him as he becomes more and more agitated.

"You have a purpose though," he says. "And that is to clean up the mess into which the world has fallen. That you do not see the full breadth of the situation at hand is regrettable, and I welcome you to venture through the alternate paths the world could have travelled."

The flames which comprise Nepiter's body intensify, burning brighter than the sun, and I blink against it, raising an arm to shield myself. His coal black eyes grow darker by comparison.

In a final burst of fiery light, he adds, "I guarantee you'll not like what you see."

With a sigh, Beluroan shakes his head, admitting defeat in the face of an angry God. "I'm sorry. It just hardly seems fair that so many should have to suffer and die."

I take a step forward, sliding an arm around Beluroan's waist. He slips his arm around my shoulders.

"Fair?" Jemarie asks. "The decisions of mortals, our decisions, the world as a whole, none of these things are governed by what is fair."

Tired of our questions, her eyes blaze a purer white than I've ever seen. "All these things are ruled by necessity. Nothing else. If you can't accept that, then there is little I can do for you. And it leaves me little hope for you when it comes time to make hard decisions. Sacrifices are necessary and inevitable."

I nod sadly, and Beluroan does too.

"We know," I say.

For us to get to Gourmaht, innocent Elves, enslaved by his Blood Magic, will likely be killed. There's no way around it. He'll use them as fodder, soaking up the blows of our daggers and our magic, attempting to tire us out.

"It is not all so terrible." Doorma says, voice gentle. "Amid struggle and strife, you have been given a gift. You share a bond truer and purer than that of anyone else alive. That is a magnificent thing."

Pulling me to face him, Beluroan leans his head against mine. My heart beats a frantic pace in my chest, but the connection with him slows it, eases the tension.

After a long moment, he whispers, "That is worth everything."

Our eyes lock, and I smile up at him.

Voice overflowing with warmth, Doorma says, "Until we meet again."

Our spirits rejoin our bodies, and we embrace. Beluroan's warmth soothes the aches in my heart and mind.

And I don't want to think, don't want to feel the pain of the Fairies or the Sirens. *This* is all I want to feel, the gift we've been given.

It comes with so many strings attached, so many responsibilities. But the heat swirling around us, the fire and the lightning flickering through the air, makes it worth it.

And it's all we have.

Our lips meet, and Beluroan's hands tangle in my hair. His fingers slide down to my neck, caressing my skin. My hands tug at his armor, his jacket, and he frees me of mine.

He lays me down and kisses my neck. He pulls my shirts off and kisses soft skin, eliciting a soft moan from my lips. I pull him up, claiming his mouth with mine.

Rolling him onto his back, I work feverishly at his clothes. His boots and armor slow me down, but he uses the time wisely, sitting up to kiss my breasts. I gasp, and my hands still for just a moment.

Desire burns through me, and I strip the remnants of my clothing away.

Flipping me to my back, Beluroan kisses my neck, my breasts, my stomach. My thighs. His fingers dip inside, working me to a fever pitch, and I let my hands roam over him. His breathing grows shallow, and he kisses me, rough with hunger.

Kneeling between my legs, he grasps my hips, pulling me close as he dives inside. Our bodies writhe. Our lips join, crushing together. I gasp, and my hands dig into his back, pulling him deeper and deeper.

"Elairie…" he whispers, ragged breath hot against my neck. "I love you."

Between moans of pleasure, I manage to answer. "I love you too, Beluroan."

We move faster and faster, bringing each other to new heights, throwing ourselves into this. I pull him deep one final time, and we fall to pieces. Gasping for air as my insides explode, I arch against him.

Beluroan collapses atop me, dropping his head on my chest. Sharp breaths fill him, shake him.

My heart flutters.

Beluroan rolls us onto our sides, and I nestle in as close as I can get. My lips find his chest, his neck, his collarbone.

Soft, fuzzy warmth seeps through me, tugging my eyelids low. Beluroan plants a soft kiss on my forehead, then tips my head back to look into my eyes. His lips find mine, soft and tender.

I fit our bodies together like puzzle pieces, and my heart slows its frantic pace. Our aura sizzles, gentles to a warm simmer, sending us gently into the land of dreams.

Chapter 23

Beluroan

After breakfast, I scour the map, outlining a route. "We should head west, around this mountain here. It's a small one, thankfully."

"What?" Elairie says. "Why not just go through this pass? We could refill our water at the lake. If it isn't frozen."

She's never been this far north.

"No, we should give that lake a wide berth. That's Aurujin's Lake."

"So? Who's Aurujin?"

"Well, more like, 'what' is Aurujin. It isn't sentient. It just imitates. No one really knows what it is though. Some sort of water and ice creature. Anyone who ventures too close to that lake…" I leave the words hanging in the air, searching for words.

"They don't survive?" she guesses.

"Most don't. A handful have in the past, but they were never the same. They shut themselves away until they died of starvation or thirst."

Elairie shivers, nodding as she says, "Okay. We'll go around."

We set off, heading northwest, as planned. By lunch, menacing storm clouds roll in, blocking out the sun. Shadows hover in the trees, hiding our path.

We should've checked the weather before we set out. We could've stayed in that cozy little cave for another day.

But weather didn't even cross my mind.

My thoughts keep slipping back up to the Great Valley, to Kaern. The Gods are on eggshells about our existence. Haedra and the Representatives might kill us once we've exhausted our usefulness.

What are we supposed to do after dealing with Gourmaht? If we're successful.

What if one of us dies?

A wave of sickness sweeps through me at the thought of losing Elairie.

Would I really be like Kaistrum?

I don't have the stomach to check, but deep down, I know I'd be just as insane. Maybe not in the same way. Or so I hope.

Desperate for a distraction, I ask, "Shall we see if Haedra administered the antidote yet?"

We check in, minds splitting to show us that place without losing sight of this one. But what we find surprises me.

She certainly put the antidote to use.

Already, her forces battle Gourmaht's army of slaves in towns nearby. Most soldiers lack aura sensing, completely oblivious to the black streaks through cloudy grey auras, the signs that denote rank. Slaves and Masters perish side by side.

But no more fall to the Blood Magic.

The town that hosts their battle lies empty, evacuated save for those who wished to fight.

I breathe a sigh of relief.

We slip from the vision, and I smile.

The mountains claim my full attention once more as we trudge through the snow, but my stomach drops. Panic slithers through my veins. We've meandered off track, heading north rather than northwest.

How far are we from the lake?

Thunder splits the sky, and the storm threatens to break over us. We push on, but I scan the cliffs, the hills, searching for anywhere to make camp and wait out the weather.

My eyes dart around, skirting over bones and talon marks. A griffin screeches overhead, pushing us from its territory.

As we hike further, a torrent of snow pours over us, obscuring everything beyond my reach. I grip Elairie's hand tight to keep her close. The wind screams, lashing the snow against my face. I squint against it but see only white as we stumble along. Only our aura keeps frostbite at bay.

We burst through a cluster of trees into a clearing coated in a thick blanket of snow. The air is motionless here, though it whistles angrily in the trees behind us, through the mountain peaks above.

Snow falls peacefully to land on a frozen lake.

My stomach drops, and a sick feeling creeps through me.

Aurujin's lake.

"This is bad," I whisper.

"We're here, aren't we? Where is it?" Elairie asks, words tumbling out in a panic. Her eyes dart around the clearing, searching.

"I don't know," I say. "But we need to leave."

A deep, husky voice coils around us, "But if you leave, you'll miss all the fun."

My heart stops.

I turn to find a man behind Elairie. He steps close, pressing himself to her back. His hands find her waist, and she freezes.

Silver-streaked black hair sweeps forward, tickling the top of her head. Vivid blue eyes sparkle against snow-white skin, untouched by the cold despite his bare chest beneath the open jacket.

But this isn't Aurujin's true form.

My blood boils as his hand snakes up to move Elairie's hair over one shoulder. He leans closer and whispers in her ear. "We could have *so* much fun."

Elairie tenses, free hand resting on one of her daggers.

"Get your hands off her," I snarl, pulling her away from this thing, spinning her to face him. *It*. I move between them, staring at the creature.

Aurujin's eyes shift to my face, taking me in, then it disappears as a cloud of snow bursts up from the ground, obscuring the creature. When the flurries land, it stares at us from a different body, a Fox Elf woman. A sheen of green sparkles in her black hair and her tight dress shows off lush umber skin.

Vivid blue eyes shine, the only thing unchanged from this creature's previous form.

Aurujin approaches me, sauntering, hips swaying. "Do you feel left out?" the creature whispers, voice smoky. It touches my neck, pressing large breasts against my chest.

"Don't touch me either," I hiss.

Elairie and I take a step back, away from this thing, and I lace our fingers together.

"So, that's how it is."

Aurujin disappears in another burst of snow. The cloud falls to its feet, revealing both forms, the mixed man and the Fox woman, holding hands.

As one, they say, "We can all play together, if that's what you want."

Elairie's other hand draws her dagger. "There are two of them now?" she asks in a panicked whisper.

"No, just one. The bodies are joined at the hands. It can't split," I say.

"Maybe it can," Elairie says. She reaches out, slashing at the joined hands.

Dark blue blood pours out, and it screams through both mouths. Chills sweep through me, and the piercing cry morphs into a roar.

A snowstorm erupts around Aurujin, and the dark shape of the two Elven bodies grows, changes. Slowly, the form of a large ice dragon materializes, silhouetted in the swirling snow.

The storm clears, and a stream of ice pours from the crystalline beast's mouth. Screams fill the air, and blue blood gushes from an immense gash on its side.

But the injury doesn't last.

The creature shifts its form, and ice crusts over it. The blood stops flowing, and the roars of pain morph into a sinister laugh. Light refracts through icy teeth, casting rainbows over the bleak landscape.

"Abyss below…"

Aurujin lashes out, gaping maw reaching for us.

Elairie and I throw up wards. They weave together, webs entwining. It takes only a heartbeat, quicker than ever before.

Aurujin's head bounces off the ward, and the beast staggers, dizzied by the unexpected blow.

But it regains composure quickly, attacking the ward in earnest. Little bits of web hang loose after each snarling bite. A few webs disintegrate completely.

But it gives us precious time to think.

How can we kill something that can just shapeshift to eliminate injuries?

If only Elairie's blade had gone straight through and split the beast in half...

Aurujin rears back, breathing icy water out over our ward and slashing with crystalline claws.

"Fire and lightning," Elairie suggests. "Neither of those mix well with water."

I call flames to my fingertips, let them build. Summoning more and more magic, I build a ball of flames in my palm. I launch it through the barrier, and it collides with Aurujin's head.

Ice melts, dripping, trickling to the ground.

The beast howls.

Vivid bolts of lightning erupt from each of Elairie's fingers, striking the creature in the heart. They glow and sparkle in the crystal body of the beast, moving from heart to head and back again. Tiny fissures form, and gas curls outward.

My heart hammers, and hope fills me. I pull fire magic to me, building another ball of flames in my hands.

But Aurujin slashes at the ward, sending bits of web flying. A hole opens over our heads, and gnashing jaws dip into our sanctuary.

Panic shoots through me, and we jump back. Teeth slash the air before us.

And Elairie stumbles, goes down. Her head hits the ground with a sickening thud, and my stomach plummets. The wind rushes out of me, and my jaw drops.

With a thought, I repair our wards and fall to my knees beside her. Blood gushes from her head, melting the snow, warming my knees. My heart lurches as I lean over her.

"No, no, no…" I say, voice breaking.

"Don't worry about me. I'm alright," Elairie whispers.

But I don't dare lift her head, and divination confirms my fear. Her skull is cracked.

"No… Please, just be still," I say, touching her cheek.

Fear slithers through me as her eyes flutter. Aurujin snarls overhead, demanding my attention.

But I focus on her, letting the wards do their job. I swallow nervously.

Panic builds in my gut, and I beg the Gods to let my magic be enough even without salves or potions. I pull forth all the magic I can, trying to ignore the roars of the beast, the sound of claws slashing at our ward.

I close my eyes, putting my hands to Elairie's cheeks, and push the healing magic into her. I urge it to close the crack in her skull, to weave the skin back together.

The blood stops pouring out, but her eyelids droop. Her breathing grows shallow, and her pulse weakens.

My heart lurches as her portion of the ward collapses around us, raining down in a shower of ethereal strands. They disappear on impact, and my heart drops into my boots.

My hands shake as I brush hair out of her face. Snow and blood soak her hair, her clothes, and I pour more healing magic into her, coursing it through her veins.

But her eyes close.

Aurujin laughs menacingly, ripping a hole in the new ward. And my mind splinters.

Rising to my feet, I spin to face the monstrous thing. I pull rock from the earth, encasing Aurujin's entire body in an instant.

Rage grips me, boiling my blood.

Lightning flows from me, curling from Aurujin's head to its tail, then out and right back in again. I whip it through the beast over and over.

And its screams spur me on.

My hands ball into fists, and I melt the stone around Aurujin. It tries to shapeshift again, tries to escape, but the molten rock oozes to coat its new body.

You'll find no escape from me…

The strands of Elairie's ward shimmer at my feet, materializing again, but only for a second. Shock spreads through me as I realize what I'm doing, what I'm becoming.

I can't be like Kaistrum…

I part the lava, dumping Aurujin to the ground. Shoving the molten rock outward, I leave it to solidify in the frigid air. Sizzling on the icy ground with all hair singed from its body, Aurujin stares at me in the form of the Fox Elf woman.

Voice firm, I ask, "Where's the nearest cave?"

I need to get Elairie out of this storm. Damn the griffin. Let it come. If it tries to hurt her, I'll destroy it.

Aurujin's hand lifts and points off to my left, west, in the direction of the pass that leads to Mount Hybar.

"Don't follow," I warn, voice hissing through gritted teeth.

Head shaking, Aurujin whispers, "No."

Steam rolls off umber skin in waves. Crisp blue eyes flutter closed for a long nap, and the thing collapses upon the icy ground.

Lifting Elairie, I dispel what remains of my ward and carry her toward the cave. Snow drifts slow my progress, and I growl under my breath. Flakes yet rain from the sky, obscuring my vision, but at long last, I find the cave.

Settling her on the rocks, I spread my bedroll, then move her onto it. I touch her cheek.

She's like ice…

My heart twists in my chest.

Retrieving her bedroll, I spread it over her. A lump forms in my throat as I gather more healing energy, pushing it into her with a touch.

I want to beg, to plead with the Gods to save her, to let her stay with me, but my voice catches in my throat.

I grip her hand as panic surges through my veins. A chasm opens inside me, threatening to swallow everything. Darkness rushes into my heart, and I sob.

Wake up, please.

I brush a hand across her cheek and lean over her. I kiss her lips, lean my forehead against hers.

"Please…" I croak. "I need you."

Dark lashes fan out over her cheeks, but they don't move, don't flutter open.

Panic surges through me, and it isn't all my own. The Gods rattle my heart, stuttering with fear in some distant corner of my mind.

Tears prick at the corners of my eyes, but the winter air freezes them on my cheeks. The heat of our aura doesn't thaw them.

Time stretches out before me, yawning like a great black abyss, and I send another burst of healing magic through her.

Her eyelids shift.

An ember of hope glows within me.

"Please, Elairie," I beg. A sob chokes me, shaking me as it rumbles through my chest.

Her hand moves, fingers flickering.

I grab her hand, lacing our fingers together.

Her eyes creep open, unfocused.

I choke out a sob and bow to kiss her lips, fingers trembling against her cheek.

The Gods sigh in my mind, sending out a whisper of warmth to flow through my veins, and the tension eases out of me.

She's safe.

Elairie whispers my name, voice sweet and soft. She touches my cheek, and I press my lips to hers.

My heart expands within my chest, and my voice breaks as I say, "I love you, Elairie. I love you so much."

"I love you too." With another kiss, she says, "Thank you."

I pull her up, crushing her against me. "Are you okay?" I choke out, voice thick with emotion.

Nodding, Elairie simply says, "I am. I'm fine." Her fingers dig into my back, holding on for dear life.

The sharp staccato beats of my heart slow, and I take joy in the warmth of her body pressed against mine. But there's too much stuff, too many layers stuck between us. In a rush, I push the bedroll off her and pull her close.

But it isn't enough.

She tears at her clothes, discarding armor and garments alike. Our aura burns around us, sparking and charging the air as I strip my jacket and shirt away. Our lips meld together, hungry and desperate.

But this isn't enough. I need to feel her, need to know that this is real, that she's here with me.

Our pants come off in a flurry of buttons and kicking legs, and I kneel between her legs, plunge deep into her. Nothing else matters. Only her.

Hearts hammering, lungs trying desperately to keep up, we move together. Elairie wraps her long, alabaster legs around me, pulling me deeper. Aching and desperate, we writhe. Fire builds within me, heavy and sweet.

Whimpering, she digs her nails into my back, raking them across my skin. Blood trickles down my spine, drips onto the bedroll, but it doesn't matter.

Our world burns around us.

She screams my name as her body quakes. I move faster, deeper, until I too find my release. I collapse atop her, panting, with my head on her chest, listening to her heartbeat.

Lying there, utterly spent, I breathe deeply and revel in the feel of her hands caressing my back. My eyelids droop, and I take another deep breath.

We roll onto our sides, and Elairie throws a leg over me. She wraps it around mine, pulling me closer. Her perfect, supple breasts press against my chest, and she trails her fingers up and down my spine, sending shivers through me.

She's here.

She's safe.

I tighten my arms, breathing in the wonderful scent of her, all citrus and spice. We drift off to sleep, warm and fuzzy as our aura simmers comfortably.

Chapter 24

Elairie

What's that sound?

Through slitted eyes, I stare at the approaching light of dawn beyond our cave. I revel in the warmth of Beluroan's strong arms around me, slowly forgetting the noise that woke me. Snuggling closer to him, I pull in a deep breath.

But the noise comes again.

The hairs on the back of my neck stand on end, and I turn to face the cave opening, straining my ears.

Snow crunches outside as someone, or something, approaches, and my heart hammers in my chest. I sit up, about to shake Beluroan awake, but waves of acrid stench reach out toward me, mingling with something sickly sweet.

Tendrils of darkness spread through my body, fogging my brain. The world grows cloudy, falling away from me.

Beluroan stirs beside me, but even the sacred details of his face blur together.

A dark figure looms at the mouth of the cave, and the smell grows stronger, pouring off the thing before me. I narrow my eyes, trying to focus, to figure out what it is that stares in at us.

But I can't.

My eyes flutter, desperate to close, and I fight them. I blink rapidly, desperate to clear the haze from my sight. I try to lift my hand to rub my eyes, but it lies on Beluroan's side, too heavy to move.

The dark shape moves into the cave, and the smell grows stronger. The fog in my mind thickens. I fall back, sprawling out beside Beluroan.

Why did I need to lift my arm?

The figure takes another step, but that can't be right.

We always put up wards. This is a dream.

That dark scent whispers to me seductively, luring me into sleep. I take a deep breath, drifting off a little further.

The figure moves closer, and realization slams into me. In the chaos of my near death and our rejoining, we never put up a ward.

There's someone in here with us.

I try to move, but the fog in my mind holds me down. I try to scream, but all I manage is a drowsy mumble.

"Wake up," I slur, trying to rouse Beluroan.

The mysterious visitor leans over us, pulls Beluroan onto his back, jerking him from my side. My hand lingers on his stomach, but every other bit of contact is lost.

I try to say, "No," try to scream it, but even that simple word comes out garbled and misshapen.

The Elven silhouette tips Beluroan's head back and pours something into his mouth.

MOVE!

Internally, I goad myself, screaming for action.

But nothing happens.

My hand flops uselessly on Beluroan's bare stomach, unable to even knock the vile drink away from his mouth.

The smell of it fills the air, pungent and sickly sweet.

But I know that smell. It tugs at some memory, hidden in the fog of my mind.

Think, Elairie.

You know this.

Slowly, it comes to me.

Belladonna. Sleep potion. Or poison in large doses.

The bottle drains into Beluroan's mouth, dumping far too much in.

"NO!" I scream, finally able to push a word past my lips.

A hand lashes out, slaps me across the face, sharp and furious. Pain blossoms through my skull, and the world tilts beneath me. My stomach churns, and I barely swallow back the bile that rises in my throat.

My gaze fixes on Beluroan, eyes open and body slack. My mind sags in its own fog, the belladonna oil the Elf wears making me hazy.

Beluroan doesn't need sleeping potion... He was already so tired from Aurujin, from saving me.

I amble through the memory of the Great Valley, welcoming me as my spirit drifted from my body after our fight.

No!

Focus.

The last drops of poison empty into Beluroan's mouth. He chokes on it, and I sag with relief.

He's still alive.

I rally every scrap of force I can muster and shove Beluroan onto his side. He coughs, spewing some of the poison out.

But he swallowed so much.

"No!" My heart breaks as the word splinters in my mouth.

But the shadow figure grabs me, dragging me away from my love. Rough, hideous hands pull a shirt down over my head, Beluroan's shirt. It reaches down well past my hips, and his scent clings to it, woodsy, yet clean.

Those filthy hands pull underwear up my legs, and I shudder, hating the stranger that sees me this way.

Focus.

I scream internally, willing myself to fight, to heal through the Belladonna.

The Elf drags me out of the cave by one leg. In my head, I hear the Gods, frantic and panicking. Their chatter freezes my veins.

The stone digs into my back, pushing Beluroan's shirt up to my shoulders. My skin breaks on the rough surface, and the metallic stench of blood fills the air.

I kick frantically, clawing at the hands that hold me and pulling in as much healing magic as I can.

The fog drifts from my mind, clearing a little at a time, and finally, my body listens to me. My hands scratch at the stone of the cave as the Elf drags me along, splitting nails and leaving a trail of blood.

My eyes dart to Beluroan, lying on his side, sputtering, coughing.

"Beluroan!"

A faint whisper crosses his lips, and my heart splinters.

The sunlight silhouettes my attacker. One ear lacks its point, something I know I've seen before, but a thin haze still lingers in my mind.

I wrack my brain, desperate for an answer. But my blood runs cold when I find it.

Waergou…

How did he find us?

Sickness moves through me as I realize my shield must've fallen when I nearly died.

Useless tears well in my eyes, dripping over my cheeks as I struggle against Waergou's grip on my ankle. My heart twists.

I let Beluroan down. I let everyone down.

But anger blossoms within me, rising up alongside my own disappointment.

My connection to Beluroan lingers, but it weakens with every second. Panic settles over me, constricting my chest.

I can't lose him.

Waergou will pay. Gourmaht. Will. Pay.

The stone beneath me turns to snow as I'm dragged outside, and I gasp as the cold soaks into my back. Mustering my strength, I kick out, and this time, I hit. Waergou lets loose a shocked gust of air.

I gather lightning at my fingertips and send it flying. The dark silhouette howls in pain, but he only grips my ankle tighter, fingers curling inward like claws.

I set my skin alight, burning his hands. He drops me quickly, but I feed the fire. It grows, reaching out for him, begging for his flesh.

But Waergou has more at stake than pain and scars. He jumps on me, pinning my arms beneath his knees. My bones creak beneath his weight, and I cry out.

He presses a finger to my temple, and ice spreads over my skin, crawling along my forehead. I scream through gritted teeth, jaw clenched tight, as cold consumes me.

Desperate, I draw the moisture from his legs, and suddenly, they aren't so heavy. I slip one arm free, clawing at his face with my nails, sending sparks of electricity outward from them.

But he catches my wrist, slamming it to the ground. Frost spreads over my skin in agonizing crystals until I fear my arm may snap.

And still, Beluroan grows weaker. The connection between us slowly fades. I hear his heartbeat growing faint, feel the agony of the Gods murmuring in the back of my heart.

With his free hand, Waergou fumbles in a pocket of his pants, pulling out another, much smaller vial.

He'd better hope he brought enough.

I'll kill him. I'll rip him to pieces for what he did to Beluroan.

Waergou pins my arm beneath his knee again, groaning in pain as he uncorks the vial. I squirm and clamp my mouth shut.

But he pinches my nose.

My lungs scream for air. My vision fades as darkness moves to take me. Gasping, I open my mouth, and he pours the Belladonna in.

Coughing, choking, I spit some of it up, spraying it over him.

But still, he pours.

I turn his damnable fingers to stone, hoping he'll drop the bottle, but he doesn't relent. Yelling, screaming in pain, he lets the last drops of Belladonna fall into my mouth.

I need to puke it back up. I need him off me, so I can help Beluroan.

But Belladonna calls, sweeping me into a dark and cloudy place, deep in the recesses of my mind. She pulls me along in her wake, smiling beguilingly, and I grow weaker as she flows through me.

My eyes grow heavy.

"Why not shut them?" Belladonna whispers, alluringly. "Just for a moment. You can open them again after that."

Surely, Belladonna wouldn't lie.

I can open my eyes again in a minute. I'll just shut them, just for a moment.

Just like she said.

Waergou's silhouette flickers as my eyes flutter, fall shut.

Belladonna, can I make him pay later? Will Beluroan be alright?

"Of course," she lies, as I drift into a deep sleep.

Chapter 25

Beluroan

Poison sloshes in my stomach, and I writhe in agony. Ice water fills my veins, my lungs, and I choke. My body shakes with deep, bone-rattling coughs. My heart slows, and the world speeds on, leaving me behind.

Elairie is gone…

The loss seeps through me, hollowing me out.

I draw myself up onto hands and knees, shaking and shivering as I vomit, time and time again. My throat screams in protest, raw and burning, and I crumple onto my side, falling onto the bedroll. My mind spins.

They took her.

Fear slithers through me, cold and vicious. My heart spasms in my chest, and my head fills with the panicked cries of the Gods. Ragged, labored breaths shake me, and my eyes flutter. Darkness closes in, eager to take me away.

But I can't die.

I have to stay alive.

For Elairie.

I force my eyes open, staring at the poisoned vomit on the cave floor. I focus on my broken breathing, trying to fix it.

But my eyelids are so heavy.

And my lungs are so tired.

Darkness reaches for me again, and my mind drifts. The forest slips through my grasp, and the battle with Aurujin fades.

And all I see is Saerine hugging Elairie.

She must be busy healing people now…

Realization dawns on me, and I reach out, grasping for healing energy. Achingly slow, I pull it inward, circle it through my entire body. With every heartbeat, I grow just a little stronger, reach for just a little more healing magic.

The pain fades.

And all the while, one thought runs through my mind.

Elairie.

The magic warms my body, tingles through me, and Elairie's face in my mind electrifies my spirit. The world stops tilting, and the ache in my head eases. I sit up, testing my stomach.

It doesn't churn at the movement.

I push myself to my feet, and winter nips at my bare flesh in Elairie's absence. I dress quickly, forsaking my missing shirt and throwing my jacket on over my naked chest.

I find no footprints at the cave entrance, only fresh snow, thick and soft.

How long was I unconscious?

My heart sinks, but I pull divination to the front of my mind. My spirit soars over the mountains, seeking her out. But all I find are Gourmaht's thoughts, his intentions with her, and my stomach drops.

I scream out, lungs aching and throat burning with the effort. Birds launch themselves into the air, and the echoes carry.

But not far enough.

I want that vile man to hear me, to feel the rage that threatens to dismantle me.

Bits and pieces of my mind fall away like loose gravel.

"It won't work," I whisper, refuting his plans. "She can't be his slave. She's immune."

But my blood boils.

Divination shows me more of his wishes, his desire for a powerful heir no matter her protests. My mouth goes dry at hazy images of his lumbering frame pinning her down, cold black eyes draining her life away as he uses her.

I double over, puking into the snow.

No. He hasn't yet.

And he won't.

My hands ball into fists, and my nails dig into my palms. But the images, the potential future, won't leave me. They circle through my mind, and my stomach churns.

I struggle to push it away, but it sticks with me, digs into my brain.

I take off at a sprint, damning the rocks and the snow and the ice. Still, I see that vile man grunting over her, and I fight not to puke, again.

My mind splinters further, showing me the battle raging in a town far below us. Unable to see their clouded auras, the Patrol unwittingly slaughters slaves alongside Masters. Swords clash and bodies fall. Blood melts the snow beneath a cacophony of fury and anguish.

But once enslaved, only a Master's death grants freedom.

So, the Patrol pushes through them toward the Masters. My mind whirls with pain and loss, a fitting backdrop for the agony scorching my entire body.

I chase the wind, racing to save Elairie and gritting my teeth.

I'll rip him limb from limb…

Divination shows me what he's *actually* doing with her now, pulling my mind in yet another direction.

Chained to a wall, she hangs limp in nothing but my shirt. Obscured by strands of lilac and mulberry, his handiwork tries to hide from me.

But I see it.

An ice scar reaches down out of her hair. It runs onto her temple, branching like the crystalline frost that put it there. And on her wrist, another scar stares out at me.

Rage burns through me, singeing my veins, and I pump my legs faster.

Waergou sits in a chair off to the side, glaring, and a cruel laugh plays on my lips as my gaze roams over him.

Malice coats my words as I spit, "Thank the Gods…"

Burns mar his hands. Stone fingers pull one hand low, drooping over the edge of his chair.

And his face…

Claw marks and slashes abound with little lightning scars branching out from each one.

A sinister smile spreads over my face.

My feet punch into the snow, pushing me farther, faster.

In my mind, I watch Gourmaht approach her, and my blood boils. A tight braid holds his dark blue hair back from his face. I clench my fists, aching to grab that braid and rip it from his skull.

His hand snakes up to the side of Elairie's face, lifting her chin with his thumb. Drowsily, she jerks away from him.

They gave her something. Poison.

A smaller dose of what they gave me.

"What happened to her face?" Gourmaht hisses.

Waergou drops his gaze and says, "The aromatic oil didn't quite work." Bitterness creeps into his tone. "She still had a lot of fight left in her."

He holds up his stone fingers to emphasize the point. "I had to wrestle her down and dump Belladonna down her throat."

Gourmaht drops his hand, letting her head fall.

Rounding yet another bluff, I push myself harder.

I have to get there. She's alive. I can still help her.

My blood screams through my veins as I run.

A sick longing sweeps through me, and I push harder, desperate to break them.

And I'll love every second of it.

"And what of the other?" Gourmaht asks. "Beluroan." He spits my name, a curse, a vile thing to be said only when necessary.

"I gave him enough to kill five Elves. He shouldn't trouble us anymore," Waergou answers.

Gourmaht steps closer to Elairie, pushing her limp form against the wall.

Fury turns my vision red.

"Elairie!" I scream.

My spirit surges toward him while my body runs. I try to grab him, try to pull him away.

He leans into her, turning her head to the side. Burying his face in her hair, he breathes her in.

Again, my spirit tries to get him off her, tries to break the chains holding her up by the arms and holding her legs apart. I ache to break the strap that's buckled around her waist and beat him with it.

But I can't.

"Godsdamnit! GET OFF HER!" I roar the words, and the echoes fill the mountains.

Elairie's eyes flicker. Weakly, she lifts her head, looking in the direction of my spirit.

Can she sense me?

"Elairie?" Fragile hope burns within me, and I hold my breath, running through snow all the while. "Elairie? You have to fight this. I know you can."

Her posture shifts, and her eyes open further.

With a hand on her face, I whisper to her. "You can get out of those chains. I promise. I'm on my way."

She nods, growing stronger every moment as she pushes through the Belladonna, as I get closer. She jerks at her chains, sluggish but moving of her own volition.

Time to make myself known.

I induce a vision in Waergou with nothing more than a thought.

He sees me sprinting through the snow, knows just how dearly they'll pay. I force my rage into his heart, let him feel the roaring of my blood.

"I'm coming for you," I growl. The words come out hoarse and rough.

And Waergou shakes before my fury.

If only Gourmaht had divination.

Every step gets me closer to Elairie, waking her, and I grow stronger. Every stride becomes easier, every breath less ragged. As I get closer to her, my abilities multiply, and I heal through my exhaustion.

Waergou sees this, sees how it effects Elairie.

He tries to push me from his mind, but his effort is laughable.

"Fine," I whisper, leaving him for now.

"Elairie," my spirit whispers, caressing her face. "I'm almost there. Break them."

Chapter 26
Elairie

I nod, comforted by Beluroan's spirit. My eyes find Gourmaht. A joyous anticipation swells in me, because I know he has news for his Master.

"B-Beluroan isn't dead," he mutters.

"What?" Gourmaht yells, spinning to face his second-in-command.

"It didn't work. I'm sorry." Dropping to his knees, Waergou says, "Gourmaht, I'm so sorry. I failed."

Gourmaht slaps Waergou hard across the face, reopening the wounds I inflicted.

"Useless," he spits, storming to a table across the room. He snatches up a small vial, uncorking it as he approaches me. "Time to make a new slave… Surely she can kill him."

Gripping my hair, he slams my head against the wall. Pain bursts through my skull, and fury roils in my gut.

Pinching my nose shut, Gourmaht lifts the vial, ready to pour it in my mouth as soon as I take a breath.

Stupid.

How could he ever think his blood powerful enough to enslave a Blessed One?

I gasp for air, and the disgusting potion pours in. I spit it over his cruel features, watching the dark liquid drip over the scar that splits his face. It clumps his eyelashes together, framing spiritless eyes.

He scowls, wiping it away with a snarl.

"It wouldn't work anyway," I say, raising one eyebrow in a taunt.

For the barest instant, genuine fear slips through the facade, creeping onto his face, but a violent fury quickly takes its place.

He slams my head against the wall, and pain blossoms through my skull.

My insides clench, and my hands curl into fists. I suck healing magic from the air around me, pulling it into my body, recovering swiftly.

But I seek more than healing.

Summoning more magic, I freeze my bindings, wrists going cold as ice forms along the links. The metal turns a frigid blue, creaking loudly. With a single jerk, I shatter the chains.

Gourmaht takes a step back, jaw falling open. "But… The wards…" he stammers.

Only then do I notice their magical attempts at binding me. The various wards lie shattered upon the ground with the frozen metal.

I laugh. "Those puny things?"

Calling forth more magic, I raise columns of stone around Gourmaht, moving them toward him. He stands transfixed, staring in horror at the encroaching pillars.

I need him to suffer, need his screams to wrench the air, need his blood to seep across the cave floor.

But he snaps from his daze and squeezes between the columns. Sprinting into a dark tunnel, he abandons Waergou.

Far braver than his Master, the Elf grabs my arm, attempts to raise a hand to me.

I set him ablaze, filling the air with the stench of roasting flesh. Hoarse screams erupt from him, filling my mind with echoes of the raw sounds that broke through my lips when he dragged me from Beluroan, when he poured the poison into Beluroan's mouth.

He falls to the floor, writhing in agony.

And I smile.

In the back of my mind, I hear the Gods pleading, frantic and desperate, hoping this ends how they want it to.

Seems their playthings aren't behaving.

My stomach sours at the thought of being used by them, created only for torment and struggle.

But I'll have my relief soon enough.

A rueful smile splits my face wide open, and I call out. "Gourmaht? Wherever did you go?" My voice echoes through the cave, down the tunnels.

He doesn't answer, but I don't need him to.

Descending into madness, I pull divination up around me, searching for him, reveling in the chase.

Gourmaht runs through tunnels, searching for a way out, a path that leads him away from me. But I see every tunnel, every cave.

He turns into a new tunnel, and I see every possible way to reach him.

He sprints, and I smile at his terror.

He's finally met his match.

I shepherd him through the tunnels, calling out, chasing him toward one specific entrance. The one Beluroan hurtles toward, even now.

It won't be long…

We can be reunited.

And then we can end this sniveling little weasel.

Chapter 27
Beluroan

Bolting over a steep incline, I face the force assembled to put me down, to stop me from reaching Elairie. They gather on a stone plateau, and right behind them, an entrance to the cave awaits.

I just have to get through them.

I don't bother counting them, don't have time. But I like my odds.

A smile twists my features, and I continue my mad dash, feet pounding the earth. Arrows fly toward me, making me wish for a shield.

I wonder...

In an instant, I build a shield out of a ward of protection, weaving the webs together until no openings remain. An arrow crashes into it, only to bounce off. I run onward, and another arrow hits. It snaps, and I trample the broken shaft underfoot.

I dash forward, dodging and blocking arrows, emboldened by the success of my new shield. Clouded auras surround me.

Slaves.

Don't hurt the slaves.

I repeat the thought, desperate to chase away the bloodlust and insanity rampaging through me, because I know the slaves don't want this.

But they rush me, keeping me from Elairie.

Hordes of them move toward me, swords drawn, pushed by ranks of Masters who cower behind them.

Don't hurt the slaves.

Don't. Hurt. Them.

I lift a hand, raising stone walls between me and the approaching forces. I move the walls, shove them back. Separating the slaves into two sections of about fifty each, I pull stone from the earth, building walls all around them.

A furious voice in my head begs me to move the walls in, to crush them where they stand.

Anger flares within me, slipping through the fractures of my mind, but I fight. Memories of my own Master flood me, and my blood curdles.

"They're slaves," I remind myself. "They didn't want this…"

I force my fingers to unfurl, sprinting forward, leaving the slaves and their stone prisons behind.

My eyes lock on the five Masters near the cave entrance, pitiful and defenseless without their living shields. They huddle together, hands trembling at their sides.

One dares to draw his weapon.

With a thought, I raise a great stone column and slam it into him, crushing him against the mountainside with a magnificent boom. Bits of stone crumble away, tumbling to the snowy ground. Blood seeps out at the bottom.

The other Masters stare at me with wide eyes, unmoving. I reach out with my magic, testing them. One has aura sensing. One can control lightning, earth, and air magic. Two have no magic at all.

I summon fire magic, setting their clothes alight. I feed the fire, melting their armor, searing their flesh. It boils their blood, and screams fill the air.

My mind begs to make them suffer, but already, they fall to the ground, dropping like flies. I move for the cave entrance, smiling devilishly, but I stop short.

Fire and lightning swirls around me, my aura rising, growing, reaching for Elairie as she draws near.

But Divination tells me that Gourmaht is closer, hurtling toward me as he runs from her, leading her to what he believes to be an ambush.

A wicked smile splits my face open.

Footsteps echo through the cave, slamming into the rock. His fear slithers through me, an undercurrent buried in the back of my heart. Even with a plan, he knows enough of us to be afraid.

His hands shake. His heart races.

My smile widens.

He bursts through the entrance, stumbling and skidding to a halt as he takes in his fallen Masters and the blood seeping out behind the stone column. His eyes trace the stone prisons, and I feel his hope leave him.

He pants, spinning in place, searching for something, anything, to tip the scales.

Elairie calmly strolls out of the cave, smiling at me.

Chapter 28
Elairie

I step through the mouth of the cave onto a small plateau, and my eyes alight on Beluroan. Waves of relief wash through me, and my shoulders sag.

But Gourmaht stands between us, holds us apart. I can't touch Beluroan, can't feel his skin beneath my touch, and my soul cries out for vengeance for such an affront.

Gourmaht spins, jaw falling as he surveys the dead, the stone prisons that can't quite hold in the auras of the slaves trapped within them.

But he doesn't have life magic, can't see the gray clouds swirling around the stone.

At long last, his eyes land upon us, switching from one of us to the other as he backs away. Fear morphs into rage, transforming his face. He squares his shoulders, gearing up for a fight.

I smile wickedly, muscles itching to unleash the tension, to make him suffer.

He conjures fire around our feet, but the snow delays him. By the time he can kindle a flame, I summon water, staunching his efforts. It turns to ice in the frigid winter air, and I nearly slip.

But Beluroan melts it, dispels it, before I lose my footing. He stirs the wind into a tornado, pulling loose stones into its grasp.

My hair whips about, and his shirt slaps my skin. Conjuring fire magic with a thought, I liquefy the rocks within his maelstrom.

Gourmaht stares at the lava flying above him, openmouthed. His eyes dart back and forth between Beluroan and me. Panic and fury shine in his black eyes.

Beluroan pushes his hands forward, and the tornado surges toward Gourmaht. My heart races, aching to see this vile man caught up in violent winds and soaring lava.

Gourmaht sends a torrent of water to cool the molten stone.

Fool…

All around Beluroan and me, our aura glows brighter, burns hotter. Lightning and fire swirl around us, reaching to close the gap he forces upon us. Agony sears the edges of my soul, ripped from its other half.

Frenzied laughter bubbles up, ringing from my lips and Beluroan's. As one, we reach out, seizing control of the water Gourmaht sent forth, ripping the reins from his hands.

"What!?" Gourmaht screams. "But… You can't do that!"

"I'm pretty sure we just did," Beluroan says, laughing maniacally.

Clenching my hands, I freeze the water we stole into fist-sized chunks of ice. The wind catches them, and I keep them away from the molten rock.

Beluroan sends lightning bolts through the tornado, and we push it off toward Gourmaht. He runs, finally seeing reason.

But we push it faster until it overcomes him.

My heart races, and I lean forward, watching eagerly as the maelstrom closes in.

Molten rock slams into Gourmaht, knocking him to the ground. His hair goes up in flames, and unbridled joy slips through me. Ice chunks pummel him and cool the molten rock, hardening it around him, pinning him to the ground.

Lightning strikes him, over and over, and my heart skips a beat each time. The wind pulls the air from his lungs, quieting his screams.

We smile, stirring the elemental tornado into a frenzy. His soul escapes, but still it batters his broken body, breaking him to pieces then freezing them in place.

Rage twists my features, demanding payment for all he did. For us. For the people he enslaved and the people he forced them to kill.

My heart burns hotter than ever before, craving violence, begging for more. Lava and ice fall upon him, obeying my will, *our* will. I turn his blood to stone, and Beluroan melts that too, sending lava flowing through his weeping veins. It oozes from him, seeping onto the plateau.

Beluroan pulls the air from his lungs, collapsing them, sucking them in on themselves. I heat the water in his body until it turns to steam.

And finally, the ache eases.

I release the magic I've summoned, and Beluroan does the same.

The elemental whirlwind falls atop Gourmaht. Heaps of molten rock and chunks of ice land with thuds and splatters and splinters. The rock beneath him cracks, sending out a spray of tiny stones.

Immediately, I shield his Blood Magic recipe, sagging as a weight falls from my shoulders. My eyes seek Beluroan, and I run to him amidst the wind and the snow.

My aura reaches for him, crackling and sparking as we grow closer. I jump into his arms, knocking him into a snow drift. Laughter bubbles up within him, and I giggle madly.

Our lips meet, shared soul fitting itself back into one piece, and our aura burns brighter, sparks hotter. My heart races, and my skin bursts to life, tingling at his touch. Our lips crush together, and our hands roam.

Panicked cries pierce the air, echoing from within the walls of Beluroan's prisons. They cry for help, screaming to be released.

The world settles onto my shoulders as madness slips away.

The caves. The slaves. The things I just did.

I glance around at the corpses, all but forgotten in our haste to be together again, to make our soul whole.

I push myself to my feet, clinging to Beluroan's hand, and he rises beside me. We crack the stone walls open, and people rush out, free from their prison and their bonds as slaves.

They stare at us, mouths agape at their dirty, half-naked rescuers.

Divination gives me the answers they need, and I let the words flow through my lips. "This storm will worsen tonight, but it'll let up the day after tomorrow. There are enough provisions in these caves to get you through until then."

Gripping my hand tightly, Beluroan adds, "Don't set off any sooner than that." He describes the route they should take to avoid encountering Aurujin.

"Head to Douhaen," I say. "General Haedra's forces will have cleared it of any remaining Masters before you reach it. She'll help you."

A thousand words of gratitude effervesce on their lips.

Beluroan and I head into the caves, hands locked together, and they follow closely on our heels.

But a fork in the tunnel divides us.

They seek food and sleeping quarters. We seek the Blood Magic.

In Gourmaht's alchemy lab, we destroy every paper we find, using them as kindling to burn every herb that won't release poisonous smoke.

The Gods will have to shield the memories. Haedra and her forces will have to eradicate the Masters and send them to the grave.

But we can take care of this cave and its contents.

My mind eases with every burnt scrap of paper. I breathe a sigh of relief, scattering the ashes of herbs.

As we work, I open my heart and mind to Beluroan, using a mixture of empath and divination to explore his.

The walls between us crumble. I feel him meandering through my thoughts and emotions, checking my feelings on what we should do next.

Wandering through his heart, I see exactly how much he loves me. I feel the rage that engulfed him when Waergou took me to the caves and the depths of insanity that gripped him in our separation, making him hope for bloodshed. I see his struggle to spare the slaves.

But I faced no such dilemma.

Without slaves to give me pause, I gave myself over to the bloodlust.

I even made a game of chasing Gourmaht...

A small shiver wanders through me as I realize what I became, and I grip his hand tighter.

Pulling divination up around myself like a blanket, I look to our future. A million possibilities lay over each other, shifting, blurring together, but I catch glimpses.

Of Saerine burning alive, my hands tight around her throat because she couldn't save Beluroan. I see myself wither away, body drying out as I reject water, reject food, shut up in our home.

Of myself slapping a child in the market for jostling us, for forcing our hands to slip apart.

I see Geeran convulsing near my dead body as lightning arcs through him at Beluroan's command, a payment for my death.

Bleak futures flicker through my head, interspersed with the joys of living with Beluroan in a little treehouse.

But then, I see him jump off the balcony, legs splintering as he hits the ground below, see him drag himself to my broken body, my shattered skull. He screams, sending flames crawling over the forest, up the trunks of Aivrard to claim one treehouse after another.

Saerine and Pakaibra carry Oran and Kraimin down the stairs that wind around their tree, comforting the screaming children as their neighbors and friends die around them.

And Beluroan draws air into himself, filling his body until he bursts, raining pieces of himself over the burning town.

I shudder, closing myself to the future. Waves of revulsion wind through me.

Returning to Beluroan's heart, I find his feelings on our current situation. It takes only a moment to see that we agree. I gaze into his eyes and nod solemnly.

"Best not to linger," I whisper.

We finish up, eradicating all traces of the Blood Magic.

As the flames die down, I search for a pair of boots to spare my feet from the rocks we'll encounter on our journey. I don't bother with a jacket or pants, knowing that our aura will protect me from the cold.

We gather paper and pens, then write letters explaining our decision. I write one for Haedra, the Representatives, and Geeran. Beluroan writes to Saerine and his nephews. We ask the Elves we freed to deliver the papers to Haedra when they reach Douhaen, trusting her to ensure that Saerine receives her letter.

The scene flashes through my mind, the future revealing itself to me without prompting. Geeran sits with Haedra, finally resting after healing her troops and consoling the recently liberated.

I blink the scene away, and we set off through the snow. A few Elves stand in the mouths of the cave, staring after us with wide eyes and shouting about the cold.

But we don't feel it.

Fire and lightning swirl around us, finally touching the world the way I always thought it should have. Snowflakes land on our bare skin, my arms, his chest, but they melt immediately. The snow seems to flinch from our feet, from my bare legs.

Beyond our little bubble, the storm rages, and ice falls to the ground. But we move forward in a gentle rain. Beluroan drapes his arm over my shoulder, and I slide mine beneath his jacket, hand leaving trails of fire along his bare skin.

Their echoes burn across my back.

The feel of him soothes me, soothes the beast I know I could be without him, and I lean my head on his shoulders as we walk.

Chapter 29

Beluroan

The cave looms, waiting for us, as if it knew we'd be back. We step inside, hands linked, to find it just as we left it.

Was it really just this morning?

Reaching for earth magic, I pull stone up over the mess I made when Waergou poisoned me, tucking it under the ground. The magic comes so easily, springing forth to do my bidding. I shudder, recalling the ease with which I smashed a man, set others aflame.

The sick glee of ending Gourmaht's life slips through my veins, and I swallow. I shudder as the visions of our future, of the people I'd kill if Elairie died, echo through me.

Elairie and I settle on our makeshift bed, smoothing the blankets. We turn to face each other, and silence wraps around us, thick and heavy.

My shoulders lift, then fall with a sigh. I nod, tracing the lines of Elairie's face, committing the colors of her hair, her eyes, to memory.

Better get this over with before we talk ourselves out of it.

Reaching over, I grab one of my daggers and one of Elairie's. I hold them up in my open palm, and Elairie takes my dagger. Her fingers brush mine, sending fire and lightning shooting across my skin.

I savor the feeling, warm and sweet. A lump forms in my throat.

Will it be the same... after?

I can't be sure, and the uncertainty rattles me.

"I love you," Elairie says, and the words sound just a little too much like goodbye.

My heart clenches, even as she places her hand on the side of my face, even as her lips meet mine.

"I love you too," I say. Taking a deep breath, I confess. "I'm scared."

Elairie nods, releases a soft, morbid laugh. "Me too."

Another deep breath. "Ready?"

Her chest rises, lungs filling. With wide eyes and furrowed brows, she nods.

I stare at the dagger in my hand, pull it from its sheath. Turning it over in my hand, I watch as the waning daylight plays along the edges of the frigid steel.

I meet Elairie's gaze and pull in a deep breath. Linking our free hands, we brace them on our laps and poise the blades over our wrists.

My heart races. "Count of three?" I ask, voice breaking.

Doubt and fear flicker through me.

But there's no other way.

Not now that we've seen what we could be.

"Ok," she replies. A single tear slips over her cheek.

Together, we count.

"One."

My mouth goes dry.

"Two."

The wind screams outside our cave, and then the world beyond disappears.

"Three."

Blades bite into flesh, agonizing and brutal, and bright red blood oozes out. I grit my teeth, squeezing

Elairie's hand as I dig the blade in deeper, dragging it up my arm. The dagger carves its way through skin and muscle. My stomach churns as it slices through a tendon with a snap.

Blood gushes, pooling on the blankets beneath us.

Elairie pushes her blade in deep, and her pale skin makes it look so much worse. I swallow bile as I stare at the dark blood pouring from her wrist.

Her grip loosens, and her eyes flutter.

Panic claws my heart, begging me to heal her, to fix the damage done to her arm and keep her here with me.

But I can't.

We can't be in this world any longer, can't put it all at risk.

I grit my teeth and stare into her eyes. With every heartbeat, every fading pulse, I remind myself of the monster I was in her absence, of the violent creature I could be if she died and left me alive.

My heart twists, but I show myself the world that Kaistrum built, the suffering he inflicted on so many after Vaerlin's death.

I show myself the madness that moved within my own mind, the fissures that opened up within me, the splintered shards of my soul that demanded the slaves' deaths.

Would I have killed them if Elairie were dead?

I shudder.

Would I have made my own slaves, just like Kaistrum?

I don't want to know. We explored so many routes, so many paths after taking Gourmaht down.

Visions of my own crumbling descent into madness haunt me.

Our lives aren't worth the risk.

I shiver, already growing cold. But this has to be it.

I lift my dagger once more, breathing heavily as I hold it over my arm. My jaw clenches, and my teeth grind together. I stare at the crimson liquid, hesitating.

But Elairie doesn't flinch. She drives her dagger into her wrist once more, carving the flesh of her arm.

My stomach roils, but I plunge my dagger into my own arm.

We can't survive this.

I need to black out before I try to heal her.

We dig deeper, and our very lives pour through our veins, dumping onto the bedroll beneath us. My head swirls, dizzy and far too light.

Finally, we set the daggers down on the cold stone and lie down. I stare into her eyes, lacing our fingers together. Our mangled wrists butt up against each other, and I wince.

But I don't release her.

With my free hand, I push strands of lilac and mulberry back behind her ear. I kiss the back of her hand, lamenting our short time together.

I didn't even get to count the purples in her hair…

"I love you," I whisper.

Tears streak her face, but her eyes shine with triumph. It looks so much like my mother's expression when she died.

"I love you too," Elairie says, voice faint.

My throat tightens as blood pools between us on the sodden bedroll. Darkness rolls in as my vision fades, and pain radiates through me. Everything in me cries out for healing, for me and for her.

I steel myself against it.

This has to be the end.

We fade together, drifting in and out of consciousness. Elairie's dark blue eyes stare deep into mine, warming my heart, and my panic eases.

With the last of my strength, I move closer, and she does the same. I feel the Gods breathe a sigh of relief in the back of my heart as our lips meet, one final time, and our eyes fall shut.

But the darkness is short-lived.

The Great Valley appears before me, lush grass soft beneath my feet. Elairie squeezes my hand, lustrous eyes gazing lovingly into mine. My stomach fills with butterflies, and my skin tingles with fire and electricity where we touch.

Elairie smiles, and I pull her against me for a kiss.

My entire body burns with it.

Fingers still laced together, we turn and walk deeper into the Valley.

Maybe we can build a treehouse.

Like the ones in Aivrard.

Epilogue
The Letters

Dear Haedra,

Gourmaht has been taken care of, as you will surely have heard by now. All tangible evidence of the Blood Magic has been destroyed, and the Masters present at the caves were killed.

By the time you get this, I assume your forces will have eradicated the remaining Masters, and the Gods will have long since blocked the information from any prying eyes. Avaencery will finally be safe from Blood Magic.

As for us…

You needn't worry. We saw what we're like apart. We can't force that risk upon anyone else. The possibility of ending up like Kaistrum… It was too much. I hope our decision will be well-received. I'm sure that, at the very least, you'll sleep easier.

If Saerine wants a funeral for Beluroan, our bodies will be in a small cave near Aurujin's lake. I'll include a small drawing detailing how to safely get there, but come prepared to fight that creature.

If a funeral is held, please bury us together. There's no one alive to fight for my burial, but… Please, don't separate us.

And if you wouldn't mind, please, thank Geeran for us. Maybe even show him this letter. He helped us so much. It really meant a lot to us. Jaetus would be so proud of him for all he's done.

Thank you, as well, for everything you've done for Avaencery.

Elairie and Beluroan

Saerine,

What can I even say to you to make this ok?

Elairie and I... Well, I'm fairly sure you knew. Somehow, it seemed like you wanted to warn us before we even left Vairsun. We're terrible creatures. Together, we're fantastic.

But... Separated... We're awful.

We just couldn't go on in this world, putting everyone at risk. I don't mean that lightly. Elairie and I agreed. We couldn't stomach the thought of becoming like Kaistrum, or worse.

I have no idea what you should tell the boys to explain why I'll never get to see them again. Whatever explanation you give them, please, please, please, make sure they know that I love them. I love them, so very much. And I love you too.

Congratulations on your relationship with Pakaibra, by the way. I really am happy for the two of you. You have the makings of a great life. Enjoy it.

I really did hope I'd be able to come home and see all of you, again. Elairie loves you and the boys. We wanted to have a house and a family. We wanted our kids to grow up with their cousins and their aunt.

Even if we'd been able to come back to Vairsun, we couldn't have had kids.

I'm sorry to ramble. I always do this when I write you letters.

Anyway, just know that things are better this way. I love you, Saerine. I love you, and I'm so sorry.

Have a wonderful life.

Kiss the boys for me.

Love,

Beluroan and Elairie

A Letter From the Author

...About Suicide

That was a rough ending, I know. And I also know that there's a chance that some of the people reading this have considered that end for themselves.

So, let me just say this.

Suicide is not the answer.

It made sense for Elairie and Beluroan, but the odds of you going criminally insane , using magic to enslave an entire continent, or trying to end the entire world are pretty slim.

That may seem like I'm not taking this seriously, but I thought you could use a laugh.

Because I know how dark depression gets. I've plumbed those depths before.

I know it makes things that aren't your fault seem like they are.

I know it makes the world seem even more daunting than it is.

And I know that sometimes it rips away all emotion, leaving you numb.

But.

I also know these things are temporary. Not fleeting. Sometimes they last a while.

But they're not permanent.

Someday, you'll feel better. Someday, you'll be glad you kept going.

And that person you *will be* deserves a chance to live.

So, please, keep going.

Talk to someone.

If you don't think there's anyone you can talk to (because I know depression makes it feel that way sometimes), call this number:

(800) 273 – 8255

Thank you!

For buying this book. For reading it all the way through. For being an awesome reader who reads.

If you liked it, please leave a review on Amazon, Goodreads, Barnes & Noble, your own blog... Anywhere, really. Reviews are the lifeblood of authors, helping books get noticed in the almighty eyes of search engine algorithms.

Other Books by this Author

Literary Fantasy Novels

Soul Bearer

The Gem of Meruna

A Heart of Salt & Silver

Allmother Rising

Literary Thriller Novellas

Annabelle

Things Left Unsaid

Literary Post-Apocalyptic Novel

World for the Broken

About the Author

Elexis Bell is a quiet nerd with too many hobbies, including everything from gaming to shower-singing and even archery, weather permitting. She specializes in sarcasm and writing stories that make people feel. She's made a home for herself with her husband, their dog, and a small army of cats.

She writes dark, gritty stories, sprinkling gut-wrenching emotions over high fantasy romance, thrillers, post-apocalyptic romance, and science fiction.

For further information, follow her on Instagram, Twitter, or Facebook, or check out her blog on her website. There, you can sign up for her newsletter to stay up to date on all future book releases, giveaways, and on-going projects.

www.elexisbell.com